SIXTEEN CARVED PIECES

An absolutely gripping crime thriller with a massive twist

MICHELLE KIDD

DI Jack McIntosh Mysteries Book 3

Originally published as *The Bishop*

JOFFE BOOKS

Revised edition 2023
Joffe Books, London
www.joffebooks.com

First published in Great Britain in 2021
as *The Bishop*

This book is a work of fiction. Names, characters, businesses, organizations, places and events are either the product of the author's imagination or are used fictitiously. Any resemblance to actual persons, living or dead, events or locales is entirely coincidental. The spelling used is British English except where fidelity to the author's rendering of accent or dialect supersedes this. The right of Michelle Kidd to be identified as author of this work has been asserted in accordance with the Copyright, Designs and Patents Act 1988.

Cover art by Nick Castle

ISBN: 978-1-80405-790-2

PROLOGUE

Sunday 29 September 2013

Blood continued to swirl around the plughole.

So much blood.

Too much blood.

He glanced down at the front of his shirt and grimaced — the stains were already beginning to dry out. He'd have to get rid of it: burn it, even. Bloodstains like that never disappeared, not entirely. They'd always be there, taunting him in his waking hours, haunting him in his dreams, and his nightmares.

And he'd had more than enough of those.

Hands shaking, he picked up the nailbrush and began stabbing at his stained fingernails.

What have you done?

It wasn't the first time he'd asked himself that question.

Even as he scrubbed, he could still smell the blood clinging to his skin, sensing its unique metallic taste on his tongue as he swallowed.

What have you done?

The same empty words echoed inside his head.

Two sharp raps on the door brought him to his senses. Flicking his eyes down at the blood still circling the plughole, he dropped the nailbrush with a clatter. Two more sharp raps were then followed by a voice — a voice that he recognised.

"Jack, it's me. Open the door." DS Robert Carmichael's tone sounded urgent. "*Now*, Jack."

Detective Inspector Jack MacIntosh glanced towards the wall clock above the kitchen sink.

5.40 a.m.

He then lowered his gaze back to his bloodstained shirt.

Shit, Jack.

What have you done?

CHAPTER ONE

Ten days earlier

Time: 11.15 p.m.
Date: Thursday 19 September 2013
Location: 3a Dolphin Close, EC1

She looked serene, with her strawberry blonde hair cascading around her shoulders. He brushed his fingertips over her pale, unblemished face, gently pulling her eyelids closed and snuffing out the vacant look from her pale blue eyes. As if in prayer, he knitted her fingers together and placed her clasped hands on to her stomach.

But no prayers would save Billie-Rose now.

She looked as though she was sleeping, slumbering peacefully in the stillness of the night. But it would be a sleep from which she would never wake.

He lightly brushed his hand alongside her cheek, running a finger over her pale pink lips. To him, she was perfect. Perfect in every sense. Which was why he'd chosen her.

Her body lay still and quiet. No breaths rasped from her mouth, life no longer coursing through her pretty veins. Her heart had stilled for the final time, the blood left within her now dormant and calm.

Humming to himself, he reached into his jacket pocket, bringing out two expertly carved wooden objects. Then, gently prising apart her laced fingers, he slipped one into the palm of her hand. Closing the fingers again, he then teased the other between her lifeless lips and watched it disappear out of sight.

He smiled as his eyes skirted the rest of her body, noting the youthful neatness of her curves. Licking his lips, he slowly rolled her on to her side.

Picking up the Stanley knife which lay by his side, he began.

* * *

Time: 10.30 a.m.
Date: Friday 20 September 2013
Location: Metropolitan Police HQ, London

James Quinn.

Detective Inspector Jack MacIntosh leaned back in his chair and sighed. The man was an enigma, or at least a magician. Wherever Jack looked, he came up against a brick wall — a dead end. Quinn had managed to disappear into thin air: a feat even David Blaine would be proud of.

But no one could truly disappear, could they?

Jack's thoughts were interrupted by a hesitant knock at the door. He looked up as the door creaked open and DS Amanda Cassidy's head, with her familiar jet-black hair, appeared around the doorjamb. She wore a broad smile while brandishing a takeaway coffee cup and greaseproof paper bag. His stomach gave an appreciative grumble.

"Morning, guv," she grinned, depositing the coffee cup and paper bag on the desk. "I'm just moving in next door."

"Thanks." Jack nodded his head towards the coffee. "Settling in?"

Cassidy's grin widened. "I've bagged the desk by the window. It's bigger than the other one, so technically Chris should probably have it, but he's so loved-up with Jenny I don't think he's even noticed." Her dark eyes sparkled with childlike excitement.

"Good choice." Jack reached for his coffee cup and noted the tantalising smell of a freshly prepared bacon and cheese toasted sandwich wafting from the paper bag. "So, how does it feel? Promotion suiting you?"

The grin widened even more. "I can't thank you enough, guv. For making me go for it. I couldn't have done it without your backing."

Jack sipped at his coffee. "Like I said. You're a great detective. Certainly sergeant material. You deserve it."

Cassidy turned towards the door, pausing with one hand on the handle. "How does it feel in here now? With Chris next door with me?" She glanced back over her shoulder, eyes twinkling. "Are you lonely?"

Jack smothered the laugh behind his coffee and took a look at Cooper's old desk opposite. Now stripped bare, the piles of paperwork had disappeared, as had the scrunched-up bacon sandwich wrappers and Coke cans that would normally have littered its surface.

And he also noticed the quiet.

"I'm fine," he replied. "This suits me just fine."

And it did. Renowned bachelor – and part-time recluse, according to some – Jack MacIntosh smiled at the solitude now surrounding him.

It was just the way he liked it.

Cassidy disappeared and Jack turned his attention back to the two words decorating his notepad.

James Quinn.

Where the hell are you?

The man Jack increasingly suspected as playing a role in his mother's death was proving hard — if not impossible — to trace.

Feeling the grumbling in his stomach intensifying, he reached for the toasted sandwich. He'd barely taken the first bite when the chirping of the desk phone interrupted his thoughts. Finding it buried beneath a mass of paperwork, Jack lifted the receiver.

"DI MacIntosh." Listening to the voice on the other end of the line, he made short work of the rest of his breakfast and scribbled the brief details on to his notepad. He nodded and swallowed at the same time. "We'll get out there right away."

Draining the rest of his coffee, Jack shrugged into his jacket and grabbed his car keys, making the short walk to the office next door. DS Chris Cooper was sitting at his new desk, munching on his own trademark bacon sandwich. The smell of greasy fried meat and ketchup hung in the air.

"I hope you've both been playing nicely. Remember, I'm only next door."

Cooper raised his sandwich towards Jack. "Of course, boss."

Cassidy was busily arranging her desk space. Jack noted a broad-leafed potted plant had appeared from nowhere, placed next to a complicated-looking pen and pencil holder.

"Get that down your neck quickly, Cooper. And get your coats — both of you." Jack waved his car keys in the air. "We've pulled a case."

* * *

Time: 11.30 a.m.
Date: Friday 20 September 2013
Location: Tannochside B&B, Scotland

Isabel Faraday carried the drinks over to the small oak table by the window. The day had dawned bright and clear, with only a handful of clouds skipping through the pale blue sky on the tails of a gently stiffening breeze.

"It's so lovely here," she sighed, taking her seat on a tartan-covered wooden stool. "I'm surprised Jack wanted to come home at all."

Sitting on his own tartan stool, Stuart 'Mac' MacIntosh reached for the pint glass. "Well, I could certainly get used to this." Taking a sip of the cool lager, he closed his eyes to savour the taste.

"You go easy. One's enough at this time of day — it's still early."

"It's my first one for months!" Mac grinned before taking another mouthful. "And I don't think you can get pulled over for being drunk in charge of these." He nudged the pair of crutches on the floor with his foot. "It's just nice to be out of that bloody hospital."

Isabel placed her hand on Mac's forearm and gave it a gentle squeeze. "It is. And this is just what the doctor ordered."

Mac's forearms and hands had healed remarkably well. Caught up in a catastrophic fire some seven months ago, his life had hung in the balance. After several skin grafts, the burnt skin was starting to become a distant memory. He'd regained movement and feeling in his fingers, and his ability to grip a pint glass was a particular relief. The only hint of the horror that came before lay in the slight mismatch in colour where the natural skin met the grafts. It was a small price to pay.

But the arms had been the easy part.

With both legs also severely burnt, the threat of amputation had never been far away. The latest skin graft operation had taken place eight weeks ago and, with the extensive debridement of the burnt tissue, plus the enforced bed rest afterwards, Mac needed to rebuild his muscles and regain his stamina — ready for the next round of grafting.

The physiotherapist at the West London Acute Burns Unit had been pleased enough with his progress to sanction a short break away, and they'd chosen the Tannochside B&B with which to start the process. With a strong recommendation from Mac's brother, Jack, it had been an easy enough decision.

"You do know I can't walk far." Mac eyed the map Isabel had spread out across the table.

She smiled. "Don't worry. I'm not planning any mountain climbing."

"And how was your first night with us?" Mac and Isabel both looked up to see a tall, burly man dressed in a cable-knit jumper striding towards them. "Everything to your taste, I trust?"

"Everything's just fine," replied Isabel, smiling up at Willie McArthur, landlord of the Tannochside B&B. "The breakfast was just fabulous."

"Aye, you'll not go hungry around here." Willie McArthur's eyes sparkled. "Not if my Margaret has anything to do with it. So, where are you two heading off to today?"

Isabel glanced down at the map. "I thought we'd start with just a drive around — with a few stops along the way to stretch our legs."

Willie McArthur leaned over the table and tapped a section of the map. "Aye, your best bet would be that road there. It'll take you all the way down to Loch Tannoch. You can park up and take a wee stroll around. It's nice this time of year."

"That sounds perfect." Isabel grinned across at Mac.

"And if you need a piece to take with you, just give my Margaret a shout. She'll fix you up with something tasty." Willie McArthur turned away, heading back towards the bar. As he did so, a young girl appeared in the doorway. She was fair-skinned with long, blonde hair tied up in a messy ponytail. A small Scottish terrier yapped around her ankles. "This is my granddaughter, Lily." Pride oozed from every pore of Willie McArthur's body. "Off to university in a couple of days."

Isabel gave a wave from her seat by the window.

Lily bent down and snapped a lead on to the excitable dog, and began to head towards the front door. "Just taking Banjo out for a walk, Grandad. We won't be long."

Willie watched the door close behind Lily and Banjo before starting to straighten the chairs and tables in the bar. "Mighty proud of her we are. University in London, no less."

His eyes glistened with pride. "She's not had it easy, bless her. But she's done us proud."

"She's very pretty, Mr McArthur." Isabel sipped her orange juice, glancing out of the window to see the slightly built girl striding off over the bridge, Banjo jumping around her feet. "But you don't look old enough to have a granddaughter going to university!"

"Aye, she's a bonnie wee lassie, that's right enough," agreed Willie. "Takes after her mother, God rest her soul." He straightened the last of the chairs and smiled back over at Isabel. "And I'm sixty-two, by the way. Getting on a bit now."

"Well, it must be all this wonderful fresh air keeping you looking so youthful!"

"Aye, maybe. Anyway, I'll leave you to it. Remember to ask Margaret if you'll be wanting to take anything out with you. Just go through to the kitchen — you'll more than likely find her out there." Willie turned towards the door that led to the guest bedrooms. "And it's Willie," he called back over his shoulder. "No more Mr McArthur. Makes me sound like my grandfather. I had to keep telling that policeman friend of yours the same thing."

Isabel watched as Willie McArthur disappeared out of sight. As she did so, she felt something tug at the back of her mind, and a faint frown touched her forehead. Something about the landlord of the B&B was familiar. It didn't go unnoticed.

"Problem?" Mac sunk another few mouthfuls of his pint, eyeing Isabel cautiously.

Hesitating only briefly, Isabel shook her head. "No. Not really. I just . . ." She broke off and drained the rest of her drink. "Ignore me." Pushing herself up from her chair, she gathered up the folded map and reached for Mac's crutches. "Come on, iron legs. Let's get out into that fresh air."

* * *

Time: 11.35 a.m.
Date: Friday 20 September 2013
Location: 3a Dolphin Close, EC1

Jack pulled the Mondeo to a stop a few doors down from where the white tent had been erected, enclosing the front porch and entrance to number three.

Exiting the car, he scoured the rest of the street for the Volvo he knew would be around somewhere. It was. Parked behind one of the scene of crime vans, it looked newly polished and waxed, reflecting the early morning sun. Jack cast a brief look back to the Mondeo, noting the mud splats decorating each wheel arch and the general dust and grime hugging the rest.

Where were the boy scouts when you needed them? Was 'Bob-a-job' week even a thing anymore? Jack resolved the take the Mondeo to a car wash — a promise he knew he was unlikely to keep, but it momentarily made him feel better.

"Let's go. Eyes and ears open at all times." Jack motioned for Cassidy and Cooper to follow him towards the white tent. "And don't get in anyone's way."

Once they were all clad in protective gear and overshoes, they each crossed the threshold into number three. It was a traditional two-up-two-down property that'd been converted into flats. The building looked well-maintained and cared for with freshly installed UPVC windows and a recently decorated hall. A set of narrow stairs led to flat 3b above.

Metal plates were arranged on the carpeted floor to indicate where they should and, more importantly, should not step. Jack saw a huddle of white-suited bodies congregating outside a small kitchen on the ground floor and, treading carefully, started making his way towards them. He hadn't got far when he heard someone call his name.

"Jack." Dr Philip Matthews stepped away from the commotion inside the kitchen and headed in Jack's direction, meeting him halfway along the narrow hallway.

Jack nodded in greeting at the tall, wiry police pathologist. "What've we got, Doc?"

Dr Matthews — whom Jack knew would be impeccably dressed in a three-piece suit, complete with bow tie, beneath his protective white gear — glanced back over his shoulder. "Young woman. Rough estimate of eighteen to twenty-five years of age. Found lying supine on the kitchen floor."

Jack raised his eyebrows. "Do we know how long she's been there?"

"Difficult to say. Rigor mortis has set in, but it's been a warm night. My best guess at this stage is anywhere between eight and twelve hours."

"Cause?"

Dr Matthews smiled. "You know me, Jack. I'm not one to speculate until I've got them on my table."

"But?"

"There are signs of substantial neck compression. A ligature of some kind would be my guess at this stage. I'll know more after the post-mortem."

Jack stepped to the side to allow Cassidy and Cooper to shuffle past. "Eyes and ears," he reminded them, before turning back to Dr Matthews. "Anything else of note?"

The pathologist hesitated, his eyes momentarily flicking back towards the crime scene. "You'll want to take a look yourself, Jack."

"So, there *is* something else?" It was more of a statement than a question. Jack felt his gaze follow that of the pathologist's back towards the kitchen.

"As I say, Jack. You'll need to take a look at this one."

"Boss?" Cooper's voice carried down the hallway. Jack looked up to see both he and Cassidy were heading back in his direction.

"I'll be seeing you, Jack." Dr Matthews turned towards the door, ready to discard his protective clothing and step out into the fresh air. "I'll let you know when she's on the table."

Jack met his two detective sergeants at the threshold to the kitchen. "What do we have?" Neither spoke: they merely shuffled to the side to let Jack past.

Elliott Walker, a crime scene manager Jack had worked with many times before, was kneeling down beside a pale, motionless body. He looked up as Jack approached.

"Good to see you, Jack." Elliott was a small, slight man in his mid-thirties. A keen triathlete, his lean and toned body was dwarfed by his oversized protective suit. His face was sharp and angled, with high cheekbones and piercing blue eyes. His closely-shaved head glinted, as it reflected the harsh lighting from above. "Mind where you tread."

"Elliott." Jack knelt down on a metal plate, hearing the cartilage crack in his knees as he did so. His eyes immediately focused on the blood pooled around the body, and splattered in waves across the nearby kitchen units. The lower half of the victim's body was stained crimson.

Elliott's face was pensive. "Looks like a strangulation, from the markings to the neck. But then we have the deep cut to the upper thigh. And then . . ." Jack followed the crime scene manager's gaze to the kitchen wall beside them. "And then there's this."

Two crime scene investigators parted to reveal the blood-stained wall beyond. Jack felt the bacon and cheese toastie from earlier begin to churn inside his stomach. The blood had dried but it still looked and smelled fresh.

Elliott placed his gloved hands on the young woman's body and gently pulled her to the side, careful not to disturb her overall position. A gaping wound was visible on her left buttock.

"Looks like a sharp instrument," continued Elliott, letting the body roll gently back down on to the cold linoleum floor. "Dr Matthews confirmed the edges look clean."

"Do we know who she is?" Jack found his eyes drawn back towards the blood daubed across the kitchen wall, trepidation growing.

"The ground-floor flat is rented to a Billie-Rose Blackburn. We've located a handbag with some personal effects." Elliott nodded towards a plastic evidence bag in a box by the kitchen sink. "We've bagged it up. There's a purse and a driving licence inside."

"Anyone else live here?"

Elliott shook his head. "Not known at this stage, Jack. I'll leave that one for you."

Jack returned his gaze to the body. "I probably don't need to ask, but . . ." He nodded towards the young woman's hands, still laced together in her lap. "The same?"

The crime scene manager nodded before placing his own gloved hand on the woman's fingers. "Rigor mortis has set in, but you can still see it."

Jack leaned in, peering at the gaps between the woman's delicate fingers.

It was there.

"And the mouth?" Jack almost didn't want to ask.

Elliott merely nodded. "The same."

Hearing his knees protest once again, Jack pushed himself up and turned to Cassidy and Cooper who were still hovering by the door.

"He's back," he said, simply, taking another look over his shoulder at the crime scene. "He's back."

CHAPTER TWO

Time: 1.45 p.m.
Date: Friday 20 September 2013
Location: Metropolitan Police HQ, London

"Four murders." Jack pinned four colour photographs to the incident room cork pin board. "All in the summer of 2009." DS Cooper and DS Cassidy both reached for the small bundle of paperwork in front of them.

Jack tapped the first photograph on the board. "First, we have Stacey Fairbrother. Age twenty-five. Found dead in her flat in Chelmsford in July 2009."

Jack then moved on to photograph number two. "Next, we have Shona Michaels. Age twenty-three. Also found dead in her flat in Chelmsford some two weeks later."

Moving to the other side of the pin board, Jack pointed at the third photograph. "This is Frankie Robinson. Age twenty-one. Her body was found in a flat above a tattoo parlour in Brentwood in August 2009." He then tapped the final picture. "Then we have Esther Faulkner. Age twenty-seven. Found dead in her home in Braintree at the end of August 2009.

"All had been strangled, and all had a deep laceration to their upper thigh, catastrophic blood loss. Blood that the killer then used to write on the walls next to his victims." Jack pinned up four more crime scene photographs. "Each time it's the same symbol, written in the victim's own blood." Jack paused, watching both Cooper and Cassidy take in the graphic images. "The killer was dubbed The Bishop."

Cassidy dragged her gaze away from the gruesome crime scene photos and down to the paperwork in her hands. "Because of the wooden chess piece found in each victim's hand?"

"Partly. A hand-carved bishop was found with each victim — but the symbol painted on the wall in blood at each crime scene was that of a mitre — a bishop's hat." Jack pulled a chair across to sit by Cassidy's desk. "You'll see that a separate chess piece was inserted into each victim's mouth." He pulled out four more photographs from Cassidy's bundle of paperwork.

Cassidy eyed the images. "Not a bishop this time?"

"No, a different piece each time. Stacey Fairbrother had a knight placed in her mouth. You know — the horse. Shona Michaels had a king. Frankie Robinson, a castle or rook. And with Esther Faulkner, it was a queen." Jack tapped the photographs of the wooden chess pieces. "And the chess pieces aren't his only calling card."

"There were the flesh wounds." DS Cooper woke up the interactive whiteboard and pulled up several bloodied images of gaping wounds. "Each victim had a portion of flesh removed from their body."

Cassidy pushed away her half-drunk chai latte and wrinkled her nose. "They're certainly not pretty."

"Indeed," agreed Jack. "The cause of death for all four victims was strangulation and exsanguination. The killer makes a fatal cut to the femoral artery in the thigh while at the same time choking the life out of them." Jack let the words sink in. "He needs to be caught."

"DNA?" asked Cassidy, more in hope than anything else.

Jack shook his head. "Nothing from any of the scenes in 2009. The only DNA retrieved belonged to the victims themselves."

"What would he do with a lump of flesh?" Cassidy shivered as she began to think of the possibilities.

"Nobody knows. The initial investigation never discovered a motive."

"And we're sure our body from this morning is a victim of the same killer?" As well as the abandoned chai latte, Cassidy returned her unopened cereal bar to her pocket, her appetite diminished.

"Has to be. The chess piece in the mouth was never made public during the original investigation. Neither was the bloodied mitre symbvol on the walls." Jack paused. "Unless there's been a leak of classified information, we have to be looking at the same killer."

"Or someone known to them?" suggested Cooper.

"Perhaps," conceded Jack, getting to his feet and pinning another colour photograph to the cork board next to those already there. "We believe this morning's body to be that of Billie-Rose Blackburn. Lived alone in a ground-floor flat on Dolphin Close. Next of kin are being traced to get a positive ID. House-to-house is currently underway."

"Why now?" asked Cooper, frowning. "If it's the same killer, why have a break for four years and then start killing again?"

Jack's eyes narrowed, not taking his gaze from the photographs lined up on the pin board. "That I don't know. We'll check out the usual recent releases from prison and liaise with the probation service."

"So, what's next?" Cassidy eyed the paperwork in front of her. "It says here a DCI Graham Hobbs was in charge of the previous investigation in Essex. Should we give him a call?"

"Ordinarily, yes." Jack hesitated. "But in this case, I think the personal touch is required — leave that one with me."

Picking up his own bundle of paperwork, Jack grabbed his jacket. "I'm needed upstairs. While I'm gone, sift through the previous investigation papers. You need to know those four cases inside and out. When I get back, we'll go over what we have."

* * *

Time: 2.00 p.m.
Date: Friday 20 September 2013
Location: Lorimer Street, NW1

Thick curtains blocked out the early afternoon sun, plunging the room into a murky dimness — just the way he liked it. Switching on the anglepoise lamp on the corner of the battered workbench, he directed the light towards the wooden block in his hand and sat down.

He loved the feeling of wood against his skin. It felt solid: almost alive beneath his touch, as if it were breathing. And from that one simple block, he could mould and create whatever he wanted.

He was in control.

Running his fingers across the light grain, he felt a brief quickening of his heart. Opening a drawer, he brought out a selection of tools and lined them up on top of the workbench. He let his fingers caress the length of the chisel and then each of the wood carving knives, straightening each until he was satisfied they were all aligned perfectly. He felt like a surgeon laying out his instruments before an operation.

Which, in a way, he was.

He was almost ready to begin, but there was just one more job he needed to do first.

At his feet lay a watertight plastic bag, its contents hidden behind a watery red smear. He smiled as he felt its weight in his hands.

Pulling down a set of digital scales and an empty glass jar from the shelf above, he carefully placed the plastic bag on to the scales, his smile broadening. Almost exactly sixteen ounces. Perfect. He was getting good at this.

Unscrewing the lid on the glass jar, he broke the seal on the plastic bag and carefully tipped its slippery contents into the jar. It gave a satisfying wet thud as it hit the bottom. Reaching for a second jar, he wrenched off the cap and poured the liquid inside over his new specimen. The familiar odour of formaldehyde grazed his nostrils and tickled his throat.

He smiled again.

Billie-Rose's buttock flesh floated among the watery suspension, the liquid turning a very pale shade of pink. Screwing the lid back on, he placed the glass jar back up on to the shelf next to the others.

Five jars lined up together in a neat row.

Waiting.

Waiting for another.

Dragging his gaze away from his trophies, he sat back down on his workman's stool and picked up the chisel.

It was time to start again.

* * *

Time: 2.30 p.m.
Date: Friday 20 September 2013
Location: Metropolitan Police HQ, London

"Jack." Chief Superintendent Douglas 'Dougie' King waved Jack towards a vacant chair and busied himself pouring two mugs of Colombian coffee from the machine behind his desk. "How are things?"

Jack dutifully sat down. "All fine, sir. New investigation up and running."

"Ah, yes. The Bishop, so I hear. News travels fast." The chief superintendent placed a steaming mug in front of Jack. "I take it you're accessing the previous investigation?"

"I've left the team going through the first four murders, seeing what we can find — if anything."

"How are you intending to play this one with the press?" Dougie King slipped himself back behind his desk. "As soon as they get wind of the Bishop being back, you know the kind of shitstorm that'll inevitably follow."

Jack took a sip of his coffee, the scalding liquid burning his lips. "I haven't really given the press much thought yet."

"I know your feelings about the media, Jack, but we can't ignore them. Not anymore. They'll find out about this, one way or another, no matter how tight a ship you think you have. They have their sources." The chief superintendent nursed his mug in his hands. "And it's best not to be on the back foot with this one. Take the news to them, Jack — not the other way around."

Jack nodded. He expected the news to hit the tabloids any moment. The press, as a rule, weren't slow to react — and the Bishop was too good a story to be passed up. "I know," he conceded. "I'll think of something."

"Make sure you do, Jack. And fast. Press conference is booked for tomorrow morning, first thing."

Jack hid a groan behind his coffee mug. "I'll get on to it right away, sir."

Chief Superintendent King drummed his fingers against the side of his mug, the only sound in the room bar the ticking wall clock and the faint trill of a ringing telephone from Penny's office next door. The silence continued, as did the drumming. Jack knew there was something else coming. He and the chief superintendent knew each other too well — and he didn't have to wait long.

"As well as the media, Jack, I need you to bring the profiler in on this one."

And there it was.

Jack's eyebrows shot up above the rim of his mug. "The profiler? Again?"

Chief Superintendent King nodded. "I know it's not your thing. Believe me, we're all well aware of that. But in a high-profile case such as this — and it *will* be high profile — you're going to need to keep your wits about you. Once this hits the media, the eyes of the whole country will be on you, Jack. If not the whole world. We can't be seen to mess this one up."

Jack ran a tongue over his coffee-singed lips. Profiling. Even the word sent a shiver through his body. More of a fan of good old fashioned police work, he couldn't help but bristle when it was mentioned. But he found himself nodding in agreement; there was no point holding out. "I'll get the papers sent over today."

Relief seemed to flood the chief superintendent's cheeks. "Good to hear, Jack. And how are things, generally? Your brother?"

Jack placed his half-drunk mug down on to the desk. "Things are good." It wasn't strictly true, but Jack wasn't about to divulge how he was trying, and failing, to track down a dead man — a dead man he suspected of having killed his mother and staged her suicide.

No, the chief superintendent wasn't quite ready to hear that.

So, Jack let the same words spill from his mouth — just like he always did. He was getting good at it now.

"Everything's fine, sir. Stu's recovering well." He took another mouthful of rich Colombian coffee. "Everything's fine."

CHAPTER THREE

Time: 6.20 p.m.
Date: Friday 20 September 2013
Location: King's Cross Underground station, London

She was the one. The next one. Of that he was certain.

He'd been following her for the last week — at one point even standing next to her on the station platform, although she'd been oblivious to his presence. Hiding in plain sight. He was good at that.

She'd been working late again today, and hadn't left the office to run for the Tube until after six. But he'd waited. He was patient. And he knew she'd be worth it.

Billie-Rose had excited him — reawakening a feeling that he'd missed for so long. Just seeing that look of terror in her eyes had instantly resurrected that exquisite thrill. Four years was a long time.

But now he was back. And he wouldn't leave it so long next time.

Next time.

He watched as she hurried across the plaza and headed towards the entrance to the Tube, and followed at a discreet distance.

Not long now.
Not long at all.

* * *

Time: 6.45 p.m.
Date: Friday 20 September 2013
Location: Metropolitan Police HQ, London

His chat with the chief superintendent had set Jack's nerves jangling. The strong coffee hadn't helped either. Pippa Reynolds from the force's PR department was organising the press release for tomorrow, which they both knew Jack would only loosely follow, and before the end of the day Dr Rachel Hunter – the force's criminal profiler – would have a new case to work on.

Jack pushed both thoughts from his cluttered mind.

"We need to go back to the start." Although it was beginning to get dark, he pushed the window open to the maximum allowed. With only a slight breeze outside, not one breath infiltrated the stuffy incident room. He turned back towards his team. "Too many assumptions were made last time. We need to start afresh with an open mind. Cooper — summarise again what we have so far, starting with the first victim from 2009. Stacey Fairbrother."

DS Cooper brought Stacey's file up on to the interactive whiteboard screen. "The previous investigation focused on her job at a local pub in Chelmsford. On the day of her murder, she left work at a little after one o'clock in the morning. It was a short five-minute walk to her ground floor flat." Cooper clicked the mouse and brought up a different image. "Very early on, they focused their attention on this man — Vince Butler. He worked locally, lived in Colchester – which isn't a million miles away from Chelmsford – and was a regular at the Six Bells pub. The landlord confirmed Stacey had worked for him for several years, working roughly five evenings a week. He wasn't aware of any ex-boyfriends and didn't think she had a current partner at the time."

Jack's face tightened. "You see, that's their first error right there. They had Vince Butler in their sights and focused all their energy on him. They didn't delve any deeper into Stacey's background."

"Then the second murder happened, fifteen days later." Cooper clicked the mouse and brought up the file on Shona Michaels. "She lived quite close to Stacey — about fifteen minutes away on foot. Similar scenario — body found in the flat, alone. Apparently, a flyer for the Six Bells pub was found in her handbag."

"Error number two," sighed Jack. "Another assumption. Believing she went to the Six Bells pub purely from that flyer. If I manage to teach you two anything, it's this. *Never assume anything*. There was no evidence Shona Michaels ever frequented the Six Bells — the landlord didn't recognise her. And there was no evidence that she knew Stacey, either — despite living close by. But again, by focusing on Vince Butler, they failed to dig any further into Shona's family background or personal life." Jack nodded at Cooper to carry on.

"There was then a gap of seventeen days." Cooper brought up the file on Frankie Robinson. "The third murder was thirty miles away in Brentwood. She had no known links to either of the first two victims, or the Six Bells pub."

"Or Vince Butler," added Jack, his tone sharp. "But, as you'll see from the file, they still focused the investigation on him. There's very little in the paperwork about Frankie. They had such a hard-on for Vince by that time, he completely blinkered their vision. Carry on, Cooper."

"The fourth murder was nine days later in Braintree. But, by then, they'd already arrested Butler and he was being held at Colchester police station when Esther Faulkner was killed."

"Which was their downfall." Jack rubbed the back of his neck. "Vince Butler was in a police cell at the time of the fourth murder. Probably the greatest alibi anyone could hope for. Later that year, Butler was convicted of two particularly nasty murders, details of which are in the case files. He was certainly a killer, just not the one they were looking for."

"What happened with the investigation after that?" Cassidy had been studiously making notes in her notebook

"Not a lot by all accounts. The post-mortems for all four victims confirmed there were no traces of drugs or alcohol in their systems. They were not subdued or incapacitated. No signs of forced entry at any of their homes. It seems they invited this guy in. None of the victims had any defensive wounds to speak of." Jack paused and looked at his team. "They trusted him."

An uneasy silence descended as three pairs of eyes studied the five photographs on the cork pin board. Jack soon found the thought of tomorrow's looming press conference disturbing his mind and glanced at his watch. "That's enough for today. Get yourselves off home. We'll pick this up again in the morning when we might have some forensics results in. I want you both in bright and early. We've a press conference scheduled for eight thirty." Jack noticed the look of alarm crossing Cassidy's face and afforded her a grin. "Don't worry, I'll be on my best behaviour.

"There'll be a hotline number for the public to call with any information." Jack shrugged back into his jacket. "I'm expecting it'll be jammed with the usual time-wasters, but we need to be prepared for the unexpected. Pippa's drafting in bodies to answer the calls." Jack eyed both of his detective sergeants as they rose from their chairs. "Anything else before we call it a day?"

"I heard you're involving the profiler again?" Cooper failed to hide the smirk on his face.

Jack felt his own mouth twitch. "Then your ears are working just fine, Cooper. I'm about to send it all over to her now." He picked up a thin manila folder and waved it in the air while heading towards the door. "Until tomorrow."

* * *

Time: 7.30 p.m.
Date: Friday 20 September 2013
Location: Lorimer Street, NW1

He'd resisted the urge to sit next to her on the Tube. That would have been both foolish and reckless. Instead, he'd boarded the carriage at the last minute and hovered by the door. She sat with her handbag on her lap, reading a battered paperback, not once looking up at her fellow passengers. If she had, she would have noticed one of them watching her intently.

He'd stayed for a few stops then alighted and left her to continue her journey alone. He already knew where she was going — he'd followed her before — and their time together would come soon enough.

He lined up the beautifully crafted chess pieces on his work bench. A bishop and, this time, a queen – the most majestic and powerful of all the pieces. They were almost perfect — just a little more sanding and they'd be ready.

Feeling the familiar quiver of excitement bubbling inside, he picked up his notepad and began to write.

I need to tell him what's coming next.

* * *

Time: 10.30 p.m.
Date: Friday 20 September 2013
Location: Kettle's Yard Mews, London

The evening was still warm and sticky, so Jack threw open the window in his living room as far as it would go. A faint breeze wafted past the curtains. His head felt thick and the beginning of a headache thumped at his temples. The floor was littered with papers and reports from the first four murders attributed to the Bishop, plus the remains of his Indian takeaway. The more he'd read, the more incensed he was with DCI Hobbs' handling of the case. The man was an imbecile. And, in Jack's opinion, could have cost the lives of innocent women. Now the Bishop had resurfaced and landed on his patch, Jack wanted to know why.

Billie-Rose's mother had travelled up from her home in Bournemouth and formally identified her daughter's body two hours ago. With a name now attached to the victim, Jack was intent on finding justice for her.

And justice meant catching the Bishop.

Stepping over the post-mortem reports, he made his way to the kitchen and pulled a cold beer from the fridge. Grabbing his phone, he tapped out a message to his brother. He hadn't heard from Stu or Isabel since they'd landed in Scotland, although he knew they'd be more than well-looked after by Willie and Margaret McArthur. And right now, Jack would give anything to be up there with them.

Placing the phone on the coffee table, he collapsed onto the sofa and closed his eyes. He knew that sleep would be a distant dream tonight. The new investigation would be circling his brain for hours, and the thought of tomorrow's press conference was already leaving a bad taste in his mouth. He washed it away with a mouthful of beer.

The new investigation would be taking up all of Jack's time now, and he knew he should bury his desire to locate Quinn. The man had been declared dead — so the usual avenues for tracing him would be closed off. It would be like trying to find a speck of dust in the dark. But Quinn wasn't the only skeleton rattling Jack's closet.

There was Joseph Geraghty.

The gangland boss was meant to be living the life of luxury on a Cuban beach, but Jack knew better. The Met's most wanted had been seen back in the capital, and ever since Jack had learned how he'd swindled Isabel Faraday out of her inheritance – and possibly been involved in the accident that killed her parents – his loathing for the man had intensified.

The French police accident report on the fatal car crash was still lying in his desk drawer back at the station. He hadn't shown Isabel — right now she had enough on her plate with Stu's recovery. She didn't need that particular bombshell ricocheting through her life anytime soon.

So, Jack had kept quiet about Joseph Geraghty.

Draining the rest of his beer, he heard the beep of an incoming message. Expecting it to be a reply from Stu, most probably telling him what a wonderful dinner Margaret had cooked up for them, he reached for his phone.

Glancing at the screen, he frowned at the number. It wasn't one he recognised and certainly not Stu's. Clicking on the message icon he placed his empty beer bottle on the floor.

The message was short.

'I know where he is.'

CHAPTER FOUR

Time: 8.15 a.m.
Date: Saturday 21 September 2013
Location: Metropolitan Police HQ, London

Jack had tried calling the number on the screen several times last night, but each time he received the same recorded message.

The number you have dialled is no longer in service.

As he made his way towards the conference room, still feeling the exhaustion from a restless night's sleep, he tried to focus his mind. He had a serial murder investigation to conduct and there was a lot to get through today — including the press conference starting in fifteen minutes' time. The very thought still jarred his nerves.

But all he could think about was James Quinn.

For he was certain that was who the anonymous text message was referring to.

It had to be.

Someone knew where he was.

Pippa Reynolds gave Jack a warm smile as he entered the conference room. "We'll try and keep it brief, Jack — limit the amount of questions afterwards. But you know how it goes . . ."

Jack nodded and returned what he hoped passed for a smile and not a grimace. He took his seat on the raised platform in front of the bank of microphones and recording equipment and sighed. He knew the chief superintendent was right — they needed to get the general public onside if they stood any chance of apprehending the Bishop. And that meant making friends with the media. The thought still turned Jack's stomach, but he pushed it to the back of his mind and poured himself a glass of water.

Chief Superintendent King had worn a decidedly wary look when Jack insisted on handling the press conference himself. Jack's relationship with the media could be described as testy at the best of times. But it was his investigation: therefore, it was his press conference — as much as he detested them.

Jack had chosen DS Cooper to be his wingman, knowing that the dependable detective sergeant would do his best to keep Jack in check if the situation looked to be boiling over. As if on cue, the ginger-haired detective hurried in, clutching a bundle of papers and slipping into the vacant seat next to Jack. "Ready?"

Jack began to nod when movement at the front doors indicated that the circus was about to begin. He took another mouthful of water and vowed to keep his cool. The sooner they got this performance over and done with, the sooner they could get back to work.

Jack recognised many of the faces filing into the conference room and, as he watched them taking their seats, he scanned the crowd for those most likely to cause him trouble. Top of the list was Jonathan Spearing. It didn't take him long to spy the *Daily Courier* reporter sauntering in and taking a chair on the far side. Dressed in a faded Stereophonics T-shirt and scruffy black jeans, he looked like he'd just rolled out of bed. Which was more than possible.

A hush descended as Pippa took up her position in front of the microphones. With a slight raise of her hand, all eyes focused on her — only the faint rustle of paper and notepads could be heard in the background.

"Thank you all for coming here this morning." Pippa's keen eyes searched the rows of journalists facing her. "We know how busy you all are. Which is why this press conference will be short. Please let Detective Inspector MacIntosh deliver the press statement to you in its entirety. Please be respectful. No interruptions." She paused, letting her eyes seek out the habitual offenders. "Time permitting, limited questions may be posed at the end. Thank you."

Turning towards Jack, Pippa gave him a quick nod and then stepped into the wings.

Jack decided that he may as well just get started. He hadn't brought any notes with him — he didn't need them. Everything about The Bishop was already ingrained in his memory. He cleared his throat and began.

"Early yesterday morning the body of a young woman was discovered at an address in Dolphin Close EC1. A positive identification has now been made by the next of kin. Billie-Rose Blackburn was last seen walking home at approximately eight o'clock on the evening of Thursday 19 September. At 7.15 the next morning, her body was discovered by a work colleague. A post-mortem examination will be performed later today to determine the exact cause of death, but at the present time we are treating it as murder."

A photograph of Billie-Rose illuminated the screen behind Jack and Cooper, appearing underneath the logo for the Metropolitan Police. Jack paused and looked out across the sea of expectant faces, most of whom were hanging on to his every word. A variety of digital recorders were held aloft, while others noted down the salient points using old fashioned pen and paper. He sought out Jonathan Spearing once again, and momentarily held the dogged reporter's gaze. Despite the many run-ins Jack had experienced with the senior crime correspondent in the past, he held a somewhat unorthodox respect for the man. Up to a point. He could be both friend and foe during an investigation, depending on where he felt the best story could be found.

Jack cleared his throat again and continued. "In 2009, a series of murders took place across Essex. Stacey Fairbrother. Shona Michaels. Frankie Robinson. Esther Faulkner." One by one their photographs joined that of Billie-Rose on the screen behind him. Jack let the final image come into view before carrying on. "These women were all victims of the same killer."

"Is the Bishop back?" The voice rang out from the back of the conference room, but Jack didn't bother to acknowledge it, or try to locate its owner. He could almost hear Pippa tutting under her breath.

"We have reason to believe that the same individual is responsible for the murder of Billie-Rose — an individual previously dubbed the Bishop." Jack now had each and every journalist's undivided attention. He heard the rustle of paper being turned over in notebooks, and the scratching of pens over their surface. Hand-held recorders were lifted higher over heads. "I'm appealing to anyone who saw Billie-Rose as she walked home at approximately eight o'clock on Thursday evening. Anyone with a vehicle in the vicinity of Dolphin Close, who may have dashcam footage, please contact the police as a matter of urgency. You may have vital information. Similarly, anyone who saw anything unusual or suspicious in the vicinity of Dolphin Close please also contact the police. A hotline number will be disclosed at the end of the press conference."

"What's the significance of the chess piece in the hand?" Jack looked up to see a tall woman dressed in striped leggings and an oversized jumper. She was perched on the edge of her seat, spectacles balanced precariously on the end of her narrow nose.

"Was the Essex police investigation flawed?" Another question rang out from the other side of the room.

And then another. "Is this latest murder due to police incompetence?"

Jack could feel the strategically structured press conference disintegrating into freefall. The last question had been from Jonathan Spearing and Jack could feel the *Daily Courier* reporter's gaze boring into him. Tell-tale prickles began to rise on the back of his neck.

"Did you hear me say that, Jonathan?" Irritation edged Jack's tone as he locked eyes with the journalist.

"But you will be reinvestigating the first four murders?" persisted Spearing. "Seeing where the initial investigation failed?"

Jack tried to count to ten, but only got as far as three. "That will naturally form part of our current investigation into the murder of Billie-Rose. We have done this before. All evidence will be reassessed."

"Will the parents of the latest victim be pursuing compensation for the negligent handling of the initial investigation? For leaving the Bishop free to kill again?" This question came from another journalist that Jack recognised — a weasel of a man who worked for *The Telegraph*. Jack knew he didn't cover crime, being more at home in the financial and business pages. Quite what he was doing here, Jack hadn't a clue – apart from annoying him.

"My team will be concentrating on the evidence, and not supposition. Comments such as that, quite frankly, are not helpful." The irritation in Jack's voice edged towards anger.

"Why are you convinced this murder was committed by the Bishop?" Again, it was Jonathan Spearing's voice that rose above the general murmurings that were now filling the room.

"We're confident we're looking for the same perpetrator." Jack paused and took another mouthful of water. "Although the cause of death has yet to be formally established — we believe the same method was used."

"And the flesh wounds?" Spearing's eyebrows hitched above his spectacles. "I take it a similar wound was found on the latest victim?"

Jack gave a slow nod. "A similar wound was indeed found on Billie-Rose's body."

"What aren't you telling us, Inspector?" Spearing once again attempted to hijack the press conference. "You're withholding information from the media, aren't you?"

Jack felt the familiar prickles intensify. He managed to count to one and a half this time. "As with any investigation, certain information is withheld from the public domain. You know that, Jonathan. This investigation is no different."

"Have you spoken to DCI Hobbs?" Spearing wasn't giving up.

Jack flashed a look at Pippa, indicating that it was time to go. He got to his feet and nodded at Cooper to do the same.

"I think that's enough now, ladies and gentlemen." Pippa stepped in front of the microphones. "Full details including the hotline number will be on the website."

"Have you recovered, Detective Inspector MacIntosh?"

Jack froze behind his chair and sought out Jonathan Spearing once again. The *Daily Courier* reporter was on his feet, hand-held recording device still raised. Jack didn't bother even trying to count this time. "Do I look ill, Jonathan?" Jack held the reporter in a hard stare before resuming his exit from the raised platform. "I'm tickety-boo. Thanks for your concern."

Jack jogged down the steps from the raised platform and strode towards the door that Pippa had hastily pulled open, brushing past several reporters in his path. Out in the corridor, he let out a long breath and reached for the tie that was constricting his throat, pulling it loose. He could hear the scraping of chairs and murmuring voices coming from the conference room, their echoes following him as he walked.

Although it was not yet nine o'clock in the morning, Jack felt in need of a stiff drink. His head was pounding already and the rest of the day stretched out in front of him like a mirage, the end of which feeling tantalisingly out of reach. His stomach churned at the thought. As he pushed open the internal doors and began to climb the stairs towards his office, he pulled out his phone and again looked at the message that'd gone some way towards contributing to his sleepless night.

"I know where he is."

* * *

Time: 10.00 a.m.
Date: Saturday 21 September 2013
Location: Westminster Mortuary, London

Dr Philip Matthews switched on the voice recorder above his head and lifted his scalpel.

"Shall we begin?"

DS Cooper, clad in protective rubber apron and wellington boots, nodded and inched closer to the examination table, a mixture of intrigue and trepidation on his face. He found post-mortems fascinating, and in some inexplicable way he looked forward to being sent in to observe. It wasn't that he didn't find them gruesome, or upsetting: sometimes he did feel a little queasy, but he'd quickly learned the lesson not to eat beforehand — or for some time afterwards. The smell of death that clung to the insides of his nostrils really did put him off his bacon. But he found the human body a source of great fascination.

And the body before them today belonged to Billie-Rose Blackburn.

The pathologist glanced up and caught Cooper's eye, a smile tweaking his lips. It made a nice change to have someone observing who was not in danger of keeling over at the first sight, sound or smell of the initial incision. DC Cassidy, or *DS* Cassidy as Dr Matthews silently corrected himself, always made a valiant effort to stay upright, but it was not always rewarded. He could always detect the inner rumblings of nausea welling up inside her when she was dispatched to oversee the post-mortem examinations; which wasn't often. Jack was kind like that. He didn't often grace the mortuary with his own presence, either, preferring to send the enthusiastic Cooper in his place. Which suited Dr Matthews just fine. It was nice to have a kindred spirit accompanying him within the harsh confines of what could otherwise be a lonely and desolate place.

"Outwardly, we have the appearance of a healthy twenty-one-year-old female. Caucasian. No external identifying features except for a rose tattoo on the left inside wrist." Dr Matthews stepped back while the mortuary technician snapped several close-up photographs of the exposed body and the rose tattoo.

Bringing a stainless-steel bowl to the table, the pathologist carefully extracted the wooden chess piece from her laced fingers, before examining each hand in turn. "No markings or bruises on either hand. Fingernails are intact. No evidence of tissue beneath. Both arms are free from abrasions." He turned his attention to Billie-Rose's lower body and inspected each leg. "Similarly, no signs of defensive wounds on either leg or foot. One incision noted to the right upper thigh.

"Now dissecting the upper torso." Dr Matthews carefully made the first incision just below the right collar bone, adjacent to the shoulder joint. Making an identical incision on the opposite side to open up the chest cavity, he then brought the scalpel down through the abdomen to the pubic bone. A perfect 'Y' shape.

And 'why' was the reason they were here. Why a seemingly innocent young girl had ended up on this cold mortuary slab. It was something Dr Matthews hoped the next few hours would go some way to finding out.

Billie-Rose's ice-white skin appeared even paler under the harsh overhead lights. Signs of lividity were now prominent, the pooled blood confirming that she'd been lying on her back at the time of death or very soon after, and remained so for some time. Cooper watched closely as the pathologist cut away the layers of skin and subcutaneous tissue, exposing both the chest and abdominal cavities. Some rib cutters took care of the rib cage, and soon Cooper could see Billie-Rose's stilled heart, devoid of movement, devoid of life.

For the next hour, Dr Matthews removed Billie-Rose's internal organs — each one carefully weighed and measured, inspected for damage or disease. It was then time to explore the real reason the young girl's life had been so abruptly brought to an end.

"Looking at the neck, there is an extensive area of compression. Significant micro-haemorrhaging and abrasions. Discolouration is apparent. The area of compression is relatively smooth, and somewhat narrow, cutting into the flesh to a depth of six millimetres. A wire is a possibility."

Dr Matthews paused while more photographs were taken. Once completed, he again peered closely at Billie-Rose's neck. Then, taking the scalpel in his hand, he began to carefully dissect the wound. "No further external wounds visible to the neck area. Internally, the hyoid bone appears to be intact. Damage evident to the larynx and trachea. Signs of petechial haemorrhaging in both eyes, supporting the theory of strangulation."

Another stainless-steel bowl was brought to the table and the pathologist carefully extracted a wooden chess piece from between Billie-Rose's jaws.

A king.

Dr Matthews then turned his attention to the wound on Billie-Rose's upper thigh. "A clean wound, two centimetres in length. Complete severance of the femoral artery, inflicted pre-mortem. Blood loss would have been extensive." He paused and looked across the examination table at Cooper. "You ready for this?"

Cooper nodded.

Together, Dr Matthews and his mortuary technician gently took a hold of Billie-Rose's upper and lower body and turned her on to her side. They then completed the manoeuvre to leave the body prone, face down on the examination table.

Cooper's eyes widened.

Billie-Rose's left buttock was covered in congealed blood. Gently teasing the area with a fresh scalpel, Dr Matthews revealed a large wound gouged into the flesh.

"On the left buttock we see an eight-centimetre by five-centimetre wound. Both dermis and epidermis, plus subcutaneous tissue, has been exposed. Minimal blood loss suggests the wound was inflicted post-mortem. It has neat edges, most likely from a sharp-edged blade."

The mortuary technician leaned in and took more of the required pictorial evidence. Dr Matthews took the opportunity to glance once more across the table towards Cooper. He noted the shocked look on the young sergeant's face.

"I take it you've seen something similar before, detective?"

Cooper nodded, recalling the photographs they'd seen in the incident room. "Does he take it as a trophy? The flesh?"

Dr Matthews smiled. "Well, that's something for you and your colleagues to work out. What the motivations are behind the person that did this are, sadly, questions I cannot answer from this table."

Dr Matthews continued with the rest of the post-mortem, examining and re-examining every inch of Billie-Rose's body, gleaning every possible shred of evidence to ascertain how, and possibly why, the twenty-one-year-old had the misfortune to end up on the receiving end of his scalpel.

Once complete, the pathologist stepped away, handing his scalpel to his technician. He paused for a second and closed his eyes, then gave his customary bow before heading for the exit.

* * *

Time: 12.10 p.m.
Date: Saturday 21 September 2013
Location: Stansted Mountfitchet, Essex

Jack pulled the Mondeo off the M11 at Junction eight and followed the signs to the village of Stansted Mountfitchet. The journey had enabled him to push the memories of the press conference, and also James Quinn, out of his head — even if only temporarily. "Ever been to the wilds of Essex before, Amanda?"

"Not really, guv," replied DS Cassidy, gazing out of the window. "I think I might've been to a nightclub in Grays when I was training."

Jack smiled. "Well, we're going to posh Essex today — Grays this is not."

"Oh, and I've been to IKEA — but, you know, who hasn't?"

Me, thought Jack, reducing the speed of the Mondeo as they approached the outskirts of the village. Having never set foot in an IKEA in his life, Jack planned to keep it that way.

Traffic through the main high street was light, and they soon left it behind. Jack settled in behind an airport taxi and saw the sat nav suggested their destination was only five minutes away.

"Does he know we're coming?" Cassidy shielded her eyes from the sun that was slanting in through the windscreen. "This DCI Hobbs?"

"Not exactly," replied Jack, pulling down his own sun visor. "It'll be a nice surprise."

"Why do I get the feeling there's some history between you and this Hobbs fella?" Cassidy glanced sideways and gave Jack a sly smile.

Jack fought to keep a smile twitching from his own lips. "Because you would be correct, DS Cassidy. You see — I told you you'd make a great detective."

Jack pulled the Mondeo on to a single lane private road and then continued along what appeared to be nothing more than a simple farmyard track. He checked the sat nav and saw they were still, apparently, heading in the right direction. After passing several deserted outbuildings and bouncing past fields that had been harvested and laid bare, Jack pulled into a sweeping gravel drive that led to an impressive-looking detached house. Parking outside a separate four-door garage, Jack peered out of the side window. The house looked out across nothing but fields and hedgerows as far as the eye could see.

"Wow, this place looks expensive," remarked Cassidy as she opened the passenger door.

"And I'm sure it is," murmured Jack, killing the engine and stepping out into the warm September breeze.

The house sat on a gentle incline in among a sculptured lawn with immaculately clipped topiary hedges on either side. Cassidy began climbing the steps that led up to the front door, stopping and catching her breath when she reached the top. "Oh my goodness — you'll never believe what's out the back!"

Jack joined her on the top step where he saw a huge boating lake at the rear of the house. Glancing skywards, he detected several CCTV cameras attached to the outer walls, watching their every move.

"How come we're visiting him at home, then?" Cassidy turned away from the stunning views of the boating lake.

"We're here because DCI Hobbs is now *retired* DCI Hobbs and has nothing better to do than while away his days fishing in that private lake of his." Jack paused at the front door, wondering whether to knock or use the doorbell. He decided on a heavy-handed knock, knowing full well that the CCTV cameras would have already picked up their arrival some minutes ago. I bet *retired* DCI Hobbs can't believe his luck, he thought, smothering another grin.

CHAPTER FIVE

Time: 12.35 p.m.
Date: Saturday 21 September 2013
Location: The Gables, Nr Stansted Mountfitchet, Essex

Jack took great pleasure in making himself comfortable on the wide, cream-coloured corner sofa, even though a seat had not been offered. DS Cassidy hovered, warily, just inside the door. The stiff, humourless woman who'd shown them into what may have previously been a drawing room in days of old, gave him a stern and very disapproving look before striding away, no doubt in search of the master of the house.

Jack's eyes swept the room. It was a huge space, light and airy, with a decorative fireplace to one wall housing a modern wood burning stove. Several bookcases lined the walls, but Jack doubted very much reading went on in here. A well-stocked bar hugged the far corner, with decanters and crystal glasses lining the ornate sideboard. That was much more DCI Hobbs' style, mused Jack, recalling his former senior officer's penchant for a drop of the hard stuff.

But what really gave the room its wow factor was the floor-to-ceiling windows that opened out onto an extensive patio, complete with outdoor furniture and a built-in brick barbeque. Beyond the seating area, the neatly trimmed lawn stretched out to meet the shores of the boating lake.

"Sit down, Amanda — you make the place look untidy." Jack waved at Cassidy to take a seat.

"This place is amazing, guv," she breathed, edging further into the room. "Just look at those gardens, and that lake . . ."

Jack shrugged. "It's all right, I guess. If that's your thing. Whatever floats your boat." He grinned at his own joke.

"Detective Inspector MacIntosh, to what do I owe this great pleasure?" DCI Graham Hobbs strode into the room, a taut look on his face that failed to demonstrate any of the aforementioned pleasure. "I see you've made yourself comfortable." Sarcasm dripped from his tongue as he eyed Jack's relaxed form draped across the corner sofa.

Jack appraised the man striding towards him. He hadn't changed a bit. The same deep-set piggy-eyes bore into him with every step, exuding the same coldness and contempt that he remembered.

Still an arsehole, mused Jack.

As DCI Hobbs approached, Jack stifled a smile. The man was dressed in a chequered polo shirt in gaudy orange and tan-coloured shades, matched with a pair of eye-watering red, black and white harlequin-style trousers. A cream jumper was draped over his shoulders, the arms loosely tied around his neck.

Jesus, thought Jack. *It's a bloody clown.*

"I don't have long, Inspector. I'm very busy." Hobbs strode over to the patio doors and stood facing the sweeping lawns. "What is it that you want exactly?"

Jack feigned surprise. "Oh, sorry, are you off somewhere?"

"I'm playing golf with the chief constable."

"Oh, I'd never have known." Jack spied Cassidy trying vainly to suppress a snigger behind her hand.

Hobbs flashed Jack a dark look. "Make it quick, Inspector. Say what you have to say."

"The Bishop." Jack detected a slight flinch beneath the gaudy golfing attire.

"What?" An edge of irritation entered the DCI's clipped tone.

"The Bishop," repeated Jack. "He's back."

Hobbs' hostile gaze intensified, a frown darkening his tanned forehead. "What do you mean?"

Jack pushed himself out of the luxurious sofa and joined the DCI at the patio doors. "Sorry, I'll rephrase — if that was too difficult to understand. The Bishop — he's back."

Hobbs stiffened again, but continued to stare out towards the boating lake. "And what makes you say that?"

"I assume it's something to do with the fact that an identical murder has occurred on my patch." Jack's icy tone cut through the air. "And the fact that you failed to catch him the first time around. I'm reopening the first four cases — they're mine now."

"What do you want from me?" The DCI made a show of looking at his watch, a flashy gold imitation Rolex. Or maybe it was a real Rolex. Jack had no idea how you would tell, and he wasn't interested.

"Well, some common courtesy would be nice. Let's start with an insight into your investigation — something that the reports on the system don't show." Jack couldn't help the hostility beginning to creep into his tone. "You had a suspect at the time. Vince Butler?"

Hobbs turned towards Jack, maybe registering the fact that the more quickly he answered, the more quickly DI Jack MacIntosh would vacate his house. "We did. It's all in the file."

"You spent a lot of time and resources focusing on him." Jack took a step towards the DCI. "Took your eye off the ball, if you don't mind me saying."

"I don't think you're in any position to judge, Detective Inspector MacIntosh." A flash of anger crossed the DCI's taut face. "All the evidence at the time pointed to Butler being our killer."

"Except he wasn't."

"No," conceded Hobbs, averting his gaze back towards the boating lake. "He wasn't."

"Did you ever wonder why the killer just stopped? A quick killing spree in the summer of 2009 and then nothing?"

The DCI gave a non-committal shrug. "I don't profess to understand the criminal mind, Inspector. He stopped. That's all I know."

"Did you look into whether he could've been in prison? I don't want my team to waste their time if it's already been covered."

"We made the necessary investigations, Inspector. We weren't imbeciles."

Jack let his eyes rake over the DCI's choice of clothing and reserved judgement. "What else can you tell me about Vince Butler?"

A further frown darkened Hobbs' forehead. "Why? He wasn't our man."

"I realise that," replied Jack. "But he was an interesting suspect nonetheless. I can see why he was on your radar. You do know he was convicted of two murders later that same year?" Jack made a point of pulling out his notebook and flicking over a few blank pages. "Yes, here we are. October 2009. Killed a young girl by the name of Annabel Collins. Dissected her liver as a trophy. Claimed to have eaten it."

Hobbs remained silent, his gaze still fixed on the boating lake.

"Then another a month later — Matilda Renshaw. This time it was her kidneys that he removed." Jack paused. "You didn't think to re-interview him?"

"Why would I?" Hobbs turned towards Jack, the expression on his face quite clear that this line of questioning would soon be coming to an end. Another look at the wrist watch. "He wasn't our man. He was in custody at the time of the final killing. You know this from the paperwork. You're wasting your time, and more importantly you're wasting mine. Now I really must be getting on . . ."

"When interviewed about the death of Annabel Collins, he mentioned the Bishop." Jack continued, ignoring the fact that DCI Hobbs was now heading for the door. "He said he admired him. Revered him, even. And you still didn't think to re-interview him? He could've given you a unique insight into the warped mind of the real Bishop."

"Look, Inspector." Hobbs wrenched open the door leading to the entrance hall. "It wasn't a line of enquiry we decided to follow."

"Clearly." Jack tucked his notebook back inside his pocket. "So, what's happened with the investigation recently?"

"I'm retired, Inspector. As you well know." Hobbs again glanced at his watch. "It really has nothing to do with me anymore. Are we done now?"

Jack flashed a look at Cassidy, who'd moved across to the mahogany bar, and indicated it was time to go.

"Well, it's my investigation now. Don't worry, I'll clear up your mess for you." Jack strode over to the open door, Cassidy following on behind. "No, you don't need to thank me." He gave the DCI a hard stare. "We'll see ourselves out."

Hobbs delivered a further contemptuous look and followed his uninvited guests out into the hall.

"Oh, and by the way." Jack hesitated at the front door, which the sour-looking woman they'd encountered earlier had already opened, overseeing their long-awaited departure. He flashed a look back at DCI Hobbs. "You look like a twat."

* * *

Time: 2.30 p.m.
Date: Saturday 21 September 2013
Location: Lorimer Street, NW1

Once he'd closed the curtains, the room immediately plunged into darkness. He switched on the anglepoise lamp at the corner of the workbench and raised his gaze to the shelf above. His prizes. His possessions. His treasures.

The five glass jars were neatly lined up with their labels facing outwards. Even in the muted light he could see the blanched white flesh suspended within. He licked his lips. Soon there would be another — another to join his collection. His eyes came to rest on the first jar on the left-hand side of the shelf. Reaching up, he took the cool glass jar in his hands, caressing it like a newborn baby. Stroking the smooth sides, he watched the liquid sloshing soundlessly within.

"It all started with you, my sweet," he murmured, his voice barely more than a whisper. "It all started with you."

* * *

Time: 1.10 a.m.
Date: Wednesday 15 July 2009
Location: Salvation Row, Chelmsford, Essex

Stacey Fairbrother's feet ached. She couldn't wait to get home and finally step out of the four-inch heels which were, she now realised, a little optimistic for a seven-hour shift behind the bar of the Six Bells. As she stepped out into the street, she felt the beginnings of a few droplets of rain brush her cheeks. Marvellous. She pulled her thin canvas jacket a little more tightly around her shoulders, now wishing she'd opted for the parka with the hood which was currently hanging up on the back of her bedroom door.

She felt the chill air hit her midriff. She tried to pull her cropped T-shirt down, but there was no way the flimsy material was going to cover the gap. She sighed and turned in the direction of home, squinting through the drizzle that was now beginning to fall. It was only a five-minute walk, if that, and she told herself that she shouldn't complain. She had a good job here, with plenty of tips, and it fitted in nicely with her studies. She'd recently enrolled as a mature student at the local further education college for an interior design course.

Mature student. At *twenty-five*. She almost laughed when filling in the application form.

The street lights along Salvation Row cast their gloom on to the damp pavement as she clip-clopped her way along.

The sound of her heels echoed off the brickwork of the terraced houses as she passed.

Five minutes. Five minutes and I can get these sodding shoes off, she thought to herself, wincing as the newly formed blisters yelled at her to get a move on. Maybe a nice hot bath, lots of bubbles. It was late, but she didn't have any classes tomorrow so a lie-in was on the cards.

The street was deserted, as was usually the case. This part of Chelmsford went to sleep early, especially on a weekday. People closed their doors behind them after the working day was finished, cocooning themselves inside their own four walls — content to settle in for the night with a box set and some supermarket beer.

The pub had been busy with the regular Wednesday night pub quiz crowd, but once all the prizes had been allocated, most of the clientele had drifted away. Only a few regulars lingered.

The landlord kept the bar open later than usual to celebrate the fiftieth birthday of one of the pub's stalwarts. There were a few rounds of free drinks, and even a few bowls of peanuts. Stacey didn't mind staying on — she thrust her hand into the pocket of her jeans and smiled as her fingers closed around the fistful of tips she'd accumulated.

Reaching the end of Salvation Row, she quickened her step and turned left into her street. Ignoring the screeching blisters that were continuing to protest, she strode in the direction of her flat opposite the entrance to the local park. She was less than a minute away and the hot bath was calling.

Just then, she heard a rustling sound coming from behind. Her heart leapt and began to thud loudly inside her chest. She whipped her head around but could only see puddles on the pavement glistening in the light of the nearby street lamps, and a lone cat slinking away across the road to seek shelter underneath a parked car.

She shivered as the drizzle intensified and continued on towards her flat. She'd walked this route countless times at this time of night. Hell, she'd even stumbled across the park on her own in the pitch black after a night out in the centre of town.

But there was always that feeling — that thought in the back of your mind. She read the papers. She watched *Crimewatch*. It was always the same — the reconstructions played out on TV always showed a lone woman walking home through deserted streets, late at night. Stacey always told herself she'd never do that; she'd never be that stupid. But, of course, she did. Regularly. But it was safe around here. It was a good area. This was *home* — this was where she lived.

Her front door was now within her sights and she began to fumble in her bag for her key. The drizzle had turned into heavier and more persistent rain. Her blonde hair stuck to her scalp. She brushed away the strands that'd plastered themselves to her forehead, and wiped the raindrops from her eyes.

She'd just turned in through the gate that led to her front door when she heard it again.

Something, or someone, was behind her; she could sense it.

Reaching towards the front door with her key ready, she glanced quickly over her shoulder once more.

And it was then that she saw him.

* * *

Time: 2.30 p.m.
Date: Saturday 21 September 2013
Location: Lorimer Street NW1

As he placed the jar containing Stacey Fairbrother's flesh back on to the shelf, the feel of the cool, smooth glass beneath his touch made him shiver. He began to brush away the wood shavings scattered across the work bench: his latest creations were almost finished.

The muffled sound of the letterbox signalled the arrival of the post. He tutted as he made his way down the narrow stairs — deliveries were getting later and later these days, sometimes not arriving until well past four o'clock. Which was irritating if you were waiting for something.

Which he was.

Padding across to the doormat, he saw the small scattering of envelopes, the exquisite feeling of anticipation making him shudder. He could see it from here — the familiar scrawl across the off-white envelope.

There was no doubt who it would be from.

He grabbed the envelope, and ripped it open in haste.

CHAPTER SIX

Time: 2.45 p.m.
Date: Saturday 21 September 2013
Location: Metropolitan Police HQ, London

"How was the PM, Cooper?"

DS Cooper was already seated in the incident room when Jack and Cassidy arrived, fresh from their trip to the Essex countryside. Jack shrugged out of his jacket. The journey back had been quick enough, but the car had been warm and sticky. Air conditioning in the aged Mondeo consisted of winding down the windows and driving at speed. His jacket clung uncomfortably to his back.

Cooper spent the next few minutes summing up the post-mortem on Billie-Rose confirming that, as expected, the cause of death was likely to be strangulation by ligature, plus cardiac arrest brought on by evidence of torrential blood loss. He also confirmed a wooden bishop was recovered from her hands, and a wooden king from her mouth.

"Well, our trip to see the delightful DCI Hobbs hasn't added a great deal to what we know already." Jack ran a finger around the inside of his collar and loosened his tie. "But your homework for tonight is to look into the cases of

Annabel Collins and Matilda Renshaw. Both were victims of Vince Butler back at the tail end of 2009. He may not be the Bishop but . . ." Jack gave a shrug and accepted the fresh water from the dispenser brought over by Cassidy. "And read again the post-mortem reports on the first four victims. You'll see how strikingly similar they are. Same method. Same ligature. Same laceration to the femoral artery. No apparent defence wounds."

"So, he takes them by surprise?" Cassidy leaned up against the open window, fanning herself with her hand.

"And they feel comfortable in his presence," agreed Cooper. "Maybe someone they know?"

Jack smiled to himself. His team was smart.

"I don't want us making any of the same mistakes as the previous investigation — we'll dig deeper into Billie-Rose's background. I want to know everything about her."

Before Jack had time to sit down, the internal phone trilled. Cooper snatched up the receiver. After listening in silence for a few moments, he replied simply with "Yes, sir," and put the phone back in its cradle. He glanced up at Jack.

"You're wanted, boss."

* * *

Time: 2.55 p.m.
Date: Saturday 21 September 2013
Location: Metropolitan Police HQ, London

Jack took the seat that he felt was increasingly becoming his own, and accepted the coffee mug as it was passed across the desk. His throat felt dry — the offer of refreshments hadn't been forthcoming from DCI Hobbs earlier, not that Jack had expected anything from his former boss. If any coffee had been offered, Jack strongly suspected it would have been laced with something none too pleasant. There was certainly no love lost between himself and the newly retired DCI.

"Good press conference, Jack." Dougie King eased himself into his swivel chair and eyed Jack over the rim of his own mug.

"By that you mean I didn't instigate World War Three." Jack blew across the surface of his too-hot coffee, grateful for the caffeine about to hit his bloodstream. His stomach felt painfully empty and thoughts of a trip to the canteen were not far from his mind.

Chief Superintendent King's eyes sparkled with good humour, and he afforded Jack a smile. "That's always a bonus, yes. I heard there were several hecklers."

Jack shrugged. "Nothing I couldn't handle, sir."

"Quite." There was a brief pause before the chief superintendent continued. "I hear you've been out to see DCI Hobbs?"

Jack's coffee mug hovered, mid-sip, as he caught Dougie King's gaze through the rising vapour. "Good news travels fast, I see. What exactly did you hear?"

King managed a smile. "Well, I've had a complaint, Jack. Let's put it like that."

"A complaint?" Jack raised his eyebrows but continued to sip his coffee. "That's interesting. Who from?"

The chief superintendent's lips twitched. "I think you know who from, Jack. DCI Hobbs contacted me almost before you'd left his driveway."

"Did he now? That was good of him. He gave me the impression he was short on time — late for a golf session with the chief constable."

"He wasn't best pleased with your tone." Another twitch from the chief superintendent's lips, this one not quite so well hidden.

"Well, he's not a serving police officer anymore, sir, so I'd take what he says with a large fistful of salt."

"Indeed." Dougie King took another mouthful of coffee, eyeing Jack across the desk. "He particularly took offence to the use of the word 'twat'."

It was Jack's turn to hide his emerging smile. "I'm not entirely sure what his problem is. I felt I was nothing but courteous towards him. I wiped my feet and everything on the way in."

"Tread carefully, Jack. Wiped feet or no wiped feet. He might be retired, but he can still cause a few ripples when he wants to." The chief superintendent paused. "I've only just been invited back to the Bar Council dinners after last summer's shenanigans. Try to be a bit more diplomatic if you can."

"Well, his investigation into the Bishop murders was woeful. He wasted time and money focusing on the wrong suspect."

"That's as may be, Jack. I'll fob him off this time, calm him down. But just stay out of his way from now on."

"Sir." Jack finished his coffee, the hot liquid burning his throat on the way down, and placed his mug on the desk.

"And stay closer to home — try to resist the urge to make any more day trips to Essex."

* * *

Time: 5.30 p.m.
Date: Saturday 21 September 2013
Location: Tannochside B&B, Scotland

Mac eased himself into the chair by the fireside and tried not to grimace. His legs ached and sharp pains stabbed towards the small of his back. They'd walked further than intended today, the weather being so glorious. Isabel had constantly asked if he was all right, suggesting they take a break, but Mac insisted they carry on. He didn't have the heart to spoil it for her. He hadn't seen her looking so relaxed and carefree in a long time.

Isabel returned from the bar with a pint of lager for Mac and a large coffee for herself. "Willie says there's roast chicken on the menu tonight. I think I can smell it already."

Mac gave a nod followed by a long sip of his drink. He'd pop a couple of painkillers later when Isabel wasn't looking.

"You OK?" she asked, sitting on the stool opposite. "You look tired."

"I'm not surprised! You had me halfway up a mountain not half an hour ago!" Mac managed a wink across the rim of his glass.

Isabel leaned across to thump him, playfully, on his good arm. "That wasn't a mountain. It was a small hill."

"Whatever it was, I'm not moving from here tonight." Mac stretched his legs out underneath the table and tried to hide the wince that followed. "What's Willie up to, anyway?" He nodded to where Willie McArthur was dragging a small suitcase and bulky rucksack behind the bar. The landlord caught their eye and sauntered over.

"You two had an enjoyable day?"

Isabel smiled and sipped her coffee. "We did, thank you. Lots of fresh air and exercise."

Mac did his best to mirror Isabel's beaming smile, before burying his discomfort behind his pint glass.

"Glad to hear it. I'll bring you some menus over in a wee while." Willie turned to go. "I've just got to help Lily with the rest of her things. She's off in the morning." He paused and leaned up against a high-backed armchair. "Margaret's in pieces, bless her. We've not been away from Lily since she was six years old. Not even for one night."

Isabel took another sip from her frothy coffee. "It'll be a wrench for you both, but exciting for her too."

"Aye." Willie's eyes began to water. "She deserves it. She's worked hard, that one. And she's not had it easy — we lost her mother, our daughter, in a car accident when she was a wee young thing. Her father and brother too. In an instant, her whole family was wiped out." Willie paused, his chest heaving. "It was a rough time — but we got there in the end."

"She's a credit to you both." Isabel found her own eyes starting to water, Lily's past being so reminiscent of her own. "I lost my parents when I was young too." She gave Willie a sad but understanding smile. "She'll do you proud, I'm sure."

"Aye, she'll do that." Willie started to head towards the bar. "I'll get you those menus. No doubt you'll both be hungry."

Isabel took another sip of her coffee and glanced across towards Mac. Her heart swelled as she watched him with his head resting back against the chair, eyes closed, gently snoring.

* * *

Time: 6.00 p.m.
Date: Saturday 21 September 2013
Location: Metropolitan Police HQ, London

Jack slid into the only other chair in the room, accepting the glass tumbler passed across the desk without a word. He took a mouthful of the whisky, savouring the burning feeling.

"Heavy day?" DS Robert Carmichael nudged a pile of files to the side, making room for the whisky bottle.

Jack nodded. "You could say that." He pushed the thoughts of DCI Hobbs and the earlier press conference as far out of his mind as he could, casting his eyes around the small office. "Looks like you're bursting at the seams in here." He nodded at the filing cabinets along the back wall, the number of which had increased since his last visit, and the stacks of additional storage boxes piled up on top.

Carmichael gave a withered smile. "Don't remind me. They've offered me a bigger office, but I'm not sure I fancy carting this lot up three flights of stairs."

"I don't blame you." Jack swirled more whisky into his mouth. "So, update me on Operation Evergreen."

"It's growing, Jack. That's all I can say." Carmichael gestured to the towers of files stacked up against each wall. "And you've seen the news for yourself. Operation Yewtree has snowballed."

Jack nodded. "It sure has."

DS Carmichael had been tasked with investigating cases of child cruelty and possible abuse at a number of local authority children's homes. Initially centred in the south-east, the investigation had soon gathered pace and now covered the entire country. Running in tandem with the more widely known Operation Yewtree, Carmichael had never been so busy.

"But I'm guessing the antics of Jimmy Savile et al aren't what's brought you to my door. What's on your mind, Jack?"

Jack scratched at the stubble on his chin, while staring into the bottom of his now empty glass. Now he was here, he wasn't sure this was a good idea. Rob was a good friend, and an even better detective. Their working relationship had got off to a shaky start, something Jack wasn't proud of, but their shared past had later created a natural bond. Jack knew he could trust Rob to the ends of the earth — but he wasn't quite sure how far he should drag him down to wherever it was he was headed.

The sound of doors closing echoed along the corridor outside. Carmichael glanced down at his watch and then back up at Jack. "You have somewhere you need to be, or do you fancy a curry over the road?"

* * *

Time: 6.45 p.m.
Date: Saturday 21 September 2013
Location: The Duke of Wellington Public House, London

The pub was quiet, even for a Saturday. Jack headed over to their usual table, tucked away in the corner by the dartboard. Carmichael followed, carrying two pints of lager and a packet of salt and vinegar crisps.

"Here's to the end of another day." Carmichael lifted one of the pint glasses to his lips and took a mouthful as he slipped into his seat.

Jack mirrored the manoeuvre. It was the end of a *very* long day. He shrugged off his jacket and placed his phone on one of the beer mats, his mind instantly returning to the anonymous message about James Quinn.

'I know where he is.'

The message continued to burn inside his brain.

"How's the Bishop investigation going?" Carmichael interrupted Jack's thoughts. "I caught the edited highlights of the press conference."

"I've sent everything over to Rachel Hunter."

Carmichael's eyebrows hitched above the rim of his pint glass. "The profiler?" He hid the smile that began to cross his lips, but not before Jack had noticed.

"I know, I know." Jack rolled his eyes, trying to hide the evolving grimace. "But I need all the help I can get right now." Jack's mistrust and, at times, reproachful indifference to the use of criminal profilers was legendary throughout the department — and probably throughout the building. "And who knows . . ." He shrugged into his pint.

"They get some cracking results sometimes. She wasn't far off with the Peter Holloway case last year." Carmichael ripped open the packet of crisps. "Don't knock it."

"I'm not, I'm not." Jack held his hands up in mock surrender. "This is the new me you see before you."

Carmichael grinned. They spent the next few minutes in an easy silence, the waitress soon arriving with their food order. Jack had opted for the classic chicken tikka masala, while Carmichael had selected the lamb bhuna. A plate of naan bread sat between them.

"I heard about your run-in with that DCI earlier today." Carmichael tore apart a piece of warm naan bread and dipped it into his curry sauce. "Sounds juicy. Spill."

Jack pushed a forkful of chicken tikka into his mouth and eyed his friend across the table, his gaze narrowing. "How did you hear about that?"

Carmichael couldn't suppress the smile that broke out on his face. "Word gets around, Jack. Rumour has it you called him a twat."

Jack swallowed his chicken and ripped off a chunk of naan. "Well, he is a twat."

Laughter erupted from DS Carmichael. "You don't say! He used to be your senior officer when you were a rookie DC, am I right? Then he transferred to Essex?"

Jack nodded and shoved a wedge of bread into his mouth.

"So, what's the beef between you two? No one around here seems to know." Carmichael's eyes twinkled. "I've already tried asking."

Jack stirred some of his pilau rice into the tikka sauce and scooped a heap into his mouth before replying. "Something and nothing," he muttered, avoiding Carmichael's gaze. Something it definitely was: nothing it most certainly was not. Jack decided to change the subject.

"You know they've demolished what was left of St Bartholomew's? English Heritage did a U-turn on the preservation order after the fire. Looks like they want to distance themselves from it all now."

Carmichael nodded. "Well, that's no bad thing in my opinion. It won't be missed. How's your brother bearing up?"

Jack stabbed at a piece of chicken with his fork. "He's good thanks. They've let him out of hospital to have a break. He's gone up to Scotland — staying at that B&B I went to a few months ago. Isabel's gone up with him."

"That'll do him good." Carmichael drained his pint glass. "He's up and about walking, right?"

Jack nodded again, chewing the last of his chicken. "It was touch and go for a while. After the first big skin graft operation they weren't sure it was going to take. They were still seriously considering amputation." Jack paused and swallowed past the lump in his throat, which had nothing to do with the chicken tikka. Sometimes, the realisation of how close Stu had come to losing one of his legs hit him when he least expected it. He took another swig of his lager. "But, thankfully, he pulled through. He'll need a couple more operations on his legs, and another on his abdomen, but . . ." Jack shrugged. "I think he's over the worst. Physically, at least."

With their plates clean, Jack brought two more pints over to their table. He didn't fancy going back to the flat just yet. He knew what would be waiting for him when he did — visions of James Quinn swam in front of his eyes once again. He glanced down at his phone and the message that he knew was still there.

The man was now haunting his daylight hours as well as his nights.

He couldn't think of anything else.

James Quinn.

With their second pints half-drunk, Jack asked the question that'd been on his mind all evening.

"Rob . . . How do you find a dead man?"

CHAPTER SEVEN

Time: 9.15 a.m.
Date: Sunday 22 September 2013
Location: 3a Dolphin Close, EC1

Jack and DS Cassidy ducked underneath the blue and white police tape that still criss-crossed the front door leading to flats 3a and 3b. The entrance hall looked much the same as it had two days earlier, although the white forensic tent outside had been dismantled. Metal plates still guided their incoming footsteps, and several white-suited figures continued to comb every inch for the minutest detail left behind. Jack nodded at Elliott Walker, crime scene manager, who looked like he'd been there for every minute of the last forty-eight hours.

Nicole Grainger lived on the floor above Billie-Rose in flat 3b, and had confirmed she would be home that morning. As Jack ascended the narrow stairs, a figure he assumed to be Nicole hovered at the top. She was slightly built and dressed in a pair of grey jogging bottoms and a faded Glastonbury 2011 T-shirt. Her hair hung in strands either side of her pale face.

Jack reached the top and gave her one of his best smiles. He stepped to the side to allow Cassidy to do the same, knowing that her smile was likely to be more reassuring than his own.

"Good of you to see us . . . Nicole, isn't it?" Jack held up his warrant card. "I'm DI MacIntosh. We spoke on the phone? This is DS Cassidy. Can we come in and have a chat?"

Nicole nodded, her eyes blinking rapidly. "Of course." Her voice was quiet and breathy, as if it were taking every ounce of her energy just to mouth those two simple words. She backed away towards a door that was already open half-way along the upstairs landing.

The door led into a flat with a very similar layout to Billie-Rose's downstairs. The main room had a small single bed up against the far wall, and a well-worn sofa facing the tiny window opposite. A single door led off to what Jack presumed would be a kitchen area. He could smell the bitter aroma of burnt toast floating in the air.

As expected, sitting on the unmade bed was Mrs Blackburn – Billie-Rose's mother. A folded newspaper sat by her side, the garish headline standing out in bold letters for all to see.

SERIAL KILLER RETURNS

After the ordeal of identifying her daughter, Billie-Rose's mother had been too distraught to face the long journey home. Initially, she'd wanted to stay in her daughter's flat below – but as the area was still an active crime scene, she was faced with trying to find a cheap hotel. It was then that Nicole had offered to let her stay in the upstairs flat with her. Having met Billie-Rose's mother on a few occasions in the past, she'd been more than happy to offer.

"Mrs Blackburn." Jack eyed the mouse-like woman sitting on the bed. "We won't take up too much of your time."

Mrs Blackburn nodded, her face drawn and pale. She, too, looked as though sleep had evaded her for much of the last two days.

Jack turned his attention back to Nicole, who was hovering by the kitchen door, unsure of what she should do. "Nicole — I know you've already spoken to officers about what happened, but could you take me again through everything you remember?" Jack had read the hastily typed statement Nicole had given the previous day, but he always liked to hear the words spoken for himself. Sometimes words had a different meaning when spoken out loud — subtle nuances that were missed by the written word. "Let's start with Thursday last week."

Nicole nodded, her face mirroring the waxen complexion of her temporary house guest. She gave Billie-Rose's mother an apologetic half-smile.

"I . . . I was home all day," she began, her voice small and hesitant. "I'd worked the previous three nights and Thursday was my day off."

"Where do you work?" asked Cassidy, smiling to try and put the terrified girl at ease.

"At the cinema on Benton Street" Nicole swallowed and took in several deep breaths to control her nerves. "I . . . I came home about two o'clock that morning, and went straight to bed. "I . . ." She faltered and frowned a little. "I don't think I woke up until after twelve."

Jack nodded. Nicole had said as much in her written statement. "And then?"

Nicole shook her head. "I'm not much use, am I?" A sob caught in her throat before she continued. "I made some breakfast and sat in bed watching rubbish afternoon TV. Then I went back to sleep."

"And what then?" Jack noticed that while Nicole was talking, Mrs Blackburn was shedding silent tears, her narrow shoulders heaving with every sob. Cassidy crossed the room and went to sit at her side.

"I woke up about five o'clock." Nicole carried on. "I made some food and then listened to some music for the rest of the evening."

"The police were called just after seven fifteen on Friday morning by a colleague of Billie-Rose's. They said that there was no answer at the door when they knocked, so they went to use the spare key Billie-Rose kept under the flower pot on the front step. But it wasn't there." Jack paused. "Did you know about the spare key?"

Nicole shook her head. "N . . . no." She wiped her eyes with the back of her hand and a pained look crossed her face.

"Billie-Rose had also given this colleague a spare key — and after much searching through her bag, she eventually found it and let herself in. You didn't hear her knocking on the door beforehand? About quarter past seven on Friday morning?"

Nicole nodded. "I heard something, yes. It woke me up. But — I didn't think anything of it at the time. I thought it might be the postman." Pausing, she choked back a fresh set of tears. "I didn't know anything was wrong until I saw flashing blue lights outside in the street."

"And you didn't hear anyone else knocking at the door — during the evening before? On the Thursday? What time did you say you were listening to music?"

Nicole frowned as she tried to force her brain to think back. "After I made myself some food. I don't know — probably from six o'clock onwards? I put my music on when the news started."

Jack flashed a discreet look at Cassidy. Dr Matthews had given an approximate time of death of between eight and midnight on the Thursday evening. Based on that, there was every chance that Nicole was happily listening to music at the very time her friend downstairs was being murdered.

"You're sure you didn't hear anything coming from Billie-Rose's flat downstairs, anyone knocking at her door during Thursday evening?"

Nicole shook her head. "No. These walls are pretty thin. The sound of people knocking at the door tends to carry up the stairs. Even with my music on, I'm sure I would've heard."

"That's very helpful, thank you Nicole." Jack turned his attention to Billie-Rose's mother. "Do you need a glass of water, Mrs Blackburn?"

Mrs Blackburn shook her head, brushing away her tears with the sleeve of her cotton jumper. "No. Thank you." She tried a wan smile.

"As I said, we won't keep you long." Jack moved closer towards the unmade bed. "A family liaison officer will be with you when you get back home — they'll be with you for the next few days, or as long as you need them."

Mrs Blackburn tried another smile.

"But if I could just take up a couple of minutes of your time, then we'll get out of your hair. Billie-Rose had lived here for several years, yes?"

"Yes. She moved out of home in the August of 2010. She was eighteen."

Jack nodded. "Did she come back home much?"

Mrs Blackburn gave a sad smile and shook her head. "No. Billie-Rose didn't get along with my second husband. They clashed almost from day one. It was one of the reasons she moved out." Her shoulders heaved. "I rue the day I chose that man over my only daughter." Silent tears began to trickle down her cheeks once again.

"When was the last time you saw your daughter, Mrs Blackburn?"

"That would be last Christmas. She came to stay for a few days."

"No clashes with your husband?"

Mrs Blackburn gave a weak chuckle. "I'd thrown him out by that time — waste of space that he was. I kept meaning to come up and see her. After Tom left, there was no reason why I couldn't. But, well . . . you know. Life just gets in the way, doesn't it?" Her face crumpled once again.

"Thank you. I'm so sorry to have had to ask such painful questions. We'll be on our way now." Jack took a couple of steps towards the door. "The family liaison officer has your mobile number. They'll arrange a time to meet you at your home address. Use them. They're there for you."

Mrs Blackburn nodded, gratefully, through her tears.

Jack waved his thanks to Nicole and led DS Cassidy back out on to the landing. They descended the narrow stairs and went outside.

"What important thing did we just learn about our victim, Amanda?" Jack turned towards Cassidy, his eyebrows raised. After a momentary pause, he knelt down by the side of a terracotta flowerpot on the front step and tipped it to the side, revealing nothing but the dusty concrete beneath.

Cassidy slowly nodded her head. "No spare key."

Jack replaced the pot and straightened up. "If Nicole is right when she says she would have heard someone knocking, then unless Billie-Rose used the key herself, I think our killer might have let himself in."

* * *

Time: 10.00 a.m.
Date: Sunday 22 September 2013
Location: The Glade, Church Street, Albury, Surrey

The house was perfect. Its seclusion behind tall leylandii trees on three sides, and aged oak trees to the rear, meant that The Glade was a recluse's paradise. Inside, the high-ceilinged bedrooms, spacious kitchen and living area with separate study gave the property an enviable floor space.

But it wasn't the space that made it perfect.

It was perfect because it had once been Isabel's.

Joseph Geraghty pushed open the patio doors and stepped out into the back garden. He closed his eyes and took in a lungful of sweet-smelling morning air. The raised flowerbeds that flanked both sides of the patio were full of pleasantly-scented phlox and bergamot, together with clumps of lavender and rosemary . The gentle breeze and the gently warming sun caressed his cheeks.

He opened his eyes and surveyed the wide, sweeping lawn — neatly trimmed by the ride-on lawnmower he'd found in the adjoining garage. Stepping out on to the spongy grass, he headed towards the wall of shady trees that stood guard at the bottom of the garden. A rush of emotions quickly flooded his brain.

Nothing had changed — it was as if time had truly stood still and, once again, he was standing in the garden of the Faraday's family home.

When his gaze came to rest on the summerhouse, still nestling beneath the boughs of the largest oak tree, Geraghty's heart gave an involuntary twitch. He could visualise Isabel's tiny face peering out from behind the gingham curtains, a wide grin plastered from ear to ear. Inside she would have set up a tea party for her favourite teddy bears and dolls — and Geraghty would be required to kneel down and pretend to drink from a tiny plastic cup, and eat make-believe cake from a tiny plastic plate.

He pushed the memories aside and backed away from the shaded summerhouse, returning to the warmth of the patio. Pulling up a wicker garden chair, he sat back and once again let the sun start to warm his pale skin as he poured himself an iced tea.

He grinned. What self-respecting crime lord drank iced tea? Heading up one of the country's most infamous organised crime rings, Joseph Geraghty had been on The Met's most wanted list for some time. Last year, several of his employees had been successfully prosecuted, and were now serving lengthy prison sentences. The temporary vacuum in his empire was soon filled with new blood, but Geraghty still smarted at how close they'd come to destroying him completely.

And then there was Isabel. He'd been a long-time family friend of the Faradays — at one point he considered both Elizabeth and Christopher Faraday to have been his best friends. Isabel had known him as her 'Uncle Clive', but he lost touch with her soon after she turned eighteen — probably something to do with him running off with her inheritance fund.

Geraghty swallowed a chuckle, along with another sip of iced tea.

Thinking about Isabel and the Faradays inevitably led to thoughts of Jack MacIntosh. The dogged detective inspector's face filled his head, and Geraghty found himself smiling. Jack MacIntosh had been the bane of his life in recent years — the thorn in his side, the itch that just wouldn't go away — along with the rest of his cronies at The Met. The detective inspector had come close to catching him several times; closer than anyone had in a long while — but he was never quite quick enough.

He would be one day, of that Geraghty was sure — he was acutely aware that his nine lives were rapidly running out.

But he had one last ace up his sleeve.

James Quinn.

The man's name had landed in his lap quite unexpectedly — and, not one to look a gift horse in the mouth, he'd done some digging. And he now had something Jack MacIntosh didn't.

Information.

Information he knew the detective inspector would give his right arm for.

Geraghty wasn't sure if he believed in fate — but something had drawn James Quinn into his world, and he wasn't about to pass up the chance to use it to his advantage.

* * *

Time: 5.15 p.m.
Date: Friday 15 February 2013
Location: Skyline Apartments, Canary Wharf, London

As much as Joseph Geraghty admired the view from his penthouse suite, he knew he'd be moving on before long. He couldn't afford to stay in one place — people would start remembering his face. And once they started doing that, recognition wouldn't be far behind.

He left the balcony and headed towards the bedroom. Although it was only just after five, his body felt wretched. Tiredness came over him in waves these days — so much so that he couldn't do much but give in. But before he made it to the bedroom door, his mobile began to chirp. Glancing at the screen, he saw a name he recognised.

"Ritchie?"

Richard Greenwood had been a new addition to his criminal enterprise — he'd come highly recommended and Geraghty was keen to find out the man's true worth.

He didn't have to wait long.

"I think I've found something you might be interested in, boss."

Geraghty liked the way Ritchie called him 'boss'. It showed respect — showed that he knew who was in charge. And that went a long way in Joseph Geraghty's book.

"And what might that be?"

"MacIntosh."

That one word banished all thoughts of a late afternoon nap and Geraghty felt a renewed vigour kick in. "MacIntosh? What about him? I'm assuming we're talking about the same MacIntosh? The DI with the Met?"

"The one and the same," agreed Ritchie. "I've just stumbled across something rather unusual."

"Tell me more."

And Richard Greenwood did just that.

* * *

Time: 10.10 a.m.
Date: Sunday 22 September 2013
Location: The Glade, Church Street, Albury, Surrey

Geraghty took another sip of his iced tea.

He had known that placing one of his men inside the laboratory would bear fruit one day — he just hadn't banked on it being this particular kind of fruit.

James Quinn.

Quite why the man's skin had been found beneath Stella MacIntosh's fingernails, Geraghty neither knew nor particularly cared. But as soon as Ritchie had given him the details, he started digging. He'd accessed the police investigation reports into the demise of Stella MacIntosh relatively easily, not having lost his touch at infiltrating even the most secure databases. He got in and out without so much as leaving a single digital footprint. Not even a sniff.

The investigation into her death was brief and contained little by way of detail.

Suicide had been the conclusion.

But Geraghty's suspicions had been piqued — in the same way he knew Jack MacIntosh's would have been as soon as he got wind of the DNA result. And, armed with that information, Geraghty dug even deeper.

Quinn hadn't been too difficult to find: not for someone with Geraghty's contacts. Sometimes the sins of your past could be put to good use. On paper, the man was somewhat unremarkable. A small-time burglar, and not a particularly good one at that. But what had been interesting, and piqued Geraghty's natural curiosity, was how James Quinn was no longer meant to be alive. A declaration of presumed death was issued in 2009 after he'd disappeared without a trace from a cross-channel ferry seven years earlier.

A smile broke out on Geraghty's thin lips. He had to hand it to him – to all intents and purposes, James Quinn was dead.

Except he wasn't.

Leaning back in the deckchair-style wicker seat, he sipped more of his iced tea. It'd been a clever stroke to play — bold, even. But Quinn hadn't quite been clever enough. It took Geraghty less than a day to discover after his 'death' in 2002, Quinn had resurfaced as David Nash.

That had been his first mistake.

Geraghty knew everything there was to know about disappearing. And coming back from the dead.

And James Quinn had got it wrong.

Which meant James Quinn could be found — if you knew where to look.

CHAPTER EIGHT

Time: 11.15 a.m.
Date: Sunday 22 September 2013
Location: St James's University, London

Dr Rachel Hunter poured chilled water into two glass tumblers, passing one across her desk.

"I got your message." Jack took the glass, nodding his thanks.

Rachel Hunter, consultant psychologist and Metropolitan Police profiler, relaxed back in her chair. "I felt we could do with a face-to-face discussion about your new investigation." She was dressed casually in a pair of dark, slim-fit jeans with a thin, knitted beige jumper. Her auburn hair was scraped into a loose pony tail, her face bright and fresh with only the faintest hint of make-up. "I looked over the papers at home last night." She paused, her pale green eyes catching Jack's inquisitive look. "Yes, I know — I have no social life."

Jack kept quiet and sipped his water. *You're not the only one*, he thought.

"I found the papers most intriguing." Dr Hunter reached for a folder on her uncluttered desk.

"I'm grateful for any thoughts you might have," replied Jack. "We need to crack this one, and fast."

"Indeed." Dr Hunter opened the folder and slid out several sheets of paper. "The original investigation — I note they commissioned a profiler at the time." She paused, scouring the papers for the name. "A Dr Heinrich Bauer."

Jack nodded. "They consulted someone quite early on. I believe it led them to Vince Butler."

"Quite. Dr Bauer isn't a psychologist known to me in the criminal profiling scene. And I do have one or two issues with his findings."

"Oh?" Jack's eyebrows shot up a notch. "Issues in what way?"

"Well," began Dr Hunter, taking a sip of water. "I'll give you a brief outline of my own findings — indicating where my thoughts differ to Dr Bauer's."

Jack pulled out his notebook. "Fire away."

"Firstly, I believe your perpetrator to be younger than Dr Bauer's estimate. At the time of the offences in 2009, I would put him in the twenty to twenty-nine age bracket. I'll expand on that in a moment. But Dr Bauer thought he was much older — forties to fifties."

Jack scribbled a note and nodded for Dr Hunter to continue.

"Secondly, I agree that the man you're looking for — and I *am* certain it's a man, Inspector, you know the statistics on female serial killers — he'll be of above average intelligence. Markedly so." Dr Hunter glanced up at Jack. "His IQ is likely to be in the top ten per cent. I believe Dr Bauer was of the same opinion."

"OK, so he's clever." Jack took another sip of water and made a note.

"Dr Bauer suggested the killer would be a white-collar worker, most likely a businessman or entrepreneur, and would be self-employed." Dr Hunter paused, a faint frown passing her brow. "However, I see an element of manual ability with your perpetrator, Inspector. The chess pieces — the wood carvings — I wouldn't be surprised if they were carved by the killer himself."

"A carpenter? That's quite specific?"

Dr Hunter gave a small shrug. "It's a possibility. I can't be any more definite than that. But a talent in that sort of area. I don't believe your killer has used shop bought, mass produced chess pieces — the pictures you sent through look more intricately carved. A lot of care and effort has gone into them. They're personal to him. I believe he's leaving behind his own creations. By placing his own markers on the bodies, he feels the victims belong to him."

"Vince Butler was an experienced chess player. He used to play on those online forums. But as far as I know he had no carpentry skills." Jack added more notes to his notebook.

Dr Hunter nodded, flicking over one of the pages in front of her. "Yes, the previous investigation team honed in on this Vince Butler from an early point. And I can understand why. Apart from the age range, he looked to be the perfect suspect according to Dr Bauer's profile."

"A profile you think is incorrect."

"To some extent, yes," replied Dr Hunter. "Butler had a high IQ, and an interest in chess. But he doesn't fulfil the rest of the criteria in my eyes. I believe your perpetrator to be artistic. I don't believe him to be a businessman or an entrepreneur like Dr Bauer suggested. I feel he has a more manual job — labouring even. He may even have had periods of unemployment. But he's also charming and likeable. None of the original four victims had any defensive wounds, to my knowledge?"

Jack shook his head. "No, none."

Dr Hunter continued. "This suggests that they went willingly with him, invited him into their homes. They felt comfortable around him. This is why I feel the original estimate of the age of the perpetrator to be wrong. All the victims were young women — the oldest was twenty-seven. They were more likely to feel at ease with someone closer to their own age bracket. The original estimate of someone in their forties to fifties doesn't fit with that."

"Butler was twenty-three at the time of the 2009 murders." Jack looked up from his notebook where he'd hurriedly scribbled more notes. "So he'd fit your profile, but not Bauer's. But, to be fair, his previous convictions probably swung it for them and placed him on their radar."

"Indeed." Dr Hunter's frown deepened. "I don't deny he's an interesting character — from a psychological point of view. Even at twenty-three, he had a long list of previous convictions." She paused while flicking through the paperwork. "Violence towards women. Attempted kidnapping. Stalking. I don't doubt that he ticked all the right boxes at the time."

"But, they had him in custody at the time of the final murder," added Jack, draining his water. "So, it couldn't have been him."

Dr Hunter caught Jack's eye. "This is by no means a straightforward case, Inspector. This man is complex. But I feel there are strong indications to put forward an almost entirely different profile." She slid an A4 sized piece of paper across the table. "These are the salient points. It's only a preliminary profile. But it's a start."

Jack took the piece of paper and quickly scanned it. "Age twenty to twenty-nine in 2009. So, twenty-four to thirty-three today. Intelligent. High IQ. Will live alone. Self-employed or unemployed. Previous or current manual labour. No previous convictions — although he will have a history of deviant behaviour from a young age such as animal mutilations, and stalking is likely." Jack paused and looked up. "Animal mutilations?"

Dr Hunter nodded. "More than likely. I don't believe this man has come on to your radar before. But he didn't just start with killing his first victim. There will be something in his past. It's well documented that animal cruelty and torture feature heavily in many serial killers' backgrounds. Also, the mutilation of the bodies post-mortem — taking a portion of flesh. That means something to him. As does the writing on the wall. I note he leaves symbols of a bishop's mitre, using the victim's own blood?"

Jack nodded.

"This points to someone enjoying their notoriety. He relishes the label being bestowed upon him. It makes him feel important. It makes him feel known. Although he'll come across as a confident character, beneath there will be many insecurities. Most likely emanating from his childhood or very early adolescence."

Jack continued to scan the rest of the profile. "Artistic. Good with his hands. Carpentry skills. Driver. Charming. Pleasant disposition. People trust him. Estranged family."

"I can flesh it out a little more, but those are the basic points that spring to mind."

Jack made to rise from his chair. "This is good, thanks."

"No problem, Inspector." She flashed him a smile. "I'll email across the polished version. Something I haven't added in yet is the chess angle. I feel that chess means something to him as well. At this juncture, I'm not quite sure how or why. But it's an area you need to explore."

On his way to the door, Jack turned. "So why the gap between 2009 and now?"

Dr Hunter hesitated, pinching her bottom lip. "Of that I'm unsure. It was an abrupt stop, which is out of character for a serial killer. It's not unheard of for serial killers to take a break, but it is most unusual. Whatever happened, something caused his routine to change after the first four murders."

Jack nodded his thanks once again and headed out the door.

* * *

Time: 12.30 p.m.
Date: Sunday 22 September 2013
Location: Isabel's Café, Horseferry Road, London

Amy Jennings pushed open the door and was immediately greeted by a comforting wave of coffee-scented air. Mixed with the smell of warm, sweet pastry, the aroma was intoxicating and made her stomach growl. She had a while before she was needed, so a drink and snack would be ideal — and it also might go some way to settling her frazzled nerves.

She seated herself by the window in a battered but comfortable looking armchair, and picked up the laminated menu. Her eyes quickly scanned the beautifully handwritten card, widening at the vast array of coffees, teas and other beverages on offer.

Sacha Greene appeared at her side. "Daunting, isn't it?" She smiled, warmly, at Amy, nodding towards the menu. "I can recommend something, if you prefer?"

Amy returned the smile. "That would be fantastic."

"Are we looking for a coffee, tea, or something else?"

"Coffee, please. Something light, not too strong, and not too bitter. And I'd love a pastry — can I smell cinnamon?"

Sacha grinned. "You can. We've got cinnamon rolls fresh out of the oven, if you'd like one? Although they're so delicious you might end up wanting another!"

Amy smiled. "Sounds great! But maybe I'll just start with the one to begin with!" She tapped the plump stomach beneath her suit jacket. "Trying to cut down!"

Sacha made a note in her order book and set off back towards the coffee machine behind the counter. "I'll get you one of our newest coffees — it's Italian, but really smooth and light. Milk?"

"Please," replied Amy, placing the menu back down on the table. "This place is amazing. All these books!" She turned and scanned the bookcases behind her. "It's incredible."

Sacha gave a chuckle, barely audible above the noise from the coffee machine. "It's my best friend's café — I'm looking after it while she's away. Help yourself to a book to read while you're here." A cloud of steam billowed out from the coffee machine as Sacha began pouring Amy's drink into a tall mug. "Dom? A cinnamon roll out here when you're ready, please."

Amy rose from her chair and began browsing through the paperbacks on the bookcase behind her. What a wonderful idea, she thought. Combining coffee with books — who didn't want a quick escape while they sipped their cappuccino? Selecting a copy of *Jane Eyre*, she sat back down at her table thinking she had time to read at least a couple of chapters from her favourite book.

Sacha arrived with the tall mug of Italian coffee accompanied by the tantalising aroma of a warm cinnamon roll.

"You really have something special here," Amy remarked, making space for the mug and plate while breathing in the wondrous scent of sweet cinnamon. "But I bet your rent is sky high. I'm an estate agent," she added, by way of explanation.

Sacha nodded. "Very. But Isabel's built up a good little business here. We're extremely busy, thankfully."

Amy took a sip of her coffee and reached into her handbag. She brought out a small, square flyer. "I have an open-house event this afternoon — for an apartment just around the corner from here. Do you know it?" She passed the flyer across the table. "I'm not really familiar with the streets around this part of London."

Sacha glanced at the flyer. "Yes, it's not far. It's a nice street — very upmarket. It was all redeveloped not so long ago. Good luck with it!"

Amy smiled and was left alone to enjoy her coffee and cinnamon roll. Looking at her watch, she saw she had plenty of time to get to the apartment, so she picked up the copy of *Jane Eyre* and began to read.

* * *

Time: 2.30 p.m.
Date: Sunday 22 September 2013
Location: Metropolitan Police HQ, London

"Have we thought any more about Billie-Rose's spare key?" Jack hung his jacket on the back of a vacant chair.

DS Cassidy got to her feet and headed across to the hot water urn, sensing Jack might be in need of some caffeine. He looked tired. "Details of everything from Billie-Rose's flat has been uploaded — no mention of a spare key. Just the bunch of keys on a key ring in her handbag. We've been watching the crime scene video, too. I can't see anywhere that it might be hidden."

Jack nodded thoughtfully, accepting the mug of coffee she offered. "So, if the key's missing then it's possible the killer knew it was there and let himself in." He retrieved Dr Hunter's draft profile from his pocket. "This is the profile we have so far — take a look when you get a moment." He dropped the A4 sheet of paper on to Cassidy's desk. "Anything new to report since I've been gone?"

DS Cooper clicked the mouse and activated the whiteboard. "I tracked down the files on Annabel Collins and Matilda Renshaw, like you asked. They're pretty horrific." Several images of the bloodied crime scenes from October 2009 filled the screen.

"That guy Butler gives me the creeps." Cassidy returned to her seat, a mug of green tea in her hand. "The things he did to those poor girls." She gave an involuntary shudder and turned her attention away from the whiteboard, picking up Dr Hunter's profile. "Anything useful come out of the profile, guv?"

Jack gave a slight shrug. "I'm not sure. Maybe. Take a look and see what you think. She's sending across a final version sometime later today. Thinks we need to follow the chess thread more than they did originally, though." Taking a mouthful of coffee, grateful for the caffeine hitting his bloodstream, Jack turned towards the pin board behind them. Stacey Fairbrother's face stared back out at him. "We need to focus on Stacey Fairbrother. She was his first victim for a reason. Amanda? Get hold of her next of kin and, if they're local, fix a time for us to visit. Tomorrow would be good."

Cassidy reached for the internal phone. "On it, guv."

Jack's eyes remained fixed on the image of Stacey Fairbrother. "We need to find out all we can about her. Background. Social circle. Whoever this killer is, his victims feel comfortable around him. No signs of forced entry, no signs of a struggle. He makes them feel safe." Pausing, he let his gaze move to the latest image of Billie-Rose, and thought about the terracotta flowerpot on her doorstep. "Safe enough to give them a spare key, or at least tell them where to find it."

* * *

Time: 11.45 p.m.
Date: Friday 13 September 2013
Location: 3a Dolphin Close, EC1

Billie-Rose felt herself swaying, and held on to the sides of the porch to regain her balance. She never usually drank on an empty stomach — history told her how it would end — but he'd been so persuasive. She didn't usually go for the pushy, overconfident kind, but he was different. She couldn't quite put her finger on what it was, but he was different.

She peered up through her matted eyelashes. Sometime during the course of the evening, her mascara had clumped together — and no amount of peering into the tiny, cracked mirror in the pub's claustrophobic toilet could rescue it. That would teach her for buying the cheap stuff from the market.

She gave him a lop-sided grin. "Oops, nearly went there!"

He smiled in return, but Billie-Rose was too tipsy to notice that the gesture didn't quite reach his steely grey eyes. He didn't reply: merely stepped closer, glancing over his shoulder into the night air.

Billie-Rose fumbled for her handbag which was draped over one shoulder. She tore at the zip and plunged a hand inside, rummaging for the door key. "Drat," she muttered to herself, prodding the four corners of the bag and peering inside once more. "Where are they?"

A further few seconds of frantic searching did not make the keys magically appear, and she flashed a sheepish look up at the handsome stranger standing by her side. Was he handsome? She pondered the question for a moment, ignoring the plight of the keys. She wasn't quite sure now. He'd seemed so in the dimly lit basement bar, but now? The alcoholic haze that she was currently viewing the world through didn't make it any easier. Well, he wasn't bug-ugly, so she shrugged her shoulders and turned her attention back to the front door.

She could knock and wake up Nicole, but that wouldn't be fair — especially if she was trying to catch up on some sleep after a late shift at the cinema. Instead, she bent down and tipped the terracotta plant pot on the doorstep to one side.

"Ta-da!" she announced, her words still slurred. Picking up the spare key from its hiding place, she swung it in front of her companion's eyes. "In case of emergencies, the flower pot never lets me down!"

He let another smile grace his lips, noting the valuable information that Billie-Rose had just imparted to a near total stranger. He tutted to himself. She really should be more careful.

Billie-Rose made several attempts to unlock the front door. He didn't step forward to help — it amused him too much to see her floundering. He could smell the alcohol surrounding her like a cheap, acidic perfume. She'd accepted each and every drink offered, and let them slip thirstily down her throat. He didn't like alcohol and women — and certainly not mixed together. It made them lose their inhibitions, dulling their sense of caution and masking their fear.

And fear was the one sense he liked to see in all its raw beauty.

As Billie-Rose finally heaved the door open, stumbling across the threshold, he dutifully followed on behind. He'd already decided tonight wouldn't be the night. He needed her fully aware of her surroundings, not dulled by a mixture of Bacardi and cheap vodka. He needed her to be in touch with her senses, to be fully conscious when the life violently left her body.

A thrill rippled through him at the very thought.

No, he would wait.

He was good at waiting.

CHAPTER NINE

Time: 2.35 p.m.
Date: Sunday 22 September 2013
Location: The Penthouse, Stevenson Street, SW1

Amy Jennings glanced at her watch for the millionth time, palpitations making her heart skip a beat. This was her first open-house event on her own. Usually, she would have either Trudy or Jacob by her side, showing her the ropes, but today she was flying solo. It was a step up — an increase in responsibility that would, hopefully, lead to an accompanying increase in salary. She could hope, anyway. The housing market was going up and down like a yo-yo at the moment.

And she desperately needed the commission. This apartment would pull in a decent one if she could just get someone to sign on the dotted line. Twenty-six and she still lived at home with Mum and Dad. She'd had a brief experience of living away from home while at uni — but once the degree was over, reality hit home pretty quickly alongside the hefty student loan. So back to Mum and Dad she'd gone. But it was only temporary, she told herself. This time next year . . .

The doorbell to the apartment rang, making her jump. She felt the palpitations quicken inside her. Smoothing down her grey pencil skirt with a sweaty palm, she ran a hand quickly over her hair. There were four couples booked in to the open house afternoon — well, three couples and a single gentleman. But with the advertising board on the street outside, and flyers on the website advising no appointments were necessary, almost anyone could turn up.

The apartment was on the top floor of the five-storey building — The Penthouse they were calling it. Just calling it that alone would push up the asking price. She pressed the button to release the communal door downstairs and made her way out on to the landing.

Plastering her face with the widest and sincerest smile she could muster, she waited to greet the first arrivals.

* * *

Time: 3.35 p.m.
Date: Sunday 22 September 2013
Location: Metropolitan Police HQ, London

Panting hard, DS Cooper burst into the incident room, his cheeks flushed. The lift was out of use, so he'd sprinted up the three flights of stairs from the basement. "Calls have been coming in on the hotline, boss." He flapped a piece of paper in the air.

Jack and Cassidy looked up from the house-to-house statements they were studying. "I almost daren't ask," replied Jack, "but is there anything useful?"

"Depends what you mean by useful, boss." Still out of breath, Cooper placed the piece of paper in front of Jack. "Take a look for yourself."

Jack let his eyes skim over the A4 sheet. It wasn't long before he saw what had made Cooper dash up three flights of stairs.

"It seems we have a name." Jack kept his voice even and controlled, but inside his stomach knotted. It was premature to get excited about just one name, but there was always the chance that this could be the key. It happened — not often, but it happened nonetheless.

As Jack skimmed through the rest of the report, a further twinge of excitement flickered. It wasn't just the one name — it was a name provided by no less than eight members of the public. Jack felt his heartbeat quicken.

"Barry Draper." Jack read out the name that'd been on the tip of so many tongues.

"They all got a bit excited downstairs," added Cooper, his breath still ragged, "So I brought it straight up."

Jack ran his eyes over the name once more. "Barry Draper," he repeated, a frown beginning to form. "Run the name through the system, Cooper . . . I've a feeling I've heard of this guy before." Something tugged at the back of Jack's mind. "Barry Draper," he repeated.

"Me too, guv." Cassidy scooted her chair across to Jack's side and took a quick look at the A4 print-out. "Definitely. His name's in the paperwork somewhere, I'm sure of it."

Without bothering to sit down, Cooper grabbed the keyboard and began typing. The interactive whiteboard sprang into life and very quickly started searching for the name Barry Draper.

Jack watched the screen as Cooper scrolled through the menus. The tightening inside his stomach intensified. Wasn't the Yorkshire Ripper's name already in the masses of police files long before they finally caught up with him? They'd even interviewed him several times. The very thought made Jack's heart thud faster.

It didn't take long to locate him. "Here you go, boss." Cooper tapped the mouse to enlarge the screen. "Barry Draper. Named by members of the public after a TV appeal went out in 2009 after the murder of Shona Michaels — the Bishop's second victim. Guy was living in Upminster at the time."

"And what did they do with that information?" asked Jack, his frown deepening. "I don't recall seeing any interviews with him."

Cooper scrolled some more, tapping a few more keys before finally shaking his head. "Doesn't look like anything came of it, boss. I can't see that he was ever questioned."

"Because they already thought they had their man — Vince Butler." Jack rubbed his eyes, the tightening in his stomach turning to one of nausea.

"Should we go back to DCI Hobbs, guv?" asked Cassidy. "Maybe they discounted him for a reason?"

The thought of being in the same room, or even on the same phone line, as DCI Graham Hobbs sent an unpleasant shiver down Jack's spine. "I doubt that'll be necessary, Amanda," he responded, trying to push away all thoughts of the retired DCI dressed in his clown-like golfing attire. "Let's pull what we can. Find out who Barry Draper is, where he lives, what he does. See what's bringing him to our attention yet again."

* * *

Time: 5.20 p.m.
Date: Sunday 22 September 2013
Location: The Penthouse, Stevenson Street, SW1

The strategically placed bowls of nibbles had more or less been emptied — only a few stray cheese twists and peanuts remained. Amy had wondered if peanuts were a good idea, with so many people suffering from food allergies these days — but Trudy had arranged for enough bags of salted and roasted varieties to sink a ship, and nobody seemed to have objected.

The glasses of free prosecco seemed to have gone down well, too.

Amy sighed with relief as the door closed behind the final potential buyers. The afternoon had gone surprisingly well — several people had made the right noises, and one or two had promised to get back in touch. As well as those already booked into the event, there had been seven 'walk-ins' — probably attracted by the free glass of bubbly.

Glancing at her watch, Amy set about collecting up the plastic plates and glasses. Trudy had told her to leave them in a box by the door and Jacob would swing by to collect them later. Taking a cheeky sip from the dregs of one of the plastic champagne flutes, she closed her eyes and slipped her feet out of her shoes. The deep pile carpet massaged her toes.

The apartment was truly wonderful — airy and spacious, with all new mod cons and energy saving devices. The kitchen had so many gadgets it looked like something from the *Starship Enterprise* — that had been one of the jokes Jacob told her to drop into the conversation with prospective buyers. She'd done so, rather self-consciously, and it received a smattering of forced laughs in return. She wouldn't use that line next time, she decided. *If* there was to be a next time. Maybe if someone put in an offer . . . ? The thought gave her a tiny thrill.

She wandered through to the master bedroom, checking all the lights were switched off and no one had left the taps running in the en-suite. Everything looked like it should. She rechecked the lounge and open plan kitchen. All shipshape. Just the plates and champagne flutes to rinse off and stack up in the box and she'd be good to go.

Amy carried some of the plates over to the sink and quickly gave them a rinse. As she did so, the door buzzer sounded again. She frowned. The open house was meant to conclude at 4.30 p.m., as it clearly stated on all the posters, and it was already long after that. Maybe it was Jacob coming to collect the plates and glasses? But he'd have his own keys and wouldn't need to buzz. Amy felt a flash of irritation — but she thought about the commission again, and the chance to finally leave home.

Padding across the soft, cream carpet in her stockinged feet, she lifted the internal phone. "Yes?" She tried not to sound too abrupt.

"Hi — it's Duncan. From the open house event earlier?"

Amy continued to frown and bit her lip. Duncan? She mentally flipped through all the faces from the last few hours, trying to place names with each one.

"I had to leave — sort out a problem at work?" Duncan's voice crackled through the intercom. "I said I might come back?"

"Ah." It was then that she managed to place him. Tall, athletic-looking, well-dressed in a tailored suit. Good looking in a rough and ready kind of way. "Yes, I remember now."

"Is it possible? To have another look around?"

Amy hesitated, glancing down at her watch once again. She was tired, and desperately wanted nothing more than to relax in a hot bath with a glass of wine. But the Tube would be a nightmare right now . . . so maybe staying on a bit longer wouldn't hurt.

"Of course, come on up."

* * *

Time: 5.30 p.m.
Date: Sunday 22 September 2013
Location: The Glade, Church Street, Albury, Surrey

Once the sun had dipped below the treeline at the rear of the garden, a chill soon started to descend. The warm Indian summer days were giving way to cooler, fresher evenings — the promise of autumn not far away. With the foundations of his plans now laid, Geraghty began tidying away the wicker furniture, and headed back inside.

Much of what he'd brought with him in the move still sat in cardboard boxes labelled 'kitchen', 'study' or 'bedroom'. In four months he'd unpacked only a handful: just the bare essentials.

He'd kept a low profile over the summer, taking an occasional stroll through the village, or a drive to a neighbouring town. He spent most of his time in the enclosed back garden, away from prying eyes. Thinking. Planning. Thinking and planning.

But now he knew he needed to act.

Geraghty laughed to himself at his own joke.

Act.

He certainly knew how to do that.

Making his way into the enormous kitchen — far too big for a single man who did no entertaining — he slipped on to one of the stools at the breakfast bar. Before him, on the granite work surface, was everything he needed to make his latest transformation. He ran some styling gel through his hair, sweeping it back from his face. He then slipped on a natural-looking wig, made from the best human hair — then a set of false teeth and a pair of tinted contact lenses. He moulded a prosthetic nose to his face, and something to give him a more rounded chin. The prosthetics were, once again, of the highest quality money could buy.

With his facial transformation complete, Geraghty applied some concealer and foundation to blend in the joins, and eyed himself in a hand-held mirror.

Roger Bancroft was a handsome man.

He quickly changed into a casual navy linen suit, opting to leave the pale blue shirt beneath open at the neck and discard the tie. He slipped a gold signet ring on to one finger.

Roger Bancroft had stepped into the local pub a few times over the last six weeks, just enough to show his face — at least his prosthetically engineered one. Just enough to get seen, but not enough to linger in anyone's memory for too long.

But tonight, Bancroft needed another outing, because the time was coming when he'd need to step up to the mark and perform.

Tonight would be his dress rehearsal.

* * *

Time: 5.45 p.m.
Date: Sunday 22 September 2013
Location: The Penthouse, Stevenson Street, SW1

Amy's eyes bulged as she tried desperately to draw air into her lungs. But the wire, or whatever it was that was around her neck, was squeezing too tightly. As she fought for breath, she waved her arms frantically in the air, in the vain hope of grabbing something, *anything*, that could help her. But there was nothing. His grip was too strong.

She could feel his warm breath on the back of her neck; hear his rasps and grunts as he tightened his hold even more. Everything swam in and out of focus as her vision began to blur.

Her chest continued to heave, her lungs fiercely craving oxygen — but none was forthcoming. She started to choke, but no sound escaped her lips other than a faint wheeze. Suddenly a sharp pain seared her thigh, followed by the warm sensation of blood soaking her skin. Through the haze she thought she saw the glint of a blade.

With both her legs and arms beginning to weaken, her knees buckled beneath her and the soft, plush carpet rose up as she slipped to the floor. She felt the grip around her neck tightening, squeezing out whatever ragged life was left within. Not long afterwards, her whole world turned to black.

Even as she lay on the carpet at his feet, he still held her tight — watching for signs of movement. There were none. Blood pooled around him, but with her heart now stilled, the blood from her lacerated artery had ceased to spurt.

Satisfied that life had now left the body of Amy Jennings, he released his grip and lay her head back down on the carpet, her glassy eyes staring lifelessly up towards the ceiling. He stretched her legs out and placed her hands together across her abdomen, taking the time to carefully intertwine her fingers.

The brushed steel wall clock continued to tick softly in the otherwise silence of the apartment. He usually liked to take his time with this part — but was conscious that time wasn't on his side. He'd taken a risk — which was most unlike him. He didn't usually take risks. He'd observed her from afar while she showed the other potential buyers around the apartment, and noticed how she self-consciously pulled her suit jacket down over her stomach. As she lay lifelessly on the floor, he gently lifted up the tails of her blouse to reveal a plump mass of flesh above the waistband of her pencil skirt.

Yes, that would be perfect.

Reaching into his pocket, he brought out the Stanley knife.

* * *

Time: 5.45 p.m.
Date: Sunday 22 September 2013
Location: Metropolitan Police HQ, London

DS Cooper clicked the whiteboard screen off. He'd replayed the crime scene videos for each of the Essex murders — the three of them watching in horrified silence as the crime scene manager took them on a tour of each scene. With the bodies still in situ, and the bloodied bishop's hat smeared on the walls, it left a distinctly unpleasant chill in the air of the incident room.

"Awful." It was the only word Cassidy could manage.

"Anything more on Draper?" Jack rubbed his eyes, feeling the grit beneath his eyelids.

"His name first appeared in the investigation after the murder of Shona Michaels — when the TV reconstruction went live. There was a swathe of calls all naming him as a suspect." Cooper flicked a page of his notebook over. "They did some initial digging — investigations showed him as being single, living in a flat in Upminster. No mention of any employment. I've found out that he's moved since then — currently living in a house on Lorimer Street." Cooper glanced up at Jack, closing his notebook. "I can't see that DCI Hobbs followed up on any of it. Didn't seem to regard him as a credible suspect."

"Anything to suggest why he's being named again?" Tip-offs were good — but the anonymous ones made Jack nervous. "Anyone willing to put their name to suggesting he's our man?"

Cooper shook his head. "All calls so far have been anonymous. And as far as I can see, he doesn't have a criminal record. There's a few incidents recorded — antisocial behaviour — shall I dig deeper?"

"Put it down as an action. What about Billie-Rose? Anything further on her?"

"Much of what her mother told us checks out." DS Cassidy glanced at her computer monitor. "Left home at eighteen. Has lived at the Dolphin Close address for the last sixteen months. Has had a few low-skilled jobs, but recently started with a recruitment agency near the university. I've had a brief chat with the office manager — she was a likeable girl, got on well with everyone. Nothing out of the ordinary. She didn't really socialise with her colleagues, so there wasn't much else they could tell me."

"Get her phone looked at. See what crops up." Jack headed for the door, pulling his car keys from his pocket. "And get yourselves off home. We'll chase forensics in the morning."

* * *

Time: 5.45 p.m.
Date: Sunday 22 September 2013
Location: Westminster Tube station, London

Jacob Bradley stepped out from Westminster Underground station and turned in the direction of Stevenson Street. He'd been to The Penthouse on several occasions, helping Trudy compile the photographs used in the particulars of sale, so he knew it was only a ten-minute walk.

He sauntered towards Parliament Square in the late afternoon light, the sun still pleasantly warm even though it had now dipped behind the buildings that lined his route. As he walked, his mind turned towards Amy. He hoped the afternoon had gone well for her and she'd had plenty of additional 'walk-ins' off the street. He knew how important it was for her to try and get a foot on to the property ladder — and the commission from such a big sale would go some way to helping her move out and set up on her own.

Jacob still lived at home, too — but he was more than happy with the arrangement. His mum washed and ironed all his clothes, and cooked his evening meal every night. Even made him a packed lunch for work. He couldn't see himself giving that up any time soon. He chuckled to himself as he continued his journey towards The Penthouse.

Stevenson Street itself was a wide, tree-lined avenue, recently redeveloped on both sides. The whole area was turning into a playboy's paradise, with smart, expensive apartments springing up along the entire length of the road. There was even talk of an exclusive, members-only sports complex being built at the end of the street — somewhere for the tired and overworked City boys to relax at the end of a hard day, with maybe even a Sunday morning squash or tennis session thrown in. The recently granted planning proposals had added several thousand pounds to the asking price of The Penthouse.

Jacob pulled out his set of keys as he approached the apartment building. The whole place still had that 'under construction' look and smell to it — the faint aroma of builder's dust and plaster hanging in the air. As he unlocked the communal door, he was met with the 'brand new' smells of paint and turpentine. There was even an element of fresh sawdust mixed in.

He took the lift to the fourth floor and headed towards apartment 4a. Glancing at his watch, he assumed Amy would have left some time ago and the apartment would be empty. Pushing the key into the lock, Jacob stepped over the threshold and into The Penthouse.

CHAPTER TEN

Time: 6.10 p.m.
Date: Sunday 22 September 2013
Location: The Penthouse, Stevenson Street, SW1

Beneath the calm exterior, his heart was pumping fast. That'd been close. *Too* close.

The sound of the apartment door opening had sent him scurrying to the master bedroom — but only just in time. A few seconds earlier and he'd have come face to face with whoever it was paying a call to The Penthouse. The visitor hadn't stayed long — just long enough to discover the bloodied scene before rushing from the building.

Which meant he didn't have long to finish what he'd started. Kneeling down by the side of Amy Jennings' limp body, he ran a gloved hand through one of the pools of blood and set about leaving his mark on the wall of the open plan kitchen. Satisfied with his work, he pulled the two wooden carvings from his pocket and slipped them into place — one clutched in Amy's dead fingers, the other inside her mouth.

Stopping just long enough to admire his handiwork, he felt the familiar smile twitching at his lips. It may have been rushed, but it was still one of his best. Careful not to step in any of Amy's blood, he picked up the bag containing his trophy and edged out into the deserted corridor outside flat 4a.

Pulling on an overcoat to hide his bloodied clothing, he stepped into the lift. As the doors closed he let out a pent-up breath and tried to steady his rapidly beating heart. He'd never come this close to being discovered before, almost caught in the act. He felt a curious mixture of concern and excitement.

Sometimes the risk was worth taking.

* * *

Time: 7.20 p.m.
Date: Sunday 22 September 2013
Location: The Baker's Arms, Albury, Surrey

Roger Bancroft, or more accurately Joseph Geraghty, had chosen a small table beneath a window at the front of the pub. Silently surveying the rest of the bar area, he concluded that this was the best choice. It gave a clear view out across the rest of the tables, and he'd see anybody who came in through the front door.

He noticed several locals gathered on the far side by the jukebox, having a good-natured game of darts. The Sunday lunch brigade had long since departed, and the bar was now only sparsely populated as they headed into the evening.

Geraghty settled back in his seat, his back against the wall, and quietly stirred his cup of full-strength coffee. He'd glanced at the bar menu on arriving, but politely declined when the amiable barman had enquired about his food order — opting for a coffee instead. He was now on his third, and the caffeine was sharpening his senses.

He'd known as soon as he'd sat down that this was the place. Bringing the coffee up to his lips, he smiled — yes, this would be perfect. With his other hand, he reached into the pocket of his jacket and brought out a mobile phone. It wasn't yet switched on — he'd wait until the moment he needed to use it. Although it was another unregistered pay-as-you-go, one of many he'd acquired in recent weeks, they were always traceable somehow. As he stared at the blank screen, another smile graced his lips. He tried to think what Detective Inspector Jack MacIntosh would be doing this early on a Sunday evening. Knowing him, he'd probably be working. The man never seemed to stop, which was a trait Geraghty quietly admired.

Luring the detective inspector down to Surrey would be tricky — but Geraghty had faith in his plan. It would work. *It had to.* Taking another sip of the bittersweet coffee, he pressed the button on the Nokia and powered up the phone.

* * *

Time: 7.45 p.m.
Date: Sunday 22 September 2013
Location: The Penthouse, Stevenson Street, SW1

Jack pulled on his protective overshoes and headed into the wide communal hallway. He'd been home for all of thirty minutes when the call came in, barely enough time to catch his breath. Metal plates on the ground instructed him where to put his feet, and after a quick glance around the lobby he headed upstairs. Dr Matthews' Volvo was parked illegally on some double yellow lines outside, so he knew the pathologist had already arrived.

The lift was being processed, forcing Jack to use the stairs.

The Penthouse.

That meant the top floor.

Jack groaned as he trudged up the four flights of carpeted stairs, still keeping to his designated metal squares. He thrust his hands in his pockets to stop himself being tempted to touch any of the bannisters that lined the walls. They would be dusted later and Jack didn't fancy being on the receiving end of an irate crime scene manager for contaminating his crime scene.

Slightly more out of breath than he should be, Jack arrived at the fourth floor. The commotion was centred around the far end of the corridor, an array of white-suited bodies drifting in and out of apartment number 4a. He dutifully followed the metal plates and stepped into a spacious living and dining area.

His eyes quickly scanned the open plan apartment. The minimalist look gave it the aura of a show home — clean, sleek and empty. No doubt the rest of the apartments in the block would look identical — nondescript spaces, bare and without character. And with everything operated by a button.

Jack's gaze then fell to the body of Amy Jennings. Kneeling at her side was a familiar figure.

"Hello, Jack," acknowledged Dr Matthews, without looking up. "Be with you in two shakes."

Jack watched as the pathologist completed his initial, rudimentary examination to confirm that Amy Jennings was indeed no longer of this world. With a perfunctory nod of the head, to himself more than anyone else, Dr Matthews pushed his tall frame up to face Jack.

Without being prompted, he answered Jack's unspoken question. "Compression of the neck — but more force was used this time. I suspect a fracture of the hyoid bone." Dr Matthews stepped out of the way of a crime scene photographer, motioning for Jack to follow him into the open plan kitchen. They stepped carefully around the pools of blood that'd already seeped into the plush carpet.

"And yes, a puncture wound," continued the pathologist. "To the upper thigh. Severing the femoral artery and resulting in catastrophic blood loss."

Jack's eyes swept the walls of the otherwise immaculate kitchen. The Bishop's infamous signature was all too plain to see — the bishop's mitre painted in wide, sweeping strokes. He didn't need to step any closer to see that the blood was still fresh.

"I would again surmise that a thin ligature was used — I'll know more once I get her back to the mortuary."

Jack nodded, tearing his gaze away from the sickening blood spatters. "And a wound?"

Dr Matthews returned the nod. "This time to the front — the lower abdomen. Again, looks to be inflicted post-mortem."

Jack felt his mind begin to churn, but his thoughts were interrupted by a figure entering his field of vision. Elliott Walker was making his way over, his thin face looking troubled.

"I'll leave you to it, Jack." Dr Matthews stepped back and headed out of the kitchen area. "I'll let you know when I'll be performing the PM. You may want to come to this one."

Jack raised a hand at the departing pathologist. "See you, Doc." He turned towards Elliott. "What can you tell me?"

The crime scene manager didn't waste much time getting to the point. "One chess piece in her hands — a bishop — and another in her mouth."

Jack nodded, his eyes flicking back to the body lying just feet away.

"And we have an ID already," continued Elliott. "Amy Jennings. Estate agent."

"Is the person who found her still here?" Jack cast another glance around the spacious penthouse apartment.

Elliott shook his head. "They shipped him off — took his details. No sense in keeping him here. He was only a young lad — goes by the name of Jacob. Works at the same estate agency and lettings business as the victim."

"Any information from him before he went?"

"He literally just walked in and saw her lying there. Says he went straight back out to call the police. As far as we know, he didn't touch anything."

Jack nodded, making a mental note to catch up with the witness later. "When the call came in, they said it was an open house type event? We'll need details of whoever was here."

Elliott nodded. "The young lad, Jacob, said those details would be back at their offices."

Jack made another mental note. "Swish place, this." He glanced around the interior of the apartment again. "I'm assuming there'll be CCTV somewhere? These apartments must cost a fortune."

Elliott shrugged. "I would've thought so. I couldn't see a camera on the door though, but . . ." He shrugged again. "One and a half million quid's worth of flat — I'd at least want something, wouldn't you?"

Jack stepped back into the living area and for a moment watched the crime scene investigators going about their work. A cardboard box by the door, stacked with plastic plates and champagne flutes, was enveloped in a transparent evidence bag. Jack edged towards it, and peered inside.

The Bishop wouldn't be that stupid, would he? Did he sip some fake champagne after choking the life out of Amy Jennings and draining her body of blood? Jack thought it unlikely, but the contents would be analysed just the same. A white-suited investigator brought several more evidence bags across and deposited them next to the cardboard box. Each one contained an individual prosecco bottle. The final bag contained a handbag, most likely the victim's.

With the main area of focus being in the living area, Jack headed towards the rear of the apartment and popped his head in the main bedroom. Again, it was devoid of any personal effects. There was another smaller room next door, unfurnished; most likely advertised to potential buyers as ideal for a nursery or study.

Jack retraced his steps to the living area, noting that Elliott was conducting another sweep of the floor. Each pool of blood was being photographed, with numerous samples and swabs taken. He mouthed towards the crime scene manager that he'd catch up with him later, and headed out into the corridor outside apartment 4a. The journey down to the ground floor was less challenging, and Jack ripped off the protective suit as soon as he reached the bottom.

Stepping out into the cool evening air, he pulled out his phone and stabbed the screen. "Cooper?" Jack walked towards the Mondeo. "We've got another one. Briefing at eight tomorrow."

Ending the call, Jack slipped into the driver's seat and rubbed his eyes. The Bishop was outplaying them. Before he had a chance to put his keys in the ignition, his phone beeped with an incoming message. Expecting it to be Cooper, he gave the screen a cursory glance.

Another number he didn't recognise.

And another message.

'*I'm waiting.*'

CHAPTER ELEVEN

Time: 7.20 a.m.
Date: Monday 23 September 2013
Location: Tannochside B&B, Scotland

Mac closed the door to the B&B behind him and stepped out into the crisp morning air. The sun had only just crawled out of its night- time slumber, rising lazily into the clear sky above. The overnight chill still enveloped him as he limped towards the small bridge that straddled the River Tannoch.

The low stone wall that bordered the bridge offered Mac a suitable resting place. He eased himself down and stretched out his aching legs. He hadn't slept well. The muscles in his thighs screamed at the slightest movement, and when he lay still they silently throbbed. He knew the exercise must be doing him some good, but right now he'd do anything just to take the pain away.

Reaching into his jacket pocket, he brought out a packet of prescription painkillers. Isabel wasn't aware he was still taking them — she thought he'd stepped down to ibuprofen and the occasional paracetamol. But he wasn't quite ready to make that leap just yet.

He popped a couple of pills into the palm of his hand and swallowed them dry. In his other hand he held his phone. He considered phoning Jack, but noted the time. It was early. If his brother was up and about, which he most probably was, then he'd be busy.

Jack was always busy.

Mac slipped the phone back into his pocket alongside the pill packet. The question he needed to ask Jack could wait a while. A few more days wouldn't matter. The gently rippling freshwater stream trickled underneath the bridge, the only sound in the bright morning air. If he breathed in deeply, Mac thought he could smell the familiar aroma of Margaret's cooking — eggs and bacon with square sausage. His stomach began to rumble. Some food would do him good — high strength painkillers on an empty stomach wasn't ideal.

Pushing himself up from the wall, he grimaced as he forced his legs to take him back towards the B&B. He envisaged a hot shower before breakfast, and massaging his muscles before the onset of whatever torture Isabel had planned for him that day.

But his grimace soon turned into a smile. Isabel. Sometimes he had to pinch himself that she was truly here with him. *Stuart MacIntosh.* The one they'd all cast aside and assumed would never make anything of himself. The smile grew into a grin as he pushed open the door to the B&B.

Sometimes the underdog really did win the day.

* * *

Time: 8.20 a.m.
Date: Monday 23 September 2013
Location: Metropolitan Police HQ, London

DS Cooper dragged the cork pin board towards the interactive whiteboard. All five faces, frozen in time, stared blankly out across the incident room. With a heavy heart, Jack added

Amy Jennings' smiling face to the board and slipped off his jacket.

The day had only just begun, but the Indian summer temperatures outside were already making everything inside sticky and warm. He rubbed his eyes and sighed. The latest message — *'I'm waiting'* — had robbed him of any chance of sleep, so he'd welcomed in the dawn sitting by his open window with a steady supply of coffee.

The number had been instantly disconnected, just like the first. Whoever was sending them was screwing with his head — maybe that was their intention. He shovelled instant coffee into three mugs, aware that his own caffeine intake so far that day was already sky high, and filled them with hot water from the urn. "We've a busy day ahead," he announced, sloshing milk into everyone's mug except DS Cassidy's. "Last night's victim, Amy Jennings, will be on Dr Matthews' table at some point today. And I'd like all CCTV in and around the scene pulled."

Cooper accepted his mug and gave Jack a nod. "Already requested, boss."

"Good man." Jack collapsed into a vacant chair. "While we wait for further information on Amy Jennings, what next of kin details do we have on the first four victims? Something links these women together. I want to know what it is."

Cooper clicked the mouse and brought up the original police investigation file.

"Victim one — Stacey Fairbrother. Next of kin is a Martin Rivers — alive and well, living in Camden Town. Stacey was his stepdaughter. Mother deceased. I've printed off the original investigation's interviews with him." Cooper nodded towards a stack of papers on one of the desks. "Then we have victim two — Shona Michaels. Her parents lived in Canterbury at the time, but have since moved to the Isle of Wight."

Jack nodded. The Isle of Wight was a bit beyond their reach today. "And the others?"

"Victim three — Frankie Robinson. Her mother moved to the USA a year or so after her daughter's death. She was American and, as far as I can tell, went back to Ohio and is still there. Her husband, Frankie's father, doesn't seem to be on the scene. Victim four, Esther Faulkner, is more problematic. No next of kin recorded in the original investigation, except an elderly aunt who lived in Brighton at the time. I'm trying to trace her as we speak."

Jack tore his gaze away from the whiteboard screen and eyed each of the photographs on the pin board in turn. "Amanda, when are we due to see Stacey's stepfather?"

"Two o'clock, guv." Cassidy nursed her black coffee and leaned up against the desk next to Jack. "I was thinking about the chess pieces last night. The wooden bishop in their hands — and the other in their mouth. It has to mean something."

Jack frowned. The chess pieces bothered him too. "The original investigation put it down to the killer playing games, but . . ." He paused and looked back at the photographs on the pin board. "I'm not so sure. Something tells me there's more to it than that. Have you both had a chance to look at Dr Hunter's profile?"

Both Cooper and Cassidy nodded.

"She thinks it has special significance for the killer — and so do I." Jack looked at his detective sergeants. "Do either of you play? Chess, I mean?" He received shakes of the head in response. "Me neither."

Pushing herself up from the desk, Cassidy's eyes sparkled and a smile crossed her lips. "I might know nothing about chess — but I know a man who does."

* * *

Time: 8.35 a.m.
Date: Monday 23 September 2013
Location: Jamieson Street, NW1

The tins of tomato soup had been lined up, haphazardly, on the supermarket shelf, and that irritated Barry Draper. His brow furrowed as he nudged each can back into line and turned them so their labels faced outwards.

Better.

He selected two tins of minestrone from the shelf below and headed back towards the household goods aisle. Anger once again flickered through him as he stepped around stacks of items waiting to be placed on the shelves by members of staff who were nowhere to be seen.

He tutted to himself and took a deep breath. Glancing at his watch, he noted it was still early — but he had a lot to do today. Today was the day he would see her: he could feel it. Yesterday had excited him, but he knew his collection wasn't yet finished. The thought sent a rippling wave of pleasure through him as he picked up two bottles of bleach and placed them in his basket. Only one more item to get and he could escape.

He detested shopping. And detested supermarkets in particular. They were dirty places, full of germs. You could never be quite sure who'd touched the products before you, or when they'd last washed their hands — if they'd washed them at all.

Barry shuddered at the mere thought, his broad shoulders heaving. He reached into his jacket pocket and pulled out a travel-sized bottle of hand sanitiser. Squirting a few spots into the palm of one hand, he rubbed vigorously until he could visualise the germs evaporating.

He made his way to the self-service checkout area, picking up his usual small white loaf as he passed. At this time of the morning, the checkout wasn't busy and he managed to quickly scan his items and pay. He'd brought his own rucksack with him, and swung it up on to his tall, athletic frame.

He needed to get back home.

Today was the day he would see her.

* * *

Time: 9.00 a.m.
Date: Monday 23 September 2013
Location: Metropolitan Police HQ canteen, London

DS Cassidy headed for a table in the far corner by the window. Jack followed, trying not to spill the mug of coffee clutched in his hand. The canteen was busy with the breakfast rush, and DC Trevor Daniels had secured what looked to be the last table.

As they approached, DC Daniels looked up and closed the magazine he'd been reading. Jack glanced at the title — *Space and Beyond.*

Jack didn't know Daniels all that well — hardly at all, in fact. He'd seen him around the station, more often than not with his nose in a book on space travel — something that had earned himself the nickname 'the nerd' if Jack recalled correctly. He was small and thin, with a pair of thick-rimmed spectacles perched on the end of his nose.

Jack cleared his throat, placing the mug of coffee in front of the young officer. "DS Cassidy here tells me you're into chess?"

Daniels peered out from behind his spectacle lenses and regarded Jack for a moment before speaking, his tone soft and quiet. "If you mean I have an interest in the strategy and intricacies of the game, then I suppose you could say I am '*into*' chess, as you so eloquently put it."

Jack felt a smile touch the corners of his mouth.

He had a feeling he was going to like Trevor Daniels.

"Well, that's just the ticket, then," replied Jack, taking a seat opposite. "I need someone with your knowledge and expertise to assist on a serial murder investigation."

"A serial killer?" DC Daniels raised his eyebrows, his dark brown eyes narrowing. "Involving chess?"

"In a manner of speaking. You've heard of the Bishop?"

Daniels hesitated, then gave a curt nod. "I saw the press conference. And I've read the newspapers."

A copy of the *Daily Courier* sat folded in half on a neighbouring table, splattered with the remnants of a bacon and egg breakfast. Jack knew that, inside, Jonathan Spearing had penned an article questioning Jack's ability to run the investigation, bearing in mind his recent 'mental struggles'. Jack turned his attention back towards the young detective constable. "That's the one."

Daniels tipped exactly one and a half sachets of sugar into his coffee and began to stir. "And you need my help how?"

"Of that, I'm not exactly sure. But we need to explore the chess angle and DS Cassidy here says there's no one better." Jack watched as Daniels continued to methodically stir his coffee. "I'll square it with your boss so you can be reassigned to my team. I hear you've recently passed your detective's exams?"

Daniels nodded, placing the teaspoon back on the table. "Six weeks ago." Jack thought he could detect a sparkle cross the young officer's eyes. "A serial murder. That would be very interesting. Very interesting indeed. I spent most of my time as a PC in Traffic."

"That's the spirit. Good to have you aboard, Daniels." Jack nodded at Cassidy and stood up. "You've got DS Cassidy here to thank — she's been singing your praises all morning. Stay and finish your coffee, then come and find me."

Jack and Cassidy threaded their way back through the canteen, leaving DC Daniels nursing his coffee mug and contemplating his temporary change in career direction.

Cassidy clapped her hands in excitement. "This is going to be so great! You'll love him!"

* * *

Time: 10.15 a.m.
Date: Monday 23 September 2013
Location: St James's House, Gold Street, London

The one room bedsit wasn't great but Lily McArthur had instantly loved it. This was London! The halls of residence attached to the university had all been full, but they recommended a block of one-bedroomed units not far from the main campus. With a single bed, a desk and a slim, single wardrobe, it was all she needed. The mattress looked new, and was comfy enough — but she needed a new duvet and pillows.

There were no cooking facilities to speak of, so as soon as she'd arrived yesterday afternoon, Lily bought herself a cheap kettle and sandwich maker from an electrical shop around the corner. The canteen at the university also offered cheap takeaway meals and, although it may not be Granny's home cooking, she knew she wouldn't starve. I'll be fine, she told herself. I'll be fine.

The only gripe she had was the communal bathroom along the corridor, shared by five other students. But she'd met a few of them yesterday, and they seemed pleasant enough. I'll be fine, she repeated to herself. I'll be fine. In any event, the university sports hall had showering facilities if she was desperate.

Lily lay back down on the bed and stared up at the ceiling. She was finally here. At university. In London! The butterflies fluttering inside her stomach had subsided a little, and she now felt hungry. She hadn't really eaten anything last night, too busy unpacking her things, so she reached for the packet of doughnuts she'd bought from the convenience store along the street.

Doughnuts for breakfast — Granny would be tutting if she knew.

But this was her first full day of university life and she could eat doughnuts for breakfast if she wanted to.

She knew Granny and Grandad had been pleased for her when she was offered her place — although she knew they would have been happier if she'd accepted the offer from Edinburgh School of Art instead. But London was where she wanted to be. She was desperate to be where all the action was. She wanted to experience Camden Town, Carnaby Street, Soho, King's Road, Portobello Market, Petticoat Lane . . . the list was endless. She had a map of London pinned to the wall by her bed, marking all the places she intended to visit.

London Fashion Week had just finished and Lily had been disappointed to miss it. But her university fund didn't stretch to the astronomical ticket price. One day, she mused. One day.

Next to the map was a photograph of Granny and Grandad, and then one of Mum and Dad too. As her gaze fell on the picture of her parents, taken on a beach on their last holiday together, she gave a contented sigh. They would have been proud of her, too — she knew they would. When she became a rich and famous fashion designer, her first collection would be dedicated to them.

Wiping the sugar from her lips, Lily resisted the temptation to reach for another doughnut. Although she didn't need to go and formally register for her course until tomorrow, there was a drinks evening happening later at the Student Union bar, and that was one event she wasn't going to miss. Pulling a hairbrush through her hair, she checked her purple lipstick hadn't smudged too badly on the doughnut and then slipped on her shoes. She just had time to pop out and get that new bedding.

* * *

Time: 1.15 p.m.
Date: Monday 23 September 2013
Location: Metropolitan Police HQ, London

"You already know DS Cassidy." Jack stood by the hot water urn as DC Trevor Daniels sat down at one of the incident room desks. "This here is DS Cooper." Jack nodded towards the ginger-haired detective, who raised a hand in greeting and then went back to scrolling through the interactive whiteboard. "DC Daniels has been seconded to our team — I'm told he's a whizz at chess which might just give us an insight into our perpetrator that we've so far overlooked. Welcome Daniels."

Jack gave what he intended to be a welcoming smile. Cassidy beamed happily from her spot by the open window, resisting the urge to start clapping again.

"You'll need bringing up to speed on where we are with things — I'll leave that to Cooper. As for the rest of today — the CCTV around yesterday's crime scene needs reviewing. Also, check if any house-to-house statements need following up — both for Billie-Rose and now for The Penthouse scene. But one of the first things I need you to do, Daniels, is check out any online chess groups. If our killer is a chess fanatic, he might just frequent them. It's a long shot, but see what you can do. Amanda and I are heading off to see Stacey's stepfather, so I'll also need you both to attend Amy Jennings' post-mortem." Jack eyed both Cooper and Daniels. "Been to a post-mortem before, Daniels?"

Daniels shook his head. "Never. No."

"Well, post-mortems aren't everybody's cup of tea." Jack flashed a good-humoured look in Cassidy's direction, who responded by poking her tongue out. "Nobody knows quite how they're going to react. It's not pleasant — it's not meant to be. But it is, unfortunately, a necessary part of the job. Cooper will show you the ropes." Jack paused and turned towards Cassidy. "Where are we on everything else?"

Cassidy pushed herself away from the window and headed over to the desk where she picked up another report. "Barry Draper still keeps coming up, guv. We've had five more calls about him overnight — all anonymous."

Barry Draper.

The man's name prickled at the back of Jack's mind.

What they'd managed to find out about him so far, which admittedly wasn't much, didn't seem to fit with Rachel Hunter's profile. At thirty-eight, he was older than the parameters of the profile and was described by most as a loner. But, if Dr Bauer could be wrong, maybe so could Dr Hunter . . .

Jack felt uneasy about discarding a potential suspect on the grounds that they didn't fit a psychological profile.

Profiles could be wrong.

And it wouldn't be the first serial murderer who surprised a psychologist.

"Leave it with me — I'll have another chat with Dr Hunter."

CHAPTER TWELVE

Time: 2.15 p.m.
Date: Monday 23 September 2013
Location: 7 Cross Keys Road, Camden Town, London

Martin Rivers showed them both into the small front room, gesturing towards a floral covered two-seater sofa. Although the sun sat in a cloudless sky outside, and was casting its unseasonably warm autumn rays across the modest end-terraced house, the curtains were closed and there was a chill in the otherwise stuffy air.

DS Cassidy obligingly sat on the sofa, but Jack remained on his feet. His eyes swept the rest of the room, taking in a stiff-backed armchair by the window and a small TV on a corner unit opposite. A dark walnut-wood mantelpiece stood above a gas fire, together with another dark wood bureau and modest bookcase on either side. Looking down, he saw what he thought was a worn Axminster carpet underfoot.

After another sweep of the room, Jack lowered himself on to the other half of the two-seater sofa. "Thank you for seeing us, Mr Rivers." He looked over at the man who'd settled into the armchair by the shrouded window. He was lean, with pale skin. His once light brown hair was tinged with grey, swept back away from his face. He wore a pair of metal framed glasses, resting on his narrow nose.

"Of course. Anything to help." His voice was quiet and Jack noted a quivering around the edges.

"As DS Cassidy here mentioned on the phone, we're reopening the investigation into your daughter's murder."

Rivers gave an involuntary shudder. "Reopening? I wasn't aware it'd been closed."

"Forgive me," replied Jack, holding up his hands. "Maybe reopening is the wrong word. The case has been reassigned to myself and my team here in London."

"W . . . why is that?" Martin Rivers' pale eyes peered out from behind his glasses.

"We have reason to believe that the person responsible for murdering your daughter is here in London." Jack paused. "And that he's killed again."

Rivers began to nod, slowly. "I saw it in the newspaper. I hoped it wasn't true, but . . ." His pale eyes took on a watery sheen. "So, what can I help you with?"

Jack glanced around the room once more. Every surface was crammed full of photographs; smiling faces staring out from every corner. But despite the happy faces, the room felt sad — empty and devoid of life. Jack turned back to Martin Rivers. "We're going over every aspect of the previous investigation. We have your witness statements here — it would help if you could read them again and let us know if there's anything else you could tell us. Anything that might've been missed first time around. No matter how insignificant it might seem."

Cassidy passed over a small selection of papers, and both she and Jack sat in silence while Rivers read through each page, tears glistening in his eyes as he did so.

Once finished, Martin Rivers placed the papers on the coffee table and wiped the corners of his eyes with a tissue. "That's all as I remember it," he said, glancing up. "I'm not sure what else I can tell you."

Jack nodded. "That's fine." He paused and cast his eyes once more to the mantelpiece and bookcase. Out of all the photographs lined up, it was impossible not to recognise the smiling face of Stacey Fairbrother.

Cassidy followed Jack's gaze and smiled sadly across the coffee table. "She was very pretty. You must miss her dreadfully."

Rivers nodded. "She was beautiful — in every way. When she and her mother came into my life, everything was complete." He looked up and caught Jack's eye. "You know she was my stepdaughter, don't you? I married her mum, Heather, when Stacey was six."

"It was in the file, yes," replied Jack.

"My first wife, Barbara, died two years after we were married. It was a bleak time afterwards — I couldn't believe it when Heather came into my life. I felt blessed. And Stacey . . ." Rivers choked back a silent sob. "She was perfect. Just like her mother was." Another heave of the chest. "Heather died of breast cancer when Stacey was fifteen."

Jack rose from the sofa and stepped across the Axminster towards the fireplace. Many of the framed photographs featured a smiling, middle aged, sandy-haired woman. She had the same sparkling blue eyes as her daughter. As he scanned the rest of the mantelpiece and across to the bookcase, he noticed there were quite a few pictures of a young man with cropped fair hair and an athletic build — in several he was pictured with Stacey. They looked to be around the same age.

"And the young man here?" Jack pointed towards a photograph at the far end of the mantelpiece.

Martin Rivers swallowed, not attempting to wipe away the tears now trickling down his cheeks. "That's Justin. My son."

Jack frowned. There hadn't been any mention of a son in any of the Essex police paperwork, or at least none that he'd seen. The slight shake of the head from Cassidy confirmed that he wasn't alone in his confusion. "Your son?"

Rivers nodded and sighed. "Yes. Justin."

Jack picked up the witness statements from the coffee table. "I'm not sure your son was mentioned at the time of Stacey's murder, Mr Rivers. Would you be able to tell us how to get hold of him?" He looked up, expectantly, noticing that Martin Rivers' watery eyes were still focused on the mantelpiece. "Mr Rivers?" he repeated. "Your son? I'd really like to speak to him about Stacey."

"You won't be able to speak to him, Inspector." Martin Rivers' voice trembled. "He's dead."

* * *

Time: 7.50 a.m.
Date: Thursday 7 July 2005
Location: 7 Cross Keys Road, Camden Town, London

"I'm going to be late." Justin Rivers eyed the fresh rack of toast that appeared on the kitchen table. "I've got to get across to the British Museum this morning — the Tube will be rammed."

Martin Rivers waved his son's comments away, placing a fresh pot of tea, complete with woollen tea cosy, next to the toast. "You've got time for another slice. It's not every day you turn twenty-one!" He turned and opened one of the kitchen cupboards, rummaging behind packets of Weetabix and Bran Flakes before bringing out a rectangular envelope and a small, square box. "Happy birthday, son."

He placed the envelope and box next to Justin's plate, which he noticed now had two more slices of thick, white toast on and Justin was busily scraping a generous portion of butter on to each. Justin looked up, the smile on his face deepening the dimples on both of his cheeks. He brushed the mop of unruly fair hair out of his eyes.

"Thanks, Dad." In-between mouthfuls of toast, Justin tore open the envelope, his pale grey eyes sparkling. "Jesus, Dad. Really?" He looked up again, mouth open. "You're sure?" His eyes fell back down to the envelope, and the cheque for £750 in his hands.

Martin Rivers nodded, picking up the teapot and pouring them both a fresh mug of tea. Always from the pot. If there was anything that Heather had taught him during their time together, it was that tea always came from the pot. None of this 'tea bag in the mug' nonsense. And always fresh water. And a warmed teapot. With a tea cosy.

"You can put it towards your travelling fund — if that's still your plan."

Justin nodded, cramming more toast into his mouth and taking a swig of tea. "Andy says he's got nine hundred quid together now. With this, I'm way past that. Thanks, Dad. You're amazing." He then picked up the square box, ripping off the hastily applied wrapping paper and pulling out a Navigator watch. "Wow, Dad!"

"It's just a little something. I didn't know what else to get you. There was a guy down the market selling them, so . . ."

Justin turned the watch over and saw it was inscribed with 'Happy 21st Justin. Love Dad'. "It's brilliant, thanks Dad. I won't wear it to work, though — I'll probably ruin it."

Martin Rivers let a soft smile graze his lips behind his mug of tea and sighed, contentedly. He'd done it. He'd successfully navigated the trials of bringing up a family alone — and his son was now a man. Both Barbara and Heather would be proud of him. "Where're you working today?" He glanced over to the small kitchen window. "Looks like a dry day, at least. Are you outside?"

Justin nodded, draining his mug of tea and pouring another one from the pot. "Yeah, most probably. We're working on a new exhibition room at the British Museum. I might be up on the roof for some of it today."

"Well, you have a good day. Keep an eye on the time." Rivers nodded towards the kitchen clock hanging on the wall above the sink. It was almost ten past eight. "You've normally left by now."

Justin gave his Dad a wink, taking another mouthful of tea. "It's my birthday, Dad. I'm allowed to be a little late." He reached across the table and took another slice of toast from the rack. "What's the worst that can happen?"

* * *

Time: 2.30 p.m.
Date: Monday 23 September 2013
Location: Westminster Mortuary, London

Dr Philip Matthews' eyes glinted in the harsh glare of the overhead lights. He loved his work, which he knew some people would find macabre or even downright disturbing. But he did, just the same. He especially enjoyed it when he had a willing audience to perform to, and this afternoon he was blessed with two eager observers.

And one of them was a post-mortem virgin.

"Detectives. How lovely to see you both." Dr Matthews glanced from DS Cooper to DC Daniels and flashed a smile. "Now, DS Cooper here is a seasoned visitor to my examination room, but I don't think I have yet had the pleasure of meeting his companion?"

Daniels hesitated. Then, realising the pathologist was meaning himself, he cleared his throat and stood a little straighter. "DC Trevor Daniels, sir."

Dr Matthews' smile widened. "Well, it's very good to meet you, DC Daniels. But let's drop the 'sir'. You'll find us a very informal bunch within these walls. I'll answer to most things, within reason. Just ask my good lady wife." The pathologist's eyes sparkled with good humour.

Daniels' cheeks coloured slightly and he nudged his glasses up a notch on to the bridge of his nose. "Thank you, s . . . er . . . doctor."

Dr Matthews gave a discreet nod, and pulled the overhead lights down a little closer. "I think it's time that we began, don't you, gentlemen?" He switched on the voice recorder and accepted a sharpened scalpel from the tray offered to him by the mortuary technician waiting patiently by his side.

With the scalpel hovering an inch above Amy Jennings' pale body, Dr Matthews glanced up and sought out DC Daniels' attentive gaze. "And just one more thing — don't feel like you have to remain in the room until the very end.

If you feel like taking a breather — for whatever reason — please feel free to step outside. Post-mortems are not for everyone."

Daniels gave a curt nod, but took a hesitant step closer to the examination table.

Satisfied he had sufficiently briefed his latest uninitiated visitor, Dr Matthews began.

* * *

Time: 3.05 p.m.
Date: Monday 23 September 2013
Location: 7 Cross Keys Road, Camden Town, London

Jack closed the door to the Mondeo and glanced across at DS Cassidy in the passenger seat. "You OK?"

Cassidy nodded, her face slack. She looked out of the passenger side window towards the neat front path leading to number seven. "How much grief can one man take? It's just not fair."

Jack shook his head and switched on the engine, lowering his window to let a degree of fresh air into the car. Martin Rivers' small front room had been musty and close, with an odd, festering smell clinging to the air. "I can't even begin to imagine."

"It's like that whole house is locked up in . . . I don't know, a coffin. A coffin full of sadness." Cassidy continued looking out of the window at the Rivers' family home. "He just sits there, in the dark, day after day. Surrounded by his memories. That's all he has left."

Jack pulled the Mondeo away from the kerb.

"Losing his first wife so young must've been heartbreaking enough," continued Cassidy, as they left Cross Keys Road and headed towards central London. "Dying in childbirth, like that. And then just when he thought he'd found happiness again, he lost his second wife to cancer." She broke off and shook her head. "Then to lose your son in the Tube bombings on 7/7, followed by your stepdaughter being murdered. That must've just ripped his whole world apart. How can one person deal with all that?"

Jack had no words and joined the queue of afternoon traffic. "We'll catch him," he murmured, gripping hold of the steering wheel, a look of quiet determination on his face. "We'll catch the Bishop. At least that might bring Mr Rivers some form of closure."

* * *

Time: 3.15 p.m.
Date: Monday 23 September 2013
Location: Westminster Mortuary, London

Amy Jennings lay on the cold, steel examination table, the harsh lighting overhead glinting off her pale skin. Three pairs of inquisitive eyes looked on.

Her heart lay in a steel bowl, waiting to be returned to the chest cavity after being weighed by the technician. Meanwhile, Dr Matthews was skilfully working his way along the abdomen, mobilising Amy's stomach. The J-shaped organ was removed and placed into another steel bowl, dutifully weighed and measured before being returned to the pathologist's side.

"Now, gentlemen, the aroma from an opened stomach can be less than enticing. So, if either of you feel you want to take a step back . . ." Dr Matthews hesitated, his scalpel hovering above the steel bowl. He glanced at DS Cooper and then DC Daniels, a look of rapt attention mirrored on both their faces. Dr Matthews afforded himself a small smile. "In that case, gentlemen . . ." He deftly sliced the organ from top to bottom.

A mixture of stomach acid and food residue, some having begun the digestion process already, slid from the opened stomach and collected at the base of the bowl. A rich, acidic and decidedly unpleasant smell wafted up. Dr Matthews' nose was desensitised to the range of pungent odours that often circulated his post-mortem room, but as he afforded another glance towards his avid spectators, he noted that neither of them seemed to flinch. He even detected DC Daniels taking an extra step forwards, closer to the steel bowl's contents. Another smile crossed the pathologist's lips.

"From the contents of the stomach it should be possible to identify what the victim last ate, and approximately how long ago that was. From that, a time of death can sometimes be concluded." Dr Matthews handed the bowl to the technician. "Although from the paperwork I don't think the time of death of this poor young lady is in any dispute."

The rest of the post-mortem progressed steadily, with both Cooper and Daniels asking intelligent questions along the way. The hand-carved, wooden bishop was prised from Amy's fingers and deposited in another steel examination bowl. Not long afterwards, a similarly expertly carved queen was extracted from her jaws.

"To conclude, gentlemen, we have a young Caucasian female, age twenty-six, who is in excellent health. No comorbidities to report. All internal organs examined show no signs of damage or disease. Externally, there are no injuries apart from two wounds I will mention in due course. There is a thin ligature mark to the neck, with extensive haemorrhaging and associated contusions. As suspected, there is a fracture of the hyoid bone, suggesting a great deal of force has been used.

"In addition, we have a puncture wound on the right upper thigh — severing the femoral artery. Catastrophic blood loss would have inevitably led to a cardiac arrest. Both the asphyxiation and cardiac arrest would've contributed to her death.

"A wound to the lower abdomen, approximately six centimetres by five centimetres was inflicted post-mortem. The wound has clean, precise edges — suggesting a very sharp blade." Dr Matthews paused and took one last look at Amy Jennings. "Due to the absence of livor mortis at the scene, I agree that the estimated time of death is between five and six p.m. on Sunday 22 September."

The pathologist stepped away from the examination table and switched off the voice recorder. Nodding at his technician, he gave a respectful bow towards Amy Jennings' body and left the room.

CHAPTER THIRTEEN

Time: 4.45 p.m.
Date: Monday 23 September 2013
Location: Metropolitan Police HQ, London

After returning from the mortuary, Jack left Cooper and Daniels sifting through the CCTV images from the streets around The Penthouse. He didn't expect much to come from it — the apartment where Amy Jennings had met her death had no cameras to speak of, and even the surrounding streets had somewhat patchy coverage. But it was a job that needed doing.

He also asked Daniels to carry on trawling the internet for any online chess forums — it was a long shot, but they had to start somewhere.

Jack returned to his office and began rummaging among the piles of paperwork on his desk before he found the telephone hidden beneath. As he slipped into his chair, waiting to be connected to Rachel Hunter's office, he found his gaze falling on the empty desk opposite. The room was quiet, and Jack began to realise how much he missed the noises Cooper used to make — the rustlings from his incessant snacking, the tapping of his fingers on the keyboard, even the occasional yawn.

“Yes? Rachel Hunter speaking.”

Jack turned his attention back to the present. “Hi. It’s DI Jack MacIntosh.” He swivelled his chair around to face his computer monitor, Barry Draper’s face staring back out at him.

“Good afternoon, Inspector,” replied Dr Hunter, her voice light. “What can I do for you?”

“I’ve a question or two concerning your profile. The one for the Bishop.” Jack plucked the single sheet of A4 paper from his desk containing a summary of the psychologist’s profile. “Could I maybe pop round to your office and pick your brains?”

“Ordinarily that would be fine, Inspector, but I’ve got a meeting in less than ten minutes.”

“Afterwards?”

There was a brief pause on the other end of the line before Rachel Hunter’s delicate tone replied. “Unfortunately, I have to attend the annual Forensic Pathologists’ Dinner tonight. Sorry, I can’t get out of it.” She paused again. “But if you’re free, you could come along as my plus one?”

“I’m sorry?” Jack let the profile flutter back on to his desk.

“To the dinner? You could come along — and we could discuss your case at the same time.” Rachel Hunter paused, and Jack heard more rustling of paperwork in the background. “I’m afraid that’s the best I can offer today.”

A dinner? Jack felt his mouth run dry at the very thought.

“Inspector?” Rachel Hunter’s voice cut through the silence that had descended. “Are you still there?”

“Yes, yes . . . sorry.” Jack cleared his throat. “That would be great, thanks.”

There was a hint of a chuckle at the other end of the line. “Good, it’s a date. And it’s black tie, Inspector. But I’m thinking you probably scrub up quite well at these sorts of events.” Rachel Hunter swiftly ended the call and Jack was left holding an empty receiver.

It’s a date.

The words echoed inside Jack’s head as his heart rate quickened.

Was that what this was? *A date*?

Unexpected heat flooded his cheeks just as his email inbox pinged with a message detailing the address and timings for the dinner. He couldn't remember the last black tie event he'd been to. He really needed to get home and see if he had anything resembling suitable attire to wear.

As he stood up he sensed a fluttering in the pit of his stomach.

He couldn't decide if it was excitement he felt, or terror.

* * *

Time: 6.05 p.m.
Date: Monday 23 September 2013
Location: Student Union Bar — St James's University, London

The Student Union bar was bigger than she'd expected, and surprisingly fresh and airy. She'd thought it would be some dark and dingy room in a basement somewhere, thick with smoke despite the smoking ban. But instead, she found herself in a light and airy space on the ground floor which opened out on to a courtyard with plenty of outdoor seating.

There were only a handful of people milling about by the bar so, as the evening was still pleasantly mild, she sat outside on a comfortable wicker chair and quickly sunk her first double vodka to calm her nerves. She watched the bar staff inside arranging the tables into groups, according to the different faculties at the university.

The Arts department had secured the tables closest to the bar, and when Lily noticed two girls sitting down she took a deep breath and ventured back inside, taking her empty glass with her. Despite the alcohol, she suddenly felt very self-conscious in her homemade pinafore dress and Dr Marten boots.

As she approached the table, one of the girls looked up and smiled. She had long, flowing black hair, dip-dyed a rich scarlet at the ends. She wore dark make-up, eyes heavy with mascara, and her sleek-looking red dress matched the hues in her hair. Next to her was a girl with short, spiky, blonde hair, dressed in a loose fitting men's shirt and a pair of baggy, faded jeans splattered with paint.

"Hey," said the girl in the scarlet dress. She stood up as Lily approached and dragged a nearby stool across. "Come join. I'm Scarlett — hence the dress. And the hair. This is Naomi." She nodded at the girl in the jeans.

Lily heaved a sigh of relief and sat down on the bar stool. She found herself grinning back, finally feeling the relaxing effect of the vodka. "Hi. I'm Lily. Pleased to meet you."

"Nervous, huh?" Naomi's large, silver hoop earrings swung as she turned her head. "So are we. That's why we've ordered these." She nodded at the glasses on the table. "Now it's after six, it's two-for-one. What d'you fancy?" Naomi nodded at Lily's empty glass.

"I'll have what you're having," she replied. Naomi nodded and headed back towards the bar.

"So, what course are you doing?" Scarlett pulled her stool in closer. "I'm doing Fashion and Textiles."

"Just the basic BA in Fashion Design," replied Lily. "I think some of our modules might overlap."

Naomi came back armed with two glasses for Lily, placing them down next to her. "Well, here's to the next three years!" She picked up her own glass and held it in the air.

Lily and Scarlett each raised their own drink and they all clinked glasses.

"Down in one!"

* * *

Time: 7.30 p.m.
Date: Monday 23 September 2013
Location: The Rose Bowl Hotel and Restaurant, W1 — Forensic Pathologists' Dinner

"I was right. You do scrub up well." Rachel Hunter flashed a smile at Jack, who noticed for the first time how neat and straight her teeth were. "Come. Let's get ourselves a drink."

Jack followed Rachel inside the hotel, discreetly running a finger around the inside of his shirt collar. The bow tie was almost strangling him and he was beginning to feel hot and bothered already. He felt like a fish out of water in among the sleek and elegantly dressed, and started to wish he hadn't agreed to come.

The foyer of the West End hotel was brimming with well-dressed, suited and booted guests — the men mostly sporting a variety of dinner suits, with even the odd cummerbund. The women were displaying a number of sparkling and glimmering evening gowns, hair coiffured to the point of no return.

Jack instinctively ran a hand over his hair, glad he'd managed to tame the tufts in the shower.

Rachel was dressed in an understated navy blue dress — it didn't sparkle or shine as many of the other women's did, but it was classy nonetheless. Not that Jack knew much about dresses. Or women, for that matter.

They found their way to the bar and after a few moments of trying to catch the attention of the bar staff, they took their drinks into the main reception room where the dinner was being held. Extravagant chandeliers hung from the ceiling, their light muted and soft. In the background, the sound of soft jazz music filled the air, which would ordinarily grate on Jack's nerves. Jazz was not one of his favourites, but here in the vast, expensively decorated dining room it seemed to fit in. So, Jack was prepared to let it go – just this once.

Rachel led the way towards a table at the edge of the room where they were to be seated. Jack followed and found his nerves, which had been fraying by the second since their arrival, begin to relax as he saw a familiar figure sitting on one of the chairs.

"Good evening, Jack. This is a nice surprise."

Dr Philip Matthews' bald head gleamed underneath the overhead chandelier. He rose from his seat and held out a hand.

Jack took the pathologist's hand, grateful for its steadying effect. "Good to see you, Doc." Rachel nodded at the seat next to Dr Matthews and Jack gratefully sank into it.

Why was he still feeling so nervous? He could feel a trickle of perspiration inching down his back.

It's a date.

Those words again.

"And just how did you manage to wangle yourself an invitation to this splendid and *very* exclusive gathering?" Dr Matthews' eyes twinkled, his gaze flitting between Jack and Rachel. "Or would that be prying?"

"Well," began Jack, reaching for his drink and taking a long gulp. He never usually drank martinis — wasn't even sure what one was — but he'd agreed to Rachel's suggestion just to get some alcohol into his system.

"I persuaded him to come," explained Rachel, a smile dancing on her lips. "Well, you could call it blackmail, I guess." She gave a sly wink towards Jack and moved her chair a little closer.

"I wouldn't quite say blackmail," replied Jack, the martini getting to work and loosening his throat.

"Maybe not, but you're doing me a huge favour." Rachel placed a hand on Jack's forearm, leaned in closer and gave both Jack and Dr Matthews a conspiratorial wink. "To be honest, I find these events so dull I might pass out."

Dr Matthews raised his glass. "And I second that. Dreadfully dull, bordering on the tedious — but I have a sneaking suspicion tonight might be different. Now I have the most pleasing of dinner guests, I feel I might actually enjoy myself." The pathologist's eyes continued to sparkle as he drained his glass and stood up. "Who'll join me in another bottle?"

* * *

Time: 9.00 p.m.
Date: Monday 23 September 2013
Location: Flat 2a, Farriers Court, London

DS Cassidy made herself at home on the comfortable two-seater leather sofa, her legs curled up beneath her. Taking a sip of her hot chocolate, she glanced around the inside of DC Daniels' flat, noticing it was the mirror image of her own just one floor below. A compact and cosy front room, with galley-style modern kitchen off to the side. Living in the same block of flats, only a short walk from the station, Cassidy had soon befriended the shy police constable, (as he was at the time) so when the need had arisen for a chess enthusiast to join them on the team, she'd known exactly who to call on.

Daniels sat opposite in the only armchair,hunched over his laptop. His face was fixed with concentration, his eyes trained on the screen. DS Cooper perched on the side.

"We're in!" Cooper slapped Daniels on the back and slugged another mouthful of the beer he'd helped himself to from the kitchen. Daniels' bottle sat untouched by his side. "We're in!"

Daniels' elegant fingers skipped effortlessly over the keyboard as he negotiated his way around the Kings and Queens online chess forum. They'd checked out seven websites over the last two hours, and demolished a giant pepperoni pizza before finally striking gold.

Cassidy wrapped her hands around her hot chocolate mug and watched. It wasn't long before Daniels looked up and winked, a smile creeping across his face.

"You'll never guess who I've just found."

* * *

Time: 9.15 p.m.
Date: Monday 23 September 2013
Location: The Rose Bowl Hotel and Restaurant — Forensic Pathologists' Dinner

After the second martini, they started on Dr Matthews' bottle of champagne. Jack slowly began to relax and, God forbid, enjoy himself. He loosened his bow tie a little, catching Rachel's sideways glance as he did so.

"Getting a little hot under the collar, Inspector?" she teased.

Jack tried to hide a smile behind his champagne glass. "A little. But nothing I can't handle."

"I'm glad to hear it," Rachel replied, coyly. "You look different out of work. In a good way."

Jack tipped the rest of the champagne into his mouth. "Likewise." He nodded towards the bottle resting in the ice bucket. "Top up?"

Rachel giggled and got unsteadily to her feet. "Just a small one. I wish they'd hurry up with the food though — I need something to soak up all this alcohol, or I'll be no use to anybody tomorrow. I'm just nipping to the ladies."

Jack watched as she grabbed her handbag from the back of the chair and threaded her way around the tables towards the exit.

"Good to see you letting your hair down, Jack." Dr Matthews reappeared at the table armed with yet another bottle of champagne which he dumped in the ice bucket to join the other. "And a very pretty companion you have, too."

Jack felt his cheeks flush. "Where's Mrs Matthews tonight?"

"Ah." Dr Matthews resumed his seat next to Jack. "Tonight's soiree clashed with her weekly pottery class. And it's the wheel tonight, not to be missed." He leaned across the table, topping up both his own and Jack's glasses from the remnants of the first champagne bottle and then handing the empty vessel to a passing waiter.

Jack's stomach began to growl as he took another mouthful of champagne. He needed to eat something before long: the alcohol was going down far too easily. As if on cue, several waiters appeared brandishing plates of exquisitely prepared delicacies. Quite what they were, Jack found hard to fathom at first glance, but he accepted several portions of each on his plate. Picking up a fork, he prodded a flesh-coloured cube wrapped in what looked like a leaf of some description. The frown that crossed his brow earned a low-level laugh from the pathologist at his side.

"Never fear, Jack. I've dealt with many an unusual specimen on my mortuary slab — but I'm pretty sure these are all fit for human consumption. Whatever they may be." Dr Matthews speared one of the flesh-coloured cubes and popped it in his mouth.

Jack followed suit, the griping from his stomach telling him that he needed to eat, whatever it turned out to be. After a few chews he decided it tasted like chicken. As most things did.

"At last!" Rachel slipped back into her seat, her eyes falling on the plates of food. "I'm starting to feel a little squiffy." She popped one of the leaf-covered cubes in her mouth, which a passing waiter reliably informed them was lemon-infused poussin wrapped in pandan leaves. She then turned towards Jack. "So, tell me — the Bishop. What's the issue with my profile? This was, at least, the reason you agreed to come tonight, wasn't it? To pick my brains, I think you said." Rachel gave a good-humoured wink and speared another poussin cube.

Jack swallowed a mouthful of rosemary-encrusted potato and washed it down with some more champagne. "It's not a problem with the profile as such — it's more a problem with a suspect. Or a *potential* suspect."

"Go on."

"After a TV appeal during the initial investigation in 2009, several members of the public named the same guy. Actually, more than several." Jack paused to stab at an asparagus spear with his fork. "For whatever reason, they discounted him. Maybe he didn't fit their profile."

"Ah yes, the infamous Dr Bauer. I remember."

Jack nodded. "The hotline we activated on Saturday has generated a lot of leads, including the usual crackpots and time-wasters. But we've also had more people ring in with the same name as in 2009. At the last count, he's been mentioned thirteen times in two days."

Rachel paused, her fork hovering over her plate. "The same name . . . that's interesting. So, he's your potential suspect?"

"Well, that's the thing." Jack placed his fork back down on his plate. "He didn't fit Bauer's profile back in 2009, and he doesn't really fit yours either, not entirely. Although we don't know too much about him. I don't know whether to rule him out, like they did in 2009, or . . ."

A slight frown crossed Rachel's face. "I don't think you should discount him *solely* on the basis of my profile. Because that's all it is — a profile. Although I'm pretty confident in the set of characteristics I gave you."

Jack nodded. "I know."

"What aspects of the profile doesn't he fit?"

"Age, for one thing. He's older. And, by all accounts, he's a bit of a misfit. A loner. Not the charming, confident perpetrator you outlined."

"I see." Rachel chewed, thoughtfully. "But you're not sure?"

"My gut tells me he's not our guy, but . . ." Jack shook his head and reached for the glass that Dr Matthews had discreetly topped up. "My gut's been wrong before. And I don't want to make the same mistakes the first investigation did. We can't let the families of the victims down again. They've been through enough."

"You know as well as I do, Jack, criminal profiles are only a guide. They're not cast in stone. We work within probabilities. There'll always be someone that comes along to surprise us."

Jack let Rachel's comments sink in while he polished off the rest of the poussin on his plate. After a while, Rachel disappeared to go and speak to someone she recognised on another table, and Dr Matthews took the opportunity to scoot his chair closer to Jack.

"How are things progressing?" asked the pathologist, keeping his voice low. "With the DNA from your mother's post-mortem?"

Jack wiped his mouth on a napkin. "They've managed to isolate a DNA profile. And we know who he is."

Dr Matthews' eyebrows raised a notch. "You have a name?"

Jack nodded. He thought for a moment whether he should tell the pathologist about James Quinn — about a dead man who was no longer dead — but decided it wasn't the time or the place for that kind of a discussion. "I'm just thinking about what to do next. If anything. His skin underneath her fingernails doesn't really prove much."

"That's true," conceded Dr Matthews. "Although it raises a lot of questions."

Jack felt his phone vibrate in his pocket. Upon fishing it out he noticed it was a call from DS Cooper. Rising from the table, and raising a hand in apology, Jack stepped away towards the side of the dining room, placing a hand over his opposite ear to cut out the noise.

"Cooper?"

"Boss. Can you talk?" DS Cooper's voice sounded strained.

"Of course. Go on."

"You know you asked Trevor to hook up with as many online chess groups as he could?"

Jack felt a strange sensation grip his stomach. "Yes. What of it?"

"Well, Trevor signed up to a load of them tonight — and we struck gold with one. Kings and Queens it's called." Cooper paused. "And Barry Draper's a member. It didn't take Trevor long to come across his profile — the guy isn't hiding. His picture's on there and everything."

"And?" The poussin started to churn in Jack's stomach. He was sure there was an 'and' coming.

"Each registered user gets to pick a username — to use when playing the online games." Cooper paused again. "Barry Draper calls himself 'The Bishop'."

* * *

Time: 1.45 a.m.
Date: Tuesday 24 September 2013
Location: Wayland Road, London

The evening had sped past so quickly, Lily hardly remembered when they'd made the decision to leave the bar. Scarlett and Naomi had been great company. Naomi was studying footwear design, so it was likely that all three would see each other from time to time in various classes. They'd been joined by several others during the course of the evening but, by that time, the alcohol had started to take hold and Lily's recollection of the rest of the night was somewhat hazy.

She looked down at the bulky, analogue-style watch that she'd picked up at a market stall in Glasgow over the summer — it was 1.45 a.m. She giggled, quietly, to herself as she walked. There'd be no one waiting at home to tell her off for being out so late, or to ask what she'd been up to until this time in the morning. She was a free spirit. *Free.*

She found herself on Wayland Road, the main road outside the university entrance, and knew that her bedsit was only a few minutes' walk away. Scarlett and Naomi were both in halls of residence so they had headed off in the opposite direction. The air was still and quiet, warm and balmy despite the hour.

The main road was well-lit with several street lights, and Lily began to walk in the direction of her bedsit. She found her legs a little wobbly, her Dr Martens scuffing along the pavement. She giggled some more. She felt good: she was having fun already and yet she had only just arrived. She couldn't wait for the next three years.

After a few more minutes staggered walking, she crossed the road opposite the convenience store where she'd bought her doughnuts earlier, knowing that her road was the next on the left. When she eventually reached it, she noticed her street was far darker than the main road, with just the one street light at the top. The buildings on either side of the road were all split into flats or bedsits, the vast majority housing university students like herself. There were one or two with lights on at the windows, but most sat in darkness.

Lily shivered. She didn't feel cold but the dark that enveloped her made her shudder. Her footsteps sounded so loud on the pavement, echoing off the brickwork as she passed by. She could hear a distant siren on the breeze, but otherwise there was nothing else to disturb the quiet.

She quickened her step, suddenly wanting to be inside the safety of her bedsit, curling up underneath her new duvet with a cup of tea from her cheap, new kettle. *Damn*, she thought to herself as she stepped into the road to avoid a section of the pavement littered with breeze blocks from a recent renovation. She didn't have any milk.

She hesitated and thought about going back to the convenience store around the corner. Surely it wouldn't still be open, would it? Not even in London. She pressed on in the direction of home, resolving to go and buy some first thing in the morning.

As she stepped back on to the pavement, a noise behind her made her jump. With her heart leaping into her mouth, she whipped her head around. The noise had sounded like a footstep, but as she scanned the gloom all she could see were dark shadows lining the walls of the buildings on either side of the street. As far as she could tell, there was no one around. She was completely alone.

Swallowing, nervously, she again quickened her pace, almost tripping over her own feet as she hurried. She began fumbling inside her shoulder bag for the front door key.

There it was again.

Not breaking her stride, she turned to look back over her shoulder. She'd definitely heard something that time – footsteps that weren't her own. Her heart thumped wildly in her chest, her vodka-infused vision now sharpening. Reaching her front door, she thrust the key into the lock and shoved the door open.

Even as she crossed the threshold into the dingy communal hallway, she felt she could still hear them; footsteps on the pavement, getting closer, heading in her direction. She slammed the door shut and ran to her room.

CHAPTER FOURTEEN

Time: 8.35 a.m.
Date: Tuesday 24 September 2013
Location: Metropolitan Police HQ, London

Jack rubbed his temples and swallowed two more paracetamol tablets. He grimaced as they slid towards his stomach, leaving a chalky taste on his tongue. DS Cassidy placed a mug of strong black coffee in front of him, a smile on her face.

"Good night was it, guv?" She giggled and turned back towards the hot- water urn to continue making three more mugs of coffee.

Jack grumbled something in response and took a sip, wincing as it scalded his lips. But the pain he felt from the hot liquid was nothing in comparison to the raging war currently being waged on the inside of his skull.

He watched as DS Cooper woke up the interactive whiteboard, the glare from the screen instantly piercing Jack's eyes. He squinted and turned his gaze back to his steaming coffee. He hoped to God that Cooper hadn't brought in his customary greasy bacon sandwiches this morning — just the word bacon made him feel nauseous. Thankfully, there was no sight, or indeed smell, of any fried rashers — just mugs of coffee. Coffee he could handle, just about.

Cassidy brought the three mugs over to the table, seating herself next to the newest member of the team. "Trevor here joined the Kings and Queens online chess club last night and managed to locate Barry Draper's profile without much difficulty. As Chris told you, he makes no effort to conceal his identity and goes by the username of 'The Bishop'." Cassidy resorted to her notebook, flicking over several pages. "He joined the site in 2006 and has been a relatively active member since then. He's ranked in their top ten."

"Daniels?" Jack risked another sip of his coffee. "You managed to interact with him last night?"

"I did." DC Daniels gave an enthusiastic nod. "I found his profile pretty quickly, as he's one of their top players. The site hosts weekly competitions, but you can also request individual games from registered players." Daniels paused. "So, last night I requested a game with the Bishop."

Jack raised his eyebrows and ignored the thumping inside his head. "And?"

"He accepted. He's a good player — a very good player. He certainly knows his chess, and he knows about strategy. He beat me hands down."

Jack nodded. "Any opportunity to chat online? Is there a message facility?"

Daniels shook his head. "Not that I could see. He played the game, then logged off at just after half eleven. I stayed online a while after, but he never resurfaced."

"Since the hotline went live on Saturday, we've had thirteen calls naming him." Cooper tapped his keyboard. "All anonymous."

Jack took another sip of the bitter, unsugared coffee. The heavy fog that had enveloped his brain from the moment he'd rolled out of bed still lingered. "Well, I managed to speak to Rachel Hunter last night about our Mr Draper." Jack detected a faint snigger coming from across the table where Cassidy was hiding her grin behind her mug. Jack felt his own mouth begin to twitch before he carried on. "I explained about how, on paper, Draper didn't match her profile, but that his name had come up in both investigations. Although she stands by her profile, which would make him a low category suspect, I can't ignore the fact that his name's been suggested yet again."

Jack rubbed his eyes, feeling the grittiness beneath his touch. "Due to the severity and high-profile nature of this investigation, and the increased risk to the public until he's caught, I feel we've no option but to follow up on our Mr Draper. Even if just to rule him out." He drained the rest of his coffee and grimaced. "I'm going to see the Chief. Play nicely while I'm gone."

* * *

Time: 8.40 a.m.
Date: Tuesday 24 September 2013
Location: St James's House, Gold Street, London

The searing morning sunlight hit her full in the face through a gap in the thin curtains, bathing her in brightness. Squinting at her watch, she noted it was still early.

As she prised her eyes fully open, she felt a familiar throbbing sensation circulating inside her head. How much had she drunk last night? After the fourth double vodka she'd begun to lose count. There was a faint recollection of shots of tequila after that, but not much else.

She turned away from the window and wrapped the duvet around herself. She wasn't due at the university until later that afternoon, to pick up some registration forms and a reading list. A reading list for a fashion design course? Lily groaned at the mere thought of having to hit the library.

The banging inside her head intensified with her change of position. Through half-closed eyes she spied the open packet of doughnuts on the floor by her discarded Dr Marten boots. Her stomach began to rumble.

Despite her headache, she pushed herself up and leaned back against the wall, propped up by her new pillows. Her mouth felt rough and dry, and she instantly regretted not cleaning her teeth before tumbling into bed last night — or, more accurately, this morning.

Glancing back down at the floor, she noticed her pinafore dress and tights had been discarded next to her boots. Somehow, in her alcohol-induced haze, she'd managed to change into her pyjamas. She could barely remember getting back to the flat, let alone getting changed. She shielded her eyes from the glare of the morning sun, and thought back to last night. Although she couldn't really remember much about getting inside the flat, she could remember with surprising clarity her journey home.

The noises.

And the footsteps.

She shuddered despite the warmth of the duvet. It had felt so real at the time, but now she felt a little silly. What did she think she'd heard? Footsteps? Someone following her? Whenever she looked around, she'd seen nothing — nothing but shadows and darkness.

She shivered once again and rubbed her throbbing head. She needed tea. And she needed some paracetamol. Pushing herself out from under her duvet, she rolled herself out of bed and pulled on the pair of jogging bottoms that were screwed up on the floor. She picked her way over to the single wardrobe and pulled out a T-shirt. She hadn't brought many clothes with her, just enough to fit inside her rucksack and small suitcase on wheels, which probably meant she'd be making regular trips to the launderette — when she could find one.

Running a hand through her bed hair, she grabbed her purse and keys and slipped her feet into a pair of trainers.

The convenience store should be open by now. She could pick up some milk and painkillers, and maybe some cereal. Her stomach growled at the thought. The lure of a hot cup of tea propelled her forwards, out of her room and along the hall towards the front door. She felt fortunate to have secured a bedsit on the ground floor — heaven only knew how she'd have negotiated the stairs last night, bearing in mind the state she was in. Grandad wouldn't have been impressed. Lily made a mental note to ring him later – one of the conditions of moving so far away was that she'd ring home regularly.

As she stepped out into the street, Lily noticed how warm it was already. The sky was a clear blue and there were only a few wispy clouds languishing lazily overhead. The bright sun felt warm on her face.

She headed along the street towards the main road, retracing her steps from last night. She began to chide herself for thinking someone had been following her. The noises she'd heard could have been a million and one other things, or nothing at all except her overactive imagination.

As she made her way along the street, she noticed several bins were upturned on the opposite side of the road. Black plastic bags had been ripped apart and disgorged their contents over the pavement.

Foxes, mused Lily as she quickened her stride. Didn't they say that urban foxes were on the increase? There were probably hundreds prowling the streets after dark, looking for food.

That's what last night's noises would have been.

Foxes.

Or maybe rats? Weren't you supposed to be no more than six feet from a rat in London at any one time? The thought made her shudder even more in the warmth of the sun.

Lily approached the junction with the main road and turned right in the direction of the convenience store. She could see, far away into the distance, the buildings that made up the main campus of the university stretching high up into the sky.

She began to smile to herself as her headache began to fade. A nice cup of tea and some cereal. And then maybe back to bed for a while.

If Lily had taken the time to take one last glance over her shoulder, she might have seen that her worries about being followed weren't entirely without foundation.

This morning he was watching her again — hovering by a set of traffic lights on the other side of the main road. Wearing a baseball cap pulled firmly down over his eyes, he held a mobile phone to his ear, pretending to make a call.

But in reality he was watching.

Always watching.

She was perfect. Exquisite even. Maybe the best one yet. She'd first caught his eye yesterday, when she'd emerged from her bedsit and headed off in the direction of the main road. She didn't once turn around and see the shadowy figure following in her wake. She called into several shops, eventually making it back to her bedsit with what looked like a new duvet and a couple of pillows.

And when he followed her home from the Student Union bar last night, he definitely knew she was the one. The *next* one. He'd kept to the shadows, silently following as closely as he dared. He could tell she'd had a little too much to drink by the way she was stumbling over her own feet, and tottering out into the road. He'd heard her faint giggles as she wavered across the pavement.

He could have made his move right there and then, but he decided he needed to watch her some more.

And the fact that she'd been drinking made him recoil. No, he'd wait. No matter how perfect she was, he needed to wait. She needed to be sober and fully aware of what was happening to her, not in some half-drunk, semi-conscious state.

He needed to see the desperation in her eyes.

He needed to hear her gasp when she knew the end was coming.

He needed to see her fear.

He would wait.

He was good at waiting.

* * *

Time: 8.55 a.m.
Date: Tuesday 24 September 2013
Location: Metropolitan Police HQ, London

"Surveillance?" Chief Superintendent King raised his bushy eyebrows and peered at Jack over the top of his spectacles. "How much manpower are we looking at?"

"Ideally, two teams of two officers, on an eight-hour rotation."

"Twelve officers per twenty-four hours?"

Jack nodded. He sipped at the glass of water Dougie King had passed him almost as soon as he'd taken in Jack's grey complexion. No offer of coffee this time.

"And how long for?" The chief superintendent puffed out his cheeks and leaned back in his swivel chair. "A day? A week?"

Jack could only shrug. "I can't really say, sir. It depends what we find — if we find anything."

The office was quiet: only the occasional rumble from the coffee machine disturbed the peace. Even the wall clock seemed to be ticking in hushed tones. Which was good for Jack's headache.

"I know it's a big ask," added Jack. "I don't really have any grounds to arrest him, but he's a person of interest. I don't want to repeat the mistakes made in the first investigation."

"Quite," nodded Chief Superintendent King. "But budgets are tight, Jack, you know that. I have to account for every penny."

"I know." Jack sipped some more water, wishing he had some painkillers to go with it.

"Look, I'll authorise one team of two officers on an eight-hour rotation." Dougie King paused. "And for forty-eight hours only — as from now. Then you report back. It's the best I can do, Jack."

Jack gingerly gave another nod, wary of aggravating his already pounding head. "We can work with that."

The chief superintendent eyed Jack from across the desk, his gaze narrowing. "You look like shit, Jack. Late night?"

Jack gave what was intended to be a rueful smile, but it came across as more of a grimace. "You could say that," he replied, taking another sip of water. He knew his appearance was verging on the shabby this morning. The taxi had dropped him home at a little after 2 a.m. — and the next thing he knew was the alarm going off at six thirty. At least he'd managed some sleep. Something that, largely due to James Quinn, had been lacking in recent weeks.

"How's that brother of yours?" Chief Superintendent King's expression softened. "Still making headway I hope?"

After exchanging a few pleasantries and updating the chief superintendent on Stu's rehabilitation, Jack excused himself, citing a need to get on with organising the surveillance operation. In reality he needed more caffeine and another box of paracetamol.

* * *

Time: 9.45 a.m.
Date: Tuesday 24 September 2013
Location: St James's House, Gold Street, London

The tea had done the trick and Lily now felt almost human. The cereal had been a bit optimistic; the mere sight and sound of the popping Rice Krispies had churned her insides, and not in a pleasant way. She wasn't used to drinking. She'd sometimes share the odd glass or two with Granny and Grandad on a Sunday, but she wasn't a big drinker. She'd have to watch herself, and not get so carried away in future.

After a short sleep and a shower, she felt more refreshed and able to face the outside world. She'd phoned Grandad after getting back from the convenience store, knowing he would have been worried when she hadn't returned his call last night. He worried a lot, she knew that. When she was younger it used to bother her, but now she understood.

The day continued to be bright and sunny, and when Lily stepped outside, she had to pull on a pair of sunglasses to keep out the dazzling rays. It also helped to hide the dark circles that were emerging beneath her eyes. Resolving to get some early nights in this week before her course started properly after the weekend — she didn't want to turn up on her first day looking like something out of a horror film — she set off down the street.

She was wearing one of her own creations — a long, flowing dress, made from a patchwork quilt she'd spied in a charity shop in Glasgow. A cropped, denim jacket across her shoulders and a pair of flip flops completed the ensemble.

The short walk to the university's main campus further cleared her muzzy head, and by the time she jogged up the front steps she was feeling excited. Apart from the day of her interview, which seemed like a million years ago now, and last night's drunken trip to the Student Union bar, she hadn't set foot inside the main building. She felt the familiar fluttering in her stomach as her excitement gave way to nervousness.

Upon stepping through the main entrance, a giant atrium opened out in front of her. Lily soon found several signs pointing in the direction of the registration desk. After joining a short queue of other nervous-looking newbies, she was given a handful of forms and papers relating to her chosen course, some of which she needed to complete and post back into a metal box by the side of the desk.

Deciding to fill out the paperwork here and now, rather than have to make the journey back again later, Lily headed through an internal door beneath a sign saying 'Student Coffee Bar'. Although busy, Lily managed to find a vacant table by the side of a large patio door.

Taking her decaffeinated latte over to the table, Lily noticed the patio doors looked out over the outdoor seating area of the Student Union bar. Taking a moment to get her bearings, she realised the coffee bar was directly opposite where she'd spent most of yesterday evening — and the early hours of this morning. As she gazed through the window, she saw several workmen in fluorescent jackets placing ladders against the outer walls and others carrying lengths of wood high up on their shoulders.

Turning her attention to the bundle of paperwork, Lily scanned the reading list for her course. She'd need to find and enrol in the student library, as many of the books on the list looked very expensive to buy. She knew Grandad would send her the money if she asked, but she didn't want to. They'd done so much for her over the years, but now it was time for her to stand on her own two feet. Or maybe her flip-flops.

The equipment list was, thankfully, shorter than the reading list. Most of the equipment she'd be using in her first year, such as sewing machines and mannequins, would be available in the classroom and students weren't expected to provide their own. But they did advise she have her own supplies of sketching books, pencils, scissors for cutting fabric, measuring tape, pins, needles and thread. Helpfully, at the bottom of the equipment list, there was a selection of local retailers who stocked the items students would need. Lily made a mental note to go shopping.

Sipping her latte, Lily began to fill out the registration forms. They asked for the usual information — name, address, mobile phone number, next of kin details. There was also a form to apply for her student ID badge which she would need to wear whenever she was on the premises.

One last piece of paper gave her timetable for the first term. Her classes would begin on Monday and she noted, after skimming through the details, that most of her days were quite busy. The only day she seemed to have any free time was on a Wednesday afternoon.

That pleased her.

She wanted to be busy. She was here to learn.

She drained her coffee and decided she'd try and find some of the shops mentioned on the equipment list. If she did it today, then tomorrow she could go to Carnaby Street or Covent Garden and start getting inspiration for her designs.

Smiling to herself, Lily got to her feet and scooped up the completed paperwork. As she started heading towards the door, she recognised Scarlett chatting to a couple of the fluorescent jacket-wearing workmen she'd seen outside. She raised a hand in greeting, but didn't intend to stop.

"Hey," greeted Scarlett, grabbing hold of Lily's arm as she passed. "Time for a coffee?"

Lily smiled but shook her head. "Sorry. I've just had one. I'm about to go in search of some of the equipment I need for my course." Lily flapped the paperwork she held in her hand. "How're you feeling after last night, anyway?"

Scarlett gave a pained look and grinned. "Not good. That's why I'm in need of coffee! Anyway." She turned her attention to the two workmen who were hanging back by the coffee counter. "These two here have agreed to buy me a coffee, haven't you?!"

Lily began to head towards the exit. "I'll leave you to it. Don't do anything I wouldn't do," she teased.

"You're coming to the Nineties Night on Thursday, aren't you?" Scarlett pointed at the poster on the wall advertising the Fresher's Week Nineties Night.

Lily scanned the poster, noting the half price drinks and special offers splashed across in large letters. She groaned inwardly. She hadn't planned another boozy night out this week, wanting to get ahead with some preparation for her course and maybe some of the reading from her reading list if she managed to find the library. The thumping still present inside her head advised caution.

"Oh, go on — I can't go on my own, can I?" cajoled Scarlett, flashing her bright smile. "I'm trying to persuade these two here to come as well! It'll be fun!"

Lily smiled and relented. "OK. I'll be there."

"Great! See you there!" Scarlett waved Lily goodbye and turned back towards the queue for coffee.

Lily pushed herself through the doors and headed in the direction of the registration desk. Maybe another night out wouldn't be so bad — if she got some reading done beforehand. She made another mental note to ask where the library was and pushed her completed registration forms into the metal box. Glancing at her watch, she decided she still had time to track down some of the equipment shops, so she jogged down the front steps and headed in the direction of the Tube.

* * *

Time: 10.45 a.m.
Date: Tuesday 24 September 2013
Location: The Glade, Church Street, Albury, Surrey

Sunday evening had gone well — Roger Bancroft had enjoyed a quiet drink at a table for one in the Baker's Arms, nodding his head and exchanging pleasantries with some of the locals. With the wig and other prosthetics now carefully stowed away, Joseph Geraghty decided a cool glass of his favourite vodka was in order. It was early, but he felt like he deserved it.

Geraghty's attention then turned to James Quinn.

He got to his feet, crossing over to open the mahogany-wood bureau standing next to the patio doors. The dark wood looked out of place in the otherwise light and airy living room, but Geraghty had insisted the antique piece make the journey to Surrey with him. It wasn't as if he'd brought much else with him.

In one of the locked compartments, Geraghty found his latest stash of mobile phones.

All simple pay-as-you-go models.

All paid for with cash.

All untraceable.

He picked up the next phone in line, stripping off the back cover and inserting the battery and SIM card. While the phone began to power up, he pulled open another drawer, reaching inside to touch the cool, hard exterior of the gun. His fingertips tingled as they came into contact with the smooth metal. With one hand still grasping the mobile phone, he curled the other around the grip of the weapon. The weight in his hand felt reassuringly heavy.

Geraghty returned to his armchair with both the phone and the gun. He checked the weapon was loaded before placing it on the glass-topped coffee table. It gave a comforting clink.

He knew he wouldn't be needing the gun just yet, loaded or otherwise, because first he needed Jack MacIntosh.

Once Jack was here, the next part of the plan could come into play.

Only then would he use the gun.

The phone had now powered up and Geraghty wasted no time in opening up the messaging screen. He knew the number by heart.

A smile flooded his thin lips as he typed.

Take the bait, Jack MacIntosh.

Take the bait.

* * *

Time: 10.50 a.m.
Date: Tuesday 24 September 2013
Location: Metropolitan Police HQ, London

Forty-eight hours wasn't ideal but it was better than nothing. He'd managed to pull some officers in to help — the lure of overtime enough of an incentive — and DS Cooper and DC Daniels had been sent out on the first shift. Jack rubbed his eyes and left the incident room. His head still throbbed and his eyes were struggling to focus. With his stomach churning almost constantly, he wondered if now would be the time to attempt some food. As the thought of eating no longer triggered instant nausea, he decided on a trip to the canteen.

Just as he started to climb the stairs, his mobile chirped in his pocket with an incoming message. Hovering on the top step, he pulled out the phone and glanced at the screen. Another number he didn't recognise.

Jack clicked on the message.

'*I can tell you where he is. Just say the word.*'

Jack's headache intensified and the pounding at his temples increased. He immediately hit the call button but knew what response he'd get even before it reached his ears.

'*The number you have dialled is no longer in service.*'

Jack looked once again at the message: almost identical to the ones before. Whatever hunger he'd felt instantly evaporated and, instead of heading to the canteen, Jack turned and walked in the opposite direction — towards the only person he knew he could trust.

CHAPTER FIFTEEN

Time: 11.00 a.m.
Date: Tuesday 24 September 2013
Location: Metropolitan Police HQ, London

"How many messages have you had?" DS Carmichael motioned to Jack to take a seat.

"Three. One just now."

"All different numbers?"

Jack nodded. "All out of service as soon as the messages were sent."

"Sound like burner phones." Carmichael eyed Jack from the other side of the desk. "I don't necessarily want the details, Jack, but I'm assuming this has something to do with you wanting to find a dead man?"

Jack inclined his head and gave the briefest of nods. "You know someone who can trace these numbers? Unofficially?"

"If by 'unofficially' you mean illegally, then yes — I know a few people who might be able to help." Carmichael pulled out a note pad and pen from his desk drawer. "Let me have the numbers."

Jack showed Carmichael the message log on his phone, giving the numbers and times the messages were received.

"I can't promise anything, but I'll do my best."

"Unofficially."

"*Unofficially*," conceded Carmichael with a wink. "Anyway, I was hoping I'd bump into you."

"How so?" Jack raised his eyebrows, feeling the familiar return of the headache at his temples.

"A little birdie tells me you had a heavy night last night in the company of a rather beautiful young woman." Carmichael's eyes twinkled. "And as this is most out of character for DI MacIntosh, certified bachelor, I'll need all the gory details. Let's go upstairs for a bacon sandwich — you look like death."

* * *

Time: 11.10 a.m.
Date: Tuesday 24 September 2013
Location: Metropolitan Police HQ, London — Canteen

Jack wasn't sure if the smell of frying bacon was causing his stomach to churn in a good way or not. It was true he hadn't eaten so far that morning, unless you included paracetamol as a dietary intake.

They found a table in the corner, Carmichael carrying the tray of tea and sandwiches — not fully trusting Jack to be able to put one foot in front of the other without colliding with something. Placing the tray down, he swept away the crumbs left by the previous inhabitant and put Jack's plate in front of him.

Jack eyed the bacon sandwich warily for several seconds before deciding to chance it. As he sunk his teeth into the soft, white bread, his stomach made encouraging noises. It didn't take him long to demolish the whole sandwich, and wash it down with a gulp of milky tea.

"Do you feel as bad as you look?" Carmichael wiped a globule of tomato sauce from his lips as he spoke. "Because you look mighty rough, mate."

Jack managed a grimace in-between more mouthfuls of tea. "I think I must've eaten something dodgy last night."

"Ha," laughed Carmichael. "Nothing to do with the copious bottles of champagne, then?"

Jack eyed his colleague and friend over the rim of his mug. "Who told you about the champagne?"

"I have my spies." Carmichael's eyes twinkled as he polished off the rest of his sandwich. "Anyhow, tell me what happened after."

"After?" A frown crossed Jack's forehead, joining the thudding headache still raging at his temples. "What do you mean 'after'?"

Carmichael shook his head as another smile spread over his lips. "Did you see her home afterwards?"

"Home?" Jack placed his empty mug down on his plate. "Who?"

An exasperated, yet good-natured, sigh escaped Carmichael's lips. "Honestly, Jack. It's no wonder you're still single in your forties. Rachel. *Your date.*"

"It wasn't a date." Jack massaged his temples as the aching continued in earnest. "It was work."

"Work?" scoffed Carmichael, his grin spreading. "But you did see her home afterwards? You were a gentleman, weren't you, Jack?"

Jack hesitated. "She got into a taxi."

"Alone?"

"Of course, alone." Jack frowned. "I went home with the Doc."

Carmichael almost spat out his tea. "Honestly, Jack. You never fail to disappoint me. You go on a date — and yes it *was* a date, before you say anything — with a beautiful young woman, and you end up sharing a taxi home with a balding pathologist."

Jack felt his own lips twitch into a smile. "Well, if you put it like that . . ."

"Have you called her, at least?"

The confused look on Jack's face gave Carmichael the answer he needed. "Well, it's a good job you enjoy the single life, mate."

Several minutes went by as Carmichael finished his tea, and one of the canteen staff came along with a trolley to take away their empty plates. Once the trolley and its owner were out of earshot, Carmichael leaned in close, his voice low.

"I'll do what I can with the phone numbers. I know a guy."

Jack nodded. "Cheers, mate."

"Tell me to mind my own business, but are you getting yourself into something deep, Jack? Something you shouldn't?"

Jack considered the question. Was he getting in over his head this time? Should he just let his suspicions about James Quinn go? For that was all they were at this moment in time: suspicions. The man was a no-good thief, that was plainly evident from his record — but was he a murderer?

"If I tell you something, you need to promise you'll keep it to yourself." Jack's voice had an edge. He glanced over his shoulder, checking that no one was even remotely in earshot.

"You know me, Jack. Soul of discretion."

He took a deep breath. "That dead man I was looking for? He goes by the name of James Quinn — or at least he did until he fell off a cross-channel ferry in 2002." Jack paused. "Except I know he didn't — fall off the ferry, that is."

"And you want to find him why?"

"I think he killed my mother."

Carmichael's eyebrows shot up. "And the phone messages?"

"Someone knows where he is."

* * *

Time: 11.30 a.m.
Date: Tuesday 24 September 2013
Location: Lorimer Street, NW1

DS Cooper unwrapped his bacon and hash brown breakfast roll, breathing in the aroma that was quickly filling the inside of the Ford Focus. "You don't mind, do you?" He paused mid-bite and glanced sideways to the passenger seat. "I've not had breakfast yet."

DC Daniels gave a quick shake of the head. "Not at all." He flipped the lid from the takeaway coffee he'd picked up at the same time as buying Cooper his breakfast roll. "They had quite a good range for a small café — I thought that one had your name written all over it."

Cooper grinned and took a large bite, tomato ketchup oozing from the sides as he did so. "How did you know?" he mumbled, his mouth full of crispy bacon and softly baked bread.

A chuckle escaped Daniels' lips as he blew across the surface of his scorching coffee. "Your dietary habits are legendary — I don't know a probationer who hasn't been told how to keep on the correct side of DS Chris Cooper."

Cooper stopped chewing, his eyes widening. "Really?"

Another chuckle from Daniels. "No, not really. Amanda gave me the heads up."

Cooper grinned and resumed cramming the greasy breakfast roll into his mouth. "Amanda's a good sort — stick with her and you'll not go far wrong." Ketchup dribbled down his chin. "If she was here now, she'd be telling me off for speaking with my mouth full."

They were parked across the road from Barry Draper's terraced house in a residents-only parking space, nestled in behind a bright yellow skip that was full to overflowing with a variety of discarded household items. No movement or sound came from number eleven.

As Lorimer Street continued to slumber in the morning sunshine, Cooper wiped the ketchup from his chin and turned to face his partner. "So, what made you join the force?"

Daniels hesitated, taking a tentative sip of the scalding coffee. It was too hot and too bitter. And it needed more sugar than the two tiny sachets that'd been thrust across the counter. "It's hard to say," he began, replacing the lid on the coffee and balancing it on the dashboard. "My parents weren't coppers — none of my family were. They're all teachers or university lecturers, every generation without fail."

"You didn't fancy the academic life, then?" Cooper cracked open the can of Coke that had accompanied his late breakfast.

Daniels shook his head. "School wasn't a great time for me." He let the sentence hang in the air before continuing. "When you're a scrawny kid with skinny sparrow legs and knock knees, and your mum won't buy you long trousers until you turn twelve . . ." Daniels paused again, a rueful smile spreading across his lips. "Coupled with the milk-bottle NHS glasses with the obligatory fabric plaster holding them together at the corner, plus the homemade haircut . . ." He glanced towards the driver's seat and gave a shrug. "Tends to make you stand out as the class target."

Cooper gave a knowing nod. "Try being the only ginger kid in a classroom full of brunettes . . . plus I was spotty."

Daniels grinned and flicked the sun visor down as the mid-morning sun began to stream in through the windscreen. "I couldn't wait to leave school. There was no way on earth I was going to voluntarily return as a teacher. I guess I wanted a job where I could feel important, feel respected. But blend in at the same time. The uniform gave me that."

"And now?" Cooper nodded at the plain-clothes detective.

"I still feel as though I've got the uniform on, underneath. It might not be visible, but . . ." Daniels tapped the side of his head. "In here I'm wearing it."

The next hour passed slowly, time seeming to slip into reverse. Cooper yawned and stretched his arms above his head. "There's not much happening with our friend Mr Draper, is there?" He again glanced over at the inconspicuous front door to number eleven. Like most of the houses along the street, the paint was faded and peeling, the window frames not faring much better. A light had come on in the upstairs window not long after they'd arrived, but hadn't been followed with any further movement.

The post-lunchtime lull brought nothing new to the street. A parking warden strolled up and down each side of the road, noting vehicle registrations and parking permits. A quick flash of Cooper's warrant card through the side window soon sent the warden on his way. Just as they watched him disappear at the top of the road, Cooper noticed a figure standing twenty-five metres or so away, staring right at them.

"Hey, take a look at this guy." Cooper nodded through the windscreen at the dishevelled looking man, dressed in more layers than the unseasonably warm September weather required. "What's his game?"

Daniels followed his colleague's gaze and a flicker of recognition mixed with annoyance crossed his face. "Bugger. That's Arnie."

"Arnie?" frowned Cooper. "Well, whoever he is, he's clocked us." He glanced up at Barry Draper's upstairs window. "Let's hope he doesn't blow our cover."

Daniels sighed and made to get out of the car. "Leave it with me," he breathed, exiting the Ford and heading across the street in Arnie's direction.

Cooper continued to watch from inside the car as Daniels greeted the man and, with a gentle hand on the arm, persuaded him to turn around and return back to the main road. After escorting the man out of sight, Daniels came back into view, jogging towards the car and slipping inside.

"Sorted," he confirmed, flashing a look up at number eleven. "Any movement from our friend?"

Cooper shook his head. "Nothing. So who was your mate? You know him?"

"Arnie," replied Daniels. "Arnold Miller. He's a well-known face with the Traffic lot. Lived on the streets for the best part of five decades. He's probably the wrong end of seventy now — although he doesn't really know how old he is. No one does. But, he's a good-natured fella — never one to get into any bother. He'd rather walk away than get caught up in anything. A useful trick for life on the streets — probably why he's lasted so long."

"And he recognised you?"

Daniels nodded. "Yeah. He wondered why he hadn't seen me out on patrol for a while. I'd see him pretty much on every shift — I'd slip him a coffee and something to eat when I could. But since I made DC, I've not been out and about as much as before. He noticed. He notices a lot, does Arnie."

"Good job you spotted him when you did." Cooper's eyes fixed once again on the windows belonging to number eleven. "We don't want our Mr Draper clocking us before we've even started." He paused. "Five decades on the streets, though. That's no mean feat."

"He's a harmless old fella, is Arnie. He'll have a few nights in a shelter every now and then, get a wash and brush up. But the rest of the time, he's happy where he is. The streets are all he knows. Carries everything he owns with him in a carrier bag." Daniels gave a small chuckle. "But he's as sharp as a pin. There's nothing he doesn't know about London. His head's like an encyclopaedia."

At a little before two o'clock, Cooper's radio crackled into life. Their replacements had arrived on scene, parking up three cars behind. Without needing to be asked twice, Cooper gunned the engine of the Ford and pulled out into the more-or-less deserted street, giving number eleven one last look.

If Barry Draper was their man, he wasn't hunting today.

CHAPTER SIXTEEN

Time: 1.15 p.m.
Date: Tuesday 24 September 2013
Location: 5 Foxglove Avenue, Hampton Wick, KT1

Jack had lost count of the number of bereaved relatives he'd visited over the years, but he never forgot a single face. Each one was ingrained in his memory, as individual as the pain that was all too evident on their faces.

The Jennings family lived in a well-maintained, three-bedroomed semi-detached house on a new-build estate. It was a quiet area, with only the sound of a random garden strimmer floating on the breeze. The house was set back from the road, as were all the other identical semi-detached properties that stretched along Foxglove Avenue. A narrow garden path led up to the small porch and UVPC front door which was flanked by two potted bay trees. Curtains were drawn on both windows that sat either side of the front door: whoever was inside clearly didn't want to embrace the outside world.

Which was understandable — the outside world had just murdered their daughter.

The front door was opened by DC James Anderson, the experienced family liaison officer allocated to the Jennings family. No introductions were needed – DC Anderson was well-known to both Jack and DS Cassidy, and the family couldn't be in safer hands.

A heavy silence enveloped the hallway as they stepped inside.

Anderson nodded towards an internal door. "They're both in there. I'm off on tea duties."

Jack gave the door a soft knock to announce their presence. As he cautiously entered the front room, he noticed that the heavy, suffocating air present in the hallway intensified as he crossed the threshold.

The tightly closed curtains plunged the room into darkness, a single standard lamp in the corner giving off the only source of light. Mr and Mrs Jennings were sitting side by side on a two-seater sofa by the shrouded window. Despite the dimness of the room, Jack could clearly see their pale complexions, all colour drained by the grief that was sucking them dry.

Stepping closer, Jack raised his warrant card. "Mr and Mrs Jennings? I'm DI MacIntosh and this is DS Cassidy. We're from the Metropolitan Police, investigating your daughter's murder." He paused, not expecting or getting any reaction. "I know this is an awful time for you both, but it would really help if we could ask you a few questions."

It was Mrs Jennings who looked up first. She had a soft face, framed by cascades of light chestnut hair that would, Jack imagined, under normal circumstances, be shiny and sleek — but presently hung in matted, dull strands. Her skin was pale and blotchy, her eyes red-rimmed and still leaking tears. She gripped a photograph in both hands.

Mr Jennings looked equally pale and drawn. A small man already, he seemed to shrink even further into himself, swallowed up by the sofa. His unshaven face looked hollow and gaunt. His short, greying hair sat up in unruly tufts, his eyes bloodshot and gritted with the evidence of a night without sleep — a look Jack knew only too well.

"Please, have a seat." Mrs Jennings' voice was quiet, barely above a whisper.

Jack and Cassidy sat in the two single armchairs facing the sofa. "Thank you," replied Jack, unbuttoning his jacket as he sat. "We'll try not to take up too much of your time."

Mrs Jennings gave a wan smile. Jack knew exactly what she was thinking. *Take up as much time as you want. Time has no meaning for us anymore.*

"I know you've already spoken to detectives, and in particular DC Anderson here — but it would really help if you could give me some further background on your daughter."

Mrs Jennings nodded. "What would you like to know?"

Jack cleared his throat, and watched as Cassidy discreetly slipped out her notebook. "Amy was working at Goodman's Lettings and Estate Agents. Did she enjoy it there?"

"I think so," replied Mrs Jennings, her voice cracking with the effort of speech. "It wasn't her first choice of career — she always wanted to be a journalist. But it was a job with some career prospects, and she desperately wanted to move out and get her own place."

Jack nodded. "Did she mention any problems at work? Or problems with clients? Anything at all out of the ordinary?"

Mrs Jennings shook her head, brushing away a tear that had strayed across her cheek. "Nothing that she mentioned. She seemed quite happy there."

"Did she socialise much? Go out with friends?" Jack had already accessed Amy's social media accounts and she didn't appear to have much of an online presence.

Mrs Jennings shook her head again. "She wasn't one for going out much. After university, most of her friends were scattered all across the country. I don't think she really saw anyone other than those she worked with."

Just then, DC Anderson appeared in the doorway, armed with a tea tray. He bent down and placed it on a small nest of tables next to the sofa.

"I took the liberty of making tea for everyone." The family liaison officer knelt down and began separating the cups and saucers, proceeding to pour both Mr and Mrs Jennings a cup first. Jack noticed he already knew Mr Jennings took two sugars, and Mrs Jennings only liked a small splash of milk. It was small details like that which made Anderson the perfect FLO. Small details mattered at a time like this. Although FLOs were more than glorified tea makers — they were a crucial link between the investigation and the family, and often uncovered details other detectives might miss.

Anderson turned towards Jack, his eyebrows raised. His tea making knowledge didn't extend to Jack's preferences.

"Just milk," replied Jack, giving an appreciative nod. "Same for DS Cassidy here."

Once everyone was nursing cups of tea that they didn't really want but would drink anyway, Jack turned back to Mr and Mrs Jennings.

"What kind of person was Amy? How was she at meeting strangers? I guess she would do quite a bit of that with the estate agency work?"

Mrs Jennings took a sip of her tea, despite it being too hot to drink. If the tea scalded her lips, she didn't seem to notice. "She was a careful person. She wouldn't have taken any unnecessary risks." She paused and glanced down at the photograph still gripped in one hand. "At least, I don't think she would."

Jack nodded. The Bishop, if the profiling was correct, was charming and confident, putting his victims at ease. Safety concerns or not, he was unlikely to have rung any alarm bells. Which made catching him all the more difficult. "When did she finish university?"

"She went to Leeds University to study English Literature, and graduated in 2008. She's been saving up for a deposit to get her own place ever since, but it's hard for them nowadays, isn't it?" Mrs Jennings broke off, realising she was speaking about her daughter in the present tense. She choked back a sob and took another sip of tea.

"How would she have travelled to work each day? The Tube?"

Mrs Jennings nodded. "She would mostly take the Tube. A bus if there were delays. She couldn't afford to run a car into the city."

Jack noticed that Mr Jennings had made no effort to join in the conversation. His teacup sat untouched in his lap, his expression vacant. The only movement Jack saw was when Mrs Jennings reached for his hand to give it a squeeze. It was so quick, and gone within an instant, but there was a momentary squeeze back.

"And on Sunday — I'm sorry to have to ask — was there anything unusual or different about that day?"

Mrs Jennings brushed another tear from her cheek. "No. It was a normal day. She got up for work as usual and left at the normal time." She paused, glancing back down at the photograph. "She was very nervous, though."

"Nervous?" Jack took a sip of his cooling tea. "In what sense nervous?"

"It was the open house event — at The Penthouse. It was the first one she would be doing on her own." Mrs Jennings hesitated and looked back up at Jack, her voice catching in her throat. "If she hadn't been on her own . . ."

"Did anyone else know she'd be at the apartment on her own?"

Mrs Jennings shook her head. "I'm sorry, I don't know. All I know is she was nervous. She sent me a message around lunchtime. She was having a coffee in a café — she texted me to say how nervous she was feeling. We try not to read the papers, but . . ." Mrs Jennings broke off, silent tears now streaming down her already glistening cheeks. "It's him, isn't it. The man in the news."

Jack slowly nodded. He saw no reason to hide the truth from the family. "We have reason to believe that, yes, the man dubbed the Bishop is responsible for your daughter's murder."

"And you'll catch him?" These were the first words Mr Jennings had spoken since Jack and DS Cassidy had entered the room and the question hung in the heavy, grief-ridden air. Jack switched his gaze to Amy's father, and the teacup in his lap. He wondered how many cups of cold tea DC Anderson had prized from the man's fingers over the last forty-eight hours.

Mr Jennings' pale grey eyes found Jack's. "You'll catch him?" he repeated.

Jack found himself nodding. "I will," he replied. "I promise."

And he meant it.

* * *

Time: 3.00 p.m.
Date: Tuesday 24 September 2013
Location: Metropolitan Police HQ, London

"The guy didn't move, boss." DS Cooper leaned against the wall by the window and stretched his neck from side to side, trying to loosen the effects of being cooped up inside the car for the last few hours. "Snapped a light on upstairs, but after that — nothing. Nada."

Jack sighed and rubbed a hand through his tousled hair. "Well, it's early days. Let's just see what the rest of the day and tonight bring." Jack knew the forty-eight hours he'd been given by the chief superintendent was tight — but it was all they had. Pushing thoughts of Barry Draper temporarily to one side, he made his way over to the cork pin board where the newly tacked photograph of Amy Jennings rested next to the other five victims.

"Not surprisingly, Mr and Mrs Jennings are beside themselves with grief. They couldn't really give much more insight into Amy's social life — she kept herself to herself, wasn't a great social butterfly. So, we need to focus on how she crossed the path or caught the eye of our killer."

"Wrong time, wrong place?" queried DS Cassidy, slipping into a chair next to DC Daniels.

"The Bishop doesn't go for random," dismissed Jack. "He does his homework. He *plans*. He knew about the open house event and Amy Jennings was happy enough to let him in. Cooper — let's get off to the estate agents and see what we can dig up there."

Cooper made his way towards the door. "What happens if nothing comes of the surveillance on Draper? What if, during the whole forty-eight hours, he doesn't make a move?"

Jack had asked himself the same question more than once. He picked up his jacket and slipped it on. "We'll deal with that as and when it happens, Cooper." It was the best he could do. Pulling the door open, he called back over his shoulder. "While we're gone, you two continue monitoring what comes in on the house-to-house. And chase up the phone records for Billie-Rose and Amy. They should be in by now. And keep going over the old case files. The answer has to be there . . . somewhere."

* * *

Time: 4.05 p.m.
Date: Tuesday 24 September 2013
Location: Goodman's Lettings and Estate Agents, Hobson's Street, Kings Cross, London

Goodman's Lettings and Estate Agents was housed in a cramped office stuck between two charity shops. The front window, which looked as though it could do with a clean, was plastered with photographs of houses and flats with their accompanying sales descriptions. Everywhere was either 'cosy', which Jack took to mean small, or 'in a sought-after area', which obviously meant it was a ridiculous price. As he peered at the window more closely, Jack noticed that some of the photographs were yellowing around the edges, giving the impression they'd been there for some time.

London was meant to be bucking the housing market slump, with prices and sales on a steady increase, but there was no evidence of this in the window of Goodman's Lettings and Estate Agents. Jack pushed open the door, an electronic beep overhead acknowledging his arrival. DS Cooper followed on his heels.

The ground floor office had six desks, three on each side, each with its own computer and monitor. The desks looked new, ergonomically designed with curved edges, and expensive-looking swivel chairs to help with posture were tucked behind each one. Only one desk seemed to be occupied.

As soon as Jack and Cooper entered, a woman in her mid-to-late thirties glanced up and rose from her chair, looking somewhat startled by the prospect of a potential customer. She stepped out from behind her uncluttered desk as Jack's gaze swept the rest of the room. The office was deathly quiet — no customers, no phones ringing, and apparently, as Jack's eyes roamed the room once again, no staff.

"Good morning. Trudy Goodman. How can I help?" Trudy took another step forwards, a well-practised smile plastered on to her face, her pale grey eyes glinting at the prospect of a potential sale. Or maybe it was a glint of desperation.

Jack gave a half-smile in return and held up his warrant card. "Detective Inspector MacIntosh from the Metropolitan Police. This here is DS Cooper." Jack nodded behind him. "We're here about Amy Jennings."

Trudy's eyes clouded over, the glint snuffed out, and her smile faltered. "Y . . . yes, of course." She brought a hand up to her mouth, and motioned for Jack and Cooper to take a seat at her desk. "Such an awful, awful thing. I can't quite believe it."

Jack slipped his warrant card back in his pocket and took the seat next to Cooper. "Although I'm sure this is a difficult time for you, it would really assist the investigation if we could have some background information on Amy."

Trudy nodded, blinking rapidly. "Of course, of course. Anything."

"How many people work here, exactly?" Jack glanced once again at the five other empty desks.

Trudy cleared her throat. "At the moment, it's just myself and Jacob. And obviously we did have Amy as well. We're a small team."

Jack nodded. "You used to have more employees?"

Trudy gave a withered smile. "Yes. After the housing crash in 2008, we had to cut back to survive. So, there's just the three . . . sorry, the two of us now." Trudy's cheeks coloured.

Cooper opened the case file he'd brought with him. "That's Jacob Bradley, yes? The young lad who discovered Amy's body at the apartment?"

Trudy nodded. She reached for a half-drunk mug of coffee and shakily took a sip. "Yes. He was so shocked by the whole ordeal, poor thing. We both are."

"Is Jacob around?" Jack flashed a look towards a door at the rear of the office which he presumed led to a staff only area. Upon entering, Jack's initial sweep of the office had noted that, although there appeared to be only one person present, there were two coats hanging on the coat stand and another mug of half-drunk coffee was sitting on an adjacent desk. "Out the back, perhaps?"

Trudy's cheeks coloured once again and she gave a slow nod. "He's out in the staff room. He's in pieces. I told him he should just go home, take the rest of the week off, but he said he wanted to be here."

Jack nodded. "It would really assist us if we could speak with both of you."

Trudy hesitated and then rose from her chair. She headed towards the rear door, returning moments later with a young man Jack presumed to be Jacob.

Jack put on one of his, hopefully, most welcoming smiles. "Thanks for seeing us, Jacob. Can I call you Jacob?"

Jacob nodded, his eyes wide and fearful. He was small and thin; his cheap, off-the-peg grey suit hanging unappealingly off his skinny frame. His face was deathly white, the only colour being the red rims around each eye.

"I know you've already given a brief statement," Jack continued, "but it would be really helpful if we could just go over a few things again. Fill in some gaps?"

Jacob nodded again, perching himself on the edge of one of the curved, ergonomic desks.

"You told officers that you attended the apartment in order to collect a box of glasses and plates that'd been used at the open house event?"

More nodding from Jacob. "I . . . I told Amy I'd call by sometime after six. She . . . she was to leave them by the door."

"How did you gain access to the building, and then the apartment?"

"I . . . I had a set of keys. One key for the communal door outside, and then one for the apartment itself."

"Anyone else have keys?" Jack turned and directed his question at Trudy, who'd sat back down behind her desk and returned to nursing her cold cup of coffee. "How many sets do you have?"

"Just two per property," replied Trudy. "Amy naturally had one set for the open house event. Then we had a further set here in the office which Jacob took with him."

"I'll need a list of everyone who was booked into the event." Jack caught Trudy's gaze. "You kept records of those attending?"

Trudy uncurled her fingers from the coffee mug and woke up her computer monitor. "I can print those off for you now."

Jack turned his attention back to Jacob. "Anything strike you as odd when you arrived at the apartment block? Did you pass anyone coming out? See anyone hanging around outside?"

Jacob hesitated and Jack could see that he was frantically searching for any seeds of memory. He eventually shook his head. "N . . . no. The building was empty when I arrived. None of the apartments are sold yet. The front door was locked. I . . . I don't remember seeing anyone outside. After I . . . after I found her, I left and ran down the road. I called the police from the corner of the street." Jacob's pale face started to flush. "I couldn't get a phone signal inside."

"And the whole building is unoccupied?" Jack looked again at Trudy, watching as she headed towards a small printer that had started to whirr on the opposite side of the office.

"That's correct," she replied, picking up a sheet of paper from the printer's out tray. "The Penthouse is the first one to be officially placed on the market. The others are just being finished off — some last-minute decorating. We'll hopefully have all of the units up for sale soon." Trudy crossed back towards her desk, handing Jack the single sheet of paper. "These are the potential buyers we had lined up for the open house."

Jack cast his eyes down, seeing seven names and addresses listed. "Just these?"

Trudy nodded and returned to her seat. "Yes. But there could've been any number of others. There was a sign outside the apartment block, and we have posters here in the office, too." She nodded at the A3 sized poster on the wall behind her. "But no one could just walk in. The doors would be locked and they'd need to ring the bell. Amy would've needed to let them in. We take the safety of our staff very seriously."

Jack looked at the poster, noticing the 'no appointment necessary' tag at the bottom. He sighed and folded the sheet of paper Trudy had given him in half, handing it to Cooper. "We'll check these names out anyway. Any CCTV in the block?" Jack remembered the lack of cameras when he'd attended the scene and already knew the answer.

Trudy shook her head. "Not yet. There is a system in place for the whole apartment block — individual cameras for each unit. The wiring's been done." She broke off and gave an apologetic half-smile. "But the cameras themselves still need to be fitted."

Jack turned his attention back to Jacob who was still perched on one of the desks, his face returning to its previous pallid tone. "Tell me what happened when you reached the apartment."

Jacob swallowed, nervously, his wide eyes blinking rapidly. "I . . . I unlocked the door, and pushed it open." He paused, lowering his eyes to his hands which were clasped in his lap. "I . . . I saw the box by the door — but it only looked half full."

"Half full?" Jack glanced across at Cooper. "How so?"

"Well." Jacob swallowed and raised his eyes to look up at Jack. "There were only a few glasses and plates inside. I was expecting more."

Cooper nodded, flicking back a few pages in his notebook. "Forensics confirm several plates and glasses were still in the sink. Others were still on the worktops."

Jack indicated that Jacob should continue.

"I thought maybe Amy was still tidying up, so I went in. And then . . ." He broke off again and brought a trembling hand to his face. "And then I saw her."

"And you didn't touch her?" enquired Jack.

A look of horror crossed Jacob's waxen face at the mere thought of touching a dead body. A sickly look entered his eyes. "No. I just turned and ran."

"I'm sure seeing Amy lying there, and the bloodied writing on the wall, would've been enough to scare anyone."

"W . . . writing?" Jacob's eyes widened in a mixture of horror and confusion. "I didn't see any writing."

Jack exchanged a look with Cooper before turning back to Jacob's panic-stricken face. "You didn't see any writing on the wall? It would've been directly ahead as you walked in — on the wall in front of you."

Jacob shook his head. "I didn't see anything . . . should I have?"

Cooper opened the case file once again and slid out a colour photograph of The Penthouse crime scene. "This photograph was taken of the open plan living room and kitchen."

Jacob's eyes lowered to the photograph DS Cooper was holding up and he physically recoiled. Jack thought that by the look of him he was going to be sick. "That wasn't there . . . that definitely wasn't there."

Jack discreetly nudged the wastepaper bin closer to Jacob's feet in case the young lad decided to vomit. "You're saying that, when you found Amy's body, the writing wasn't on the wall? Or you just didn't see it?" Jack paused. "This is quite important, Jacob."

Jacob's wan face paled even more as realisation hit. "It wasn't there," he whispered, swallowing back bile. "I would've seen it. It wasn't there."

Jack got to his feet. "OK, Jacob. That's really helpful, thank you." He nodded towards Cooper, who slipped the photograph back in the case file. "We'll leave you to it."

"He was still there, wasn't he?" Jacob's voice was barely audible. "The killer — he was still in the apartment when I found Amy."

Jack hesitated by the door before turning back round. "It would appear so, Jacob. It would appear so."

He thanked Trudy and Jacob for their time and headed outside, grateful to get into the fresh air. Cooper closed the door behind them.

"The Bishop was still inside the apartment when Jacob discovered her?" Cooper's face mirrored the same shock they had seen on Jacob Bradley's. "That's unreal."

Jack headed towards the Mondeo parked across the street. "It's the only logical explanation. When the first officers on the scene turn up, the writing's there."

"They must've just missed him . . . literally just missed him."

Jack threw the car keys at Cooper, still feeling the effects of last night's champagne. "He certainly sailed close to the wind on this one. I need that CCTV of the surrounding streets checked again."

"And I'll run these names through the system when we get back to the station." Cooper held up the paper containing the seven open house event attendees. "But if you could just turn up and knock on the door . . . ?"

"I know. We won't find our killer on that list, Cooper. He's far too clever for that. But run the names anyway. Someone may have seen something." Jack slipped into the passenger seat, his headache still throbbing. "Whoever he was, Amy Jennings felt comfortable enough to let him in."

CHAPTER SEVENTEEN

Time: 5.15 p.m.
Date: Tuesday 24 September 2013
Location: Metropolitan Police HQ, London

DS Cassidy had already placed mugs of fresh coffee on the incident room desks when Jack and Cooper entered. There was a packet of paracetamol next to one of them. "Saw you pulling up in the car park outside," she explained, catching Jack's bemused expression. "How did you get on at the estate agents?"

Jack slipped his jacket off and pulled out a chair. "The poor lad that found Amy was shocked to the core. I reckon that's the first dead body he's seen."

"And one he won't forget," added Cooper, reaching for a mug.

"Anything useful though?" Cassidy perched on the edge of one of the desks.

"Maybe. We know she let the killer in and he didn't just wander in off the street." Jack shrugged and sipped his coffee, throwing a couple of paracetamol into his mouth. "Plus, Jacob didn't see the writing on the wall. The only explanation is the killer was still in the apartment." He paused to let it sink in. "Which means he's starting to take more risks."

"Which means he could slip up?" queried Cassidy. "Make a mistake?"

Jack considered the possibility. "Maybe. Or it could just make him all the more dangerous."

"I'll check out these names." Cooper unfolded the A4 piece of paper Trudy had given them. "Even though it's unlikely our man is one of them."

Cassidy pushed herself off the desk and slipped into the chair next to Jack, reaching for a thin folder. "While you were gone, I went back into the old investigation files." She pulled out a single sheet of paper. "Despite mentioning the Bishop's possible talent for woodwork, I couldn't see that it was ever followed up as a line of enquiry. Even Dr Bauer's profile mentioned the likelihood the killer had at least a passing interest in carpentry."

Jack nodded, feeling the caffeine hit from the coffee starting to give him a boost. "We should get on to that."

"We already have." Cassidy's eyes twinkled. "I've contacted as many further education colleges as I could find in the area of the original murders — basically most of Essex. I've asked them all for details of any males enrolling in woodwork or carpentry courses from 1997 onwards."

"Good work, Amanda. Earning your sergeant's badge already."

Cassidy beamed, happily. "It might take a while for them all to get back to me. But I've lined up some help to go through any results — as and when we get them."

"And how about you, Daniels? Anything on the house-to-house? Or any further contact on that online chess site?"

Daniels shook his head. "Everything's quiet on the chess side. So I started looking back at the paperwork for the first four murders." He paused and reached for a sheet of paper that he'd been annotating. "And I noticed something unusual."

Jack's interest was piqued by the curious look on the young officer's face. "How unusual?"

"The addresses of the victims." Daniels glanced down at his notes. "Stacey Fairbrother lived in a flat on Knight's

Avenue, and Shona Michaels' home was in a block called King's Court. Frankie Robinson lived on Bermont Street, but in a flat above a tattoo parlour called Castles and Dragons. Esther Faulkner lived on a street called Queen's Parade." Daniels looked up expectantly at Jack, noticing that both Cooper's and Cassidy's eyes were trained on him too. "They're all chess piece names. I don't know how the original investigation didn't spot it."

Jack reached for Daniels' sheet of notes and scanned them quickly, a slow nod following.

Daniels continued. "And there's more. The chess piece found in their mouths — it matches their address. Maybe it's just coincidental, but . . ."

"Nothing about the Bishop strikes me as coincidental." Jack handed back the sheet of paper. "I think you may have cracked the link to chess, Daniels."

Daniels shook his head. "I don't think so. The addresses for our two recent victims don't have any links to a chess piece. Dolphin Close and Stevenson Street. That's where my theory falls down."

"Are we completely sure this isn't a copycat, guv?" Cassidy frowned over the rim of her chai tea. "It might explain how the murders in 2009 had links to chess in their locations, but the two most recent ones don't?" She shrugged and took a sip of the cooling tea. "Maybe we're not chasing the original Bishop after all?"

Jack rubbed his chin, feeling the stubble prick his fingers. Neither scenario made sense. It was a good shout from Daniels — a potential link that'd been overlooked before. But did the Bishop then abandon that link for Billie-Rose and Amy Jennings? Jack didn't think so. "I still feel it's the original killer. He knows about the chess pieces in the mouth — that was never made public before. And the crime scenes are identical. The writing on the wall is identical. It *has* to be the same killer. But I can't explain the street names."

"Maybe the street names are no longer important to him?" suggested Cassidy.

Jack continued to shake his head. "No, it's *all* important to him. *Everything*. He chooses his victims for a reason. If the street names were important before, then they'll be important now." Jack turned towards Daniels. "Stay on it, Daniels. You might have something. See what else you can dig up."

Jack drained his coffee and felt his stomach rumble. He hadn't had anything to eat since the bacon sandwich with Carmichael earlier. "Look, everyone, get off home. It's been a long day. I need you all back out in the morning keeping a close eye on where our friend Barry Draper goes. It's our last day of authorised surveillance."

"Two more calls have come in while you've been gone," added Cassidy. "Both naming him."

The sense of disquiet lodged in Jack's stomach refused to shift. Barry Draper bothered him, in the same way that Vince Butler had bothered DCI Hobbs. "Keep a close eye on Draper — anything suspicious, then we'll move in. While you're keeping tabs on Draper, I'm going to head out to see our friend Vince Butler. Something about him doesn't sit right."

* * *

Time: 6.45 p.m.
Date: Tuesday 24 September 2013
Location: Lorimer Street, NW1

DC Malcolm Sullivan and DC Paul Ashford had parked their nondescript Ford a few doors down from number eleven. In place since two o'clock that afternoon, they'd settled down with a selection of snacks to keep them occupied. Previous reports had shown that Barry Draper didn't often leave his home address, so they reasoned they could be in for a long and tedious shift. The minutes stretched into hours, with nothing moving behind the thin curtains of number eleven.

As the sun began to sink behind the rooftops of the neighbouring terraced houses, it was DC Sullivan who noticed the movement first. He nudged Ashford and both officers turned their gaze along the pavement towards the home of Barry Draper.

The front door opened, its occupant stepping out into the early evening and pulling the peeling door closed behind him. With a quick glance in both directions, he headed off towards the top of the road. Both DCs raised their eyebrows and wordlessly came to the same conclusion.

They exited the Ford and began to follow Barry Draper's shadow at a discreet distance.

* * *

Time: 6.50 p.m.
Date: Tuesday 24 September 2013
Location: Tannochside B&B, Scotland

Isabel lingered at the bar, closing her eyes and letting the warm, soothing aroma fill her nostrils. The smell was intoxicating

"You'll not be wanting to miss Margaret's lamb tonight." Isabel's eyes fluttered open to reveal Willie McArthur's beaming face smiling at her from behind the bar. "It's always a favourite with the guests."

Isabel smiled and perched herself on a barstool. "It smells divine."

Willie glanced over to the table by the fireplace where Mac was seated, one leg stretched out on a vacant chair.

"So, where did you two manage to get to today?"

Isabel stifled a yawn. "Just about everywhere! We headed out past the village, and then on towards the hills." She let her eyes flicker across to Mac. "I think I've worn him out. His legs held up pretty well, but I think he'll be sore in the morning. We'd best have a quieter day tomorrow!"

Willie reached for a pint glass and began filling it up with Mac's favourite lager. "He'll be needing one of these, then." The landlord's eyes sparkled. "And something for yourself?"

Isabel selected a bramble-infused gin from the vast selection behind the bar, and watched as Willie poured her a generous measure, topping it off with just a splash of tonic water. A slight frown flashed across her forehead as he did so. There it was again. That vague feeling of familiarity surrounding the landlord of the Tannochside B&B. She'd felt it the first day they'd arrived and the feeling had never really left. A distant memory tugged at the back of her mind, but whenever she tried to dig deeper the feeling vanished.

Willie noticed Isabel's expression as he placed her drink in front of her. "Something on your mind, hen?"

Isabel blinked, rapidly. The memory — if indeed it even *was* a memory — slipped further out of reach. "Not really," she replied. "But — have we met before, Willie?"

Willie McArthur's eyebrows shot up an inch. "Us?" He began to shake his head. "I don't think so, hen."

Isabel sighed, but the frown remained. "I just feel like I know you from somewhere." She reached for her gin and tonic, taking a long sip.

Willie McArthur's eyes continued to sparkle. "Well, I've a good eye for faces — as Margaret will no doubt tell you. I'm pretty sure I'd remember if we'd met before."

Isabel shrugged and slipped off the stool, reaching for Mac's pint of lager. As she did so, she noticed a collection of framed photographs decorating the wall behind the bar. Some had wooden frames, others plastic. Rows and rows of photographs in all manner of shapes and sizes, taking up almost every inch of wall space.

"Quite a collection," she commented. "Do you take photographs of all your customers?" She saw that each and every picture had Willie McArthur's famous beaming smile grinning out towards the camera. On closer inspection, they all looked to have been taken from in and around the bar area — some guests seated at tables, others propped up against the bar itself. In one or two, the guests had made it behind the bar, with Willie's welcoming arm around their shoulders.

Willie McArthur laughed. "No, not all of them. It's not obligatory. It started way back when we first took over the B&B. We took a picture of our first ever customer." He turned and tapped one of the black and white photographs behind him. "Something to mark the beginning of a new era, and . . . well, it kind of became a habit."

Isabel let her eyes rake over the photographs before scooping up the drinks and heading back towards the open fire. Mac was slumped in an armchair, his eyes closed and chin resting lightly on his chest. Isabel placed the glasses down on the table and stepped around Mac's outstretched leg. She'd tested his stamina today — maybe a little too much. Her own legs were tired and aching, the muscles feeling tight from their exertions. But Mac hadn't grumbled — he'd merely gritted his teeth and carried on.

He stirred as Isabel sat down, his eyes opening and spying the pint glass. "You read my mind," he murmured, shifting slightly and reaching out to grab the drink.

"Willie did — poured it without me even asking."

Mac raised the pint glass in Willie's direction, taking a long-savoured sip while the landlord returned to polishing the glasses behind the bar. As he sank another couple of mouthfuls, his mobile phone began to chirp. Glancing at the screen he saw it was a call from Jack.

"Hey, bro," Mac greeted, placing his lager back down on the table. "How's things?"

Isabel settled back in her chair and gazed out of the window at the setting sun. She gave another contented sigh, and let the bramble-infused gin seep into her veins. The delicious aroma coming from the kitchen enticed her senses once again. The last few days had been wonderful. She now understood perfectly how Jack had managed to spend so much time here. The scenery was stunning, and the air so clean and fresh. Time seemed to stand still and have no meaning — other than to mark the beginning and end of each day. If she were honest, she'd lost count of the days — it could be a weekday, it could be the weekend. It didn't matter. She had at last managed to release herself from all thoughts of the café — relaxing in the knowledge that she'd left it in more than capable hands.

She crossed her legs and winced at the continued tightening of her calf muscles. The exercise was even doing her good. She listened as Mac chatted to his brother, the sound of their conversation washing over her as the gin continued its soothing journey through her bloodstream. The bar was starting to fill up with guests, enticed down from their rooms by the smell of Margaret's cooking. Willie was in his element behind the bar, ever the congenial host, laughing and joking with his customers.

Isabel continued to watch from afar.

Willie McArthur.

She still couldn't shake the feeling that she knew him from somewhere.

* * *

Time: 6.55 p.m.
Date: Tuesday 24 September 2013
Location: Jamieson Street, London

Barry Draper entered the Bassett & Sons Hardware shop, the bell tinkling above his head as he stepped over the threshold. It was a place he'd been to many times before, so he knew exactly where he needed to go. The shop was run by a father and son, and their extended opening hours to 8 p.m. on weekdays suited Barry just fine. He preferred shopping without the crowds. Without the busybodies wondering what he was buying, and why. He headed towards the tools section located at the back of the shop.

Although a quiet area in which to live, this was still London. An array of saws, knives, chisels and other tools just inside the door would be asking for trouble. So, Mr Bassett Sr configured the shop so the tools were well away from the door and windows. A security camera also blinked high up in the far corner.

Barry was well aware of the camera, too, and turned his head to the side. He disliked cameras. They made him feel nervous. Continuing down the aisle that led to the tools, Barry came to a stop next to a gleaming array of knives. He scanned the section until he found what he was looking for.

It was a small knife, akin to a paring knife for cooking, but it would do the job. He also selected a new Stanley knife plus some fine-textured sandpaper and a roll of thin wire. Moving along to the next aisle, he picked up a roll of masking tape and a small bottle of household bleach that was on offer.

He was so engrossed in his selections, Barry didn't hear the doorbell tinkle to announce the arrival of another customer. Taking his purchases up to the counter, he again shielded his face from the security camera at his side. The young lad behind the till was new — Barry hadn't seen him before. There seemed to be no sign of the ageing Mr Bassett, nor his son.

Barry paid for his items in cash, carefully checking his change — well, you couldn't be too careful, could you? — and slipped them into a plastic carrier bag. With the smallest of nods to the gum-chewing teenager behind the till, he made his way to the exit, oblivious to the two plain-clothes detectives watching his every move.

* * *

Time: 9.00 p.m.
Date: Tuesday 24 September 2013
Location: Kettle's Yard Mews, London

Jack had brought the papers from the 2009 investigation back home, and they were again decorating his living room floor. There was still something about Vince Butler that niggled him. DC Daniels had done well to spot the link to the victims' home addresses — Jack couldn't understand how Hobbs and his team had overlooked it. But how it all tied in with Butler, Jack couldn't quite put his finger on.

Vince Butler might not be the Bishop, but there was something about him that didn't add up — one of the reasons Jack wanted to see the man in person.

The remains of an Indian takeaway littered the coffee table. Initially not intending to have a drink tonight, wanting to be up bright and early in the morning, Jack had succumbed to opening a new bottle of Glenfiddich.

He picked up the whisky bottle and poured another two inches into the bottom of his glass. It was a bit late for hair of the dog now, but it might just help to banish the persistent throbbing at the sides of his head which had been present all day long. Or it might make it worse. Right now, Jack didn't care.

He stood by the open window, feeling the fresh breeze wafting inside, and gazed out over the darkened rooftops of London stretching out before him. It was a view he never tired of. But right now, he would give anything to be looking out over the mist of Loch Tannoch.

His thoughts turned to his brother, who should right about now be sampling some of Willie McArthur's wares from behind his bar. They'd spoken earlier — Margaret was cooking lamb and Jack could almost smell it himself. Stu had sounded upbeat, if a little tired.

Stu.

Jack let his mind wander, the whisky freeing his thoughts — and it wasn't long before his thoughts turned once more to James Quinn. How would both his and Stu's lives have turned out if they'd known that their mother didn't commit suicide after all? Would it have changed anything? Would they have taken a different path? Jack took another mouthful of the amber liquid and let the fiery burn scorch his throat. Their mother would still be dead — that wouldn't have changed — and they would still have been taken into care. But would knowing she didn't choose to leave them have made any difference to their young, developing personalities? Would Stu no longer have wrestled with feelings of abandonment? Would he maybe not have ended up on the road to self-destruction and a criminal record?

Jack pushed himself away from the window and away from his thoughts.

They were questions no one would ever be able to answer. And he had enough cluttering up his mind right now without adding to it.

DCs Sullivan and Ashford had radioed in with details of Barry Draper's visit to the DIY shop. After requesting to be informed if Draper so much as put his milk bottles outside during the night, Jack added it to the list of concerns currently circulating inside his head. Despite over twenty years in the job, he was no closer to knowing what made someone a killer.

Rubbing his eyes, he took another slug of whisky and headed for the bedroom. The clearing-up could wait until the morning; he really needed to get some sleep. Something told him he'd need his wits about him when he came face to face with Vince Butler.

He checked his phone for any message from Carmichael, but knew it would be too soon. Rob was a good copper, and had some useful contacts — if anyone could trace those phone numbers, he could. But whether any of it would lead him to James Quinn was another matter entirely.

But if there was even a glimmer of hope, Jack would take it.

* * *

Time: 9.45 p.m.
Date: Tuesday 24 September 2013
Location: Tannochside B&B, Scotland

The lamb had tasted just as good as the aroma had promised. Served with a sweet redcurrant sauce and rosemary butter, both Isabel and Mac had quickly devoured it. The day's exertions in the fresh air had sharpened their appetites, and the empty dinner plates were quickly replaced with servings of homemade clootie dumpling with clotted cream.

Isabel patted her stomach and let out a contented sigh. "I don't think I need to eat for a week now."

Mac grinned. "I'll remind you of that tomorrow when you're tucking into your bacon and eggs."

Isabel returned the grin. Margaret's breakfasts were to die for. "How was Jack?" she asked, reaching for the cup of coffee Willie had brought over alongside the dessert.

Mac spooned another mound of clotted cream into his mouth. "He's good. Busy, as usual. He's on that Bishop murder investigation."

Isabel nodded. They'd both seen the newspaper headlines at breakfast. Another serial killer on the loose . . . it made her shiver despite the warmth of the open fire next to them. Her own experiences of last summer were still all too fresh in her mind.

"He said to say hi to Willie. I think those two hit it off." Mac scooped up the last of the clootie dumpling and finally pushed his bowl away. "Right, I'm done. I think you might have to carry me upstairs."

Isabel waved her hands in front of her face. "No chance, sunshine!" She glanced up at the antique-style clock on the wall and saw it was approaching ten o'clock. Most of the guests had sloped off up to their rooms, with full bellies and sleepy eyes. Only a few stalwarts remained, nursing nightcaps before making the same journey. Willie had already closed the bar and turned down the lights, and was taking a few moments to bid his guests goodnight.

Isabel struggled to her feet, her calves still protesting at the sudden movement. She helped Mac with his crutches and they both stumbled their way towards the door that led up to the bedrooms. A subdued light was seeping out of the wall lights, casting a warm glow through the dimness of the slumbering bar. As Isabel approached the door, her eyes again flickered to the array of framed photographs pinned to the wall behind.

'Old friends' Willie had called them, proudly telling her that he could remember each and every name. Isabel's tired eyes again raked over the happy, smiling faces, wondering for a moment if Jack had succumbed to having his picture taken with his host after one too many whiskies. Somehow Isabel couldn't see Jack posing for such a photograph, no matter how much he'd drunk, but she searched the faces just the same.

As she inched closer, she froze. Despite the warming gins from earlier, her blood turned to ice.

"Isabel?" Mac was holding the door open, keen to get upstairs to bed. His legs were throbbing.

But Isabel didn't respond. She couldn't. Her mouth felt dry, her throat constricted. Wide eyed, she stepped closer towards the photographs; and closer to one in particular. It was tucked away next to the fire alarm and above the fire extinguisher. It was only a small photograph, sitting in a battered wooden frame, but there was no mistaking who it was.

Those eyes.

And that smile.

She felt her legs begin to shake. With a trembling hand, she pulled out her mobile phone and snapped a shaky photograph of someone she was certain was Joseph Geraghty.

CHAPTER EIGHTEEN

Time: 5.15 a.m.
Date: Wednesday 25 September 2013
Location: Isabel's Café, Horseferry Road, London

The photo had pinged on his mobile phone at a little before midnight. He hadn't been asleep at the time — and he'd only slept fitfully thereafter.

Joseph Geraghty.

Jack rubbed a hand through his hair and across his unshaven chin. Tiredness enveloped him like an old friend. Despite his constant reassurances that the gangland leader meant her no harm, Isabel had been distraught. And seeing his face grinning out from behind Willie McArthur's bar, the landlord's arm draped around his broad shoulders, Jack felt the all too familiar trickle of fear return.

It couldn't be a coincidence.

A movement out of the corner of Jack's eye caught his attention. Dominic and Sacha were heading towards the café, ready to open up and begin their day. It was early, but Jack knew baking at Isabel's Café began way before sunrise — which was why he was here.

Just as Sacha slotted the key in the lock, Jack exited the Mondeo and jogged across the road. She glanced up, a look of surprise on her face.

"Jack? What are you doing here so early?" She pushed open the door, the bell above chiming loudly through the otherwise still and silent air. "Is everything OK?"

"Isabel called." Jack nodded a greeting at Dominic as they entered the café. "She wants me to get something from her flat."

Sacha was already heading for the kitchen. "Well, you go on up — I'll have a coffee waiting for you when you come back down."

Jack headed up the narrow stairs and pushed open the door that led into Isabel's small one-bedroomed flat. As he stepped into the living room he noticed that Livi was curled up fast asleep on the sofa. Judging by the matted clumps of cat hair that clung to the fabric, the sofa was her preferred sleeping area while Isabel was away. The cat's ears twitched, acknowledging Jack's presence.

He gave the room a quick sweep. Isabel had told him what to look for — and where to find it. He approached the bureau by the side of the bookcase, and pulled open the bottom drawer. The faint aroma of baking pastry wafted upstairs as Jack's eyes settled on to the contents — and, in particular, one large photograph album.

Pulling the album out of the drawer, he began flicking through the pages, searching for the one thing that Isabel said would explain Geraghty's link to the Tannochside B&B.

Isabel told Jack she felt sure she'd met Willie McArthur before, but also knew that was impossible. She'd never been to Scotland, let alone the Tannochside B&B. But the feeling didn't leave her. She was convinced she knew him.

It was then that Jack found what he was looking for.

Isabel hadn't imagined it. Although she hadn't quite met the man before, she was right to feel an element of familiarity at the name. Jack slid a single sheet of thick, off-white paper out of the album. It was embossed with Pearson and Chalmers Funeral Directors on the letterhead and dated 20

March 1987. Two granite headstones — one for Elizabeth Faraday and one for her husband, Christopher.

Total cost £1612.00

Paid in full — by William McArthur.

During their conversation, Isabel told Jack that, although she'd only been a child at the time, she distinctly remembered the confusion when the headstones had appeared, unbidden, in the village graveyard. Her aunt had called the funeral directors, but they could only confirm that they'd been ordered and paid for by a Mr William McArthur. After a few months, the mystery surrounding the curious benefactor died down, but Isabel never forgot the name.

Jack straightened up, once again hearing the cartilage in his knees crack. Folding the invoice in half, he slipped it into his pocket and headed for the stairs. The café was coming to life — the ovens were humming away contentedly in the kitchen, and Sacha had the radio on, tuned to Capital FM. The smell of baking pastries and freshly brewed coffee warmed his nostrils as he re-entered the café. As promised, Sacha had prepared him a coffee to take away, together with a freshly warmed croissant in a greaseproof paper bag.

"Did you find what you were looking for?" Sacha handed over the coffee and croissant.

Jack hesitated for a second, almost able to feel the weight of the funeral director's invoice in his pocket. "I think so," he replied. "I think so."

He'd found what he was looking for, but he had no real idea what it meant.

* * *

Time: 7.30 a.m.
Date: Wednesday 25 September 2013
Location: Tannochside B&B, Scotland

It had come to her almost as soon as she'd snapped a copy of the photo behind the bar.

Joseph Geraghty.

Or Uncle Clive as she'd known him.

Mac had wondered what was the matter when she eventually made her way upstairs — the colour having drained from her cheeks. She made some excuse of feeling exhausted after their exertions that day — and a good night's sleep was all she needed.

But she hadn't slept a wink. After sending the image to Jack, she'd sat in the bathroom waiting for his call, Mac dead to the world, snoring soundly.

Knowing Jack was heading to the café as soon as it opened, she'd got out of bed as soon as the sun had risen, pulled on a pair of jeans and a sweatshirt, and headed out into the crisp, morning air. Margaret was already in the kitchen, judging by the aroma of bacon and toast that greeted her — but the rest of the B&B slumbered on.

Sitting on the low wall of the bridge that crossed the small stream outside the B&B, Isabel stared once more at the image on her phone. Willie McArthur. She now knew why she felt she'd met him before. Not physically — it was his *name* that had registered with her. She just hoped that Jack could find the piece of paper that would prove she wasn't going insane.

William McArthur.

And the headstones.

Once again, she had the all too familiar feeling that Joseph Geraghty was haunting her. A shiver rippled down her spine. She scoured the skyline, looking for any evidence that she was being watched. She saw nobody. But she didn't feel very reassured. There were a thousand places someone could hide out here, if they really wanted to.

Snapping her phone shut, Isabel scrambled to her feet and ran back inside.

* * *

Time: 7.35 a.m.
Date: Wednesday 25 September 2013
Location: Metropolitan Police HQ, London

Jack shut the door to his office, grateful for the solitude. He needed peace — and he needed quiet. And above all else, he needed to think. He dropped the takeaway coffee cup from Isabel's into the bin and slipped behind his desk.

Pulling the folded invoice from his pocket, he picked up his desk phone. Although it was early, he dialled the number for the Tannochside B&B and it was answered on the second ring by a voice Jack instantly recognised.

"Willie? It's Jack. Jack MacIntosh."

A brief pause on the other end of the line was followed by a hearty chuckle. "Jack! How wonderful to hear from you! You know we have your brother and his delightful friend staying with us right now?"

Jack felt himself nodding and smiled into the receiver. You couldn't help but smile when Willie McArthur was around; the man exuded happiness. "I hope he's behaving himself."

Willie McArthur gave another throaty laugh. "Aye, he is that. What can I do for you, Jack? You wanting to come up and stay with us again for a wee while?"

A momentary vision of the peace and solitude of the Scottish hillsides and lochs filled Jack's head. He could almost smell the clean, fresh air and feel the tingle of the crisp, frosty mornings on his cheeks. "That would be grand, Willie. I will be back, I promise, but right now I've got something I need to ask you."

"Oh?" Intrigue filled Willie McArthur's tone. "Ask away, my friend."

Jack paused. He hadn't quite rehearsed what he was going to say. And now it came down to it, the words seemed to stick in his throat. "You've got a photograph, behind the bar?"

"Yes?" Intrigue was joined by puzzlement in Willie's voice. "I have quite a few of those, Jack."

"The one by the fire alarm, above the fire extinguisher?" Jack remembered where Isabel said she'd seen the photo. "In a small wooden frame?" He took out his mobile phone and brought up the picture Isabel had sent through. "You're standing with a man behind the bar."

Jack noted a few moments pause at the other end of the phone.

"Yes?" Willie's voice eventually cut through the silence. "I'm looking at it now. What about it?"

Jack noted a tinge of abruptness had entered Willie's tone. "Do you remember him? The man in the picture?" He thought it a long shot, with the amount of guests the Tannochside B&B would have had over the years, but worth asking anyway. Jack was somewhat surprised at the response.

"I do that, Jack. I remember him very well." Willie McArthur paused, and Jack thought he could hear the clink of a glass as if the amiable Scotsman were pouring himself a drink. Jack glanced at his watch. It was early, but time meant nothing in the tranquillity of the Tannochside B&B.

"Did he give you a name?" Jack's voice tightened.

"Ha!" The derision in Willie's voice was all too plain. "He gave me *a* name, Jack. But I suspect it wasn't his real one. Called himself Gerald Carstairs."

Another alias, thought Jack. "Is there anything else you remember about him? When was he there?"

"It would've been the early part of 87. We'd only just opened, so I remember it well. He was one of our first ever guests."

"You don't sound enamoured with him, Willie."

Jack detected a grunt from the other end of the line and the sound of liquid being poured into a glass. "The man stole from me, Jack. Plain and simple."

"He stole from you?"

"Indeed he did. That's why I remember him. Stole the sum of £1612 from my bank account and I've never forgotten it to this day."

Jack's eyes flickered to the invoice from Pearson and Chalmers Funeral Directors and the sum of £1612 at the bottom. "And you're sure it was him that stole it?" But Jack already knew the answer.

"No question, Jack." Contempt almost drowned out the Scotsman's words. "The man's cheque for his week-long stay bounced — the bank had never heard of a Gerald Carstairs. The cheque was a forgery with a false name to boot." Willie paused again; more sounds of clinking glasses filled the receiver. "Then my own bank in Stirling told me that the sum of £1612 had been withdrawn at their branch — the signature on the withdrawal slip was perfect."

"I'm sorry to hear that, Willie."

"When we cleaned out his room, after he'd buggered off without paying, we found a notepad full of my signatures. The bastard had been practising my handwriting the whole time he was here."

"Did you report it to the police?"

"Aye." Willie McArthur's voice sounded subdued. "They took all the details but he was long gone. Covered his tracks and disappeared."

Jack nodded. That was Joseph Geraghty all over. His loathing for the man intensified, if that were possible. "And you keep his picture behind the bar because . . . ?"

"Because if that bastard ever sets foot in here again, I'll be ready for him this time."

Jack didn't doubt it for a second.

After hanging up, having again promised to pay the Scottish hills another visit sometime soon, Jack stared back down at the funeral directors' invoice. Joseph Geraghty, for whatever reason, had paid for headstones on both Elizabeth and Christopher Faraday's graves.

Another link between Geraghty and Isabel. Another link to her parents.

Was it guilt? Jack pulled open the drawer where he knew he'd find the French police accident report on the crash that killed the Faradays. And also the detailed notes DI Geraint

Jones had sent him, outlining his suspicions that the crash had been no accident.

And that Joseph Geraghty was at the very centre of it.

'*How did he find the vehicle so easily? The car wasn't visible from the road.*'

'*Why were there no tyre marks on the road? No evidence of braking?*'

'*Why did he claim to be the closest person to the family — capable of identifying the bodies — when Elizabeth had a sister in England?*'

Jack had to agree, the more he looked at it, the more the case stunk of something unsavoury. The investigation had been wrapped up and closed down before the bodies had even gone cold in the morgue.

He made a mental note to check in with DI Jones — for Jack's own suspicions, that Geraghty was mixed up in the deaths of Isabel's parents, had just quadrupled.

CHAPTER NINETEEN

Time: 10.00 a.m.
Date: Wednesday 25 September 2013
Location: Lorimer Street, NW1

The skip was still there, so they'd parked up behind it once again. They'd changed vehicles, this time they were keeping watch in a silver Vauxhall Vectra, not wanting to arouse too much suspicion among any nosy neighbours who might be keeping tabs on the comings and goings in the street. Overnight hadn't provided anything of substance — after the excitement of the trip to the DIY store, Barry Draper had hunkered down for the night.

DS Cooper was again behind the wheel with his customary bacon roll — this time without the hash browns. Instead, there was a square fried egg in its place. His stomach grumbled in anticipation as he took his first bite, a dribble of runny egg yolk trickling down his chin.

"You're such a disgusting eater," commented Cassidy from the rear passenger seat, tutting and shaking her head. "Your mother would be horrified."

"My mother's seen far worse than this," replied Cooper, wiping his chin with the back of his hand. "Anyway, you can talk — that tea of yours smells rank."

Cassidy dropped her gaze to the takeaway cup of green tea that she'd balanced on her knee, and found herself in agreement. It'd sounded nice written on the blackboard — green tea flavoured with honey, lemon and ginger — but it smelled like something you'd be given for a sore throat.

DC Daniels remained silent in the front passenger seat while Cassidy and Cooper continued to trade good-humoured insults, ranging from their choice of food and drink to their taste in music and film.

"What do you think, Trev?" Cassidy poked her head in between the two front seats.

"Huh?" Daniels tore his gaze away from number eleven.

"Chris has never seen *The Shining*. I find that incredible."

"Not really my thing either, to be honest — horror. I'm more of a science fiction movie goer."

"I loved *Back to the Future*." Cassidy snapped the lid back on her green tea, finally admitting defeat. "That counts as sci-fi, doesn't it?"

Daniels flashed her a smile. "In a way, yes. They're good films."

"Heads up. Movement." Cooper shoved the rest of his breakfast roll into his mouth and tapped the steering wheel.

Cassidy and Daniels turned just in time to see the front door swing open and a tall, broad-shouldered man step out on to the pavement.

"That's our man," confirmed Cooper, gently switching on the Vectra's engine. "What do you reckon? Follow him in the car, or on foot?"

They watched as Barry Draper crossed in front of them and headed towards the main road, walking quickly and purposefully with a battered brown satchel slung across his back.

"Let's see where he goes." Cassidy peered through the windscreen as Barry Draper headed away from them. "If he turns left, he's heading towards the park — I'll get out and follow on foot. If he turns right,he could be going anywhere. We'll have to follow at a safe distance by car."

Cooper nodded, his hand poised over the handbrake, ready to pull away if needed. "Looks like he's heading straight over towards the crossroads. Not turning left or right."

They waited another few seconds before Cassidy flung open the rear door of the Vectra and swore. "Shit. He's heading for the bus stop." In a split second, she was striding quickly towards the crossroads, just as a red double decker approached.

Barry Draper was, by this time, hovering by the bus shelter, reaching into his pocket for change or an Oyster card. Cassidy spoke quietly into the microphone embedded into the collar of her jacket. "Suspect boarding the number 33 bus. I'm following."

Cooper and Daniels watched as DS Cassidy jumped aboard the double decker and disappeared out of sight.

* * *

Time: 10.05 a.m.
Date: Wednesday 25 September 2013
Location: M11, Essex

The drive had been verging on pleasant – if negotiating central London and then the M11 could ever be described in such words. Jack had used the time to go through the evidence, such as it was, in his head — trying to put Willie McArthur and Joseph Geraghty to one side. Today his focus had to be on the Bishop.

And Vince Butler.

The man bothered him. Although there was no way he could have been the Bishop, there was still something about him that niggled at the back of his mind.

Jack left the M11 at junction 5 and switched on the sat nav. The road took him through a section of Epping Forest, somewhere he was relatively unfamiliar with, but as traffic was light, his mind began to wander. The rest of the team would be out keeping tabs on Barry Draper, and Jack's stomach tightened at the thought. The report from the DIY store had unnerved him, and Jack wondered if he was wrong to hesitate in making an arrest. Should they be moving in on Draper now? He began to feel the same pressures that DCI Hobbs would have felt back in 2009 — but any sympathy for his former boss soon evaporated and he again turned his attention back to Vince Butler.

The psychiatric unit was approximately six miles outside Epping and, according to the sat nav, there was meant to be a turning up ahead. He swung the Mondeo on to a B road and carried on deeper into the Essex countryside. Jack saw signs for several golf courses — but no psychiatric unit.

Assuming the sat nav had got it wrong, he nudged the Mondeo up to 40 mph — and noticed the small turning ahead fractionally too late. He jumped on the brakes and pulled the Mondeo hard to the right. Thankfully nothing was behind to see him skid impressively towards the ditch. Just about managing to keep two wheels on the grass verge, he turned a full one hundred and eighty degrees to face the opposite direction.

Glad Cassidy wasn't in the car with him to criticise his driving, Jack gunned the engine and wrenched the Mondeo off the verge, heading down one of the smallest side roads he'd ever seen. It was barely wide enough for a bicycle.

Branches and twigs glanced off the Mondeo's bodywork, and the rutted mud-caked track tested its suspension to the limit. It wasn't long before the narrow track widened into a broad driveway and New Green Psychiatric Unit came into sight.

The Mondeo crunched over the gravel as Jack pulled up in a 'visitor' space close to the front entrance. Six wide, well-worn steps led to a broad front door flanked by two stone pillars. The rest of the impressive three-storey building stretched up into the pale blue sky, its windows closed to whatever lay within.

Jack jogged up the steps and pressed the buzzer next to a sign that read 'Please ring ONCE. Your presence has been noted!' He raised his eyes to spy a modern CCTV camera positioned above the door. He tried a smile and a wave.

And then pressed the buzzer again.

* * *

Time: 10.25 a.m.
Date: Wednesday 25 September 2013
Location: 33 bus route, London

DS Cassidy made her way along the centre aisle of the packed double-decker, her eyes scanning those already seated. She'd made it on to the bus by the skin of her teeth, earning a disapproving frown from the driver when all she could produce was a ten-pound note. It didn't take her long to realise that Barry Draper wasn't there and must have gone upstairs. Pushing past a disgruntled young mother carrying a wailing child on one hip, Cassidy headed towards the upper deck.

The bus had already pulled away from the bus stop, slipping back into the mid-morning traffic, lurching her from side to side as she climbed the stairs. A quick scan of the upper deck saw Barry Draper sitting on a seat by himself next to a window. Careful not to catch his eye, she walked past and seated herself at the back.

As the bus jerked forwards, Cassidy tapped out an urgent message. "*Bus route 33. Heading?*"

A few seconds later, the incoming message read, '*circular route via the university*'.

Cassidy could feel the blood pulsating in her ears as her heart pounded. She tried to control her breathing and plastered a suitably vacant look on her face to match her fellow passengers. Barry Draper had his back to her, and he appeared to be staring directly ahead towards the front window.

The bus made several stops, but Draper made no attempt to move. After a few more minutes, the bus pulled in again. Cassidy glanced out of a side window that was in dire need of a clean, and recognised the exterior of St

James's University. Wide sweeping steps led up to the main entrance which was already swarming with students. Some clutched their brand-new timetables, others chose beer and cider bottles. It was Freshers Week, and Cassidy noted the look of excitement on each of their faces at the adventures that awaited them. In the meantime, they were clearly getting into the swing of things, judging by their exuberant behaviour and the alcohol that was being consumed. And it was barely mid-morning.

The hiss of the double-decker's brakes could be heard from downstairs, and then the mechanical sliding of the doors opening. A sudden rush of noise was soon followed by the sound of heavy footfall on the stairs. Cassidy's gaze flickered towards the throng of students now piling up the stairwell and into the upper deck. Their loud, raucous voices filled the air, their bodies swinging into every available seat.

And still they came. More and more students continued to spill up from the lower deck, and with all the seats taken they gathered in the gangway, shouting at each other and jostling for position. Looks of irritation flashed across the rest of the passengers' faces, but none of the students took any notice. Bottles of beer and cider were still clutched in their hands as they scrambled past each other. Despite an alcohol ban on all public buses, the driver had clearly been powerless to prevent such an influx.

The air was thick with noise and Cassidy soon realised that her view of Barry Draper was now completely obscured. Her already thumping heartbeat quickened as she strained her neck to peer around the side of a student with a large, rugby player's physique, who was blocking her way. Her mouth started to turn dry as she struggled to see past the increasing throng of bodies.

She could hear the bus driver shouting from downstairs that no standing was allowed on the upper deck, but his cries were largely ignored — although several students did eventually relent and begin to make their way back down the narrow stairs. Cassidy caught a faint glimpse of the side of Draper's head as he turned towards the commotion. For a split second, she felt their eyes connect through the melee.

A message beeped on her phone and Cassidy lowered her gaze. It was Daniels. '*What's the hold-up? We're four cars behind you.*'

Abandoning her phone, Cassidy spoke directly into her comms device. With the commotion going on around her, she doubted anyone would be able to overhear. "Students. Blocking the gangway. Blocking my view. Trying to keep eyes on the subject."

The comms unit crackled in her ear as she shifted in her seat to try and get a good view of Draper. Several more students were pushing towards the back of the upper deck, and again her view disappeared. All she could see were bodies. The rugby-playing student in front of her suddenly stepped to the side, affording her a clear view ahead. It wasn't long before a sick feeling began to creep into the pit of Cassidy's stomach.

He wasn't there.

She shot up from her seat and pushed violently past the cluster of remaining students who were refusing to move from the gangway of the upper deck. More shouts from the driver below rushed in and out of her head, but she only had eyes for Barry Draper. Or, more accurately, the seat that he'd been sitting in only moments before.

A seat that was now empty.

"Shit," she cursed, shoving her way between two students. As she jostled one of the student's arms, a spray of lager hit her in the face.

"Hey, lady," called the student, the two simple words coming out slurred.

Cassidy flashed him an angry look and pressed her warrant card within inches of his nose. "It's the police, sunshine. Now move!" She pushed on through several more bodies, reaching the top of the steps just as the bus started to lurch forwards. She found herself thrown against the side of the railings as she frantically tried to hurry down to the lower deck. The driver had clearly given up trying to restore order; he had a timetable to keep to.

As the doors to the bus hissed shut, Cassidy reached the bottom of the steps, "Subject has left the bus," she shouted into her comms device. "I repeat, subject has left the bus!" She hurriedly searched through the dusty side windows for any sign of Draper.

But there was nothing.

Barry Draper had disappeared.

CHAPTER TWENTY

Time: 10.35 a.m.
Date: Wednesday 25 September 2013
Location: St James's University, London

Lily exited the main doors and stepped out into the pleasantly warm sunshine. Squinting, she held up a hand to shield her eyes against the glare of the mid-morning sun. Spending the last two hours in the university library, she immediately felt the intense glare as she made her way down the steps.

Clutching several books under her arm, she pulled her shoulder bag close to her body and decided to head back to her bedsit — she could spend the rest of the day getting a head start on the reading list. The library had been almost deserted when she arrived at a little after eight o'clock that morning, with only one or two other intrepid students seeking an early start to their own reading lists.

The library assistant had been helpful in locating most of the books she needed, and put her name down for those that would have to be ordered in. Lily had been pleased to find a comfortable reading area, complete with coffee machine, and settled down for a couple of hours reading.

She skirted around a cluster of students larking about on the university steps. One had a skateboard and was trying to show off their skills while sipping from a bottle of beer. Lily shuddered at the thought of alcohol so early in the day.

Putting her head down, she jogged to the bottom of the steps. The number 33 bus had just left the bus stop, and Lily quickly crossed the road in its wake, glad to leave the raucous hubbub of Freshers Week students behind her. Reaching the pavement on the other side, she headed towards her bedsit. Now a familiar route, it didn't take long to pass the small convenience store and head towards the traffic lights.

The sun was now behind her, so she no longer needed to squint, enjoying instead the warmth of the rays on her back. The noise of the university was slowly receding into the background as Lily made her way towards the less populated end of the road. As she walked, the traffic began to thin out and she was even able to hear her own footfall.

It was then that she thought she heard it again. The footsteps. And the unnerving feeling of being followed.

Just like before.

She whipped her head around and saw that the pavement behind her was empty — the only people she could see were far away in the distance. She shook her head and carried on, pulling her shoulder bag even closer towards her body and clutching her books tightly underneath her arm.

Don't be silly, Lily, she scolded herself. *It's broad daylight in the middle of London. What are you afraid of?*

She passed a recruitment agency with a betting shop next door, before finally reaching the turn for her road on the left. Glancing back over her shoulder, she quickened her stride. There still seemed to be nothing behind her, but she couldn't quite shake the feeling of being watched. It caused the back of her neck to prickle and a faint sheen of cold sweat to break out on her brow. Suddenly the warm September sunshine didn't seem to penetrate her skin.

Her road was deserted — its student population either out socialising for Freshers Week or lying in bed recovering from the night before. The feeling of being followed still clung to her so she broke into a jog, skirting around the builder's discarded breeze blocks, until she arrived outside the block of bedsits she now called home. Fumbling inside her shoulder bag for her keys, she admonished herself for not having them ready in her hand. People used keys as a weapon, didn't they? She'd seen it in a film once – holding a key hidden between your fingers, then giving your assailant a quick jab.

Lily pulled out her keys and took one last look behind her.

Nothing.

* * *

Time: 10.35 a.m.
Date: Wednesday 25 September 2013
Location: St James's University, London

Barry had watched the number 33 bus pull back out into the slow-moving traffic, and a small smile flickered across his face. He wasn't stupid. He'd seen the female police officer follow him on to the bus from the top of his road. It wasn't exactly difficult – she'd made it quite obvious.

And the succession of vehicles that'd been sitting outside his house for the last twenty-four hours — they hadn't made much effort to try and blend in, either. He knew all the cars that parked in his street, so it didn't take him long to notice the unmarked police cars turning up at regular intervals — for he was certain that was who they were. Police. They stood out like a sore thumb.

Barry's experience of the police wasn't great, so it had made him smile how easy it had been to outfox them. He was sure he'd managed to leave the female officer on the bus, just slipping out through the doors as they began to close. The horde of loud, yet good-natured, Freshers Week students had done him a favour — creating a suitable diversion so he could give his follower the slip.

Following a group of students along the pavement, he glanced down at his watch.

He still had time, if he hurried.

He headed past the small convenience store, his footsteps fast but soundless. The familiar trickle of excitement flickered through his senses — she wasn't far away.

* * *

Time: 10.55 a.m.
Date: Wednesday 25 September 2013
Location: New Green Psychiatric Unit, Epping, Essex

"Mr Butler is undergoing a word association test with his psychologist," explained a petite woman bearing the name badge Ava. She looked young — too young to be working in a place like this, thought Jack. "He's in the room opposite. He shouldn't be too long." Ava gave Jack a hesitant smile. "Erm . . . would you like a coffee while you wait?"

Jack shook his head and returned the smile. He detected that maybe this was Ava's first day on the job, whatever that job turned out to be – her name badge gave no clue. And she very possibly had no idea where the coffee machine was. If, indeed, they even had one.

"I'm fine, thank you," he replied, noting the brief flash of relief that crossed Ava's face. He watched as she turned and hurried back down the corridor. She'd shown him into a small, windowless room and left the door open — maybe that was a rule in a place such as this, mused Jack. He hadn't been in very many psychiatric hospitals to know the protocols. Maximum security prisons, yes — where doors were always very firmly closed — but places like New Green he'd rarely set one foot inside.

There was no clock on the wall; indeed, nothing adorned the regulation pale grey walls that closed in on him from all four sides. The only thing that stood out was a large, square red button by the door with 'PANIC ALARM' emblazoned across the centre. Glancing around the bare room, he also noted that nothing was bolted down like it was in Belmarsh. Jack sat down on one of the uncomfortable looking wooden chairs and inched it a little closer to the button — just in case.

The journey hadn't taken as long as he'd expected, the roads uncharacteristically clear. His appointment with Dr Erskine had been scheduled for eleven fifteen, albeit rather reluctantly, so he was a little early. Jack suspected the doctor wasn't relishing his visit — her tone had made that abundantly clear.

Word association.

Jack gazed across the corridor, to where Ava had informed him Vince Butler was undergoing his psychological assessment, and felt a flicker of curiosity. Rising from the chair, he stepped out into the corridor, noticing two doors opposite. 'CONSULTATION ROOM' was printed across the first, with an ENGAGED sign in the centre. The one next to it was blank.

Jack took a glance over his shoulder to check the coast was clear. With nobody in sight, he grabbed hold of the handle to the unnamed door and found it unlocked. It opened into a small, cupboard-sized space with a bench-like table along one wall, and what looked like recording equipment and a TV monitor sitting in the corner.

Two chairs were tucked under the table and faced the largest two-way mirror Jack had ever seen. It looked directly into the consultation room next door, and Jack immediately saw Vince Butler sitting, straight-backed at a wooden table, opposite a bored-looking man dressed in a white coat.

Jack shut the door behind him, pulled out a chair and sat down.

* * *

Time: 11.05 a.m.
Date: Wednesday 25 September 2013
Location: Metropolitan Police HQ, London

Cooper handed round fresh mugs of coffee, but Cassidy waved hers away.

"It wasn't your fault, Amanda." Cooper eased into the chair opposite, eyeing his friend and colleague across the desk. "Really it wasn't."

Her face said otherwise. "He knew I was there." She leaned forwards and buried her face in her hands. "He knew I was there."

"He'd probably already clocked us outside his house, to be fair." Cooper nudged the mug of coffee closer to her elbow. "So — still not your fault."

Cassidy shook her head, keeping her face hidden.

"If he was that intent on giving you the slip, there was nothing you could've done about it." Reaching into his pocket, DC Daniels brought out a bar of milk chocolate and pulled out the chair next to her. He slid the chocolate bar next to the coffee mug and sat down.

Cassidy lifted her head. She spied the chocolate bar and gave a half smile.

Daniels nudged the bar closer, and then reached for the pile of files relating to Vince Butler. "I, for one, am not going to lose any sleep over it. It just means we need to refocus."

"Don't forget," added Cooper. "We were behind the bus and still didn't see him jump off. No one's to blame."

"But what if he's out there now, on the prowl? What if he's already seen his next victim?" Cassidy's face remained crestfallen.

"The boss isn't even convinced it's him." Daniels flicked open the first set of papers and began to read. "Don't beat yourself up over it."

"Innocent people don't run from the police." Cassidy reached for the chocolate bar and gave Daniels a rueful smile. "But thank you for trying to make me feel better." She bit into the bar and relished the sweet, velvety chocolate melting over her tongue.

But it didn't take away the painful churning of her stomach. Pulling out her phone, she sighed. She had to tell Jack.

"Let me do it." Cooper nodded towards her phone. "I'll fill the boss in — you go out for a breath of air."

Cassidy rose from her chair and shook her head. "I'll go outside for a breather, but I'm dealing with it myself. It's my mess." She pushed another square of chocolate into her mouth and headed for the door. "I just hope we haven't let another girl die."

* * *

Time: 11.05 a.m.
Date: Wednesday 25 September 2013
Location: New Green Psychiatric Unit, Epping, Essex

"Cat." The psychologist had a short, clipped and somewhat disinterested tone.

"Mouse."

Jack's gaze fell on Vince Butler: the man who'd been suspected, for a while at least, to be the Bishop. He was tall — Jack could tell by the way his legs almost touched the underside of the small wooden table — and dressed in a pair of beige trousers, with a pale blue shirt untucked. His face looked freshly shaven. From his side-on view, Jack noted the man's sharp features; his skin smooth and taut, with a pair of piercing green eyes. His blond hair was cropped short and he wore small, round-rimmed spectacles.

"House." The psychologist's eyes were lowered to the sheet of paper in front of him. He didn't look up when his subject responded. Jack noted the camera blinking in the corner of the room, focused on Vince's face, and the recording equipment on the table. Every word, every facial expression, every movement, was being analysed.

"Garden." Vince's reply was controlled, devoid of expression or emotion.

"Chicken."

"Dinner."

"Man."

"Boy."

"Woman."

Vince hesitated. Jack detected a slight flash of something crossing the man's face. Irritation? Anger? It was so subtle and fleeting that, as soon as Jack noticed it, it was gone. Vince briefly flicked his eyes towards the camera. "Mine," he replied, in a measured tone.

"Fork," continued the psychologist, still not making eye contact with his patient.

"Spoon."

"Knife."

"Death." Jack's curiosity intensified as he listened to Vince's controlled response, noting the hint of a smile on an otherwise impassive face.

"Home."

"Sadness."

"Prison."

Vince paused for the briefest of seconds. "Happiness."

"Detective Inspector." Jack whirled round, startled as the door to the viewing room slammed open. "I'm not entirely sure you have permission to be in here."

Jack looked up to see a stern looking woman of indeterminate age bearing down on him. Her arms were folded in front of her ample chest, her stance reminiscent of an aggrieved headmistress. She had a round face with pudgy eyes, and a chin that wobbled as she spoke. Her head was covered in short, tight curls.

"I'm not entirely sure I have, either," remarked Jack, getting to his feet and giving the irritated headmistress one of his best smiles. "But then again, no one told me not to. No harm done." He paused and held out his hand. "I'm not sure we've had the pleasure of an introduction. Detective Inspector Jack MacIntosh."

"Yes, I know who you are." A short arm encased in a woollen jumper, despite the warmth outside, was reluctantly thrust towards Jack. "Dr Erskine — manager of New Green."

Jack felt the woman's sturdy grip and maintained his smile. Dr Erskine had initially refused Jack's request to visit and had only relented when he'd threatened certain consequences for obstructing a police officer in the course of his duties. Jack had been very unspecific as to what those 'consequences' might be, but it had done the trick.

The hostility that'd been all too apparent in her telephone manner was mirrored in her eyes. "I still don't believe you have permission to be in here."

"Quite right, my apologies." Jack meant nothing of the sort as he stepped back out into the corridor. "Very interesting though — word association."

Dr Erskine escorted Jack back to his uncomfortable wooden chair in the room opposite before she stalked back off to wherever it was she'd been disturbed from. Jack sat and drummed his fingers on the side of his chair. Vince Butler had intrigued him on paper and even more so, now, in the flesh. His cool and calm exterior reminded Jack of the many cold-blooded killers he'd had the misfortune to interview over the years. He may not have turned out to be the Bishop, but he was a killer nonetheless — and just as dangerous.

Jack's thoughts were interrupted by the opening of the consultation room door. The beleaguered psychologist emerged first, closely followed by the tall presence of Vince Butler, so tall he had to duck down to avoid banging his head on the door frame.

The psychologist led Vince across the corridor and towards Jack's box-room. "Detective," he nodded, not quite making eye contact. "This is Vince." He stepped back to allow his patient to enter the room. With three bodies inside, it now felt very claustrophobic. "Sit over there, Vince. I'll be outside."

Jack got to his feet and was about to comment, but the psychologist held up his hand. "This is non-negotiable. If you want to speak to Vince, then the door remains open and I sit outside. Dr Erskine's rules." He paused. "It's for everyone's safety, not just yours."

Jack felt his eyes being drawn back towards the PANIC ALARM button by the door, wondering how many times it had been activated. He brushed the intrusive thoughts aside. "Of course."

Vince dutifully stepped over to the far side of the tiny room, which in reality was no more than six or eight feet away from Jack, and sat on an identical wooden chair. He crossed his legs, brushed some imaginary dust from his trousers and then rested his hands in his lap.

"Vince," began Jack, sitting back down on the uncomfortable chair and pulling out his notebook and pen. "I'm Detective Inspector MacIntosh with the Metropolitan Police. I'd like to ask you a few questions, if that's OK?"

Vince Butler raised his gaze and Jack noted the same piercing green eyes he'd seen in the consultation room. "Of course, Inspector. I'm happy to help in any way that I can." His calculated, quiet tone carried softly through the cramped room.

Jack felt an involuntary shiver ripple down his spine. He shook his head and glanced down at his notepad; the pages were blank, bringing it more as a prop than anything else. He paused, tapping his biro against the edge of his chair.

"Do I make you nervous, Inspector?"

The question was unexpected, and Jack looked again into the pair of cold, penetrating eyes. He instantly wondered what Vince's victims had felt like when they, too, saw those eyes staring back at them. A chill descended into the otherwise warm and stuffy room.

Jack shook his head. "Not at all, Vince. I can call you Vince, can't I?"

Vince shrugged, a smile twitching at his thin lips. "You can call me whatever you wish, Inspector. Did you enjoy the show, by the way?"

"The show?" Jack frowned.

"In there." Vince nodded towards the open door and the corridor beyond. "Word association, I believe they call it. I know you were there, Inspector. Watching. Just call it one of my special senses."

Jack cleared his throat. "If we could get back to the reason for my visit. I'd like to ask you about the Bishop."

Vince's fair-haired eyebrows rose a notch. "The Bishop? What makes you think I know anything about him?"

Jack studied Vince's face. The twenty-seven-year old's skin was taut — not a wrinkle or a blemish in sight. Even when he spoke, the skin barely creased. "I just wondered what you thought about him. The original investigation had you as their number one suspect at one time."

"Indeed they did. And very honoured I felt — to be considered so important. I mean, I could see why they thought it could've been me. We are very similar, after all." Vince paused, his glassy green eyes sparkling. "Even *I* would've thought it was me."

Jack felt the hairs on the back of his neck prickle. The man was gloating, proud to have been considered a suspect, almost disappointed that it wasn't true.

"Can you tell me anything about what type of person he is? If you think you're so similar?" Jack held Vince's gaze in his. "What kind of person should I be looking for?"

Vince paused for a moment, theatrically placing his delicately thin fingers together while he thought. "That is a very good question, Inspector. I feel we're somewhat kindred spirits in many ways — he's very intelligent, you know? *Extremely* intelligent, I would add. And careful. Fastidiously careful." Jack detected an element of excitement in Vince Butler's tone. "And a great thinker. A great planner. He really is one of a kind. Very much like myself."

And narcissistic, thought Jack, an edge of irritation creeping into his thoughts.

"You do know he's playing with you, don't you?" continued Vince. It wasn't really a question. "These chess pieces. He's playing a game. Testing you."

"But you have no idea who he could be? A friend of yours? An acquaintance maybe?"

Vince's taut face broke out into a wrinkleless smile, and a deep, throaty laugh escaped his lips. He clapped his hands together in merriment. "Really, Inspector. You think all us deviants know each other? Like we have some sort of secret club?" He continued to laugh and pretended to wipe tears from his eyes.

"It was just a question." Jack continued to watch the theatrical clapping, his intense dislike for the man in front of him increasing by the second. He'd been watching Vince's eyes from the moment they sat down. Jack didn't subscribe to the suggestion that you could tell if someone was lying by the direction of their eyes. In any event, Vince's eyes had remained dead centre throughout. His gaze never deviated once.

"What about Barry Draper? Is he someone you know?"

Vince continued to laugh, shaking his head "You do amuse me, Inspector. You really must come again. I haven't enjoyed myself like this in a very long time."

Jack snapped his notebook shut and slipped it back into his pocket. "I think we're probably done here." He made to stand up. He'd been wrong to come. Vince Butler wasn't going to help him find the Bishop. If he knew Barry Draper, he wasn't going to tell.

"In many ways, Inspector, the man you're looking for is nothing like me." Vince's words were cool and crisp, the laughter having subsided. "You take one look at me and you know I'm different. I look the part. I'm the very epitome of a *deviant*. You don't want to meet me in a dark alley. But your Bishop . . ." Vince paused and watched Jack hovering in the doorway. "He's not like me at all. Yes, he's a killer, and yes he's dangerous. But he's normal, Inspector. In ways that I am not." Vince licked his thin lips, a smile still dancing at their edges. "I ate mine, Inspector. My trophies. You know that."

Jack found himself nodding, while a series of sickening visions flickered through his mind. Both Vince's victims had their organs removed, liver and kidneys according to the reports. Butler had confessed to eating them, frying them in a pan with a little garlic butter.

Vince continued. "But your Bishop — no. He won't be eating his, Inspector, *that* I can guarantee. His trophies mean something else to him entirely." Vince got to his feet, his head almost brushing the ceiling. "Good day to you, Inspector. Happy hunting!"

Jack backed out of the cramped room, taking one last look at the convicted killer before heading back along the corridor. After that encounter, he badly needed some fresh air. Ava hurried to buzz him through the security doors, and as he neared the reception area, Dr Erskine stepped into his path.

"I trust we won't be seeing you again, Inspector?"

Jack plastered a fresh smile on his face. "Oh, I wouldn't go that far, Dr Erskine." He felt like coming back just to annoy her. "Not when you've made me feel so welcome." With that, he turned away and headed out of the main door, his phone beeping with an incoming message as he went.

CHAPTER TWENTY-ONE

Time: 3.45 p.m.
Date: Wednesday 25 September 2013
Location: Metropolitan Police HQ, London

Jack's request for tactical support had been authorised without objection, which both surprised and concerned him in equal measure. Barry Draper was the only name they had in their sights. The house-to-house and CCTV had thrown up nothing useful — nobody had seen or heard anything unusual. With a population of over eight million, Londoners seemed to neither see nor hear anything on a regular basis.

Following and losing him from the number 33 bus earlier this morning had been an error of judgement. DS Cassidy was convinced Draper knew he was being watched. And the Bishop, whoever he was, was clever: they knew that much. He'd know by now that the whole of London was looking for him — you only had to open any one of the tabloid newspapers to have an idea of the scale of the manhunt that was underway. Every police officer, uniformed or not, was scouring the streets for him.

Jack knew this could now go one of two ways. The Bishop would either go to ground, disappearing from sight — or he would kill again. It was that simple. But the window on catching him before he murdered again could be closing fast. And with his visit to Vince Butler drawing a blank, Jack found the decision to move on Draper an easy one to make.

With their bulky protective stab vests on, Cassidy, Cooper and Daniels emerged from the incident room, their pensive faces speaking for them. They knew as well as Jack did that they couldn't mess this one up.

Wordlessly, Jack motioned for them to follow him downstairs and out into the rear car park where the vehicles were amassing. "Cooper, with me." Jack indicated towards the patrol car nearest to him. "Amanda, Daniels. You're in the car behind."

Cassidy nodded and she and Daniels made their way to the second car, which was idling behind the first. Three more patrol cars and two police vans completed the ensemble. Firearms officers had been authorised as backup due to the high-profile nature of the forthcoming arrest.

Guns made Jack nervous. The Bishop had never been known to be armed, but any killer could be unpredictable. When cornered, who knew how he might react?

The afternoon surveillance team had confirmed that Barry Draper was now at his home address, having arrived back on the number 33 bus and calmly walked into number eleven as if nothing had happened. Usually, an arrest warrant such as this would be executed early in the morning, before the sun came up — but time was not on their side. If Barry Draper was the Bishop, he'd managed to give them the slip once already — and Jack couldn't afford for him to do it again.

"Ready?" Jack glanced around the rest of the car park. He received a curt nod from each of the assembled officers. "Then let's do this."

* * *

Time: 4.15 p.m.
Date: Wednesday 25 September 2013
Location: 11 Lorimer Street, NW1

She'd been exquisite. Even better than he'd remembered. He'd never seen anything quite like her before. In his mind's eye, he could recall her every sleek and slender curve as his well-trained eye observed her every movement. She moved with such grace, almost as if she were walking on air. He'd seen beauty before — he cast a glance up at the shelving above his work bench — but he'd never seen anything quite like this.

He poured exactly 350ml of water into the kettle and flicked the switch. It would take precisely fifty-five seconds to boil. He knew that, because he'd timed it.

As he waited, he lined up a clean mug and dropped a single tea bag inside along with exactly half a teaspoon of sugar.

Precise.

Just how he liked things.

Once the kettle had boiled, he poured the water into the mug and waited exactly forty-five seconds, stirring ten times in each direction. Then he added exactly 20ml of milk and stirred again, six times in each direction.

Now it was ready, he took the mug across to his work-bench and sat down. The room was dim with the curtains tightly closed as they always were. He'd taken a look out on to the street earlier and noticed that the unmarked police car from before was nowhere to be seen. Maybe they'd given up watching him, or they were getting better at it.

He switched on the anglepoise lamp, placing his mug of tea on a wooden coaster. He was very proud of his wooden coaster. He'd carved it himself, one of his very first projects. Lined up before him on the work bench were the tools he would need. The new Stanley knife blade gleamed under the light of the lamp. Next to it, his favourite craft knife and chisel, both aching to be held, let loose to create their masterpiece.

He ran his fingers over the waiting fresh block of wood. He liked wood: wood came alive in your hands. You could almost feel its heartbeat as you held it next to your skin. And wood could be moulded — moulded into anything you desired. Whatever you wanted to create, it would succumb. It became your servant, and you were its master.

He reached for the mug of tea. After exactly two minutes, it was ready for the first sip, his eyes closing as he tasted the first mouthful.

Perfect.

As it always was.

He replaced the mug on to the coaster and returned his gaze to the shelving above the workbench. A flicker of pride coursed through him as his eyes roved from left to right. They were all his. Each and every one.

And there was still room for one more. There was *always* room for one more. And this one was going to be his best.

With a ghost of a smile on his lips, he reached for the chisel and began to work.

* * *

Time: 4.20 p.m.
Date: Wednesday 25 September 2013
Location: Tannochside B&B, Scotland

Isabel stared at the open suitcase on the bed. They still had a few more days until their flight home, but the thought of staying in the same place as Joseph Geraghty once had was chilling her to the core. What if he'd stayed in this very room? She shuddered and pushed the vision from her mind.

Mac had been more than happy to take a day's rest from walking, content enough to sit downstairs in the bar and play cards with Willie. Isabel had claimed a migraine and spent the day lying down, her head thumping with visions of Geraghty.

Uncle Clive.

Sighing, she closed the empty suitcase and slipped it back under the bed. She couldn't ruin Mac's first break away from the hospital. He had colour in his cheeks that had been absent for the last six months. The fresh air and exercise was doing him the world of good. She knew she was pushing him a little too hard sometimes, and that his legs must be aching at night — but she saw such a renewed vigour and lust for life in him that she just couldn't bring herself to spoil it.

She could last another few days. She wouldn't let Joseph Geraghty ruin things.

He'd ruined enough as it was.

* * *

Time: 4.25 p.m.
Date: Wednesday 25 September 2013
Location: Lorimer Street, NW1

Two police vans had sealed off the road at either end, and any pedestrians in the vicinity were quickly ushered away to a point of safety. The procession of patrol cars, silent with no flashing lights or sirens, crept along and parked several houses away from number eleven.

Jack stepped out of the lead patrol car and adjusted his protective vest. It felt bulky and uncomfortable, already starting to chafe during the short drive over. He squinted into the low-lying sun behind him, noting that the rest of his team had all exited their vehicles and were awaiting instructions.

Nobody spoke. Nobody moved. Nobody seemed to want to dare to breathe.

Although the busy main road was only a stone's throw away, silence descended on Lorimer Street. If any residents inside the other terraced houses had noticed the late afternoon procession, they kept it well hidden. Nobody opened their front doors; nobody stood at their windows. Net curtains failed to twitch.

Without a sound, Jack waved the Territorial Support Officers to approach the front door of number eleven, watching them position themselves either side of the blue painted door. With no other way in, or out, of the property, if Barry

Draper was to make a run for it, he would have to come this way. Cassidy, Cooper and Daniels kept their distance, waiting behind a patrol car.

Jack found his lips were dry. Taking a deep breath, he stepped forwards to thump a fist on the peeling paintwork of number eleven.

* * *

Time: 4.25 p.m.
Date: Wednesday 25 September 2013
Location: 11 Lorimer Street, NW1

The mug held exactly sixteen mouthfuls. He knew that, because he counted each and every one. Savouring the last sip, he replaced the now empty mug on the wooden coaster. In his other hand he held the beginnings of the wooden creation that would be his next masterpiece.

This one was going to be his best. He could sense it.

Because she was perfect. He knew that the moment he'd seen her.

Yes, that was what this one would be: perfection.

He glanced up once more at the shelving and felt the same flood of excitement that he'd felt earlier.

One more. There was definitely room for one more.

The perfect end to his perfect collection.

Just as he was placing his chisel back alongside the other tools, he sensed movement from outside. The muffled sound of a car door closing, followed by several more. It was unusual for this time of day; he knew his neighbours' movements, and the sound was out of character.

For the next few seconds there was only silence. All he could hear was the heavy tick-tock from his wall clock, and his own ragged breathing.

The hairs on the back of his neck stiffened when the silence was broken by a thump on his front door.

* * *

Time: 4.25 p.m.
Date: Wednesday 25 September 2013
Location: 11 Lorimer Street, NW1

"Open up, it's the police." Jack stepped back and squinted up at the solitary window. The one-bedroomed terraced house was narrow, just the width of a single window, one upstairs and one down. Both had thick curtains firmly pulled across, shutting out the diminishing daylight. Jack trained his eyes on both windows, but neither showed any movement.

Stepping forwards, he thumped once more on the door. "Last chance," he bellowed. "In ten seconds your door's coming down."

Moving to the side, he nodded at the Territorial Support Group leader behind him, indicating that the door was all his. The TSG officer dutifully brandished the 'enforcer', a heavy piece of kit used to batter down offending doors such as the one now facing them.

As Jack returned to the kerb, he continued to train his eyes on the upstairs window. "Five seconds," he shouted.

Just as the TSG officer heaved the enforcer into position, ready to take a swinging shot at the already battered looking front door, a brief flicker of a curtain caught Jack's eye.

"Wait!" Jack held up a hand. The curtain across the downstairs window flickered once more. Squinting against the sun, Jack shielded his eyes with a hand across his brow. "Mr Draper. Barry Draper. It's the police. Open up right now, or your door will be forced."

The curtain gave a final flicker and the ghost-like face at the periphery disappeared almost as quickly as it'd come into view.

Several more seconds dragged by — the TSG officer gripped the enforcer, ready to move at a moment's notice, his eyes trained on the front of number eleven. As Jack took another hesitant step forwards, there was a discernible click.

The door to number eleven creaked open.

* * *

Time: 5.15 p.m.
Date: Wednesday 25 September 2013
Location: The Glade, Church Street, Albury, Surrey

Joseph Geraghty faced the bathroom mirror.

Roger Bancroft stared back out at him.

Tonight was the night — if his plan was going to work, then everything had to fall into place tonight. He'd made a lot of assumptions about James Quinn. Assumptions that could make or break his final plans for Jack MacIntosh.

But if there was one thing Joseph Geraghty was good at, it was reading people. You didn't get to where he was in life without honing that skill. He may never have met James Quinn in the flesh, but he knew his type. And he knew exactly what would reel him in.

Greed.

The one characteristic he suspected James Quinn had in spades.

Slipping the tinted contact lenses into place, Joseph Geraghty smiled at his reflection. Roger Bancroft was a handsome man.

Pulling on his linen jacket, Roger Bancroft left The Glade and headed towards the Bakers Arms.

* * *

Time: 5.35 p.m.
Date: Wednesday 25 September 2013
Location: 11 Lorimer Street, NW1

Barry Draper's house was small, and it didn't take long to give it an initial sweep. With their suspect safely under arrest and handcuffed in the back of a police van, Jack took the opportunity to have a look around the inside of number eleven.

The initial euphoria he'd felt at gaining entry to the house was slowly starting to evaporate. And it was rapidly being replaced with a more familiar feeling.

Disquiet.

Draper lived a simple life. There was one small bedroom upstairs, sparsely furnished. The main living room was downstairs, together with an even smaller kitchen. Jack stood in the centre of the downstairs room, noticing a threadbare sofa and ancient looking TV tucked away in one corner. Most of the room was taken up by a long workbench resting against one wall, housing a scattering of DIY tools and equipment. Jack's heart initially fluttered when he saw the blocks of wood and the wood carving equipment.

Barry Draper was a carpenter.

But the feeling didn't last long. Jack's attention was drawn to the shelving that sat above the work bench, and his mouth instantly turned dry.

DS Cassidy approached cautiously from the door that led to the tiny galley-style kitchen. "Can't see too much in here, guv. The cupboards are quite bare. He lives pretty frugally. Everything is spotlessly clean, though. There's bleach everywhere." She stepped across the worn carpet and came to stand by Jack's side, her gaze following his to the rows of trophies lined up on the shelving above. As she did so, her foot caught against something on the floor. Bending down, she picked up a small, hand-carved piece of wood.

Turning the object over in her hand, her forehead creased. "But this is . . ."

"A horse . . . I know." Jack inclined his head towards the row of perfectly carved wooden horses that adorned the shelving above the workbench. "Not bloody chess pieces — just bloody horses."

CHAPTER TWENTY-TWO

Time: 6.00 p.m.
Date: Wednesday 25 September 2013
Location: The Baker's Arms, Albury, Surrey

Joseph Geraghty brought the drinks over to the table by the window where James Quinn was waiting for him. Or, more accurately, David Nash, as he was now known. The man had been much as Geraghty had expected — for an ex-burglar. He was tall, but had a stocky build, and where once he might have carried muscle, the intervening years had turned much of that to flab.

He looked a million miles out of place at such a genteel country pub.

Which was exactly Geraghty's plan.

The years had turned Quinn's previously dark hair into a dull, wispy grey. It was cut short, close to the head; and by the looks of the strands of hair still clinging to the collar of his jacket, there'd been a recent trip to the barber. His face was rough and pockmarked — several scars evident along the left cheek and chin. He wore a faded grey T-shirt underneath a tatty leather jacket.

Geraghty watched as Quinn removed the jacket and hung it on the back of his chair. Several tattoos decorated his forearms, with more across his knuckles. Although they were mostly faded, Geraghty knew prison tattoos when he saw them.

The Baker's Arms was a pleasant country pub nestled in the heart of the village. With its oak beams and olde-worlde charms, Geraghty knew it would be perfect. He pushed the pint of bitter towards the hulk of a man sitting opposite and forced a smile on to his lips. "Cheers."

He raised his glass of crystal-clear vodka, noticing Quinn hesitate before taking hold of his pint and clinking glasses. "Cheers," the man mumbled, before taking a sip of his bitter. "So, we gonna get down to business, or what?"

Geraghty smiled and sipped his drink. He'd asked for it to be chilled to his chosen temperature, and he savoured the burn as it slipped down his throat. "Of course," he replied, fixing Quinn with an inquisitive stare. "But maybe we should get to know each other a little — *if* we are going to do business."

James Quinn shrugged and necked some more of his pint. His double chin wobbled as he swallowed. "How come we needed to meet here? It's a bit out the way, innit?"

"Exactly," replied Geraghty. "Which is precisely why it's perfect. Nobody knows us here." He tried to keep a straight face as the first lie of the evening escaped his lips.

"How did you find me?" Quinn's voice was low. He looked furtively over his shoulder as he spoke. "I'm not that easy to track down — been out of the game a while."

"I have my ways, Mr Quinn."

A dark look crossed James Quinn's face and he flashed another look behind him. "Don't ever use that name in public. I'm David Nash these days."

"My apologies, Mr Nash," replied Geraghty, his tone suggesting nothing of the sort. "You came highly recommended for the business I'm interested in putting your way."

James Quinn's pudgy eyes narrowed. "Just what exactly's on the table here? I've retired. I'm not sure you could make it worth my while."

"Oh, I'm sure I can do that, Mr Nash." Geraghty fixed Quinn with a penetrating look, his pale green contact lenses glinting in the muted light of the bar. "I will shortly have some items in my possession that, shall we say, need a temporary home until the heat caused by their disappearance dies down. After that, they can be returned."

"You want me to babysit stolen goods?"

Geraghty inclined his head into a nod. "In a manner of speaking, yes."

"And that's it?" A frown crossed Quinn's brow. He fiddled with his half-empty pint glass while Geraghty took another opportunity to survey the man's tattooed knuckles.

"Indeed. It's as simple as that."

"Sounds too easy. And why me?"

"As I said, you come highly recommended. I need someone I can trust. Can I trust you, Mr Nash?" Geraghty's piercing gaze locked on to James Quinn.

Quinn hesitated. He was being offered a lot of money — *a lot* of money. And to do what? Look after a few stolen items? Retired or not, it was money for old rope.

"You can trust me."

"Good. Then that's settled." Geraghty beamed across the table. "I'll get us some more drinks to celebrate. Same again?"

* * *

Time: 8.25 p.m.
Date: Wednesday 25 September 2013
Location: Metropolitan Police HQ, London

"What's happening with Barry Draper, guv?" Cassidy looked pale, not touching the mug of tea Cooper had deposited in front of her.

Jack ran a hand over his head and rubbed his eyes. His team were exhausted. The heightened levels of emotion and adrenaline from the raid on Lorimer Street were all too evident on each of their faces. And they were now back to square one — Barry Draper was not the Bishop.

"He's been given a cup of coffee and a sandwich — a uniform will eventually drive him back home."

Jack's words sounded flat. The last few hours had sapped his energy, leaving him feeling defeated once again. Although he'd always had misgivings about Barry Draper, the realisation he'd been right didn't come as any form of reassurance.

Cassidy had led the brief interview with Draper and within the first ten minutes Jack's fears had been confirmed. He wasn't their man.

"I liked him." Cassidy pulled her jacket closer around herself. Despite the warmth of the room, a sudden chill had descended. "He came across as an ordinary bloke. Keeps himself to himself. Doesn't bother anyone."

Cooper had joined her in the interview room and nodded in agreement. "I dug into those reports of antisocial behaviour. Seems like he was the victim, getting a fair amount of stick from local youths. They taunt him if they see him on the street — you know the type. Bang on his front door and scarper. Push things through his letterbox, even throw paint at his windows. All because they think he's a little bit odd. I wouldn't be surprised if some of them were behind the anonymous calls to the helpline."

Cassidy gave in and reached for the mug of tea. "Several PCSOs have seen him about the antisocial behaviour, but nothing's ever come of it. In fact, he thinks it made it even worse. So, the poor guy doesn't trust the police — which is why he was intent on giving us the slip on the bus." She took a grateful sip of the hot tea. "He's obsessed with horses. Wanted to be a jockey when he was a boy, but grew too heavy. Spends his days sitting in betting shops watching the racing, studying the horses." Cassidy gave a sigh, the warmth of the tea beginning to sink in. "He commits them to memory, then recreates them in wood. Some of his work's amazing. He's really talented."

Jack had seen as much back at Lorimer Street. Exquisitely carved horses lined up on the shelving above Draper's work bench. *At least we didn't break his door down*, he mused, standing up to slip his jacket back on. "Let's call it a night. Go home. Switch off. We'll regroup in the morning."

"I don't feel quite so bad about losing him on the bus now," remarked Cassidy, finishing her tea and rising from her seat. "Now we know he's not the Bishop."

Jack gave a rueful smile. "Forget it. Get yourselves off home." He glanced round at the rest of his team. "All of you."

Cassidy hesitated by the door. "But he's still out there, guv. The Bishop. If we don't find him soon . . ."

"Home," repeated Jack. "It's been quite a day."

CHAPTER TWENTY-THREE

Time: 8.30 p.m.
Date: Wednesday 25 September 2013
Location: The Baker's Arms, Albury, Surrey

Geraghty studied James Quinn from his side of the table. The man was repulsive. The alcohol had loosened Quinn's tongue — but every word that escaped his mouth grated on Geraghty's nerves. His views on women were archaic at best, bordering on vile. He viewed them as objects — his property to possess and do with as he pleased.

Geraghty thought about Stella MacIntosh and how their paths might have crossed. And more importantly, how the skin of the brute sitting opposite him had ended up underneath her dead fingernails. For a moment — a very fleeting moment — Geraghty felt a glimmer of sympathy for Jack MacIntosh.

Quinn's views on ethnic minorities and homosexuals were equally repugnant. The man was nothing but a stain on human society. He wouldn't be missed.

Geraghty took another sip of his 'vodka' — after the first glass, he'd changed to chilled water. He needed to keep a clear head, and James Quinn was in no fit state to notice.

By the end of the evening, he'd obtained all the information and, most importantly, evidence that he needed from James Quinn — the man was now surplus to requirements. "I'll be in touch, Mr Nash." Geraghty held out a hand and fought back the bile as the man's pudgy, sweaty hand gripped his. "Are you sure you're all right to drive?"

Quinn grinned, his eyes struggling to focus. "I'm as right as rain." He slipped his battered leather jacket back over his beer belly, and began to stagger towards the exit. Geraghty followed, smiling to himself as the inebriated Quinn stumbled into chairs and tables on his way out. Making a discreet exit he was not.

He watched from the pavement outside the pub as Quinn unlocked his rusting Ford Escort at the third attempt and heaved himself behind the wheel. With any luck he'll end up in a ditch or wrapped around a lamp post, Geraghty thought to himself as he waved off his new best friend.

Failing that, Joseph Geraghty had plans for James Quinn.

* * *

Time: 9.35 p.m.
Date: Wednesday 25 September 2013
Location: Metropolitan Police HQ, London

Jack closed the door to his office and sank into his chair. It was happening again; he could feel it. The investigation was spiralling out of his control. Barry Draper had been remarkably good-natured, with no hint of hostility at having been arrested and his house searched. With any luck, there'd be no repercussions. But Jack knew from bitter experience how some things had a habit of coming back to bite you.

All it would take would be one leak to the press and Jack would be front-page news — again. Another wrongful arrest. Another mistake. Jonathan Spearing wouldn't be able to smile wide enough. Suddenly, an unwelcome image of

DCI Hobbs in full golfing attire grinned out at him from all four corners of his mind, delighting in Jack's predicament. '*Not so cocky now*' — he could almost hear his former boss's gloating words.

Jack shut down the computer and ignored the increasing pile of paperwork. All he could think about now was the glass of Glenfiddich waiting for him at home. Glancing at his watch, he wondered what the odds were that the chief superintendent was still in the building. Dougie King wasn't someone he fancied meeting on the stairs right now. News of the arrest and subsequent release of Barry Draper would no doubt have reached the senior officer's ears. It was only a matter of time before the call came through.

Jack switched his mobile on to silent and headed for the door.

* * *

Time: 9.40 p.m.
Date: Wednesday 25 September 2013
Location: The Baker's Arms, Albury, Surrey

Joseph Geraghty waited until the battered Escort turned the corner and disappeared out of sight. A ditch would be too good for the likes of James Quinn. Turning to push the pub door back open, he stepped inside to find warmth and laughter enveloping him as he made his way over to the bar where the barman was busily drying glasses with a cloth.

"Good to see you again, Roger. Another glass of our finest chilled tap water?" A broad smile stretched across the barman's face, his ZZ Top style beard twitching.

"I think I'll partake of a glass of your best vodka instead, before I call it a night." Geraghty inclined his head towards the row of spirits behind the bar. "Your best Russian please."

The barman's bushy eyebrows arched. "Are we celebrating?" He reached for a clean glass and began to pour out a generous measure.

"In a way." Geraghty leaned up against the bar, watching the huddle of pub patrons still crowding around the table by the dartboard – the game of cards appeared to be reaching its climax.

"Your friend not staying to celebrate with you?" The barman placed the glass on a bar towel next to Geraghty's elbow. "I'm not sure I've seen him here before. And you know I never forget a face."

Geraghty grimaced and took a sip of his drink. "He's no friend of mine," he replied, catching the barman's enquiring eye. "And with any luck, neither of us will see him again."

"He did appear somewhat out of place," agreed the barman, resuming the drying of the row of glasses by his side. "With yourself being such an eminent banking executive, he looked a little — how can I put it delicately? Rough around the edges?" He paused, briefly sweeping his eyes around the pub. "And I'm not the only one who noticed."

Geraghty allowed a smile to escape his lips.

Good. James Quinn's presence had been noted.

"Hey." The barman caught the attention of one of the crowd breaking away from the card game. Several whoops and back slaps for one of the players suggested the game had just finished, the victor holding up his glass amid cheers. "Have you met our newest resident?"

A tall, broad shouldered man approached the bar and regarded Joseph Geraghty with an inquisitive look. With a weather-beaten, rugged complexion, the label 'farmer' oozed from every pore. Dressed in an open-necked chequered shirt with brown corduroy trousers and heavy work boots, he grabbed hold of Geraghty's hand and gave it a vigorous shake. "I'm not sure I've had the pleasure. Always good to have some new blood in the village. Simon Treacher — I own the land behind the church."

"Roger Bancroft," replied Geraghty, extricating his hand from the farmer's rough textured grasp. "Retired banker. I used to work in the City, but spent most of my time in the US." The lies tripped off his tongue like an old friend.

"Ah, I thought I could detect a slight American twang there," smiled Treacher, his eyes twinkling. "Welcome to the village. Whereabouts are you?"

Geraghty took a sip of his drink before replying. "I've bought The Glade. At the end of Church Street."

Treacher reached for the pint of bitter the barman placed in front of him. "The Glade? That's a beautiful house. Backs out on to my land at the rear."

"Yes, I fell in love with it as soon as I saw it."

"Such a sad story, though."

"Oh?" Geraghty raised his eyebrows. "Why's that?"

"The family that used to live there — the Faradays." The twinkle in the farmer's eyes faded. "Such bad luck."

"What happened to them?" Geraghty let his glass hover before his lips. "If you don't mind me asking?"

Treacher pulled up a bar stool and settled his large frame on to the upholstered cover. "They were killed in a car accident. So terribly sad. I remember my dad telling me about it. He knew the Faradays quite well. They had a little girl at the time, too. Such a sweet little thing, by all accounts."

"That does sound like a sad tale. I had no idea." More lies spilled from Geraghty's mouth. "Where's the daughter now?"

Treacher shrugged his broad shoulders. "I'm not sure. She was looked after for a while at The Glade, by an aunt I think my dad said. Then she just seemed to have drifted away. The house was sold a few years ago. I hope she's doing well, wherever she is."

Geraghty drained the rest of his glass and set it back down on the bar towel. "Well, it's certainly a lovely house. I'll do my best to look after it." He bade farewell to the barman and his new farming friend, before stepping back out into the cool evening air.

Roger Bancroft had set the scene perfectly.

* * *

Time: 9.55 p.m.
Date: Wednesday 25 September 2013
Location: 13 Lorimer Street, NW1

The commotion from earlier had now died down. Peering out from behind the thick curtains of his upstairs window, he'd seen the man from next door being swiftly escorted towards a waiting police van. A stream of people had then disappeared inside number eleven, one of whom he recognised. He'd seen his picture in the newspaper; a police inspector. A trickle of amusement flooded his senses, and a smile caressed his lips. If they were looking for the Bishop, they'd come to the right place — *almost.*

With everything now quiet outside, he turned his attention back to the creation he still held in his hand.

A pawn.

It was almost finished — almost perfect.

And it was definitely the right piece for her. She was so delicate, so pure. And although the pawn was thought to be the weakest piece on the chess board, she was anything but. That's what made it the perfect choice. She had a hidden strength and resistance within her, he could tell — and that was what he was looking forward to the most.

Yes — he would enjoy her immensely.

Reaching for a sheet of fine sandpaper, he began to gently rub the head of the pawn, smoothing the wood to an even, perfect finish. As he did so, his gaze lifted once more to the shelving unit above — and the six jars sitting there, waiting to be joined by one more.

Another ripple of excitement caused him to shiver once again.

Tomorrow.

CHAPTER TWENTY-FOUR

Time: 9.45 a.m.
Date: Thursday 26 September 2013
Location: 7 Cross Keys Road, Camden Town, London

"Thank you for seeing us again." DS Cassidy flashed a sympathetic smile as Martin Rivers stepped back to allow her and DC Daniels to enter the small hallway.

"It's no problem." Rivers' voice was barely above a whisper and Cassidy noticed his face looked even more pale and drawn than last time. "Come through."

He led them through into the front room, again waving his hand towards the floral two-seater sofa. Cassidy led the way, taking a seat closest to the fireplace. She noticed the curtains were still drawn, shutting out the beautifully warm September sunshine outside. The room was dim and smelled musty. And, if she wasn't very much mistaken, Martin Rivers also had on the same clothes as before. She recognised the thick brown corduroy shirt missing several buttons.

"This is my colleague, DC Daniels." Cassidy nodded towards Trevor.

Martin Rivers lowered himself back into his armchair.

"We won't take up too much of your time, Mr Rivers," began Cassidy. "We just need a little more background on Stacey's personal life."

Rivers nodded. "Of course. Anything to help. Oh, where are my manners?" He pushed himself back out of the armchair. "Would you like a cup of tea?"

Cassidy began to shake her head. "No . . ."

"Yes," interrupted Daniels, taking a seat. "That would be really great. If you don't mind? White with one for me."

Cassidy frowned. They'd literally just finished a takeaway coffee from the Starbucks down the road as they arrived at the front door. She tried to catch his eye, but Daniels' head was turned towards the mantelpiece.

"I won't be long." Once Rivers had shuffled out into the hallway, Cassidy turned to her partner, her frown deepening. "You don't really want tea, surely?"

Daniels continued to avoid Cassidy's gaze, getting to his feet. "Not really, but — you know. It's always useful to have that extra bit of time to have a look around." He glanced back towards the door and the sound of the kettle being filled in the kitchen down the hall. "Something I learned during training."

Cassidy pursed her lips and watched Daniels proceed to inspect the array of photographs decorating the mantelpiece and nearby bookcase. At the sound of the kitchen door opening, he made his way back to the sofa in time for Martin Rivers' arrival with the tea tray.

"Let me take that for you," said Cassidy, still flashing an irritated look in Daniels' direction. "It's most kind of you."

"It's no trouble, really." Rivers allowed Cassidy to pour the tea, seating himself back in his armchair. "It's nice to do something useful."

After splashing a little milk in each tea cup, Cassidy handed them around, still trying to catch Daniels' eye as she did so. "As I was saying," she continued, seating herself back down and taking a sip of the tea she didn't really want. "We just need a little background information on Stacey's life. Where she liked to go. Friends. Boyfriends. That kind of thing. Did she have many friends?"

Martin Rivers' eyes glazed over for a few seconds. "I'm not sure," he eventually replied, shaking his head. "She left home when she was eighteen. I never met any of her friends. But I suppose she must've had some."

Cassidy took another sip of tea. They'd accessed Stacey's Facebook account and discovered she had quite a limited social circle — mostly people from the Six Bells pub and a few from her school days. "How about a boyfriend? Was there anyone special in her life?" There'd been no trace of anyone on Facebook, or indeed from any of the messages on her mobile phone, to suggest this, but it was ground they needed to cover again.

Rivers gave another shake of the head. "I think she had a boyfriend during college, but after that . . . I don't know. She never said. But then again, she probably wouldn't have told me."

Cassidy made a few entries in her notebook, noticing Daniels was still staring at the mantelpiece, not touching the cup of tea he'd asked for. "That's fine. We're just revisiting everything. How was she after her stepbrother died — Justin, wasn't it? That must've been a tough time for her."

Martin Rivers' shoulders shuddered. "It hit her hard. She and Justin were quite close. They were the same age, you see. He took her under his wing and really looked out for her — especially after we lost Heather, her mother." With his breath catching in his throat, Rivers brought his shaking tea cup to his lips.

"I can imagine." Cassidy closed her notebook. "Did she have any grief counselling?"

Rivers shook his head. "No, I don't believe so. It was one of the reasons she wanted to move out. She wanted a fresh start, away from all the memories. It was too painful for her to remain here. I had to let her go." He paused. "She went back to using her mother's maiden name. I think it made her feel closer to her."

Cassidy took the last mouthfuls of her cooling tea and placed her teacup back on the tray. She didn't feel there was much more Stacey's stepfather could tell them.

"You take care now, Mr Rivers. If you have any questions at all, please get in touch. You have our details."

Cassidy stood up, watching Daniels hastily finish his tea. With a nod of the head at Rivers, Daniels followed her out to the front door and back along the garden path towards the car. When they were out of earshot, she turned round and fixed him with a confused look.

"Just what was that all about?"

Daniels hovered by the passenger door, casting a glance back up towards the house. Martin Rivers had already shut the front door, no doubt settling himself back down into his armchair, staring at nothing.

"Trevor?" Cassidy unlocked the car. "What went on in there?"

Daniels tore his gaze away from the front of number seven.

"It's just . . . I wondered where the photographs of Jamie were."

* * *

Time: 9.25 a.m.
Date: Friday 21 May 1999
Location: The Den, Colchester, Essex

"Come on, don't be a wimp." Kenny Bateman ran through the bushes at the back of old man Crocker's back garden, throwing a taunting look back over his shoulder. "Or are you going to run back home to Mummy?" Kenny's mocking tone floated on the sultry breeze as he pushed his way through the thorns and prickles.

Jamie Rivers' face flushed red, feeling tiny stabbing sparks of anger rage through his body. He broke into a run and thrashed his way through the bushes. Thorns grabbed at his skin but he blundered on.

On the other side of the bushes was the Den. They'd built it last summer, during the long six weeks' summer break from school, and it looked to still be intact, save for a few fallen branches and extra leaves, weeds and brambles.

Kenny had brought what Jamie thought looked like a hunting knife, and was hacking through the unwanted, twisting thorns, clearing them both a path to the centre of the Den. Jamie noticed that the metal tin they used to collect insects and other tiny creatures was still there, buried beneath a tangle of branches. It had rusted badly over the winter, but he could just about make out the OXO logo on the lid. He'd snuck it out of the kitchen when his stepmum wasn't looking. To this day, she never did know what'd happened to it. She used to keep her recipe cards in it.

Jamie chuckled to himself, wondering what she would say if she could see what it contained now. Slugs, snails, butterflies, the odd worm. They captured all things creepy-crawly and transferred them to the tin — dead. By now they'd all be decomposed into a mush at the bottom; the thought made him smile.

Kenny was kneeling on the floor, brushing away the biggest of the branches and twigs. He turned round to face Jamie, his piercing green eyes penetrating the gloom beneath the undergrowth. "You ready for this?"

Jamie nodded, rapidly. He eyed the plastic bag Kenny had brought with him — a grubby Co-op bag that'd seen better days. Kenny placed the bag down next to the OXO tin and Jamie watched, holding his breath, as the bag began to move and rustle of its own accord.

Whatever was inside was alive.

A ripple of excitement rushed through his veins.

"I can't believe this place is still here — look, it's even still got the planks of wood we put up at the sides." Kenny pointed at the broken wooden pallets they'd shoved at the sides of the Den last summer. They were still standing, locked in place by bindweed and other crawling vegetation. "It's like we never left!"

Kenny tucked the hunting knife back in the waistband of his jeans and nodded at Jamie to kneel down next to him. He pulled the grubby plastic bag towards him. "This is going to be so much fun!"

Jamie knelt down in the dirt, feeling sharp twigs poke through to his knees. He didn't notice the discomfort — all he could focus on was the wriggling plastic bag and what lay inside. "How many did you get?"

A broad grin lengthened over Kenny's face. "Three. They're dopey buggers — they don't move all that fast, even the bigger ones."

Jamie licked his lips and felt his hands begin to tremble with anticipation. It was all they'd talked about for weeks. And when Kenny had called round earlier that morning and told him that today was the day, he could barely contain his excitement. He hadn't been able to eat any of his Rice Krispies at breakfast and had run from the house as soon as he was dressed in his school uniform. His stepmother had called after him to have a good day at school and not get into any more trouble.

As he ran away from the house he couldn't help but laugh out loud. They weren't going to school today — they had far more important things to be doing.

Jamie's eyes fixed on the plastic bag. "Go on, then."

Kenny held the bag with both hands; whatever was inside was getting agitated. Carefully opening the bag and tilting it towards Jamie, he caught his friend's eye and smiled. "Your job is to hold them still."

The olive green skin of the frog didn't feel quite as Jamie had expected. He'd imagined it would be rough to the touch, but it felt surprisingly smooth and moist. He let his fingers glide over the frog's back.

"Pull it out, quick." Kenny tipped the bag to the side. "And make sure the bugger doesn't escape."

Jamie put both hands into the bag and grabbed one of the frogs. It wriggled and tried to jump out of his clutches, so he gripped it even tighter. Pulling the squirming animal out of the Co-op bag, he placed it on the ground and pressed down hard. He could feel it twisting beneath his grip in a vain attempt to free itself. Excitement built within him: a feeling more intense than he had ever felt before. He watched, wide-eyed, as Kenny drew out the hunting knife from the waistband of his jeans and dangled it above the frog's head and began to laugh.

"What do we have here, little Freddie the Frog?" Kenny's eyes gleamed and danced manically in the dimness of the Den. He touched the top of the frog's head with the tip of the blade.

Jamie held his breath and gripped the frog's legs even more tightly. His heart was thumping, wildly, and his mouth had started to run dry. He kept his eyes trained on the blade.

Watching.

And waiting.

* * *

Time: 10.55 a.m.
Date: Thursday 26 September 2013
Location: Metropolitan Police HQ, London

"Guv, you need to listen to this." DS Cassidy burst into the incident room where Jack and Cooper were going back over the CCTV images from both crime scenes.

Jack looked up from the computer screen. "What is it?"

She glanced over her shoulder at DC Daniels, who'd followed her in, noting how his cheeks were flushed a pale shade of pink. "Trevor here . . . well, you tell them Trev." She gave him an encouraging nod and a wide smile. "It could be just the lead we've been waiting for."

Jack's eyebrows hitched. "What kind of lead?"

DC Daniels was still out of breath from racing up the stairs two at a time. "Justin Rivers — the lad that was killed in the 7/7 bombings." He paused and glanced across at Cassidy who was still nodding, vigorously. "Well, I noticed it just now — when we called round to see the father. He's got all these photographs in his front room of Justin and Stacey. Every surface is full of them."

"Yes?" Jack nodded, remembering the array of pictures on their last visit. "What about them?"

"Well." Daniels' cheeks flushed darker. "Justin had a brother."

Jack's face dropped. "He had a what?"

"A brother," repeated Daniels, hovering by the pin board that still showed the Bishop's first four victims plus the two most recent, Billie-Rose and Amy Jennings. "Jamie Rivers. People sometimes called him Jay."

"It's true, guv," confirmed Cassidy, noting Jack's bemused look. "Trev knew them as kids."

Daniels continued. "I didn't click at first — the name Rivers. I thought I'd heard it before but, well it's a pretty ordinary name. It was only when I walked into his front room and saw the photographs of Justin that it all started falling into place."

Jack flashed a look at Cooper. "Bring up Martin Rivers' statements again — those he made in 2009." Cooper nodded and woke up the interactive whiteboard.

"I was a year younger than Justin," added Daniels. "We didn't go to the same school, but I knew him from football. He was a good player. Jamie was younger by a couple of years. I knew there was a sister, but I never met her or knew her name."

"What can you tell us about him?" asked Jack. "This Jamie."

"I didn't know him that well, but he was odd." Daniels paused. "He used to hang around with this other kid, Kenny Bateman. Nobody particularly liked them. Most kids were scared of them. Thick as thieves they were — never saw one without the other."

"How were they odd?"

"There was a rumour — I don't think it was ever more than that. Most kids around the estate thought they'd made it up just to look cool, or to frighten people." Daniels swallowed. "They told everyone that they killed animals."

"Animals?" Jack's eyes widened.

Daniels nodded. "Like, you know — torturing them."

Dr Hunter's profile pricked at Jack's memory.

Animal mutilation.

* * *

Time: 10.30 a.m.
Date: Friday 21 May 1999
Location: The Den, Colchester, Essex

"It's your turn next time." Kenny nodded down towards the carcasses of the three dead and dismembered frogs. "Bring something good."

"More frogs?" Jamie raised his eyebrows.

"No. Something better."

Jamie nodded. A sheen of sweat covered his forehead and several trickles had made their way down his back beneath his school shirt. The air in the Den was thick and humid, not even the hint of a breeze infiltrated the undergrowth. It surprised him how much of a thrill it had given him, just holding the creatures still while Kenny sliced into them with his knife. He hadn't been able to take his eyes off the blade. The surge of pleasure that engulfed him, as he watched the life seep out of the frogs and their legs quiver for the last time, was something he'd never felt before.

And he wanted to feel it again.

Jamie reached for the OXO tin but Kenny shook his head. "We need something bigger." He pulled the battered chess set out from underneath a pile of leaves and waved the metal box in front of Jamie's eyes. "This'll do!"

Kenny removed the contents of the box, placing the chess board and pieces down by his side and, wordlessly, tossed the limp carcasses of the three frogs inside. He grinned across at Jamie. "Perfect, eh?"

Jamie glanced down at his beloved chess set, resting on the dry, dusty ground. He'd had that set since before he could remember, one of his most treasured belongings.

Kenny noticed the look on his friend's face. "Hey, we'll get you another box." He scooped up the pieces and unfolded the board. "Let's have a game before we go."

* * *

Time: 11.05 a.m.
Date: Thursday 26 September 2013
Location: Metropolitan Police HQ, London

"All Martin Rivers' statements are here, boss." Cooper nodded at the whiteboard screen which had now been populated with several files.

"I'm pretty sure I know the answer, Cooper," replied Jack, "but do any of them mention he had another son — Jamie? He didn't mention his first son, Justin — so I'm guessing the answer's no."

Cooper scrolled through the statements on the screen. After a few moments, he shook his head. "No, boss. Nothing about either son Justin or Jamie."

Jack's heart rate quickened as he began rummaging in the paperwork strewn across his desk. "Daniels. Tell me where you lived when you knew Justin and Jamie Rivers."

"Colchester. They both went to the local comprehensive school. I went to an independent school just outside the town."

Colchester.

"Bear with me." After some more fervent foraging among the stacks of paper on the desk Jack finally found what he was looking for. He pulled out the six-by-six-centimetre colour photograph and strode over to the pin board, stabbing it to the cork with a drawing pin.

Jack tapped the picture. "What about him? Do you recognise him?"

Daniels stepped towards the pin board peering closely at the image, nudging his spectacles further up towards the bridge of his nose as he stared intently at the man's face. A frown crossed his forehead. "It looks . . ." He paused and stepped even closer. The man looked older, but the eyes were the same piercing green. He hadn't seen that face in over ten years, but he was sure.

"It's him," replied Daniels, turning back towards Jack. "It's Kenny. The boy Jamie used to hang around with. The one that boasted how they'd both torture and cut up animals."

Jack reached for his jacket and swiped his car keys from the table.

"You may know him as Kenny, Daniels — but to the rest of us he's Vince Butler."

CHAPTER TWENTY-FIVE

Time: 12.05 p.m.
Date: Thursday 26 September 2013
Location: 7 Cross Keys Road, Camden Town, London

"Why didn't you mention you had another son, Mr Rivers?" Jack remained standing, his eyes fixed on the photographs lining the mantelpiece and every other surface of the room. "Jamie." He turned round to face Martin Rivers who'd just lowered himself back into his armchair. DC Daniels hovered by the doorway.

A flicker of distaste crossed the man's pale face, but he remained silent.

"Because it's been brought to my attention that your son, Justin, had a brother." Jack flicked his gaze back to the photographs on the mantelpiece, noting the happy, smiling face of Justin Rivers staring out of many of them. "Which makes me wonder why you didn't think to mention him when we last spoke, or indeed to any of the previous investigating officers in 2009? And also, why you don't seem to have any pictures of him? These are all of Justin, correct?"

Martin Rivers slowly began to nod, but still remained silent. His face had lost even more colour, if that were possible, to the point of being almost transparent.

"So, I ask you again, Mr Rivers. Why not mention Jamie?"

Rivers' voice, when it came, was barely audible. "He was born wrong. There was no place for him in my family."

"I want to find your stepdaughter's killer, Mr Rivers. Withholding information, no matter how small and insignificant you think it might be, makes that all the more difficult." Jack sighed, noting how crushed the man looked. Taking a breath, he tried to soften his tone. "Where is he now? Jamie? When did you last see him?"

Rivers gave a shrug. "I have no idea. I haven't seen or heard from him in years."

"Going back to my previous question — why no photographs? What did he do that was so bad?"

Martin Rivers' jaw clenched. "Detective Inspector. My family has all but been destroyed. Both my wives. My daughter. My son. All taken from me." A sob caught in his throat. "All I'm left with is a lying, cheating, stealing waste of space. Barbara died because of him. She died giving him life. He's nothing but evil."

Jack saw the anguish etched on to Martin Rivers' pale face. "I understand your pain, Mr Rivers, but I really need to find him. What do you know of this man?" Jack held up a photograph of Vince Butler.

Rivers peered out over the top of his wire-rimmed spectacles, his eyes glassy. "I don't know him."

"This man was the prime suspect for Stacey's murder in 2009. Didn't the officers show you his picture at the time?"

Rivers shook his head. "I don't know. I don't remember. I didn't hear from them much."

"He changed his name by deed poll to Vince Butler when he was seventeen. He isn't the killer, but he knew both your sons. He went to school with them. In particular, he was good friends with Jamie." Jack thrust the photograph in front of Rivers' face once again. "Take another look. You might know him better as Kenny Bateman."

Martin Rivers took the photograph this time and cast his watery eyes down to take in Vince Butler's face. The picture shook in his grip before he began to nod.

"Kenny Bateman," he said, faintly. "I remember that name. Heather wouldn't have him in the house."

Jack took back the photograph and slipped it into his jacket pocket. He caught Daniels' eye, noting the young officer raising his eyes to the ceiling.

Jack returned the gesture with a nod. "Mr Rivers? Would you mind if I took a look upstairs? Do you still have any of Stacey's belongings?"

Martin Rivers gave another shudder. "Stacey's room is just as she left it. I didn't have the heart to clear it out — in case she came back. And now . . ." His voice broke off and his shoulders heaved.

"I understand." Jack nodded towards the door. "I'll take a look if you don't mind?"

"Upstairs, first on the left."

Jack headed for the stairs. They were narrow with a worn carpet runner in the centre. Once on the landing, Jack noticed there were five doors, all of which were closed. He stepped towards the first door on the left, as instructed, the door creaking slightly as he pushed it open. It was a good sized room for a house that looked so small from the outside. The curtains were drawn, shrouding the room in a muted light. A single bed hugged the wall beneath the window, topped with a pink and white striped duvet that looked freshly laundered.

Jack's eyes swept the rest of the room. It was as if Stacey Fairbrother had just stepped out to the shops, and would be back again soon. Her dressing gown lay draped over the end of the bed, a pair of pyjamas neatly folded on the pillow. A small dressing table at the side of the bed housed all manner of pots and potions. A hairbrush was still matted with her hair.

The mirror on the dressing table had a strip of passport-sized photographs stuck to one side. Jack instantly recognised Stacey's heart-shaped face grinning out at him. At her side, squashed into the photo booth with her, was another face that Jack recognised.

Justin Rivers.

Brother and sister in happier times.

As Stacey wasn't living at home at the time of her murder, Jack doubted the room would be of much forensic significance. His real reason for wanting to take a look upstairs lay behind one of the other doors. He padded back out on to the landing and made his way towards the rest of the closed doors. The one next to Stacey's room was a family bathroom, and next to that was what looked like Martin Rivers' bedroom.

Jack headed towards the final two doors at the back of the house. He tried the first door and it swung open to reveal another decent sized bedroom. Again, it was swathed in muted light from the curtains that were tightly closed across the window. Even before he took another step into the room, Jack was sure it belonged to Justin Rivers.

A single bed on the far wall was covered in a navy blue duvet. The single wardrobe by its side, when Jack nudged open the doors, revealed an array of shirts, jeans, jackets and T-shirts. A small bedside table was home to several cans of Lynx antiperspirant and a pot of hair gel.

Jack's eyes scoured the rest of the room. There was a bookcase at the end of the bed where Justin had kept his CD player and collection of CDs. There were precious few books — a couple on learning to play the guitar and a few on travelling. On the very top of the bookcase was a small, square box — its transparent lid revealing a watch.

"He never got to wear it."

Jack jumped at the sound of Martin Rivers' voice behind him. Turning around, he saw the gaunt looking man leaning up against the door frame, DC Daniels behind him. "The watch," he added.

Jack turned his attention back to the Navigator watch in its display box. It looked brand new.

"It was a birthday present — on the day he died." Rivers shuffled further into the bedroom. "I set it to 8.49 a.m. — the time the bomb went off. It was his birthday. I'd made him an extra round of toast so he was running late. If I hadn't done that . . ." He broke off, his face collapsing beneath the guilt that threatened to crush him.

Jack looked up into Martin Rivers' eyes, but only saw a hollow, haunted expression reflected back at him. "I'm sorry." It was all he could think to say.

"You'll be wanting to see Jamie's things I take it? There's not much." Rivers turned and headed back out on to the landing. "But you're welcome to have a look."

* * *

Time: 12.15 p.m.
Date: Thursday 26 September 2013
Location: St James's House, Gold Street, London

Lily stood and stared at the contents of the single wardrobe. What did you wear to a Nineties Night?

She rifled through the various clothes and sighed. She'd have to try a few things on, see what looked the best. She hadn't brought much with her, and what she did have was mostly her own creations. She didn't really have any 'party' clothes to speak of. She wasn't really a 'party' girl.

She closed the wardrobe door and slipped her feet into a pair of trainers. Before she decided anything she needed a drink. The thought of another night out in a room full of people she didn't know sent an unsettled feeling through her stomach. She knew Scarlett and Naomi would be there, but she still felt the nerves building. She wished she hadn't said she'd go — but she didn't want to let Scarlett down. And maybe it would be fun. Maybe.

Grabbing her purse and keys, she left her bedsit to go and see what she could find in the convenience store.

* * *

Time: 12.20 p.m.
Date: Thursday 26 September 2013
Location: 7 Cross Keys Road, Camden Town, London

The room was tiny in comparison to the others. More of an oversized cupboard, mused Jack, as he peered inside. Martin

Rivers had opened the door but immediately shuffled away, declining to enter, and headed back downstairs. He clearly wanted no part of this. He couldn't even bring himself to step across the threshold.

Daniels entered first. It was a narrow squeeze when Jack followed. Once again, curtains were drawn across the tiny window. There was no bed, no wardrobe, no bookcase. Nothing to indicate that a person had, indeed, ever lived in here. Instead, there were a series of cardboard boxes lined up against the walls, stacked up one on top of the other. From the layers of dust, it looked like none had been moved for some time.

Daniels took one of the boxes and, kneeling on the floor, pulled open the flaps. A mass of loose papers and notepads, with a few vinyl records, littered the base. Jack looked up and counted the boxes — twelve in total. It could take some time to trawl through them all – time they didn't have.

"You think there might be something in here?" Daniels got back to his feet and put the box back where he found it.

Jack shrugged. "I doubt it. But it was a good call — coming upstairs. You've got a good detective's brain in there."

Daniels beamed and his cheeks flushed pink. "Thank you, guv. I remember it from my training." He followed Jack out on to the landing. "Always ask for tea, and always go upstairs."

They jogged back downstairs, leaving Martin Rivers alone with his memories, and headed for the Mondeo parked outside.

"Did he say much after I went upstairs?" Jack opened the driver's door and slipped inside.

"Not a great deal." Daniels slid into the passenger seat. "I asked about Jamie but he really doesn't like to talk about him. He visibly flinches at the name. All he did say was that he left home at eighteen, he thinks he went to college and ended up living in a squat somewhere."

Jack drummed his fingers on the steering wheel. "We need to trace this Jamie, and fast."

Daniels opened his mouth to speak, then closed it again.

"What is it, Daniels? Spit it out."

Daniels hesitated, then looked down at his notebook. "It might be nothing, but I took Vince Butler's interview transcripts home last night." He flicked over a few of the pages. "I went through each of the four taped interviews he gave when arrested in 2009. Some of his answers concern me."

Jack's hand hovered over the ignition. Vince Butler still concerned him too. "How so?"

"When Butler's questioned about the murders, he gloats. He doesn't seem to be concerned that he's been arrested. It's like it's all a game to him — he's enjoying it." Daniels flicked over another page. "When they question him about his movements and motives, his replies are unusual. Here, look." He handed his notebook across to Jack. "I copied a few sections down. See how he responds to the questions in the third person?"

Jack's eyes skimmed Daniels' neat handwriting.

DC Stimpson: What did you do with the flesh removed from Stacey Fairbrother, Vince?

Butler: The Bishop keeps his chosen ones close to him. They won't be far away.

DC Stimpson: Where are they, Vince? You keep flesh from each of your victims, we know that. Where are they?

Butler: You'll have to find the Bishop before you find them.

"And the bit over the page?" Daniels urged Jack to keep reading.

DC Stimpson: Why did you kill Shona Michaels, Vince? We know it was you. We can put you at the scene. Did you follow her home from the Six Bells pub, like you did Stacey?

Butler: You have no evidence from any crime scene. The Bishop leaves his crime scenes spotless. He takes instruction well. He learns fast. You'll need to do better than this if you want to stop him.

"All his interviews are along the same lines," continued Daniels. "He talks freely. He never once reverts to 'no comment'. Refuses the offer of legal representation. And he's right — they didn't have any evidence linking him to the crime scenes, it was all bluff. They brought him in on the basis of Dr Bauer's psychological profile and his links with the Six Bells pub. But any question that's put to him about The Bishop — if he's asked directly about the offences — he answers in the third person, each and every time."

Daniels nudged his glasses up a notch. "If we're thinking Jamie Rivers might be the Bishop — then I think Vince Butler, his old childhood friend, might know where he is."

CHAPTER TWENTY-SIX

Time: 2.35 p.m.
Date: Thursday 26 September 2013
Location: New Green Psychiatric Unit, Epping, Essex

The journey didn't seem to take quite so long this time, and Jack was able to navigate his way without the assistance of the sat nav. He remembered the tight, hidden turn, managing to avoid the ditch, and soon New Green Psychiatric Unit came into view.

Parking the Mondeo in the same spot as last time, Jack motioned for DC Daniels to follow him up the steps to the front door. Once inside, the first face that greeted them was Dr Erskine — and the experience wasn't a pleasant one, judging by the thunderous look on her face.

"We weren't expecting you, Inspector." The statement was short and not particularly sweet.

Jack plastered his most patronising smile on to his face. "I know — I thought it would be a nice surprise."

"Well, I'm not sure we can accommodate you today." Dr Erskine's flabby jowls wobbled as she spoke. "It is most unacceptable to just turn up without an appointment."

"I don't need an appointment," replied Jack, watching as the diminutive doctor's face darkened even further. "I'm conducting a murder investigation. And I need to speak to one of your inmates."

Dr Erskine bristled. "We have patients here, Inspector. Not inmates. This is not a prison."

"Quite," smiled Jack, looking past Dr Erskine and towards the corridor beyond. "So, if you could run along and get him ready for us, that'd be great. I'm sure you know which patient we've come to see." He made a show of looking at his watch. "Right now would be great."

Without a word, Dr Erskine turned abruptly on her heels and stormed off along the corridor, thrusting her electronic pass, angrily, at each security door. As she disappeared from view, Jack wandered up to the reception desk, noticing that this time it was manned by a young man in his mid-to-late twenties, neatly shaven and dressed in an immaculately pressed suit. He looked up as Jack approached.

"Ava not here today?" Jack remembered the name of the timid young woman who'd shown him in last time.

The young man shook his head. "No, she left."

"Ah," nodded Jack, "Smart girl."

After a few minutes, Dr Erskine returned. "He'll see you now." Her curt tone made it overwhelmingly clear that Jack's sudden arrival was extremely inconvenient. "You have twenty minutes. Not a second longer, Inspector."

Jack gave another smile and motioned for Daniels to follow. "We'll see, shall we? Lead on."

This time they were taken to a different consultation room — still windowless, still claustrophobic, and still with the large red PANIC ALARM button on full display by the door.

Dr Erskine stood, stiffly, by the open door, her displeasure at Jack's unannounced visit still all too evident on her face. "Twenty minutes, Inspector," she repeated, sourly, proceeding to take a seat in the corridor outside.

Jack smiled and winked at Daniels. "I think she likes me," he whispered, moving further into the tiny room. He could have phoned in advance and let them know he was coming — that would have been easy enough to do, and probably courteous. But where was the fun in that? The sheer look of contempt on Dr Erskine's face was worth any ripples his unannounced visit might have caused.

Jack's attention turned towards the figure already seated on the far side of the box-like room. Vince Butler sat, as before, with his legs crossed and hands held loosely in his lap. He had a mildly bemused expression on an otherwise impassive face.

"Inspector," he greeted. "How nice to see you again. So soon?"

Jack remained standing, nodding at Daniels to take the only remaining seat. "Jamie Rivers." Jack fixed his gaze on Vince Butler. "Tell me how you know him."

"And what makes you think I know him, Inspector?" Butler held Jack's stare, a flicker of a smile teasing his lips. After several seconds he glanced towards Daniels. "Oh, and I see you've brought a friend this time."

Jack took a step forwards. "I asked you a question. How do you know Jamie Rivers?"

Vince Butler hesitated, averting his gaze back to his lap where he began to pick at his neatly manicured fingernails. "Jamie . . . Jamie . . . let me see . . ."

"Quit with the messing around, Butler," barked Jack, his voice failing to mask his impatience. "It's a simple enough question."

Butler smirked. "He was an extraordinary young man back in the day. We were pals. Friends. Call it what you will. Why do you ask?"

"I'm the one asking the questions." Jack motioned for Daniels to get his notebook ready in the unlikely event Butler gave them anything useful. "So, you were school friends. You lived near each other?"

"You already know we did, Inspector — that's why you're here."

"When did you start calling yourself Vince?"

Vince Butler smiled. "My, my, we have been doing our homework, haven't we?"

Jack felt the rising need to bite his tongue. "I know your real name is Kenny Bateman and you were school friends with both Jamie Rivers and his brother, Justin. Tell me about Jamie."

Butler raised his eyes to the ceiling while his face flickered with a thin smile. "He was my best friend. We did everything together."

"Such as?" Jack noted that Butler's attention was now focused on the seated DC Daniels.

"I know you, don't I?" Vince Butler's green eyes sparkled as he cocked his head in Daniels' direction. "You were that nerd who went to the posh school . . . always had your head in some sci-fi comic."

"I asked you a question . . ." continued Jack, bristling. "Tell me about Jamie."

It was then that Jack noticed the figure hovering by the open door. Dr Erskine stood in the doorway with her arms folded. "That's your time up now, Inspector."

Jack frowned, not even attempting to hide his irritation. "You said twenty minutes, I'm not finished."

Dr Erskine's frosty gaze remained impervious. "Well, I've changed my mind. Mr Butler is needed in the therapy room."

Jack considered flashing his warrant card again, but decided against it. Instead, he fixed Vince Butler with a cool stare. "We're not finished here, Butler. Don't leave the country. I'll be back."

"I can't wait, Inspector." A sickly smile stretched across Vince Butler's lips.

Dr Erskine tapped her feet, impatiently, a look of disdain plastered to her face. "If you would make your way back to the reception desk, Thomas will see you out." She buzzed Jack and DC Daniels through the security doors, before turning back to escort Vince Butler to his therapy session. If there even was such a thing – Jack suspected otherwise and that Dr Erskine was just making life difficult for them.

Well, two can play at that game, he thought, as the basis of an idea rapidly formed in his head.

"Daniels." Jack leaned towards the detective constable as they headed towards the reception desk. "Follow my lead. Find out where Butler's room is."

Thomas greeted them at the desk, stepping out from behind the counter. "I'll let you out," he smiled, heading towards the main door.

"Before we go, I couldn't just use your bathroom, could I?" Jack flickered a discreet look at Daniels. "It's a long journey back to London."

Thomas hesitated but then gave another smile. "Of course. I'll get you a visitor's security pass. You'll need it for the door. Bear with me." He stepped back behind the counter and quickly authorised a temporary pass. "I'll show you where it is — bit of a trek I'm afraid. It's upstairs."

Jack returned the smile and flashed another quick look at Daniels. *Always go upstairs*. The young detective constable's words echoed through his head. "That's most kind of you, Thomas. Lead on."

Once Jack had disappeared through the first set of security doors and was out of sight, Daniels slipped behind the desk and eyed the computer screen. The young receptionist had helpfully left the computer logged on, and it took seconds for him to locate the whereabouts of Vince Butler's room.

* * *

Time: 3.00 p.m.
Date: Thursday 26 September 2013
Location: Metropolitan Police HQ, London

With Jack and Daniels out paying another visit to Vince Butler, Cassidy took advantage of having the incident room to herself. Cooper had taken an extended break to go and see Jenny, the lab technician he'd been seeing for a while now– so now she had peace and quiet.

And, more importantly, time to think.

The tumultuous last twenty-four hours following the Barry Draper debacle had rocked her confidence. She looked up at the pin board, seeing the same six faces staring back at her — faces of six young women cut off in their prime. There were so many pieces of the jigsaw that didn't quite fit — they needed that one last piece to bring it all together.

But it was a piece they had yet to find.

She tore her gaze away from the faces and fired up the whiteboard. Calls had started coming in on the investigations she'd made at various further education colleges across Essex. As the screen flickered into life, she saw that a catalogue of calls had come in since yesterday. Each one would need following up, checking and then double checking. No stone could be left unturned in their hunt for the Bishop.

Dragging her notepad towards her, Cassidy began to take down the numbers she needed to call.

* * *

Time: 3.10 p.m.
Date: Thursday 26 September 2013
Location: New Green Psychiatric Unit, Epping, Essex

The text from DC Daniels had pinged just as he left the toilet cubicle. Thomas had trusted him to make his own way back downstairs, and Jack felt a twinge of regret for the nuclear fallout that would be heading the young receptionist's way once Dr Erskine discovered his mistake. Pushing the thought from his mind, Jack headed along the corridor in the direction of rooms 12-20.

Even the briefest of glances inside room seventeen told Jack all he needed to know about Vince Butler. The neatly made bed, the precisely folded pyjamas, and the orderly arrangement of books on the small bookshelf. Jack had seen inmates' cells at many a prison, but this was unlike anything he'd cast eyes on before. It was common for prisoners to have photographs of loved ones stuck to the wall beside their bed, or even 'page three' style magazine cut-outs for those without family. Sometimes there were both.

But Jack had never seen a room like this before, and it made his blood run cold.

Dozens of newspaper articles had been neatly cut out and pinned to all four walls. Every available space was covered, floor to ceiling, in newsprint. Page after page, article after article. As Jack stepped closer he saw that they were in a strict chronological sequence — some form of order in among the chaos.

The sickening feeling deepened within Jack's stomach as he recognised the faces of each of the Bishop's victims staring out at him. Stacey, Shona, Frankie and Esther—joined by the two newest victims, Billie-Rose and Amy. Jack noted there was even a recent extract from the *London Evening Standard*, depicting his own mugshot at the press conference.

A highlighter pen had been used to mark several newspaper headlines.

'*The Bishop strikes again!*'

'*Police no nearer to catching the Bishop.*'

'*The Bishop is back!*'

Jack's gaze then rested on a small desk tucked away next to the neatly made bed. Its surface contained nothing but a stack of writing paper and envelopes, and a pot of pens. Jack didn't have time to contemplate who Vince Butler might be corresponding with.

"Inspector." Dr Erskine's sour tone cut into the room.

Jack turned to see an expression bordering on irate flooding the doctor's face.

"Yes?" he enquired.

"I believe you must have taken a wrong turn." Dr Erskine stepped back and motioned for Jack to vacate the room. "The bathroom facilities are in completely the opposite direction."

"Are they?" replied Jack, taking one last look at the walls before stepping out into the corridor. "Geography was never my strong point."

"Clearly." Dr Erskine's tone was clipped. "Entering a patient's private room without permission is highly inappropriate. If you would care to follow me, I will escort you from the premises personally. And I'll take that pass from you." She snatched the visitor's pass from Jack's hand. "This way."

Jack followed Dr Erskine towards the stairs. "I'll tell you what *I* find inappropriate, shall I? Allowing your inmates, sorry *patients*, to adorn their walls with this kind of material." Jack waved in the direction of room seventeen. "Surely this is counterproductive to whatever therapy it is you perform here?"

Dr Erskine didn't break her stride as they began to descend the stairs towards the ground floor. "What patients are allowed to have in their rooms is of no concern to the Metropolitan Police. We have our own guidelines and we adhere to them." Upon reaching the bottom of the stairs, Dr Erskine turned to face Jack. "We follow rules here, Inspector. Unlike yourself, so it seems. I shall be making a formal complaint about your conduct here today, make no mistake about that."

Join the queue, thought Jack, as she buzzed them both through the security door. Daniels was hovering by the reception desk, but before he reached the detective constable, Jack turned and faced Dr Erskine. "What policies do you have on censoring letters received by your patients?"

Dr Erskine bristled. "What policies we may or may not have is of no concern to yourself, Inspector."

"Well, that's a matter for debate." Jack headed for the door. "Don't get comfortable — I'll be back with a warrant."

* * *

Time: 4.45 p.m.
Date: Thursday 26 September 2013
Location: St James's House, Gold Street, London

She took another large gulp of the acidic-tasting red wine and shuddered. The £2.99 price tag should have given her fair warning. But it was doing the job, notwithstanding the eye-watering aftertaste.

Lily resumed applying the final coat of mascara and then considered her reflection in the tiny, hand-held mirror. A pair of smoky eyes and sculptured eyebrows were reflected back at her. Not bad, she thought to herself. Not bad.

She took another swig of wine and grimaced. She tried to push the thought of the nineties themed night far from her mind. Discos weren't her thing. Neither was clubbing. Her home village had neither and that suited her just fine. Her idea of a perfect evening was taking Banjo for a walk down at Loch Tannoch.

Banjo. She missed that daft dog like crazy. She hoped Grandad was finding the time, and the energy, to take him out for a walk each day.

Turning her attention back to tonight, Lily knew it would be very different to a moonlit walk alongside the loch. She shuddered at the thought and took another gulp of wine, hardly noticing the bitter taste now that the alcohol had successfully dulled her senses. She didn't really want to go, but Scarlett hadn't taken no for an answer.

Lily applied a thin coating of lip gloss as a smile flickered over her features. Maybe tonight would be fun after all. It was the last Freshers event before classes started next week, and Lily felt lucky to have found two good friends in Scarlett and Naomi already.

Glancing at her watch, she got to her feet and slipped on a pair of open-toed sandals. She was wearing another of her own creations, thankful that the dreaded words 'fancy dress' hadn't been added to the Nineties Night invitation. Her denim dress, made out of old pairs of jeans, hugged her body and came to a stop just above her knees. She pulled on a homemade crochet cardigan and grabbed her shoulder bag. It was still early, but Scarlett had suggested they meet for a drink or two beforehand.

Draining the last mouthful from her wine glass, she left her bedsit and headed in the direction of the university.

* * *

Time: 4.45 p.m.
Date: Thursday 26 September 2013
Location: Metropolitan Police HQ, London

Jack waved away the offer of coffee even though he could do with the caffeine hit. He took the seat opposite the chief superintendent's desk and watched as Dougie King poured himself a cup from the machine behind him. While he was waiting, Jack's eyes skimmed across the contents of the senior officer's desk, coming to rest on what looked like a new photograph next to the computer monitor.

A beachfront house, nestled at the edge of a strip of golden sand, looking out over an azure blue sea. "Nice photo," remarked Jack, as Chief Superintendent King settled back into his chair. "Holiday home?"

"Not quite." The chief superintendent placed his coffee mug down and turned the photograph towards him. "It's my brother's place in Kingston. Well, it used to be our parents' house, but he lives there now, with his new wife. They've asked me to go out there and join them. Take my retirement and end my days in the Jamaican sunshine."

Jack raised his eyebrows. "And?"

"And I have to say I'm severely tempted, Jack." Dougie King sighed and cast a look around the contents of his desk, which was groaning under a mass of folders and files; his in-tray housing even more correspondence than Jack's. "Leave all this bureaucratic red tape nonsense behind."

"Ah, but you'd miss the job here, sir."

It was the chief superintendent's turn to raise his eyebrows. "Would I?" He shook his head and took a sip of the scalding coffee. "The job's changed, Jack. You know that as much as I do. The whole police service has changed. I didn't join up to push paper around my desk and attend meeting after meeting discussing budget cuts."

"Fair point," conceded Jack, now wishing he'd accepted the offer of coffee as the rich scent reached his nostrils.

"Filling my days relaxing on a beach with nothing to do but play cards with the locals and drink rum . . ." Dougie King let the image hang in the air between them, a wistful look crossing his tired face.

"Have you seen the latest crime statistics for Kingston? It makes this place look like a kid's playground."

"Hmmm, maybe," murmured the chief superintendent, sipping more hot coffee and turning the photograph back round. He cleared his throat and eyed Jack above the rim of his steaming mug. "Not wanting to sound like a school headmaster, Jack, but do you know why you're here? Again?"

Jack had a pretty good idea what was behind the latest summons to Dougie King's office. He detected the glimmer of a smile dancing across his senior officer's lips. "Well, I've lost count of the number of people I've rubbed up the wrong way this week . . ."

"Have a guess." Chief Superintendent King's lips twitched again. He took another sip of coffee to prevent a broad smile from breaking out.

"Well, I think number one on the list would have to be my dear friend, Dr Erskine."

A chuckle escaped the chief superintendent's mouth. "And you would be spot on, Jack. You want to know what she said?"

Jack gave a shrug. "Go on, surprise me. I'm guessing she wasn't praising my politeness and charm."

Chief Superintendent King pulled a sheet of paper towards him.

"It's written?" Jack's eyebrows hitched up another notch.

"Oh yes — emailed across only minutes, I'm guessing, after you left the premises." Chief Superintendent King paused and glanced back down at the piece of paper. "You appear to have made quite an impression. First of all, she makes it *very* clear that she didn't appreciate your latest unannounced visit. And I quote . . ."

Jack shook his head. "You know as well as I do, sir. I don't need to make an appointment for visits made during the course of an investigation."

Chief Superintendent King held up a hand. "I'm saying nothing of the sort, Jack. That isn't even the good bit — it gets better. Apparently, you then unlawfully accessed parts of the unit that were out of bounds and trespassed into a patient's private room."

"Trespassed?" Jack gave another shrug and watched the chief superintendent's mouth twitch once more. "I lost my way, that's all. The place is a maze of corridors, and I took a wrong turn. The door was open. What can I say? I apologise profusely for any inconvenience I caused."

Dougie King let the paper fall back on to the desk. "What were you really up to, Jack? Whatever it is, you've made an enemy out of this Erskine woman. I think it's safe to say she's not your number one fan."

"That's a shame," replied Jack, rubbing his chin. "Because I haven't quite finished with her yet."

Chief Superintendent King took another sip of his coffee. "Good God, Jack, what else have you got planned for the poor woman? I take it it's likely to attract another complaint?"

"Quite possibly. I wouldn't close the file on that just yet." Jack paused and waited for the chief superintendent to swallow his coffee. "I need a search warrant for one of the inmate's rooms."

"And this might be the room you accidentally stumbled into earlier today?"

"It would."

"Grounds?"

Jack paused. Did he have grounds? It was questionable but he thought he'd be able to swing it. "Our main suspect is Jamie Rivers — the stepbrother of the first victim. And he was childhood friends with one of the patients at New Green — Vince Butler — one of the original suspects from the first investigation. I think they've been in contact."

"What makes you say that?"

"It's a hunch at this stage," admitted Jack. "Butler idolises the Bishop. You should see his room. Wall to wall newspaper cuttings. It's creepy. If The Bishop does turn out to be Jamie Rivers, I'd bet my life on them being pen pals."

Chief Superintendent King sighed and rubbed his tired eyes. "Is it an offence to be a pen pal with a killer?"

"No, not yet. But if there are letters in Vince's possession from Jamie Rivers, we just might get an address for him."

"I say it to you every time you set foot in here, Jack — tread carefully. There's only so many of these that I can make disappear." Dougie King picked up the letter from Dr Erskine and slid it into one of his desk drawers, out of sight. "And I'm not even going to mention the spectacular cock-up with Barry Draper. I've managed to keep that under wraps so far, Jack — but I'm no magician. I can't keep making everything go away."

"What about Dr Erskine?"

"Don't you worry about her." Chief Superintendent King looked at Jack with his soft, brown eyes. "You go get your warrant and catch me a killer."

CHAPTER TWENTY-SEVEN

Time: 7.45 p.m.
Date: Thursday 26 September 2013
Location: New Green Psychiatric Unit, Epping, Essex

Jack sped into the car park at New Green, the Mondeo's tyres kicking up plumes of gravel. Cassidy braced herself against the dashboard as the car came to a rapid stop. Looking through the windscreen, Jack saw he'd come to rest in the designated parking bay of none other than Dr Erskine. A satisfied smile crossed his face as he turned to Cassidy. "Ready?"

"Ready," she confirmed, waggling the search warrant in the air. "I'm looking forward to meeting this Dr Erskine you speak so fondly of." Opening the passenger door, she noticed the parking sign nailed to the wall. "You do realise you've parked in her space?"

Jack merely shrugged and began jogging up the steps towards the front door. "I'm sure she won't mind. We're old friends." Just as he lifted a hand to press the bell, the sound of a vehicle flying through the gravel and screeching to a halt behind them caught his attention.

The door to a shiny new Mazda was flung open and Dr Erskine came storming towards them with a sour expression. "Detective Inspector MacIntosh — you're back. Again."

"So it would seem." Jack watched the doctor hurry up the steps, her face an intense shade of crimson.

"Those parking spaces are reserved," she continued, hotly. "Visitor spaces are on the other side."

Jack flashed a smile. "I'll try and remember that for next time. Anyhow, we've a warrant to search Vince Butler's room." Cassidy once again waved the search warrant in the air., "So, if you'd be so kind . . ." Jack nodded at the front door which was still barring their entrance.

Dr Erskine's face creased in distaste, as she swiped her electronic key fob and released the door.

"That's the ticket." Jack pushed past and stepped inside, motioning for Cassidy to follow.

"This is most inconvenient, Inspector." Dr Erskine hurried through, letting the door swing shut behind her. "You can't just turn up here, out of the blue . . ."

"Oh, but I can, you see," replied Jack as he made his way towards a familiar face at the reception desk. "It's called being a policeman." Cassidy smothered a grin as she quickened her step to keep pace by his side. "Ah, Thomas. Good to see you again. We'll need access to Vince Butler's room."

Cassidy once again held up the search warrant. Thomas flashed a worried look in Dr Erskine's direction, just as she managed to catch up with her uninvited guests.

"It's all right, Thomas." Dr Erskine's clipped tone informed everyone within earshot that it definitely was *not* all right. "I'll deal with this. Follow me."

Dr Erskine stiffly strode towards the stairs, her displeasure etched into her every step. Jack almost expected to see smoke billowing out from her ears as he and Cassidy jogged to catch up. "Mr Butler will be at evening recreation." She led them up a flight of stairs and through several sets of security doors. "You'll have five minutes."

"I think you'll find we'll have as long as it takes," replied Jack, recognising the corridor that led towards room seventeen.

Dr Erskine came to an abrupt halt outside Vince Butler's open door. "As I said." She turned towards Jack and Cassidy, her lips pursed. "Five minutes." With that, she turned on her heels and stormed back along the way they'd come.

Cassidy sniggered behind her hand. "Wow, she just oozes charm."

"Let's just say I don't think I'm invited to their Christmas party. Shame, really. I bet they have a ball." Jack handed Cassidy a pair of gloves. Although technically not a crime scene, if they didn't follow protocol he knew it would come back to bite them at some point. And he couldn't afford to make any more mistakes. Too many had been made already.

Jack again cast his eyes around the four walls. He heard a slight intake of breath from Cassidy behind him as she saw, for the first time, the newspaper articles and headlines staring back out at them.

"Oh my days." Cassidy's eyes widened. "Is this man for real? No wonder they had him down as prime suspect number one."

Jack snapped on his gloves. "He's an oddball, that's for sure. And he's a killer. But he's not the Bishop."

They headed towards a small desk nestled next to Vince Butler's bed. Its surface was empty, except for the same stack of notepaper and envelopes Jack had seen before. "Letters, postcards, notes. Anything that connects him to the outside world. I want to know who he's communicating with, and more importantly, what he says."

"You think it'll be Jamie Rivers?" Cassidy pulled on her gloves.

Jack paused. "I think it's more than likely."

For the next ten minutes they worked in silence, the only sound being the rustle of paper and envelopes as they studied the piles of correspondence Vince Butler seemed to have accumulated during his incarceration. Jack noted the horror etched on to Cassidy's face as she read through the disturbing contents.

"Pretty vile stuff, eh?" Jack selected another bunch of letters from the top drawer.

"Disgusting." Cassidy held up a lilac-coloured piece of notepaper. "He gets fan mail. These women, and they *are* mostly women, revere him. They're not at all turned off by him being a murderer that ate body parts. If anything, it turns them on more." She waved the scented pale purple letter in the air. "This one's proposing marriage." She shuddered. "It's sick."

Jack's portion of correspondence had revealed something similar. Vince Butler had a level of notoriety that was reserved for the most evil and twisted of society — and, for some, that made him all the more attractive. He didn't understand it any more than Cassidy did — and nor did he want to.

He returned the bundle of letters to the top drawer, finding nothing even remotely linking Butler to the Bishop. There was one final drawer to look through, but when Jack tried to open it, it remained firmly shut.

"This one's locked." Jack pulled at the drawer once more. "You see a key anywhere?"

Cassidy rummaged among the notepaper on top of the desk, but no key was forthcoming. A quick glance at the shelving gave the same result. Jack merely shrugged his shoulders and selected a sturdy metal ruler from the pen and pencil pot. He turned it over in his hands. "The things convicted murderers are allowed to have in their rooms."

Using the ruler, Jack forced the drawer open with a crack of splintering cheap wood.

Cassidy glanced over her shoulder towards the open door. "Are you sure we're allowed to do that, guv?"

Jack gave another shrug. "Don't know what you mean, Amanda." He placed the ruler back in the pen pot. "The drawer was already busted open when we got here." He gave a sly wink and began to rifle through the contents.

Jack noticed almost immediately that these letters were different. Up to now, they'd been reading correspondence on shades of pink, lilac or pale yellow paper, some infused with perfume, others tied up with fancy pieces of ribbon. The handwriting was beautifully crafted, with kisses and love hearts by the signatures.

But these letters were *very* different.

No scented paper this time, no hearts and flowers decorating the edges — no declarations of undying love. In this drawer, the letters were written on paper that'd been torn from ordinary cheap A4 notepads, some with rips at the sides as if removed from the pad in haste. The writing was scrawled and urgent, often with smudged ink.

Jack opened up one letter and began to read. It wasn't long before his heart quickened.

"Jesus," he breathed, hastily grabbing another letter. "Take a look at these."

Cassidy stopped her trawl through a bundle of lavender scented notepaper and looked across at the busted drawer. Jack handed her an envelope. "Tell me what you see."

It wasn't long before Cassidy gave the same exclamation. "Jesus." She paused and glanced up at Jack. "Trevor was right."

Jack pulled out several plastic evidence bags. "Bag up the contents of that bottom drawer."

While Cassidy began filling the bags, Jack got to his feet and pulled out his phone. "Cooper? Good, you're still there. See if you can find out the address behind this PO Box for me. PO 4578 Uxbridge. And tell Daniels I owe him a pint."

* * *

Time: 8.00 p.m.
Date: Thursday 26 September 2013
Location: Metropolitan Police HQ, London

"Thanks, mate. I owe you." DS Carmichael put down the phone and frowned. The phone numbers Jack had asked him to trace hadn't turned up much — his contact had managed to trace the origins of the text messages, but that was about it. The phones were all disconnected within seconds of the messages being sent. Whoever it was, they knew what they were doing. The phones themselves were untraceable. Pay as you go, most likely paid for in cash.

But the tech trawl had thrown up something.

Carmichael pulled his notepad towards him and wrote down a location he knew Jack would recognise in an instant.

With a deepening frown, he dialled Jack's number, wondering just what it was his friend was getting himself caught up in.

* * *

Time: 8.05 p.m.
Date: Thursday 26 September 2013
Location: New Green Psychiatric Unit, Epping, Essex

"How nice to see you again, Inspector. Doing a spot of spring cleaning?"

Jack turned to see Vince Butler standing in the doorway, the familiar figure of Dr Erskine bristling at his side. He pulled off his gloves and slipped them in his pocket. "Vince."

"I trust you've finished invading my patient's privacy now, Inspector." Dr Erskine stepped into the room, her face taut.

Jack glanced at the bundle of sealed plastic bags by his feet. He shrugged. "It's a start. We might be back." Jack caught Dr Erskine's eye and relished the look of horror that darkened her features. He bent down and scooped up the bags. "Thanks for your hospitality, Doctor," he breezed. "We must do it again sometime."

Vince Butler began to chuckle and clasped his hands together in apparent joy. "I do hope you find what you're looking for, Inspector. I'd so hate for it to have been *another* wasted journey."

Jack fixed Vince with a cold look. "I'm not finished with you, Butler. Not by a long shot. You've been holding out on me." He waved the evidence bags in Butler's face. "Jamie Rivers. That name ring any bells, does it?"

Vince's expression remained impassive, a small smile still plastered to his lips.

"You knew who the Bishop was all along." Jack's jaw was clenched tight. "And the minute I can prove you've been inciting him to murder, then I'll be back. Have no doubt about that."

Jack turned away from Vince Butler's cold expression and instead faced Dr Erskine. "And, as for you and this . . . this *institution*. How you let material like this through uncensored is beyond me. In my eyes, you're just as guilty as he is."

Jack pushed his way past Dr Erskine and strode off in the direction of the security doors, Cassidy hurrying after. "If you'd be so kind as to buzz us through, we'll see ourselves out."

CHAPTER TWENTY-EIGHT

Time: 9.10 p.m.
Date: Thursday 26 September 2013
Location: St James's University Student Union bar, London

Even with the best part of half a bottle of cheap red wine and several double vodkas from the pub around the corner inside her, Lily's stomach flipped with ever increasing butterflies as she entered the Student Union bar. She'd had the same feeling of someone behind her as she made her way to meet Scarlett. But every time she looked over her shoulder, there was nothing to see.

Inside the sanctuary of the bar, Scarlett found them a corner table and went to get the first round of drinks. It was two-for-one all night on spirits and shots, the thought of which made Lily feel even more queasy. But she needed the numbness only alcohol could bring. When Scarlett returned, Lily picked up a glass and immediately downed its contents, not caring what it was.

"Steady on," grinned Scarlett, nodding at Lily's empty glass. "I don't fancy carrying you home later!"

Lily returned a half-grin of her own, and reached for the second glass. The alcohol quickly flooded her bloodstream, her empty stomach aiding its swift progress.

Lily bought the next round of tequila shots and quickly forgot about the unease she'd felt earlier. The DJ turned up the volume and the walls of the Student Union bar pulsated to the music.

* * *

Time: 9.10 p.m.
Date: Thursday 26 September 2013
Location: New Green Psychiatric Unit, Epping, Essex

Lying back on his neatly made bed, Vince Butler clasped his hands behind his head and stared up at the ceiling. His light was still on, past the regulation 'lights out' at nine o'clock — just one of the many privileges afforded him by Dr Erskine.

His eyes flickered towards the desk and the splintered wood of the busted bottom drawer. A spark of irritation crossed his face. He'd been expecting the detective inspector to return, but not quite so soon. The man really didn't know when to leave something well alone.

He knew, by now, that they'd be searching for Jamie. The Bishop had finally been unmasked. But they'd had a good run — him and Jamie. And all good things eventually come to an end, as the saying goes.

Jamie had come a long way since their first experiments inside the Den. Vince let a smile cross his lips. *The Den*. At one time, it had been his favourite place. The two of them would spend hours cocooned in their own little world, away from the teasing and disdainful looks of their so-called school friends. Inside the Den, they could be anything and anybody they wanted.

And he'd done well in selecting Jamie, he was sure he had. The boy had come on leaps and bounds with only the barest of instruction — almost as if he was born to do it. Vince could remember the turning point like it was yesterday — the time when he finally knew he'd found something very special in Jamie Rivers.

* * *

Time: 11.30 a.m.
Date: Friday 28 May 1999
Location: The Den, Colchester, Essex

"What did you bring?" Kenny led the way through the bushes at the bottom of old man Crocker's garden, just like before. The way through to the Den wasn't so overgrown this time and, once inside, he made his way over to the battered chess tin where the remains of last week's experiment were now safety entombed.

Jamie followed on behind, clutching a small cardboard box under his arm. Its cargo could be heard scrabbling frantically inside, tiny claws scraping against the inside of the box. He knelt on the ground and placed it next to the tin. "It's in there."

"Yeah, but what is it?"

Both boys fell silent as the scrabbling sound intensified — the box rocking a little from side to side. Jamie let a smile creep across his face as he leaned in and opened it up.

Hammy had been easy enough to catch — he was a friendly little thing. He liked to be handled and would happily curl up in the palm of your hand while his cage was being cleaned.

But he wasn't content right now. Right now he was agitated, and most probably scared. That alone caused Jamie's smile to widen.

Jamie lifted up the flaps of the box and put his hand inside. The hamster wriggled beneath his grasp, and he made sure he kept his fingers away from the little rodent's sharp teeth. "Put the knife down on the ground," he commanded, relishing taking control.

Kenny did as he was told and placed the hunting knife down on the soil next to them. He then held out his hands towards Jamie.

"He's a wriggler," said Jamie, tipping the agitated hamster into his friend's hands. "You'll need to grip hold of him tightly."

Kenny nodded and closed his hands around the furry animal. He felt the hamster's sharpened claws scratching at the palms of his hands.

Jamie reached for the knife, another ripple of excitement washing over him as he took hold of the handle. It felt surprisingly heavy.

Neither boy spoke: the only sounds were the ragged breaths escaping their lips. Even the birds that had been chirping constantly around the bird table had fallen silent. There wasn't a breath of fresh air to be felt.

"You ready?" asked Jamie, quietly.

Kenny nodded, tightening his grip on the hamster. "Do it."

* * *

Time: 5.15 p.m.
Date: Friday 28 May 1999
Location: Friar's Lane, Colchester, Essex

"Mum?" Stacey Fairbrother stepped on to the landing and looked towards the closed door of her mother's bedroom. Hovering for a moment, she strained her ears for any sign or sound that her mum was awake. Mum was sick. Very sick. And Stacey hated waking her unless she really had to. Some days she didn't even have the energy to get out of bed, and then Justin would get her breakfast ready and make sure she had everything for school.

Today had been one of those days.

That morning, Justin had made her a packed lunch, poured her a large glass of orange juice and gave her a bowl of her favourite cereal. It made her smile how he liked to look after her, even though she was more than capable of doing it for herself. He even did the washing up before they left for school. Jamie hadn't shown up for breakfast — presumably off somewhere with that weird friend of his.

She'd had gymnastics club after school, and after it was over she'd raced home to get out of her school clothes. It was half-term now and she couldn't wait for a break from the never-ending schoolwork. As soon as she'd flung her schoolbag on her bed, she'd noticed it.

"Mum?" Stacey took another tentative step towards her mother's bedroom door. As she did so, it creaked open. "What's up, poppet?" Heather Rivers' voice was soft and raspy. She looked pale, but had brushed her cheeks with some hastily applied blusher to give herself some colour, and pulled a hairbrush through her thinning hair. She took a step towards her daughter; it was clear that every movement she made was causing her considerable pain. "What's happened?"

Stacey glanced back over her shoulder towards her own bedroom. "It's . . . it's Hammy. He's gone."

Heather's face clouded, her pale blue eyes tinged with concern. A frown creased her pallid brow. "What do you mean, gone?" She took another hesitant step towards Stacey, grabbing hold of the door frame as she did so.

"H . . . Hammy." Stacey's eyes filled with tears. "The cage is open — and he's gone."

* * *

Time. 9.20 p.m.
Date: Thursday 26 September 2013
Location: New Green Psychiatric Unit, Epping, Essex

Yes — that day had marked a change in the direction of Jamie Rivers' life. Vince knew, from that very moment in the Den, that his best friend was destined for greater things.

Vince afforded himself another smile and let his eyes flicker towards the newspaper articles pinned to his walls. Jamie had been a good student — compliant and attentive to detail. Each killing had been planned to perfection, and then executed exquisitely.

Executed.

Vince's smile widened. It was a good enough word as any to describe the Bishop's exploits.

But things were finally coming to an end — the Bishop would be caught, Vince had no doubt about that. Not even Jamie Rivers could escape detection now. But *when* he would be caught was an entirely different matter. If he knew Jamie as well as he thought he did, then he'd be hunting right now.

The only real question that remained was whether Detective Inspector Jack MacIntosh would find him in time.

CHAPTER TWENTY-NINE

Time: 9.45 p.m.
Date: Thursday 26 September 2013
Location: Metropolitan Police HQ, London

"We're now looking for Jamie Rivers." Jack paced up and down in front of the cork pin board. "Son of Martin Rivers. Stepbrother of our first victim, Stacey Fairbrother. The letters found in Vince Butler's room confirm they've been in touch on and off for the last ten years. Certainly throughout 2009 and the first four murders. We'll go through each and every one, but I think we'll find that Vince Butler was somehow orchestrating his fantasies through Jamie. Encouraging him to murder — revelling in the details when Jamie reported back."

"The PO Box address you gave me only gives a forwarding address to the Rivers' family home," added Cooper. "And we know he hasn't lived there for a long time."

Jack stood in front of the pin board, staring at Vince Butler's impassive face. "Butler was arrested in October 2009 for the murders of Annabel Collins and Matilda Renshaw. After that he was shifted from pillar to post, through a variety of prisons and psychiatric facilities, where any communication he sent out or received would have been closely monitored. It wasn't until he settled in New Green that he would've been able to resume his correspondence with Jamie — I think that explains our break of four years."

Cassidy joined Jack at the pin board. "I came back to a message from the admissions officer at St George's Technical College — Jamie enrolled on a carpentry course in 2002. They sent through the only photo they had on file." She pinned a small, square picture of Jamie Rivers to the board.

"Daniels. You knew him when you were a kid. Does that look like him?" Jack tapped the photograph and glanced across at DC Daniels.

Daniels nodded. "Yep. That's definitely him."

"Although it's old, I want that picture sent everywhere. I want to know where he is — now."

"On it, guv." Cassidy sprang towards the door.

"And tomorrow we go back to see Martin Rivers. I'm not convinced he's telling us everything. Amanda, head out there first thing — take another look at what's in Jamie's old bedroom. There wasn't much, but take a look anyway." Jack glanced at his watch and rubbed his eyes. "Everybody, go home. It's late. Thanks for staying on." Before turning away, Jack let his eyes rest on the heart-shaped face of Stacey Fairbrother. "At least we can now guess how Stacey Fairbrother invited a killer into her home."

* * *

Time: 1.00 a.m.
Date: Wednesday 15 July 2009
Location: The Six Bells, Salvation Row, Chelmsford

The rain hadn't let up for hours, but still he watched.

The first batch of drinkers had left the pub three hours ago, followed by a handful more as midnight approached. Then everything had gone quiet. Just as he was beginning to wonder if he'd missed her, the door to the pub opened

— a shaft of light from within momentarily lighting up the pavement outside. Instinctively, he shrank further back into the shadow of the doorway that had become his hiding place.

He couldn't let her see him.

Not yet.

He watched as she pulled her tiny jacket around her, then turned her head up towards the sky. Setting off in the direction of her flat, the only sound along the deserted terraced street was the clicking of her heels.

He let her walk a few more metres ahead before starting to follow. His footsteps were light and barely audible above the gentle patter of raindrops hitting the parked cars that lined the street. She hurried along Salvation Row, and he followed as discreetly as he could, watching her turn into the side street that would lead to her home. He already knew where she was going — he'd been there before.

Closing the gap between them, he could see she was almost home now: almost at the end of the street, and within reach of the comfort of her ground floor flat.

He felt a trickle of jealousy mixed with anger begin to seep through his frozen body. She'd left home, finished college, got a job and secured herself a flat. All the things that *he* should have had. All the things that *he* deserved. Even his own father preferred her to his own flesh and blood. It made him seethe how easily everything had come to her; she'd never had to struggle the way he had.

Bitterness welled up as he clenched his fists tightly inside his pockets. Lengthening his stride, he closed the gap even more, breaking into a silent jog around the final line of parked cars. As he did so, he saw her flinch. He watched her head whip round, searching through the darkness as he ducked down behind the rear wheel of the final car.

He watched her push open the small gate that led to her front door, stumbling slightly in her heels as she fumbled for her keys. Her hair was plastered to her scalp and her thin cotton jacket soaked through. He saw her body flinch, her head swivelling around in his direction, eyes wide with fear.

It was then that he decided the time for waiting was over.

He stepped out of the shadows and strode towards her. As their eyes locked, he saw the initial fear dissolve — replaced by confusion.

"Hello, Stacey," he said, taking another step towards her. "Long time no see."

"Jamie?" A frown crossed Stacey Fairbrother's forehead. "What on earth are you doing here?"

"I'm just passing through. You know me — rarely settle in one place for long." Jamie Rivers paused, glancing up at the sky as heavy raindrops hit him squarely in the face. "Can I come in and ring for a taxi?"

* * *

Time: 11.30 p.m.
Date: Thursday 26 September 2013
Location: St James's University Student Union bar, London

Lily didn't need the stacks of shot glasses on the table to tell her how much she and Scarlett had drunk. The evidence was in the steady throbbing at her temples, and the numbness seeping into her legs. Her vision was becoming hazy around the edges, everything sounding muffled and distant. The cheap red wine she'd drunk in her bedsit hadn't been the greatest way to line her stomach.

She glanced down at her watch, but found it almost impossible to see through the dimness of the Student Union bar. The strobing disco lights weren't helping either. She'd shaken her head when Scarlett had suggested another round of shots — at least, that's what she thought her friend had said. The music was so loud, thumping against her eardrums, she hadn't been able to make out a single word. Scarlett had then gestured that she was heading to the ladies.

And that'd been how long ago now? Lily rested her forehead against the table, not caring that it was sticky from their various spilt drinks. A half-eaten packet of salt and vinegar crisps sat inches from her nose — the acidic aroma of the vinegar caused her stomach to churn. *Good job Granny and Grandad can't see me now*, she thought to herself, suppressing another heave from her insides.

"You had enough?"

The words didn't particularly register the first time around. Lily's head remained slumped on the table, her eyes closed. It wasn't until she felt someone bump against her shoulder that she peered out from underneath mascara-caked eyelashes and vaguely saw the outline of another human being.

"I said, have you had enough? Want to get out of here?"

Lily pushed her head up from the table, instantly feeling dizzy. Her eyes came to rest on a face that she vaguely recognised. "Sorry?" she mumbled, frowning against the noise. "What did you say?"

Jamie Rivers smiled 'that smile', inching closer so his lips were only millimetres from Lily's ear. His breath tickled her skin in a not unpleasant kind of way. "I said," he repeated, slowly, mouthing each word carefully. "Do you want to get out of here?"

The wink that followed finally caused the penny to drop.

"You're Scarlett's friend," slurred Lily, reaching down for the bag that, thankfully, was still between her feet. "You work here."

Jamie Rivers nodded and flashed 'the smile' again. "Working on the renovations."

Despite the haziness clouding her mind, Lily could now picture him standing at the student coffee bar with Scarlett. There'd been two of them; workmen from the university. She hadn't recognised him without his hi-vis jacket and hard hat.

"So, what do you think?" He cocked his head to the side. "Go someplace else? This music is doing my head in."

Lily giggled. "Mine too!" She pulled her bag up on to her lap. "But what I really need more than anything is just to go home. I'm shattered."

Jamie Rivers' smile didn't falter. "Well, I can help with that. I'll walk you home."

CHAPTER THIRTY

Time: 2.30 a.m.
Date: Friday 27 September 2013
Location: St James's House, Gold Street, London

He watched her slumbering form and gritted his teeth, nose flaring. This wasn't how it was meant to be. He thought he'd dragged her away in time — but he'd been wrong. It had been naive to think she would have turned up to the Student Union bar sober — it was Freshers Week, after all.

Irritation spread through him once again. It wasn't like him to make this kind of a mistake; he was usually so careful. If she wasn't so perfect, he would have abandoned the idea and chosen someone else. Someone less difficult.

But there was something about her — something that drew her to him. He needed her on his shelf with the others — part of her anyway.

Maybe this was what he needed — someone difficult. Someone to test his patience. The thought gave him a twinge of excitement. Vince had taught him well and encouraged him to widen his boundaries, so maybe Lily was just the challenge he needed. Vince would be impressed.

He glanced around Lily's bedsit and was pleasantly surprised at how clean and tidy it was. *At least she doesn't live like a pig*, he muttered to himself, taking in the neatly made bed that she was currently sprawled over. He sat propped up against the wall by the side of her single wardrobe, and waited.

It was a little after two thirty when he heard the chirping of her mobile phone. He bristled at the intrusion. It had rung four times since they'd arrived back and Lily had slipped into her self-induced unconsciousness. He reached for her shoulder bag and pulled out the phone, peering at the screen through the subdued light. Five missed calls. All from someone called Grandad.

The voicemail icon was flashing on the screen, with three waiting messages. He pressed play and brought the handset to his ear.

Grandad's voice sounded cheerful to begin with — asking how Lily was and what she'd been doing that day. By message number three his tone had changed to one of concern. The relaxed Scottish tone of earlier was clipped — Jamie could almost hear the fear wrapped around each word. Grandad was urging Lily to call him back to let him know she was OK.

But Lily was indisposed right now.

Pressing the message icon, he began to type. The last thing he wanted was Grandad interrupting his plans for Lily. That wouldn't do at all. He tapped out a brief message, signed it from Lily and then closed the phone.

Grandad was sorted.

Now all he needed to do was wait.

* * *

Time: 3.15 a.m.
Date: Friday 27 September 2013
Location: Tannochside B&B, Scotland

Willie McArthur wasn't usually one for hitting the bottle this late at night — or early morning, depending how you looked at it. But he couldn't sleep, and nothing short of the fiery burn of his best whisky would take away the gnawing sense of unease that was settling in his stomach.

He took the drink and sat down by the dormant fireside, its flames long since died down. Pulling out his phone, he stared at the screen. The message had come through forty minutes ago and had caused him nothing but concern ever since. It was usually his prostate that kept him up at night these days, not worrying about his granddaughter living over 400 miles away.

Holding the phone at arm's length, he squinted at the tiny screen while taking another mouthful of whisky. A sound from the other side of the empty bar caught his attention — then he saw the door to the guests' bedrooms being nudged open by a wet black nose.

Banjo padded across to Willie and jumped up on to the bar stool by his side. Willie noticed that the small Scottish terrier wasn't alone. He broke out into a tired smile. "Isabel. What brings you down here at this time of night?"

Isabel threaded her way past the empty chairs and tables, pulling her dressing gown tightly around her. "I could ask the same about you," she smiled. "I found this one scratching at our door. I think he wanted to play." She bent down and ruffled the terrier behind his ears. "Then he led me down here."

"Ach, Banjo," scolded Willie, good-naturedly. "What have I told you about disturbing our guests in the middle of the night?"

Isabel perched on the edge of a nearby table and stifled a yawn. "It's OK. I wasn't really sleeping. What are you doing up, anyway?" She eyed the almost empty glass tumbler in Willie's hand. "Nightcap?"

Willie gave a sigh and sank the rest of the whisky. "I couldn't sleep. I had a message from Lily." He waved the phone in the air.

"Oh? Is she OK?"

Willie paused. "I'm not sure." He handed Isabel the phone. "See for yourself."

Isabel lowered her eyes to the small Nokia screen. "Hi Grandad," she read out loud. "All good here. Sorry I didn't ring, so busy! Talk soon, Lily." Frowning, she looked up. "I'm not sure I understand. Sounds like she's fine. The first week at university is always hectic."

Willie nodded, taking the phone back and staring at the screen once again. "I know, but . . ." He broke off, his eyes having lost their customary sparkle.

"What is it? What's wrong?"

"Lily," replied Willie, simply, his voice grave. "I think she's in trouble."

"Why would she be in trouble?"

"The message." Willie looked again at the screen. "Lily never sends me text messages. She knows my eyes are so poor these days I cannae see the words." His voice wobbled as he spoke, the words catching in his throat. "I phoned her four, maybe five times — she didn't answer. Then this comes through — but I don't think it's from her. The few messages she has sent me, she always signs them with 'L'. Never Lily."

Isabel let Willie's words sink in, all thoughts of sleep instantly swept aside.

"Let me phone Jack."

"Ach, no, don't bother the poor wee man in the middle of the night." Willie waved a hand in Isabel's direction and got to his feet. "I'm probably imagining it all. Ignore me." He gave Isabel a tired smile. "That's what happens when you get old. The old brain goes into overdrive."

Isabel let herself be ushered out of the bar and back towards the stairs, Banjo sniffing at her heels.

"You just see — I'll ring her in the morning and she'll be as right as rain." Willie squeezed another smile across his face. "Now get yourself to bed."

Isabel watched as Willie turned away, heading back towards the bar. For all his reassuring words, she wasn't convinced that the landlord of the Tannochside B&B would be getting any more sleep tonight.

* * *

Time: 6.25 a.m.
Date: Friday 27 September 2013
Location: St James's House, Gold Street, London

The first thing Lily felt as she stirred was an intense banging at the sides of her head. She slowly peeled open her eyelids, the mascara she'd so carefully applied the night before sticking her eyelashes together like glue. A wall of pain stabbed her between the eyes.

The room was still bathed in darkness. She gingerly turned her head towards the window, wondering what time it was. She managed a tentative frown. The flimsy curtains that came with the bedsit usually let in a dim light from the streetlights outside, even in the dead of night, and the first rays of sunrise would cast the room in pale light. But right now, all she could see was black.

A trickle of fear crossed her senses. Was she even at home? She slowly turned her head away from the window, her eyes searching the gloom for any signs of familiarity. As she peered through the shadows and her eyes began to adjust, she could make out the outline of the single wardrobe, her desk, and even a pile of clothes on the floor.

Fear and confusion was replaced by relief. She was home. All was well:except for the thumping headache and wave of nausea rising up from her stomach. She'd had hangovers before and could recognise the signs. Her tongue felt dry, as if she'd swallowed a mouthful of sand, and her gums ached.

As she began to move, she realised she was still fully dressed — still wearing her homemade denim dress, the crochet cardigan still around her shoulders. Even her sandals were still on her feet.

Jeez, I must have been wrecked when I got home last night, she mused, closing her eyes once again to quell the stabbing pain. I don't even remember *getting* home last night.

With her tongue feeling rough and swollen, Lily craved a glass of water but didn't have the energy to move. Moving meant opening her eyes again, and along with movement came the nausea. She didn't fancy vomiting on the carpet of the one and only room she lived in. The smell would never disappear.

Instead, she clamped her eyes shut and turned her face towards the wall. She would sleep until the sun came up. Willing the nausea to subside she took in a deep breath, but found that it merely caught in her throat. Despite the pain, her eyes snapped open.

There's someone in my room.

* * *

Time: 7.20 a.m.
Date: Friday 27 September 2013
Location: Kettle's Yard Mews, London

The weather was finally turning at last — September no longer fooling anyone into a false sense of summer warmth. The dawn had been overcast, the sun shrouded behind thick grey clouds, and the air had taken on a seasonably fresh chill.

Jack flicked on the kettle and yawned. Last night's sleep had been patchy at best. Before leaving the station, he'd made sure Jamie's picture was circulated nationwide so every police officer would now be on the hunt. And time was crucial. For all they knew, he had another victim in his sights already.

But it hadn't just been the Bishop keeping him from sleep.

Rob's text had come in late last night — just two simple words. '*Albury, Surrey.*' Followed by a '*call me*'. Jack's finger had hovered over the call button, but instead he'd resorted to another glass of whisky. Albury was where Isabel's family home had been — and Jack was sure that fact wasn't without significance.

He hadn't managed to speak to Isabel — not since the discovery that Geraghty had paid for her parents' headstones. It was an unexpected development that he couldn't quite get his head around.

But both Quinn and Geraghty would have to wait.

He dumped an extra spoonful of instant coffee into his mug, feeling strong coffee was going to form an integral part of the next twelve hours or so. Chief Superintendent King had notified him there would be another press conference at 4 o' clock today — news of Barry Draper's arrest had leaked and Dougie King needed to put out some fires.

The debacle over the targeting of Barry Draper was likely to be in the headlines of every newspaper that morning, and Jack could almost see the smile stretching across Jonathan Spearing's face as the *Daily Courier* crime correspondent prepared to inflict as much pain and humiliation as he could muster in a 250-word front page article.

As Jack took the first sip of the scalding hot coffee, wincing as it seared his lips, his phone beeped with an incoming message. Glancing at the screen, he saw it was DS Cooper.

'*On my way over — 5 mins. Something you need to see.*'

Jack frowned and checked the time. Cooper was up and about early. He looked down at his creased boxer shorts and crumpled T-shirt. Five minutes. He just had time to jump in the shower.

Cooper was true to his word and exactly five minutes later knocked at Jack's front door. Still dripping from the shower, he wrapped a towel around his waist and let the detective sergeant in.

"The lock on the door downstairs is still broken, boss," said Cooper as he stepped inside. "Any Tom, Dick or Harriet could just walk in off the street."

"I know, it's been reported." Jack ran a hand over his wet hair. "You want a coffee?" He nodded towards the kitchen but Cooper was already shaking his head.

"No, I've already had a bacon butty and a mug of tea from that all-night café along Stockton Street."

Jack reached for his own half-drunk mug and drained the rest of the strong, bitter liquid. "How come you're up with the dawn chorus?"

Cooper grinned. "Jenny had an early start at the lab. I dropped her off and then called in at the café for a bit of breakfast — took it back to the station."

"The station?" Jack dropped his empty mug into the sink. "You've been in already?"

"And it's a good job I did. Something came in overnight." Cooper brought out a folded piece of paper from his pocket. "More phone records for Billie-Rose and Amy Jennings."

"And?"

"Nothing of significance on Billie-Rose's phone. She barely used it. A few calls here and there. No great social media presence except for an Instagram account. But take a look at this." Cooper handed Jack the piece of paper. "Amy Jennings sent this text only hours before she was killed."

Jack cast his eyes down to the typed message. Cooper let the significance sink in before he spoke again.

"It can't be anywhere else, right?"

Jack passed the note back to Cooper and headed for the bedroom. "Give me two minutes to get dressed. You're driving."

CHAPTER THIRTY-ONE

Time: 7.45 a.m.
Date: Friday 27 September 2013
Location: Tannochside B&B, Scotland

Isabel was up and about as soon as the sun started to appear above the horizon. Despite Willie's assurances that all was well with Lily, and that he was just overreacting, she hadn't been able to sleep a wink. Not wanting to disturb Mac any more than she had already, she slipped on her dressing gown and stepped out into the corridor.

All was quiet. There was a faint smell of cooking bacon in the air: no doubt Margaret was already up and about in the kitchen preparing the breakfasts. She padded to the end of the corridor, where she knew there was a quiet space with a huge window seat looking out on to the craggy hillside that bordered the B&B.

Lily's message had played on her mind all night. She was sure Willie was more worried than he was letting on — playing his fears down to make Isabel feel better. She'd seen the look on his face, the worry in his eyes.

She pulled out her phone and quickly scrolled down to Jack's number. The call went to voicemail. She decided against leaving him a message and instead rang the number for the station. After several connections, she was put through to the incident room where the call was answered by an unfamiliar voice.

"Hello, DC Daniels speaking."

"Oh . . . er . . ." stuttered Isabel, suddenly unsure what to say. "Sorry. Is Jack there? DI MacIntosh?"

"He's not here right now. Can I help?"

Isabel hesitated. Just what was it that she wanted to say? She didn't know Lily. She had no real idea whether Lily sending a text message was as unusual as Willie seemed to think it was. Maybe she'd just wanted to reassure him, but didn't want to get into a lengthy phone conversation? Maybe she'd forgotten his eyesight was so poor?

Maybe.

Isabel made a decision. "It's probably nothing. But a friend of Jack's is concerned about his granddaughter. She's at university in London and he hasn't heard from her in a while."

"OK." Isabel heard the sound of paper being rustled in the background. "If you give me the details, I'll pass it on when he gets in."

Isabel reeled off what details she knew — which she soon discovered wasn't much. She had no idea where Lily was living, or what her mobile number was. Promising to call back with Lily's address and contact details, Isabel ended the call.

It was probably nothing, she mused, making her way back to the room, the smell of frying bacon waking up her senses. But, just in case it wasn't, she felt better about passing the details on to Jack. She hoped Willie wouldn't mind.

Slipping back into the room, she threw open the curtains to let in the sun's early rays, telling Mac he had precisely five minutes to make himself decent for breakfast.

* * *

Time: 8.00 a.m.
Date: Friday 27 September 2013
Location: 7 Cross Keys Road, Camden Town, London

DS Cassidy pulled up outside number seven and sighed. As she exited the car, she saw that, once again, every window was shrouded by curtains. As she made her way up the garden path, she could almost feel the sadness seeping out of the brickwork as she approached the front door.

She composed herself before knocking firmly. It wasn't going to be an easy visit. Martin Rivers had yet to be told that his youngest son was now their main suspect in the Bishop murders, but she secretly wondered if he already suspected. She raised her hand and knocked again before she saw signs of movement through the frosted glass.

Martin Rivers slowly pulled the door open, as if even that effort was too much for him and sapped him of whatever energy he had left. To Cassidy, he looked to be even paler than before. His eyes were sunken, with large bruise-like rings around them. He still wore the same brown corduroy shirt with the same missing buttons.

"Good morning, Mr Rivers," greeted Cassidy, noting how his watery gaze barely raised to meet hers. "I'm sorry to call on you so early. May I come in?"

Martin Rivers gave the briefest of nods and shuffled backwards to make space in the narrow hallway. As Cassidy stepped inside, she noted the same musty smell as before — as if the house hadn't seen a breath of fresh air in months, or maybe even years.

Wordlessly, Martin Rivers closed the front door and shuffled back into the front room. Cassidy followed on behind. The TV was turned off and the only sound was the gentle tick-tock from the mantelpiece clock. Rivers returned to his armchair.

"As I said, I'm sorry to call on you so early, but would it be possible to have a look in Jamie's old bedroom?" Cassidy raised her eyes towards the ceiling. "Upstairs?" Martin Rivers flinched at the sound of Jamie's name, but remained mute. "Mr Rivers? Your son's room?" Cassidy stepped a little closer. "It could help us in a murder investigation." She didn't want to come right out and say it so kept the details vague.

Martin Rivers lifted his head, fixing Cassidy with an empty look and simply nodded. "Of course. Help yourself."

* * *

Time: 8.10 a.m.
Date: Friday 27 September 2013
Location: Isabel's Café, Horseferry Road, London

The familiar aroma of coffee and sweet pastry filled their nostrils as soon as they stepped through the door.

"Jack!" Sacha threw a tea towel over her shoulder and brushed away several stray hairs from her flushed forehead. "Take a seat. I'll bring you both a coffee."

Jack held up a hand. "We're not here on a social call, unfortunately."

A frown crossed Sacha's flushed complexion as she stepped back behind the counter. "Oh?"

"Nothing to worry about," added Jack, watching Cooper casting his hungry eyes over the laminated menu. "Just a few questions when you've got a moment."

The café was relatively quiet, but several tables had an assortment of empty mugs, cups, plates and cutlery as evidence of a recent influx of early morning breakfast visitors. Sacha flicked on the coffee machine. "Dom? Can you come and clear the rest of the tables and give everything a wipe down? We've got about half an hour before the post-school-run hits us."

Sacha made her way across the café armed with two mugs of fresh coffee, Dominic soon emerging behind her from the kitchen. He immediately began work clearing the tables.

"Busy morning?" enquired Jack, as Sacha placed the mugs of coffee on the table and collapsed into a nearby armchair.

Sacha exhaled loudly and grinned. "Very. But that's when I enjoy it the most. Isabel will be pleased with the books this week!"

"We won't take up too much of your time." Jack reached into his pocket and brought out his notebook, slipping a small coloured photograph out from between its pages and placing it on the table. "Do you recognise this woman?"

Sacha leaned forward, casting her eyes at the image of Amy Jennings. Recognition soon followed. "Oh my, isn't that the poor girl from the newspapers?"

Jack simply nodded. "Amy Jennings. Do you recognise her? Other than seeing her in the media?"

Sacha picked up the photograph to take a closer look, and then began to nod. "I think I do, yes. I'm sure she's been in here, now you come to mention it. Why didn't I realise before?"

Jack went back to his notebook. "We searched Amy's phone records. She sent a text message to her mother at 1.45 p.m. on the day she was murdered. We believe it was sent from here." Jack began to read the message out loud. "'*Feeling nervous! First open house event on my own! Hope I don't stuff it up.*' Her mother then replied, '*You'll be fine. Have faith. Try to relax.*' Amy messaged back, '*In a fabulous café. It's full of books and has an adorable tabby cat — I'm in heaven!*'"

The poignancy of Amy's last words echoed around the otherwise silent café.

"She has to be talking about here," continued Jack. "It can't be anywhere else. Can you think back to last Sunday and see if you remember anything about her coming in — before she went to her open house event?"

Sacha's eyes widened. "Oh my goodness, yes. Yes, I do now. When you just mentioned the open house . . . she sat right over there." Sacha indicated towards the window. "She said she was an estate agent, going to an event just around the corner. I remember . . ." Sacha faltered. "She had one of our new Italian coffees and a cinnamon roll."

"Anything else you can remember about her?"

Sacha frowned again, passing the photograph back to Jack. "I don't know. We were so busy — it was lunchtime." She looked crestfallen. "I really don't remember much else, sorry. Other than she said she was an estate agent and didn't know the area very well. I . . . I don't think I even saw her leave."

Jack slipped the photograph and notebook back into his pocket. "Don't worry, it was a long shot. And you don't have CCTV in the café, do you?" Jack already knew Isabel hadn't installed any cameras. He picked up his coffee and downed half of it in one go.

"No," confirmed Sacha, forlornly. "We don't." Her eyes moistened. "That poor girl," she whispered.

"There was a man."

Jack's coffee mug hovered in front of his lips. All eyes turned behind them, to where Dominic was wiping down a table and balancing two trays on top of each other, ready to take back to the kitchen.

"A man?" Jack lowered his mug, his jaw tightening. "What man?"

Dominic straightened up and reached into his back pocket, his cheeks colouring. "There was a man," he repeated, lowering his gaze from the three pairs of eyes that were now focusing on him. He began to side-step, one foot to the other, counting to three on each side as he brought out his notepad.

Jack's stomach tightened again. Of course. The notepad. Anything and everything that happened in Dominic Greene's life was duly noted down. Dates. Times. People.

People.

"Can you tell me anything more about the man, Dominic?" asked Jack. "Anything at all?"

Dominic continued to side-step, his eyes focused on his notepad. After what seemed like an eternity, he lifted his gaze and began to nod. "He came in at 1.28 p.m. and sat there." Dominic nodded towards a table near the window. "He had a black coffee."

Jack didn't take his eyes off Dominic for a single second. "Go on." He pulled out Amy's photograph once again and held it up. "Did he speak to this woman at all?"

Dominic nodded again. "At 1.48 p.m. he sat at her table. He took his coffee with him." Dominic paused, colour still flooding his cheeks. "I . . . I didn't see him again after that. I went to load the dishwasher and start on another batch of baguettes."

Jack's heart began to thump while he reached into his pocket for his notebook. "Was this the man you saw?" This time he pulled out Jamie Rivers' photograph.

Dominic nodded, wide eyed. "Yes. That's him. That's the man."

* * *

Time: 1.45 p.m.
Date: Sunday 22 September 2013
Location: Isabel's Café, Horseferry Road, London

The delicious Italian coffee went some way to calming her nerves, but just looking at the flyer on the table next to her empty plate made her stomach flip. She really needed this to go well — to prove to Trudy she was capable of handling things solo. The cinnamon roll had been fantastic — melting in the mouth — but now it made her stomach churn all the more.

Amy pulled out her phone and decided to tell her mum she was heading over to the apartment. She'd been just as nervous as Amy this morning – she could tell from the look on her mother's face over the early morning teapot. She'd tried to hide it, of course, but Amy knew. Her mum had been her rock since she'd landed back on the doorstep of the family home, armed with a degree and a shedload of debt. Dad had been great too. They'd both welcomed her back with open arms, her room already made up for her. Naively, Amy had thought that once she had her degree, she'd move into her own flat and start living the life she'd always dreamed of.

But that was all it was now. A dream.

Reality dawned on her every single morning.

She had some savings now, thanks to the estate agency job, and she hoped it wouldn't be too long before she could step out on her own, make her own way in the world. And today was an important step towards that.

So long as she didn't mess it up.

Amy had been so wrapped up in texting her mum about the fantastic new café she'd stumbled across, spying several books by her mum's favourite author and getting a glimpse of the most beautiful tabby cat weaving in and out of her legs, that she didn't hear him speak the first time.

So, when he spoke again, it startled her.

"Can I borrow your menu?" he repeated, nodding down at the laminated card propped up against a salt and pepper shaker.

Amy looked up. He was tall, she could see that, and his grey eyes crinkled at the corners as he smiled. "Oh, of course," she replied, blushing slightly as she handed the menu across. "Sorry. I was miles away."

Jamie smiled one of the smiles he knew always worked. He had it perfected now. If you had a nice smile, women trusted you. And trust was the key. His eyes flickered towards the flyer: the real reason he was standing by her table. The real reason he'd followed her here from her home address in Richmond. "What's this?"

"Oh, it's an open event for an apartment near here," Amy replied. "I'm an estate agent. I'm hosting it in . . ." She glanced down at her watch. "Forty-five minutes."

Jamie picked up the flyer, plastering another well-rehearsed expression on to his otherwise featureless face. "Really? I'm looking for something like this. Would I be able to come along?" He forced another well-practised smile on to his lips. "I'm new to the area, you see."

Amy felt a tinge of excitement. Another potential buyer. "Of course," she breezed, getting to her feet and brushing stray pastry flakes from her blouse. "Take a flyer." She pulled another from her handbag. "It starts at two thirty. You'll need to ring the bell at the entrance to the block."

Jamie took the flyer and slipped it into his back pocket. He didn't need to read it. He already knew what it said and where it was. And it was perfect. *She* was perfect. Vince would be pleased with his choice.

"I'm Duncan, by the way." Jamie stretched out a hand as he slipped into the seat opposite. In his other hand he carried his half-drunk cup of black coffee. "Duncan Foster. Do you have five minutes to fill me in on the details?"

* * *

Time: 8.20 a.m.
Date: Friday 27 September 2013
Location: 7 Cross Keys Road, Camden Town, London

The room was small and smelled just as stuffy as the rest of the house. Cassidy resisted the urge to crack open the window. She saw a dozen or so cardboard boxes lined up against one wall, but after picking up a couple she realised the majority were only half full.

Not much for twenty-odd years of someone's life, she thought as she began peering into more boxes. It became apparent quite quickly that the contents weren't likely to help them in their hunt for Jamie Rivers. Most contained clothes, shoes and belts, as if the contents of a wardrobe had been scooped up and deposited inside. There was just one other box that contained a few papers, a selection of books and some old vinyl records.

After a brief rummage, one book caught Cassidy's eye. It was a battered copy of *The Merchant of Venice*. As she pulled it from the box, it fell open at a section marked with a tatty bookmark. Shakespeare wasn't her first choice for reading pleasure, but she remembered this one from school.

"A pound of flesh," she mused, her eyes tracking down the page to a line that'd been highlighted. "A pound of flesh."

Before she knew it, her head flooded with images of the flesh wounds from each of The Bishop's victims. Was it really that simple? A pound of flesh?

Pulling out a plastic evidence bag, she dropped the paperback inside just as her mobile beeped with an incoming message. Scanning the screen, she noted she was needed at Isabel's Café — there was a lead on Jamie.

Satisfied the rest of the boxes held nothing of any significance, Cassidy got to her feet and made her way downstairs. The musty smell intensified as she reached the bottom: all the doors along the hallway were closed fast. She poked her head into the front room and saw Martin Rivers was exactly where she'd left him — sitting in his armchair, staring into space. Hesitating in the doorway, clutching the plastic evidence bag to her chest, she cleared her throat. "Mr Rivers? I'll be off now, thank you."

Martin Rivers didn't react immediately, but eventually he turned his gaze towards her. He nodded, but made no attempt to get to his feet. "I see. I hope you found what you were looking for."

Cassidy glanced down at the plastic evidence bag. "I think so. Thank you once again." She paused and took a hesitant step forwards. "Is there anyone I can call for you? Someone to come and sit with you?"

Rivers slowly blinked, then shook his head.

"OK, well . . . I'll leave you in peace." Cassidy turned and made her way back towards the front door, glad to step outside into the fresh air.

Martin Rivers turned his attention back to staring into space.

CHAPTER THIRTY-TWO

Time: 8.30 a.m.
Date: Friday 27 September 2013
Location: St James's House, Gold Street, London

He'd had to restrain her — and that both concerned and excited him. None of the others had required such a step to be taken — they'd been compliant; they'd trusted him.

But Lily was different; he could see that.

He cocked his head to the side, regarding her limp body as it rested against the wall behind her bed. At least she was calm now. He was grateful that he'd had the foresight to bring the plastic cable ties with him, and the masking tape. Something in the back of his mind must have foreseen Lily McArthur was going to be a handful.

She was staring at him now, her eyes wide and fearful. A thick piece of masking tape had hushed her screams, and her hands were tied behind her back. Resting his head back against the wall by the side of the wardrobe, he looked at her. He could spend hours watching her — indeed he already had.

He thought back to his time in the Den with Kenny. The time between holding the poor, defenceless animals in his grasp, and inflicting the first injury — it was the most exquisite time of all. Looking into their frightened eyes was a feeling like no other. He began to feel the same rush of excitement now, anticipating what was to come.

He'd taken down the blanket that was strung up across the window, which had kept the room bathed in darkness all night, snuffing out the moonlight, and masking the sunrise. But now he wanted light. Now he wanted to see the fear etched onto her face.

Fear was everything.

Kenny had taught him that.

Although he could sit and watch her for an eternity, he knew he didn't have long. The noise she'd made earlier had concerned him — hence the masking tape. Once she'd been alerted to his presence, she became quite vocal — and she was surprisingly strong for someone so petite. He rubbed the swelling on his chin where she'd kicked him. So far nobody had knocked on the door to enquire about the noise — hopefully the block was full of equally comatose students nursing hangovers.

Usually, he'd ended the lives of his victims by now: gaining their trust and then swiftly turning it to fear and horror. Usually, the production of the knife was enough to render them silent — then the wire around the throat soon choked out any desire to scream.

But he knew he'd need a different plan with Lily. The masking tape would do for now, and the cable ties would prevent her trying to escape. But to satisfy his desires, he needed to see the fear in her eyes, to hear the gasp in her throat as realisation dawned that her life was about to end.

It would take patience and exquisite timing; ripping off the masking tape just at the right time to hear her gasping for her final breath, but not so soon as to give her the force and energy to scream. A fraction of a second too early, or too late . . . he shook his head to rid himself of the thoughts. He didn't like to think of failure. Failure was not an option.

Reaching for the wire that lay by his side, he wrapped it around his hand and got to his feet.

* * *

Time: 8.30 a.m.
Date: Friday 27 September 2013
Location: Metropolitan Police HQ, London

Within minutes of getting Jack's message, DC Daniels hopped into the unmarked patrol car. Isabel's Café wasn't far, and he could easily walk — but there was no telling where the boss might send him next. The boy scout in him told Daniels to be prepared.

Pulling out of the rear car park, he headed south towards Horseferry Road. It didn't take long before he noticed there was trouble ahead. On what was usually a clear route, albeit busy during the morning and late afternoon rush hours, Daniels came to a halt behind a long line of stationary traffic.

Knowing Jack was waiting, Daniels threw the steering wheel hard right, and performed a perfectly executed U-turn. Several car horns blared in his direction, which he silenced with a flash of his warrant card and a cold stare. Knowing there was a side street not too far away, he pulled the patrol car across the waiting line of traffic. More angry car horns greeted him.

Cutting down a second side street, Daniels swung the car into a one-way street and was instantly confronted with another obstruction. His heart sank. Why was London so gridlocked on a Friday morning?

As he inched the car forwards, he noticed a group gathered in the middle of the street. His first thought was that it was a protest of some sort — the capital had seen several anti-capitalism protests in recent months — but try as he might, he couldn't see any of the usual placards or banners, or hear any of the associated chanting.

Two cars in front had managed to negotiate their way around the gathering, gesticulating out of their windows as they passed. Daniels intended to do the same — maybe minus the gesticulating — when he caught sight of a familiar face.

Arnie.

As his car crept forward, a number of raised voices floated towards him over the noise of the car engine. Things were getting heated. He watched as Arnie stumbled to the side, almost falling to his knees. Several members of the group started jeering, stepping towards the old man with raised hands; one started kicking Arnie's carrier bag across the street.

Without stopping to think, Daniels activated the dashboard blue lights and steered the unmarked patrol car towards the angry mob. Almost before the car came to a halt, he'd flung open the door and rushed out.

"Police!" he yelled, holding up his warrant card. "Move!"

Within seconds the youths, dressed in a uniform of jeans and dark hoodies, had turned on their scruffy heels and disappeared from sight. Daniels turned his attention back to his friend, who was trying to retrieve his worldly goods from the tarmac. "Jesus, Arnie, what happened?"

* * *

Time: 8.40 a.m.
Date: Friday 27 September 2013
Location: St James's House, Gold Street, London

The sight of the Stanley knife had the desired effect.

Fear.

He could see it now. He could *feel* it now. The air was so thick with it; you could almost touch it.

And it *had* been worth waiting for.

Lily's eyes widened so far he could see the whites etched with horror. Inside, he knew her heart would be thumping wildly. How he longed to feel it pulsating beneath his touch — and then, when the time finally came, to feel it reduced to nothing.

It was that part of the whole process that made him ache with pleasure. The time when life finally turned into death. When he could feel the last shuddering breath leave her body, her lungs deflated and stilled.

And then there would be silence.

Death might be quiet; but it was the most exquisite sound there was.

Then he would hear his own ragged breathing and his own heartbeat pounding — both reminding him that he was so very much alive.

Not that his father cared. As far as he was concerned, Jamie was very much already dead. They'd never been close, not like Justin. Justin had been the golden child, the favourite. Justin could do no wrong in their father's eyes — unlike Jamie; *the disappointment.*

And he knew why — it wasn't hard to figure out. He was the reason his mother had died. It was something that'd been drummed into him from the very moment he could comprehend the difference between life and death. His mother had died giving life to him. He had lived, she had died.

It was his fault.

When Justin died in the terrorist bombings, Jamie wondered if his father would finally reach out and accept him. But instead, Justin's death had only pushed his father further and further away from him.

He shut thoughts of Justin and his father out of his mind and turned his attention back to Lily. She was still cowering on the bed, pressed up against the wall, but there was nowhere to go — and he could see in her eyes that she already knew that. He'd bound her legs together at the ankles with strips of masking tape, but they would soon loosen, especially if she kept kicking. But what he had planned wouldn't take long.

He approached the bed and felt that all too familiar trickle of elation start to feed into his senses. He'd been right. She *was* perfect. The more she fought him, the more perfect she became. He placed one knee on the bed, testing the water. Lily didn't move.

"There, there. It'll all be over soon enough," he chuckled.

With one hand, he reached out to touch her leg, delighting in how Lily immediately flinched beneath his touch.

She was ready.

* * *

Time: 8.45 a.m.
Date: Friday 27 September 2013
Location: Balmoral Street, London

"You can't keep winding people up like that, Arnie. Not these days." DC Daniels led Arnie to the side of the road, picking up the remainder of his scattered belongings as he went. "You've no idea who they are, or what they're capable of. They could've been carrying knives."

"I know, I know." Arnie wiped the sleeve of his grubby jumper across his forehead, where a small cut was oozing blood. "I thought they were interested in the old Masons' building. They were hanging around outside." He nodded towards a nondescript terraced house behind them.

"Arnie, people like that aren't going to be interested in the history behind some old building, I can assure you." Daniels began slipping the rest of Arnie's belongings back inside his carrier bag. "Not everyone has your hunger for knowledge. You need to be careful."

"It's one of the oldest masonic lodges in the whole of England." Arnie dismissed the warning and continued with his history lesson. "Dates back to the eighteenth century. Survived the redevelopment of this part of the city and still stands to this day."

"And they weren't interested in that?" Daniels gave his friend a lop-sided smile. "Youth of today, huh? What can you do?" Passing him the carrier bag, Daniels led Arnie back towards the waiting car. "Come . . . I'll give you a lift somewhere."

Arnie dutifully followed, but he wasn't finished. "There were plenty of lodges around here, you know — that's why the street was named Masons' Lane. Of course, it's all gone now — everything cleared away and flattened. Rebuilt. All except that house." Arnie nodded back towards the terraced building that had caused all the commotion in the first place. "Changed all the street names around here, too, they did. This one was changed to Balmoral Street in 1925."

Daniels hesitated as he rounded the driver's side of the car and slowly turned back towards Arnie. "You're saying this street used to have a different name?"

Arnie nodded, clutching the carrier bag tightly to his chest. "They all did around here. Once an area is redeveloped, sometimes the street names change, too."

Daniels fumbled for his notebook, his heart hammering. Surely it wasn't as simple as that, was it? Hurriedly, he flicked the pages open then held the notebook up towards Arnie. "What about Dolphin Close, EC1?"

A smile crossed Arnie's chapped lips, his unruly beard beginning to quiver. "That would've been the Old King's Road — before the houses were knocked down after the war and rebuilt."

Old King's Road. Daniels felt his mouth turn dry. "And what about this one?" He flicked to a separate page in his notebook and again held it up towards Arnie. "Stevenson Street, SW1?"

"You're testing me there, detective," grinned Arnie, showing his broken teeth as he smiled. "That area was redeveloped not so long ago. Used to be called Queen Victoria Avenue — after Queen Victoria, obviously."

Old King's Road and Queen Victoria Avenue.

Daniels swallowed back his sense of elation. The Bishop's pattern was still there: they just couldn't see it. He flipped his notebook shut, stomach tightening. "Arnie, you're amazing. Hop in — I'll drop you wherever you need to be." He gestured towards the car.

"Well . . ." Arnie hovered by the passenger door, glancing up at the sky where a covering of thick, grey cloud was threatening rain. "I guess a lift wouldn't hurt — I was going to head down to the shelter to get a bit of a wash and a change of clothes."

Daniels nodded and herded Arnie into the front passenger seat. "No problem. It's not far."

"It's a long time since I've been inside a police car," commented Arnie, snapping his seatbelt into place, a grin stretching across his bearded face.

"Glad to hear it." Daniels jumped into the driver's seat and started the engine. He swung the car back out on to the road and mentally calculated his route. He shouldn't be too late for Jack, so long as he didn't run into any more obstacles.

"And that one was The Pawnbrokers."

Daniels frowned as he negotiated the junction ahead. "Sorry, what?"

"The Pawnbrokers," repeated Arnie, nodding at the post-it note stuck to the car's dashboard. "You've got Gold Street written there. Full of student housing I think now, but it used to be called The Pawnbrokers. It's not far from here."

Daniels' eyes flickered to the yellow post-it note he'd stuck to the dashboard after Isabel had rung back with further details on the girl she was worried about. He'd intended to give it to Jack at the café.

Arnie's eyes began to shine as he carried on. "That whole area had the highest number of pawnbrokers in London at one time. After the industrial revolution, pawnbrokers sprang up everywhere, but especially in that part of the city. Whole area was dubbed 'The Pawns' by the locals. They renamed it Gold Street when they pulled all the old tenements down — after the three golden balls you used to see outside a pawnbroker's shop."

Without warning, DC Daniels snapped on the blue lights and swerved violently across to the opposite side of the road.

"Sorry, Arnie. We need to make a detour."

CHAPTER THIRTY-THREE

Time: 9.00 a.m.
Date: Friday 27 September 2013
Location: St James's House, Gold Street, London

Daniels screeched to a halt at the entrance to Gold Street and shot a look at Arnie in the passenger seat. "The Pawnbrokers — you're sure?"

Arnie nodded, enthusiastically. "You couldn't move for pawnbroker shops all around here. This was the most famous street in the whole of London at one time."

With no more time for a history lesson, Daniels exited the car and quickly looked around. He'd called Jack on the way over and requested backup. It'd been a garbled conversation at best — he just hoped he'd got the message across.

But there were no sounds of sirens in the air, and no patrol cars within sight. The sick feeling in his stomach intensified. He couldn't have got this spectacularly wrong, could he? The girl was missing, and she lived in a street that once had a chess title in it. Apart from those two facts, his hunch was all he had to go on.

Daniels felt a faint prickle of fear at the back of his neck, and with one last glance behind him, decided he couldn't wait any longer. Throwing the rule book and most of his training out of the window, he jogged towards St James's House.

A student was coming out of the communal entrance and stared, wide-eyed, as Daniels thrust his warrant card inches from his nose.

"Is there another way into this block? A back entrance?"

The student shook his head and inched out on to the pavement. "N . . . no. Just this way in. And out."

"Room number 1a?" Daniels stood his ground, warrant card still visible.

"First door on the right. Ground floor."

Daniels gave a curt nod as the student scuttled away and pushed his way into the communal hallway. He detected the familiar mixed odours of takeaway food, cigarettes and stale alcohol. The first door on the right was shut tight. Daniels placed his ear to the wood but heard no sounds from within above the blood pulsating through his own head.

The door looked strong — and locked.

With nothing about his person other than his warrant card, which wasn't going to get him through the thick wooden door anytime soon, Daniels retraced his steps back to the pavement outside. Arnie had followed him from the car and was standing by the ground floor window of number 1a, an oversized hunk of concrete in his hand and a wide grin plastered across his face.

* * *

Time: 9.00 a.m.
Date: Friday 27 September 2013
Location: St James's House, Gold Street, London

Jamie moved silently up the length of the bed, his eyes firmly fixed on Lily McArthur's increasingly pale face. She'd ceased kicking now and merely watched his approach with wide, staring eyes.

Fear paralysed them all in the end. And it was the moment he enjoyed the most. The complete and unadulterated fear that he could inflict on someone by his mere presence. He'd stood by her side for a full fifteen minutes, saying nothing, merely staring at her — enjoying the terror that multiplied with every passing second.

There'd been some shuffling noises from the communal corridor outside, and the sound of the front door opening. He'd paused for a while, listening, but was satisfied it was nothing more than students going about their day. So, he'd turned his attention back to Lily. With her hands still tied behind her back, and her legs bound at the ankles, she remained motionless on the bed.

Gripping the thin wire in one hand, he grabbed hold of Lily's upper arm and twisted her face down on to the bed. A muffled moan escaped her lips, quickly absorbed by the masking tape. He yanked her head back by grabbing hold of her hair and slipped the wire around her neck, pulling it tight.

But not too tight — not yet. Otherwise, it would be over too soon.

He slowly twisted the wire to increase the force, hearing a faint gurgle from Lily's throat. An adrenaline-fuelled shiver of excitement flooded his body. Lily's eyes bulged as she turned her head to the side, her lungs desperately screaming for air that was not forthcoming. Her limbs began to twitch, and it wasn't long before her chest heaved and her eyes flickered and lost focus.

Jamie held the wire steady and reached for the Stanley knife.

The sound of the concrete crashing through the window startled him. Whipping his head around towards the noise, he narrowly missed being struck by the hurled breeze block that crashed into the side of the wardrobe. His grip on the ligature tightened as he turned to protect himself from the splintering glass raining down on the bed.

The next thing he saw was a shadow hurtling through the open window. Jamie abandoned his grip on Lily McArthur and she fell, limply, back on to the bed — face down on the duvet, with no signs of life.

DC Daniels landed in a heap on the floor, the force of the impact winding him and squeezing the air from his lungs. Within seconds, Jamie was straddling the prone detective, pinning him to the floor. Daniels tried to wrestle himself free, but his captor was too strong and easily subdued his efforts. With one hand, Jamie pinned Daniels' arms beneath him, and in the other he brandished the blade of the Stanley knife.

It would have to be quick, and not necessarily clean. He'd have no time to enjoy the thrill this time.

Jamie considered the quickest and easiest place to inflict most damage would be the neck — one well-placed slice and it would all be over. He brought the knife close to Daniels' skin, continuing to press down to keep the man still. The first cut didn't go as deep as he'd wanted, as the detective began to kick out with renewed strength and managed to dislodge the blade.

Jamie repositioned his weight and sliced him again.

* * *

Time: 9.00 a.m.
Date: Friday 27 September 2013
Location: St James's House, Gold Street, London

DS Cooper yanked the wheel hard to the right and careered across the carriageway. The number 27 bus braked sharply and the driver could be seen gesticulating madly through the windscreen as the unmarked police car turned almost on two wheels into Gold Street. The street was deserted, except for DC Daniels' car which was sitting abandoned with its doors wide open not far from the junction with the main road.

"Stop here," barked Jack, already flinging open the passenger door and jumping out. He ran past Daniels' empty car and headed towards the end of the street, Cooper following in his wake. As he neared the entrance to St James's House, all he saw was a shabby looking old man clutching a battered carrier bag to his chest, hovering next to a shattered window.

Cooper caught up with Jack and instantly recognised him.

"Arnie? What's happened?"

Arnie gestured towards the broken window, now merely a gaping hole with lethal splintered pieces of glass around the edges. "In there," he shouted, his eyes wide. "He's gone in there!"

"Find out where the goddamn backup is, Cooper," yelled Jack, shrugging out of his jacket and facing the window. "And stand well back." Before he could talk himself out of it, Jack took a run up and leapt through the jagged glass.

Landing almost directly on top of Jamie and DC Daniels, Jack first collided with the corner of a cheaply made wooden desk. Briefly winded, he took a split second to assess the scene. There was a young girl lying face down on the bed, but his main concern was Daniels who was lying trapped beneath someone Jack could only guess was Jamie Rivers.

The Bishop.

In the same split second, he noticed the gleam from the blade of the Stanley knife and then the blood. As if powered by slow motion, Jack heaved himself to his feet, noticing for the first time that both his arms were streaked with blood. His own blood. Ignoring the pain, he grabbed hold of the nearest thing to a weapon he could find.

He flung the breeze block at the back of Jamie Rivers' head, satisfied to hear the crack of concrete on bone. Jamie instantly slumped to the side to reveal Daniels' body beneath — the front of the detective's shirt already saturated with blood. Jack grabbed a discarded T-shirt from a pile of clothes by the bed and immediately pressed down hard on the gaping wound to his colleague's neck. More blood was seeping from a wound on his abdomen.

"I need an ambulance," he yelled over his shoulder, towards the shattered window. "And I need it now!"

CHAPTER THIRTY-FOUR

Time: 12.15 p.m.
Date: Friday 27 September 2013
Location: St James's Hospital Accident & Emergency Department, London

Nurse Tina stepped out of cubicle number seven, discarding her gloves in a nearby bin. "Is he always like that?" She flashed a look at DS Cooper who was leaning up against the nurse's station. "He needs to stay still. If he keeps on moving, he'll burst his stitches."

Cooper stifled a grin behind a plastic cup of weak tea. "I'll make sure I tell him."

The nurse pursed her lips and strode off along the corridor to attend to her next patient, calling back over her shoulder. "He needs to wait for his TTOs. And remain on the trolley until he's discharged."

Cooper took the opportunity to poke his head in-between the plastic curtains that shrouded the cubicle. "You being an awkward patient, boss?"

Jack was lying back on a hospital trolley, his head propped up by several pillows. Both of his forearms were heavily bandaged, his left temple sporting several steri-strips.

"I'm taking up a bed when I don't need one," he grimaced, wincing as he changed position.

"Technically, it's a trolley not a bed, boss." Cooper stepped into the cubicle and pulled the curtains closed behind him. "Anyhow, they said you can be discharged as soon as your medication's sorted. So long as you take it easy at home."

After hurtling through the window and landing in a heap on the bedside desk, Jack's forearms had both suffered deep gashes from the shattered glass. An X-ray confirmed there were no glass fragments in the open wounds themselves, so it was a quick shot of local anaesthetic and Nurse Tina had been more than willing to stitch him back together. His head had a minor laceration from headbutting the corner of the desk, and his abdomen would soon be sporting some spectacular bruising.

"Any news on Daniels?"

Before Cooper could respond, the curtains were pulled open once more and Chief Superintendent King's head appeared. His normally jovial face bore a decidedly grave expression.

"Good to hear you're on the mend, Jack."

"Any word on Daniels?" repeated Jack.

The chief superintendent shook his head sombrely. "Not yet. Still in theatre, so they tell me."

Nobody said anything for a moment or two. Jack's eyes clouded over as he replayed the scenes from Lily's bedsit once again. He felt himself shudder beneath the thin hospital blanket. He'd seen some pretty horrific scenes in his police career, but nothing quite like that. "And the girl? Lily?"

When the ambulance crew had arrived, they bundled Lily straight into the back of the first ambulance, performing CPR along the way. The vision of them pumping her chest as they wheeled her out of the bedsit would stay with Jack for some time to come.

"She's alive," confirmed the chief superintendent. "They restarted her heart and she's up in intensive care as a precaution." He paused, letting his eyes rest on Jack's. "You saved her life, Jack. You and your team saved that girl's life."

Nobody asked about Jamie Rivers. Nobody cared — not when one of their own was critically ill and fighting for his life in surgery.

"It was Daniels, sir. He was the one that put it all together." Jack swung his legs around and sat on the edge of the trolley. "Lily owes her life to him."

"And he owes *his* life to *you*, Jack." Chief Superintendent King watched as Jack gingerly got to his feet. "Don't forget that."

"Only if he survives," muttered Jack, reaching for his wallet and keys that were on the side.

"Should you be getting up, boss?" Cooper flicked the curtains to one side to see if Nurse Tina was in the vicinity. "You're supposed to be on bed rest."

Jack waved Cooper's comment away. "I can't lie around here doing nothing, Cooper. I'm going up to wait for news on Daniels."

The chief superintendent moved back, allowing Jack to step out of the cubicle, patting him on the shoulder as he passed. "Good work, Jack. Good work."

Jack headed towards a set of stairs which he assumed led up into the main hospital. His head was banging and he felt groggy — a mixture of the bang to the head as he collided with Lily's desk, and the concoction of painkillers foisted on him in A&E. He wasn't convinced the drugs were doing much for the pain: he could still feel the wounds on his forearms throbbing underneath the bandages.

As he reached the stairs, he noticed an old man sitting on a plastic chair next to a bank of vending machines. Notwithstanding his fuzzy head, Jack instantly recognised him. During the ride over in the ambulance, Arnold Miller had told him all about Daniels and the role they'd both played in the apprehension of the Bishop.

Jack stood in front of the old man, waiting for him to raise his gaze from the floor. He hadn't had a chance to have a proper look at him before, with the events unfolding so quickly, but he now saw the man seemed to be wearing every item of clothing he possessed, one layer on top of another, topped off with a frayed donkey jacket. On his feet he wore a pair of dusty work boots, the sole of one flapping loose. His white hair was unkempt and in need of a cut — his face covered in a rough looking beard.

But as Arnie raised his gaze, Jack saw brilliant blue eyes shining back at him, full of warmth and compassion as deep as the ocean.

"You must be Arnie," said Jack, taking a seat on another plastic chair. "Cooper's told me all about you."

The old man nodded, slowly, his hands folded in his lap. Jack noticed that his fingernails had been bitten to the quick, but were scrubbed clean. "Is Mr Trevor all right?" he asked, his voice quivering around the edges. "He looked in a bad way."

"He's in surgery," replied Jack.

"And the girl?" Arnie's blue eyes began to water.

Jack nodded and gave Arnie a smile. "She's doing well, by all accounts."

Arnie lowered his eyes back down to his lap. "I'll just wait here, then — until I know Mr Trevor is all right." The old man paused. "He's a good sort, Mr Trevor. Always looked out for me on the streets, he did. Got a heart of gold."

Jack gave another nod. "You helped solve the case and save that poor girl's life, too, you know. We owe you."

Arnie shook off the compliment. "I just hope he's gonna be OK."

Jack got to his feet and patted the old man on the shoulder. "You just let us know if there's anything you need. And I mean anything. As I say, we owe you."

Arnie glanced up as Jack turned to leave, his bright eyes shining. "Well, you couldn't stretch to a cup of tea, could you?" His eyes flickered to the vending machines.

Jack gave a small laugh, and fed the machine a succession of coins until it spat out a scalding hot cup of tea. As well as passing the cup to Arnie, Jack fished around in his trouser pocket and pulled out a series of notes. Handing him three ten-pound notes, Jack smiled. "Go get yourself something hot to eat."

* * *

Time: 2.25 p.m.
Date: Friday 27 September 2013
Location: St James's Hospital Intensive Care Unit, London

Jack peered through the glass of the Intensive Care Unit at Lily McArthur's bed space. He could see a nurse attending to her, then writing in her hospital charts, documenting her observations. Jack hadn't wanted to get in the way, so had remained outside by the window. It was a large ITU department, with eighteen bed spaces and several side rooms, but there was an air of tranquility about the place — in sharp contrast to the hustle, bustle and noise of the A&E department directly beneath them.

Lily was doing well and was now conscious. They'd briefly intubated her in the back of the ambulance, but she was now breathing for herself. Initial examinations reported little physical injury except for a nasty compression wound around her neck. Her heart had briefly stopped beating after the attack, but the emergency crew had started CPR almost immediately and managed to bring her back. A CT scan was being organised to look for any signs of damage to the brain from the brief interruption of oxygen, but all the signs were looking positive and the doctors were happy with her current condition.

Willie and Margaret McArthur were getting the next flight down to London, having had a brief yet emotional conversation with Jack several hours ago.

Jack turned his attention to the bed space closest to the window. It was empty and in the process of being cleaned ready for the next inhabitant, which was more than likely going to be DC Trevor Daniels. Jack's stomach churned and a wave of nausea rose up from within. His head still hurt and his forearms throbbed.

He intended to wait until Daniels came back from theatre — he couldn't possibly go home until he knew that the young detective was going to pull through. Cooper had followed Jack upstairs and was heading in his direction, armed with two coffees from a vending machine by the entrance to the unit. They were an unappetising wishy-washy colour, but Jack didn't care and immediately took a gulp. It was hot, and the heat blocked out the pain.

"You looked in on our suspect?" Cooper nodded towards one of the side rooms in the corridor. Side room one had two uniformed officers standing guard outside.

Jack shook his head and grimaced. "No. And I don't intend to. He's not going anywhere."

Jamie Rivers had been admitted to the Intensive Care Unit at almost the same time as his victim, suffering from a severe head trauma caused by the concrete breeze block Jack had flung at him. An initial trauma CT in the A&E department had confirmed a fractured skull and associated brain haemorrhage. He was unconscious and had been placed on a ventilator.

Jack knew there'd be an enquiry, and if Jamie Rivers died then by all accounts it could get quite messy — but he wasn't in the slightest bit concerned. Given the same situation, he wouldn't hesitate to act in the same way again.

Jack took another sip of the scalding hot coffee. "I guess one of us should go and see Martin Rivers before this gets splashed all over the front pages tomorrow."

Cooper nodded "Amanda's already volunteered — I think she's got a soft spot for him."

"OK." Jack glanced towards the side room. "Once Rivers regains consciousness, we'll come back and formally arrest him. Get the ball rolling."

Just then, the swing doors that led to the emergency theatres swung open and a hospital bed surrounded by all manner of equipment rushed past. Jack dropped his half-drunk coffee into a nearby bin and followed the procession into the Intensive Care Unit. DC Trevor Daniels looked deathly pale as he was quickly hooked up to his bedside monitors.

Jack caught the eye of one of the surgeons who'd accompanied the bed from theatre. "How's he doing?"

"Jeremy Coulson, Consultant General Surgeon." A tall, lean-framed man in surgical scrubs leaned forward with a hand outstretched.

"DI Jack MacIntosh," responded Jack, taking hold of the proffered hand and glancing back at Daniels. "He's one of my team. How is he?"

The surgeon pulled the cloth cap from his head and wiped his brow. "Mr Daniels has had a rough time in theatre, I won't lie. The neck wound didn't turn out to be so bad — it missed the carotid artery by a centimetre or so — so we repaired that pretty easily. But he also had a penetrating wound to the side of the abdomen. It lacerated his spleen and caused a huge amount of internal bleeding. We've removed the spleen, and repaired two small lacerations to the liver." Coulson paused. "He's lost a lot of blood and his body could go into shock. The next twenty-four hours will be critical."

* * *

Time: 4.15 p.m.
Date: Friday 27 September 2013
Location: 7 Cross Keys Road, Camden Town, London

DS Cassidy drew up once again outside number seven, wiping her eyes and checking her face in the rear view mirror. Jack and Trevor's brush with death had shaken her. The text she received from Jack assured her that he was fine — just a few stitches — but she noted he couldn't be quite so reassuring about Trevor.

With her eyes still a little red-rimmed, she stepped out of the car and made her way up the short garden path. Once again, all the curtains were closed and nothing appeared to be moving inside. As she held up her hand to rap on the front door, she hesitated. The early morning newspaper was still poking out of the letterbox, and two pints of milk were sitting on the doorstep.

Frowning, Cassidy gave the door a sharp knock. She didn't expect to see Martin Rivers' shuffling figure immediately, so she stepped backwards on the porch and glanced at the upstairs windows. He wouldn't still be in bed, surely? More likely he was sitting in his armchair in the front room, staring into space, surrounded by his memories. She glanced at her watch and stepped forward to rap on the front door once again, a little harder this time.

After another minute or so, she peered in through the front window. Thick curtains shielded her view and all she saw was her own blotchy face reflected back. Returning to the porch, her concern mounted and her frown deepened. Martin Rivers never left the house, as far as she could tell. He was unlikely to have just popped out to the shops, or gone for a walk. He would still be inside — somewhere.

Unease started to creep in. Wondering if there was a back door, she followed the narrow garden path around the side of the house towards the rear garden. If you could call it a garden. There was a small patch of lawn in the centre, which had been overrun by every weed known to man, and thick, overgrown bushes full of thorns flanked the sides. A small, square patch of slimy green patio slabs sat in the shade of the rear of the house and the entrance to what Cassidy presumed was the kitchen.

The wooden back door was in need of repair: its edges warped by the weather, its paintwork peeling. A rusty barbeque sat forlornly in the corner, next to an overflowing metal dustbin. Cassidy wrinkled her nose. It didn't look like anyone had stepped out here for a long time.

She approached the back door and tried the handle, surprised to feel it give beneath her touch. With a firm push, it opened into a darkened kitchen and Cassidy's nose once again twitched at the faint smell of rotting food. There was a pile of plates next to the sink, caked in leftovers; empty tins and cartons sat on every available surface, waiting to make their way outside to be disposed of. A couple of flies buzzed around the scraps.

Cassidy moved out of the kitchen towards the front room, expecting Martin Rivers to be sitting in his usual armchair, staring emptily into nothingness. Why he hadn't heard her knocking, or her entrance through the back door, she couldn't understand.

Unless he was asleep.

Or . . .

A trickle of unease dripped into her veins as she made her way towards the door that led into the front room, pushing it open and stepping cautiously inside.

Martin Rivers was, indeed, sitting in his usual armchair, and to the untrained eye he appeared to be asleep.

But DS Cassidy knew better.

Sighing, she stepped across the faded Axminster carpet, her heart thumping painfully inside her chest. She could see the empty pill bottles littering the small coffee table next to yesterday's paper.

No, Martin, please no.

One simple touch of his hand confirmed her fears.

Martin Rivers was dead.

CHAPTER THIRTY-FIVE

Time: 10.15 a.m.
Date: Saturday 28 September 2013
Location: Kettle's Yard Mews, London

Jack hadn't slept beyond ten o'clock for as long as he could remember. The knock-out painkillers he'd been given when he was finally discharged from A&E had certainly done the trick. That and the not so small helping of Glenfiddich.

He yawned and padded through to the living room, heading towards the kitchen and the kettle. He'd been signed off work for seven days and instructed by the chief superintendent, in no uncertain terms, not to set foot inside the station or visit the hospital during that time. Jack gave the impression he'd heard and understood — but he knew, as well as everybody else, that as soon as Jamie Rivers regained consciousness he'd be there to arrest him. Sick leave or no sick leave.

But time was on their side, for once. The man they believed to be the Bishop currently remained in a deep coma in the Intensive Care Unit.

There was no possibility of regaining consciousness for Martin Rivers. A suspected overdose of both prescription and non-prescription drugs had ended his life sometime during Thursday evening. A post-mortem would be carried out in due course, but Jack wasn't expecting any notion of foul play. The grim discovery had upset DS Cassidy, but it hadn't been altogether unexpected.

On each of their visits to the Rivers' house, she'd remarked how desolate and devoid of life Martin Rivers had appeared; the weight of grief burdening his ever-shrinking shoulders.

'At least he didn't get to hear about Jamie,' she'd commented to Jack, when they'd spoken over the phone the previous evening. 'That would've crushed him.'

Jack had agreed but, in his heart of hearts, he wondered whether Martin Rivers had already known. There'd been something about the man's eyes — beneath all the pain and suffering, there was a hint of resignation and the possible realisation that his sole surviving child was a killer. And, that being so, he'd decided to end his own suffering.

And who could blame him, thought Jack, as he sloshed the last of the milk into his mug. Slumping down on to the sofa, he nursed the hot coffee in his lap and contemplated the day ahead. His forearms still ached, but the pain was subsiding now. He was meant to go to the local minor injuries unit for a dressing change later, which was shaping up to be the highlight of his day.

One upside of being signed off and banished from the station was that he couldn't take part in the postponed press conference which was due later this morning. Every cloud, he mused, taking a sip of his coffee and closing his eyes. As he sat back and contemplated how to fill the rest of his day, his mobile phone began to ring.

Prising open an eye, Jack frowned and reached across to the coffee table, scooping up the ringing phone.

It wasn't a number that he recognised.

"Hello?"

There was a brief delay at the other end, and Jack contemplated hitting the 'end' button, convinced it was one of those irritating recorded messages enquiring about his latest car accident, or whether he had the correct life insurance. But then a voice spoke — a voice that was all too familiar.

"Hello, Inspector. I think you've been waiting for my call."

* * *

Time: 11.30 a.m.
Date: Saturday 28 September 2013
Location: New Green Psychiatric Unit, Epping, Essex

He'd seen the news that morning — it was impossible to get away from. Every newspaper from broadsheet to tabloid had it emblazoned across the front page.

The Bishop had been caught.

Vince felt a mixture of disappointment and intrigue at the news. Disappointed that his work with Jamie would now be at an end, but intrigued as to how, finally, he'd been captured.

Jamie had been a good student, as Vince had always known he would be. Their days spent alone in their childhood den had not been wasted. He folded the newspaper that had arrived with his breakfast that morning and placed it to one side. With Jamie's reign of terror now over, Vince strongly doubted he'd be able to contact his protégé again.

There wouldn't be much point, anyway. There was nothing he could do for Jamie now. If he was lucky, he'd end up somewhere like this. Vince looked around at his environment. Somewhere safe and secure: *protected*. If he wasn't so lucky . . . Vince felt a shudder ripple through him. Prisons could be dangerous places for people like Jamie. He would need to be strong and have his wits about him.

But Jamie Rivers was no longer his concern.

Vince had known, as soon as the detectives had ransacked his room and taken away his treasured correspondence with Jamie, that the hunt for the Bishop would soon be over. And now that it was, he felt strangely calm.

He flexed his fingers and a cruel smile crept across his thin lips. Jamie who? He laughed a little to himself and reached for that morning's post. The bundle of letters was tied up with a thick rubber band, which Vince quickly snapped off to release the contents.

He felt a chill of renewed excitement wash over him as he flicked through the envelopes, some feeling thicker than others. He knew he was fortunate — Dr Erskine afforded him certain special privileges: uncensored mail, for one. She understood him, she knew what made him tick. If Vince didn't know better, he thought Dr Erskine harboured a perverse attraction towards the unit's most infamous patient.

Pushing that thought from his mind, he let his eyes rake, hungrily, over the envelopes.

Someone in here could be his next friend.

His next puppet to take over from the Bishop.

His next protégé.

* * *

Time: 6.30 p.m.
Date: Saturday 28 September 2013
Location: Kettle's Yard Mews, London

His arms were throbbing again — reminding him he needed another dose of painkillers. The practice nurse at the Minor Injuries Unit had redressed his wounds, but hadn't been too gentle about it.

Jack knocked back another couple of tablets with the remainder of his cold coffee.

As well as a trip to get his bandages reapplied, he'd slipped into the station and retrieved the police accident report into the Faraday's car crash. No one saw him — at least, those that did kept out of his way — and he was in and out within a few minutes. Certainly not long enough for the chief superintendent to be alerted as to his presence. He then spent the afternoon reading, then rereading, the contents — with the assistance of Google Translate.

A brief conversation with Geraint Jones in Surrey had cemented the suspicion in both their minds — Joseph Geraghty was up to his neck in it. Which led Jack back full circle to the phone call earlier that morning.

He hadn't mentioned it to DI Jones. He didn't want to pull the unsuspecting detective into whatever quagmire he was already knee deep in — and rapidly sinking further. He also resisted the temptation to call Rob Carmichael — he'd already bent the rule book on Jack's behalf.

No: if he was going to do this, then he was doing it alone.

Geraghty's instructions in the phone call had been specific — even to the exact time Jack needed to leave. And the exact items of clothing he needed to wear.

Jack glanced at his watch.

He had thirty minutes. Thirty minutes to change his mind. Thirty minutes to come to his senses.

But the lure of finally locating James Quinn was too strong, so he ignored the warning signs that raged inside his head and sat in semi-darkness, waiting for the minutes to tick by. He knew he was stepping into the unknown, into danger, even — almost certainly breaching any number of police procedures and risking his career to boot.

The man was a killer.

So, what was he doing?

A simple phone call was all it would take and they'd have Geraghty behind bars.

One simple phone call.

But that simple phone call would also close the door on finding James Quinn once and for all. Geraghty had made that crystal clear. Do as he said, and Quinn's current location would be disclosed.

So Jack would follow the instructions.

Just as Geraghty knew he would.

CHAPTER THIRTY-SIX

Time: 7.15 p.m.
Date: Saturday 28 September 2013
Location: The Glade, Church Street, Albury, Surrey

The evening was cool but still pleasant enough out on the patio with the heaters on. Joseph Geraghty's eyes flickered towards his watch for the umpteenth time.

MacIntosh should have left by now.

The final part of the plan would be in motion.

Bypassing the vodka bottle on the patio's wicker table, Geraghty reached for a freshly poured glass of water instead. Tonight he needed to keep a clear head.

Everything was in place; he'd checked numerous times. But he knew he would check again. *Nothing* could go wrong.

He let his gaze rest on the handgun he'd placed next to the vodka bottle. Checking once more that the gun was fully loaded, a smile crossed his lips.

All set.

All he needed now was Jack MacIntosh.

* * *

Time: 8.45 p.m.
Date: Saturday 28 September 2013
Location: The Glade, Church Street, Albury, Surrey

Jack pulled up outside The Glade and switched the engine off. He'd done as instructed, avoiding the main roads as far as possible.

Geraghty had been quite clear on that.

The hire car had tinted windows, and Jack had dutifully worn the baseball cap tugged down low over his eyes. But probably the most alarming instruction, and one that Jack knew he should have questioned at the time, was the wearing of gloves and covering the seats in plastic sheeting before setting out.

And leaving his mobile phone at home.

He sidelined the creeping disquiet that had intensified throughout the ninety-minute journey. Finding James Quinn was more important. How Joseph Geraghty knew of Quinn's whereabouts, he wasn't quite sure — but Jack had long ago stopped trying to second-guess men like Geraghty.

He had never visited Isabel's childhood home, although he'd seen it in photographs. The house was set back from the small, single-track lane and nestled in among mature trees and gardens. A gravelled garden path led up to a wooden front door beneath a shady front porch. On all sides, the house was concealed behind tall, leylandii hedges.

Perfect for hiding behind, mused Jack, as he left the hire car parked by the gate and made his way up the garden path. As he approached, he could see the front door was already open. Hesitating only momentarily, Jack pushed it wider and stepped inside the dimly lit entrance hall.

About to announce his arrival, Jack noticed a movement up ahead. A connecting door swung open and the doorway filled with the imposing presence of Joseph Geraghty.

"Detective Inspector." Geraghty took several steps forward and came into view. He looked pretty much as Jack remembered him — perhaps a little thinner in the face. His hair was light, with flecks of grey — but whether that was his natural colour, who could tell? The man changed his appearance as often as others changed their socks.

What hadn't changed, however, was the intensity of his piercing gaze. His eyes were coloured green this time, from what Jack suspected were tinted contact lenses. His true eye colour was anyone's guess.

As Geraghty continued towards Jack, he noticed there were lines around his eyes that hadn't been there before. The man's cheeks looked a little sunken, his skin tone looking pale even in the dimness of the hallway.

If Jack didn't know any better, Joseph Geraghty looked unwell.

"Do come in." Geraghty waved Jack into the house, gesturing towards a connecting door to the right. "I'll get us some refreshments."

Geraghty led the way into a light and airy living room. It was sparsely furnished, with just one three-seater sofa and one armchair surrounding a low-level glass-topped coffee table. The room opened out on to a generously sized patio area, where Jack could see pieces of wicker furniture and a brick-built barbeque. The patio doors were open and a cool evening breeze was wafting in from the garden.

Jack removed his baseball cap and felt a thin line of sweat sticking to the inside of his collar. The drive down had been warm and sticky, with no air conditioning in the car and the strict instruction not to open any of the tinted windows. Geraghty had already brought through a tea tray laden with a china teapot and two cups with saucers.

"Tea, Inspector?" Geraghty picked up the teapot and Jack noticed a slight tremble in the man's hand. "Or do you require something a little stronger?"

Jack accepted the cup of tea that he didn't really want, and went to sit on the edge of the sofa. His arms were beginning to throb once more beneath the freshly applied bandages.

"Let's sit outside." Geraghty headed towards the patio doors. "It seems a shame to waste such a beautiful evening."

Jack frowned a little but followed him out into the darkness that was now enveloping the garden. The motion-sensitive outdoor lights sprang into action as Geraghty settled into one of the wicker chairs. It was at that moment that Jack could clearly see the waxen appearance of Geraghty's skin.

As if in response to the question that hadn't yet been asked, Geraghty raised his gaze to meet Jack's.

"I'm dying, Inspector."

Jack's tea cup hovered in front of his mouth. "I'm sorry to hear that."

Geraghty gave a small laugh. "I don't think we need to pretend. I've been a thorn in your side for far too long for any false pleasantries. You're probably thinking, and not without foundation, that karma has finally caught up with me."

Jack sipped the lukewarm, weak tea and took a seat in one of the other wicker chairs.

"Pancreatic cancer," continued Geraghty. "Stage four. It's inoperable. Already spread to my lungs, liver and bones — so it's only a matter of time now."

Jack placed his tea cup on to the wicker table and looked across at Geraghty's pale face. "I don't understand why I'm here. You said you had information on James Quinn."

Geraghty nodded. "And indeed I do, Inspector. But all in good time. Before I impart to you my knowledge about the elusive Mr Quinn, I need you to understand something. Something about this house. And something about Isabel."

Hearing Isabel's name spoken by the man who'd caused her such grief made Jack's neck prickle. "Why bring her into this? She has nothing to do with Quinn. Haven't you caused her enough heartache already? I have grounds to arrest you right here, right now."

"I know you do, Inspector." Geraghty paused and took a sip of his tea. "And if that's the course of action you wish to take, I'll not stand in your way. But . . ." Geraghty's pale green eyes hardened slightly in the muted light. "I will then take my knowledge of James Quinn with me to the grave."

Jack gave a slow nod. He knew he was breaking all the rules by merely being here, but something told him he needed to hear what the man had to say. He could always arrest the man afterwards, couldn't he?

"As I said, I'm dying. There's no escaping that fact. My diagnosis was made in Cuba last year — a doctor friend of mine gave me the good news. The paperwork will never see the light of day, so my disease is only known to myself and my doctor. And now you." Geraghty paused. "I took out a life insurance policy a few months ago — but it won't pay out if there is any suggestion I didn't disclose the full extent of my diagnosis — which of course I made no mention of when I applied."

Jack's frown increased. "I still don't . . ."

Geraghty held up a hand. "As I said, Inspector, let me explain. The life insurance has one beneficiary — Isabel Faraday. And in my will, everything I own goes to her. Including this house." Geraghty paused. "And, indeed, her parents' trust fund money that I misappropriated."

"Don't you mean stole?"

Geraghty let the comment slide. "Upon my death, everything will go to her. I made a promise to her parents and I intend to keep it."

"You've got very strange loyalties." Jack watched for Geraghty's reaction. "You killed them. I've seen the accident report — you were there."

"I've done many things I'm not proud of, Inspector. But I never wanted to hurt Isabel. I've always tried to protect her."

"Is that why you've been stalking her?"

"Stalking is a harsh way of putting it."

"You've been watching her at the café."

Geraghty took another sip of his tea. "I needed to see what had become of her. How she'd fared in adult life. I can see she's grown into a remarkable young woman, with a thriving business. She deserves to have everything returned to her."

"Look, where are we going with all this?" A tinge of irritation entered Jack's voice. "I came here because you said you had information on James Quinn."

Geraghty nodded. "And I do, but bear with me a few more minutes. As I say, cancer is consuming my body. It's eating away at me every single day. I don't know precisely how much time I have left, but I know it's not long. And, let's just say, it's not the way I wish to die."

It was then that Jack spied the gun hidden behind the vodka bottle on the wicker table. "So, you want to kill yourself?" Jack shrugged. "I don't see why you need my help."

"Oh, but I do need your help, Inspector." Geraghty reached into his pocket and brought out a folded piece of paper which he passed across the wicker table. "My insurance policy."

Jack took the document and unfolded it. He nodded as he scanned the details. "And this is the name you're going under now, is it? Roger Bancroft?"

Geraghty managed a thin smile. "Yes. I'm a retired banker."

Jack scanned the rest of the policy and nodded. "Isabel is your sole beneficiary in the event of your death. You already said that."

"Indeed, but look at the clauses at the bottom — the exclusions."

Jack's eyes scrolled to the bottom of the paper.

"You'll note how the policy is void if I die by my own hand. Suicide."

Jack began to nod.

"I cannot die from cancer, Inspector. Although I've covered my tracks as best I can with regard to my diagnosis, it's a risk I cannot afford to take. And I cannot die by suicide. The policy will be null and void either way."

Jack's gaze flicked towards the handgun. "You're not asking me . . . ?" Geraghty gave another small laugh. "No, no — nothing quite so abhorrent, Inspector. Although I'm sure there's a small part of you that might relish the thought of pulling that trigger. No — I need you to do something else for me. For Isabel." Geraghty paused. "I need you to stage a murder."

CHAPTER THIRTY-SEVEN

Time: 9.15 p.m.
Date: Saturday 28 September 2013
Location: The Glade, Church Street, Albury, Surrey

The sun had long ago sunk below the tree line at the rear of The Glade and the evening air had taken on a decisive chill. But the drop in temperature didn't account for the ice-cold ripple of fear seeping through Jack's veins.

"You can't be serious?"

Geraghty pushed himself up out of his wicker chair. "Indeed I am, Inspector. Deadly serious. And I've thought it all through, every aspect. Come."

Geraghty motioned for Jack to follow him back inside the house, leading him through into the spacious kitchen accessed through an archway from the living room. The gangland leader halted just inside the doorway and turned.

"That's far enough, Inspector. It's best you don't come any further. I don't want you to contaminate the scene."

Jack stopped, looking past Geraghty into the country-style kitchen. It was huge: almost the size of his entire flat. In the centre was a large family dining table set with two dinner plates, knives, forks and spoons. A jug of water sat in the centre, plus three empty pint glasses. The plates themselves were decorated with half-eaten food.

Jack felt another frown deepen his brow.

"I've taken the liberty to set the scene for my own murder, Inspector."

Jack remained silent, his mouth dry.

"The pint glasses on the table will have fingerprints and DNA belonging to our friend Mr Quinn. As will the handkerchief at the side of his plate." Geraghty paused and picked up a small, pocket-sized diary from the kitchen work top. He flicked through to today's date and held the page up in front of Jack's confused gaze. "See? James Quinn was due to come here for dinner this evening. I took the liberty of writing it in my diary — I can be so forgetful, you see."

"How . . . ?" Jack stopped. He wasn't sure he wanted to know.

"Oh, it was really quite simple in the end."

* * *

Time: 7.25 p.m.
Date: Wednesday 25 September 2013
Location: The Baker's Arms, Albury, Surrey

The pub was filling up, which suited Joseph Geraghty just fine. More people meant more witnesses. His first glass of vodka had gone down extremely well, but he now resisted the temptation and opted instead for chilled water. He needed to keep a clear head. To the uninitiated, they looked the same.

Geraghty carried the drinks over to the small table by the window, nodding at several regulars that he recognised from his previous visits. As the new resident at The Glade, Geraghty had been keen to get his face noticed among the locals, so had popped into the pub several times over the preceding weeks. It was all part of his plan.

Roger Bancroft was settling down well into village life.

James Quinn repulsed him more and more as each laborious minute ticked by. Not blessed with even a moderate amount of intelligence, Geraghty found him both boorish and uncivilised. It was a struggle at times to keep the conversation heading in the direction he needed, but he persevered. The end result would be worth it.

"Tell me more about the job," slurred Quinn, draining the final dregs from his fourth pint and accepting the fresh one Geraghty handed to him. "How much space do I need? I have lock-ups all over London."

Geraghty settled back down at the table and sipped his ice-cold water. "It's high value — but won't take up a lot of space. Mostly jewellery. Some cash. My clients are targeting safety deposit boxes in one of the capital's leading banks."

"A bank job?" James Quinn's eyebrows shot up. "That's high-end stuff."

"Indeed," conceded Geraghty, plastering yet another fake smile on to his face. "For which you will be more than generously compensated."

Quinn nodded, taking another mouthful of bitter. Geraghty could see the man's eyes glinting with greed — the proverbial pound signs dancing in front of them. "Well, I'm in. Just tell me when."

Geraghty gave a slow nod. "That's good news, Mr Nash. I knew I could rely on you. I'll contact you with the final details as soon as I have them. Please stay close to home for the next few days."

It took a few more gulps of bitter before Quinn rose to his feet. "I just need to take a piss."

Finally, thought Geraghty, watching as Quinn staggered off in the vague direction of the men's toilets. Once he was out of sight, Geraghty placed his glass back down on the table and pulled out a small holdall hidden beneath his seat. Reaching inside, he brought out several plastic bags and a pair of gloves. With a quick glance towards the bar, he ascertained that no one was looking in his direction. The card game was still in full swing, the focus of everyone's attention.

Geraghty snapped a glove on to one hand and lifted up Quinn's latest empty pint glass. Depositing it inside the plastic bag, he repeated the process with two more pint glasses that still littered the table.

With another glance towards the bar, and an eye on the entrance to the men's toilets, Geraghty rose from his seat and walked around to the back of Quinn's chair. Opening up another plastic bag, he carefully lifted as many strands of hair that he could from the collar and shoulders of the tatty leather jacket, together with what looked like dandruff flakes.

He considered It a stroke of luck to hear that his new best friend had frequented a barber's recently — with the evidence still plain to see. You're making this far too easy for me, mused Geraghty as he returned to his seat and stowed the plastic bag containing Quinn's hair into the holdall.

Finally, with still no movement coming from the men's toilets, Geraghty leaned across the table and plucked the handkerchief that he'd seen Quinn wipe his nose with. Within seconds, it was safely concealed inside a plastic bag and hidden in the holdall.

Satisfied, he sat back in his seat and took a long, cool sip of his water.

* * *

Time: 9.45 p.m.
Date: Saturday 28 September 2013
Location: Hawthorne Street South, London

James Quinn sat in the near-darkness, his eyes trained on the front door. Roger Bancroft had said tonight was the night — the night the package would be delivered.

All he had to do was stay home.

And wait.

The street was quiet, as it usually was. Being a cul-de-sac, it had no through traffic. The only cars to pass his window would be his neighbours, or maybe the occasional takeaway delivery.

Other than that, all was quiet.

Except for James Quinn's thumping heart. And his jangling nerves.

Roger Bancroft was paying him a lot of money — *a lot* of money — so whatever was in those packages must be very valuable: to someone, at least. A fact that both excited and unnerved him. He'd been out of the game for so long, he'd forgotten what the adrenaline rush of a job felt like.

He dabbed at the fine dots of sweat resting on his brow, and waited.

* * *

Time: 10.00 p.m.
Date: Saturday 28 September 2013
Location: The Glade, Church Street, Albury, Surrey

"So, are you going to help me?" Geraghty's cool voice interrupted Jack's thoughts. "Finally get your revenge?"

Jack opened his mouth but no words were forthcoming.

Geraghty took the opportunity to continue. "The car you picked up earlier this evening was hired in the name that James Quinn now goes under — David Nash. His current address is on all the hire company's documentation — so he should be easy enough to find when the time comes." He followed Jack back into the living room and pulled out a small plastic bag from his pocket. "I've planted some of his hair in the kitchen, the rest I'll give to you. Scatter it on the driver's seat once you've safely delivered the car back to the agreed location — after the deed is done."

Realisation hit Jack full in the face. The plastic sheeting in the car. The tinted windows. The route meticulously planned to avoid major ANPR cameras, and the baseball cap to hide his features. The man had thought of everything.

Jack had been set up.

"I trust you took the route I suggested?" Geraghty raised his pale eyebrows.

Jack nodded that he had.

"Good. I researched it so it avoided too many cameras that could cast doubt on who was driving — although the tinted windows should help to some extent. But also just enough cameras to prove that the car made the journey. Do tell me if I've missed anything, Inspector."

Jack felt the ground shift slightly beneath his feet. "Tell me," he replied, finally managing to find his voice. "How did you find out about James Quinn?"

"Oh, that was just a happy coincidence!" smiled Geraghty, clasping his hands together in delight. "But not one you need trouble yourself about. I know how hard you've been trying to find him, Inspector. And I also know why." Geraghty let the statement hang in the air. "But I also need to die — I have a feeling that, with our shared history, you'll be more than happy to help me in my quest. Am I wrong?"

Jack shook his head, unable to quite believe he was having this conversation. "Just supposing this plan of yours works. What if he has an alibi for tonight? Quinn. What if he can prove he wasn't here?"

"All taken care of." Geraghty's smile widened, his pale, sunken cheeks wrinkling. "At this precise moment in time he's waiting at home for a package to be delivered. I promised him some business, you see — to look after some property of dubious origin. He was only too happy to oblige. Needless to say, there aren't any packages. He lives alone, and keeps himself to himself. Well, you would, wouldn't you? If you were meant to be a dead man."

Geraghty let the thought hang in the air and continued.

"After the struggle, in which I am fatally injured, Quinn will flee the scene leaving behind his car hire documentation, plus papers disclosing his real identity. I trust that will be enough for the detectives that show up to put two and two together?"

Jack shook his head. "I can't believe you're even contemplating this."

"I've had plenty of time to think about it, Inspector. This is the only way to guarantee Isabel inherits everything that I own. And, in addition, you get to frame the man who murdered your mother. You have every right to want to hunt him down. This way, he'll be convicted of murder — just not the murder he really committed."

Jack felt his legs sway and he grabbed hold of the back of the sofa. His heart was racing, his blood beginning to boil. Pain tore into his skin beneath his bandages. Geraghty had ruined countless people's lives for decades — including Isabel's family — and was now seeking the easy way out. Even the cancer wouldn't make him suffer to the very end.

Justice was never going to catch up with Joseph Geraghty. For people like that, it never did.

Geraghty dropped a length of rope and some cable ties onto the sofa. "I'll need you to tie me up and make it look as though I was incapacitated at the time of my murder. As a detective, I'm trusting you to make it look authentic."

Jack shook his head in disbelief.

"And this is the handgun we'll use." With gloved hands, Geraghty had retrieved the gun and the vodka bottle from the patio table. "It's untraceable. And I've wiped Quinn's handkerchief over the handle — it'll have his DNA on it."

Jack eyed the weapon as Geraghty placed it on top of the glass topped coffee table

"We'll obviously need to do a bit of housekeeping before we get down to it." Geraghty went to the small bureau and brought out two pairs of gloves and some antibacterial wipes. "Here." He threw a pair of gloves at Jack. "Put these on. And then start rubbing down everything you've touched."

Jack caught the gloves but remained motionless.

"I'm fully prepared to shoot myself, Inspector. Although it would be far more authentic if you'd do the honours." The smile stayed on Geraghty's lips as Jack raised his gaze. "And don't tell me you're not tempted. I'm handing you a golden opportunity to end my life, and avenge your good friend

Isabel at the same time. I won't stop you. Vengeance can be yours tonight, Inspector — *if* you want it. All you need to do is pick up that gun. You know deep down you want to."

Still Jack was unable to speak. His eyes locked on to the gun as his anger swelled. He couldn't do this . . . could he?

"I can see that you're still undecided." Geraghty took a step towards Jack.. "And that's OK. We have time. All I can say is that I *am* going to die tonight. The only question is by whose hand?"

CHAPTER THIRTY-EIGHT

Time: 5.40 a.m.
Date: Sunday 29 September 2013
Location: Kettle's Yard Mews, London

The blood continued to swirl around the sink, turning the water a shade of deep pink. He hadn't realised he'd managed to get quite so much blood on himself . . . it was everywhere. Everywhere except in the car. The plastic sheeting had taken care of that.

Geraghty really had thought of everything.

As he glanced down at his shirt, he knew he'd have to dispose of it. Washing wouldn't get rid of these stains: not entirely. And he'd never be able to wear it again anyway– not with the knowledge of what had gone on inside The Glade.

What have you done?

The same question bounced around inside his head, on a relentless and depressing merry-go-round.

What have you done, Jack?

He turned off the water and squeezed some bleach around the inside of the sink. He'd do a proper clean later, but for now he needed to get out of these clothes. He could smell the unique aroma of blood every time he moved. It clung to the insides of his nostrils, like the smell of death inside Dr Matthews' mortuary.

A knocking at the door froze him in his tracks and he instinctively dropped the nailbrush with a clatter.

Two more sharp raps were followed by a voice that he recognised.

"Jack, it's me. Open the door." DS Robert Carmichael's voice sounded urgent. "*Now*, Jack."

Jack hesitated, swallowing past the lump that'd just formed in his throat, and again sensing the metallic taste of blood on his tongue.

Shit.

He stepped forward and pulled opened the door, glad to see that Carmichael was on his own. Without a word, he stepped back into the flat, folding his arms across his chest in a vain attempt to conceal the bloodstains on his shirt.

The expression on DS Carmichael's face confirmed that he needn't have bothered. "Shit, Jack. What . . . ?" Carmichael took in Jack's appearance, but he merely shook his head and looked away. "Tell me another time — if I even want to know."

Jack's gaze twitched back to the clock on the kitchen wall. Five forty a.m. Carmichael noticed and carried on. "I came straight over. I rang your mobile a while ago, but there was no answer."

Jack's gaze switched to his phone which was lying, as instructed, on the living room coffee table — where it had been all night.

"I . . ." began Jack, the words stalling in his mouth. He had no idea what to say. This hadn't been part of Geraghty's plan. The man had thought of everything — everything except Jack stuffing things up the moment he got home.

"No matter." Carmichael waved Jack's words away. "But I thought you'd want to be one of the first to know

— something's happened regarding that chap you were trying to trace. The dead one? James Quinn?"

Jack's stomach tightened. "Quinn?" he managed to reply, his voice a few octaves higher than normal. "What about him?"

"I've been on-call overnight — catching up with some paperwork. I was keeping an eye on the reports coming in — and one caught my eye." Carmichael paused, again running his eyes over Jack's dishevelled and bloodstained appearance. "James Quinn's name flagged up."

Jack's eyebrows shot up. "In what regard?"

"Murder enquiry. Down in Surrey. They want our help in nabbing him."

Jack's eyebrows remained hitched. He kept his arms folded across his chest. "Murder? Who's dead?"

"Unofficial reports say a chap by the name of Roger Bancroft. No formal identification as yet." Carmichael paused once again. "But they're pretty sure it's Quinn they want, so . . . you coming to watch?"

"Watch?"

"There's a team going round to pick up Quinn as we speak. I thought, with your history, you might want to swing by and take a look."

"How?" Jack's frown deepened. "How did they track him down?"

"Seems like the muppet left his ID at the scene — seems to go by the name David Nash these days, but there was also something to link him back to the name Quinn. I'm a bit hazy on the details. Shall we go?"

Jack swallowed, the taste of blood still on his tongue. Slowly he began to nod, casting an eye down at the front of his shirt.

"I'd probably change first, though, mate," added Carmichael, raising an eyebrow. "I'll be waiting outside."

* * *

Time: 6.10 a.m.
Date: Sunday 29 September 2013
Location: Hawthorne Street South, London

Hawthorne Street South had been cordoned off and Carmichael brought the car to a stop just outside a launderette. Both he and Jack jogged the rest of the way, ducking under the police tape after flashing their IDs. The sun had yet to rise so the street was bathed in darkness — the only pale light in existence was emanating from several street lamps, one of which was located outside number six.

Jack's stomach was in knots. His eyes flicked across to the car he'd left at the roadside barely an hour ago. He could still smell the blood in his nostrils, certain it remained embedded beneath his fingernails. He glanced up at the buildings that hugged the street, searching for any cameras that might've caught his presence earlier.

Even as he looked, Jack knew there would be none.

Geraghty wouldn't have made a mistake like that. His preparation would have been meticulous. But no matter how many times Jack tried to convince himself that the gangland leader's plan was watertight, he couldn't stem a trickle of fear from seeping through. Geraghty was dead. What did it matter to him if Jack was linked to his death and the setup of James Quinn? What loyalty, if any, did Geraghty owe him now? Jack was police — and the police and Geraghty had never seen eye to eye. The more Jack thought about it, the more concerned he became.

"You all right, mate?" Carmichael frowned at Jack, noting his friend's pallid complexion even in the darkness of the near-dawn.

Jack nodded and followed Carmichael across the street towards number six. There was a strong police presence with two uniformed constables either side of the open front door, and several more clearly visible inside. A police van and three marked police cars, still with their blue lights flashing, were parked close by.

"Who's in charge?" asked Carmichael, as they approached the front door.

"The SIO is DI Hooper," replied one of the uniformed constables.

Just as the SIO's name was uttered, a tall woman stepped out of the open doorway. "Did I hear my name?" Snapping off a pair of gloves, she flashed both Jack and Carmichael a quizzical look. "News appears to travel fast, gentlemen. What brings you both here?"

"What's happening?" Carmichael craned a look over the DI's shoulder and into the house. "Looks busy in there."

"That depends who wants to know." The quizzical look remained. "You have an interest in this chap?"

"I saw the shout come in overnight," continued Carmichael, still trying to get a glimpse inside number the house. "Request to pick up David Nash on behalf of Surrey."

"And what interest is our Mr Nash to either of you good fellows?" repeated DI Hooper, stepping to the side to allow two more detectives to enter the premises.

"His name's come up in another investigation," answered Jack, finally finding his voice. "We've been looking for him."

It was true. Partly.

DI Hooper took Jack and Carmichael off to one side. "Well, you've had a wasted trip. He's not here."

Jack's already pale face drained further. "What do you mean he's not here? He has to be."

"He's not here," repeated DI Hooper, shrugging her shoulders. "The place is empty. Looks like he left in a hurry, though."

Jack and Carmichael exchanged a look.

"My guess is someone spooked him before we got here," continued the DI. "Either that or he was tipped off." She pulled out her mobile phone and began to turn away. "If you'd both excuse me — I have to make an awkward call to Surrey Police and explain how their murder suspect has disappeared into thin air."

Carmichael grabbed hold of Jack's arm and led him back across the street, away from the house. "He's gone, mate," he breathed, making sure nobody was close enough to overhear. "He must've got wind of someone being on to him."

"I heard." Jack's stomach had tightened so much he felt physically sick. He gave an involuntary shudder at the thought of the last twenty-four hours, and at everything Geraghty had made him do. *What have I become?* he thought. *Just what have I become?*

"I guess there'll be a nationwide manhunt," continued Carmichael. "The guy's a murder suspect, after all. They'll catch up with him eventually."

Jack shook his head, looking back across the street. James Quinn had been living not ten minutes from his own front door all this time. His mother's killer. And now he'd gone — leaving Jack the one with blood on his hands. Literally.

It was then that Jack uttered the words that hadn't escaped his lips for some time. "Rob — give us a smoke."

Carmichael reached into his inside pocket and produced a packet of Marlboro cigarettes and a lighter. He wordlessly handed them across.

"They won't find him," Jack breathed, slipping a cigarette into his mouth and lighting it. He drew in a deep lungful before exhaling the smoke and passing the packet back to Carmichael. "He's disappeared before — he'll do it again."

* * *

Time: 6.15 a.m.
Date: Sunday 29 September 2013
Location: Hawthorne Street South, London

The rapid appearance of the police before the sun had even risen had caused not an insignificant amount of commotion in this usually quiet street. With no sunrise yet to illuminate the skies, it was flashing blue lights that had pulsated through the gloom, leading several net curtains to twitch as their occupants were disturbed from their slumber.

James Quinn watched the scene unfold.

He'd known Roger Bancroft was up to something: something about the guy just didn't sit right. And he'd been right to trust his instincts. The deal had been too good to be true. Initially, he'd been ecstatic at his own good fortune, his greed overtaking his common sense. It was a quick way to make some easy money — *a lot* of easy money. And he'd almost fallen for it — *almost*.

It hadn't taken long after his meeting with Bancroft in the Baker's Arms for the disquiet to set in. If there was anything that his time in prison had taught him over the years, it was deals that looked too good to be true usually were. He'd tried to delve into Roger Bancroft's past, using a few of his contacts that still owed him a favour or two, but he'd found nothing. Literally. The man was a shell.

And that worried James Quinn.

Fearing he was being set up for the bank robbery itself, and not just handling the stolen goods, he'd grabbed a holdall and stuffed it with the bare necessities before leaving his lodgings.

And not a moment too soon, either.

He'd made it across the street with only minutes to spare, breaking into an empty flat above an abandoned taxi office that had dispatched its last taxi several years ago.

He nervously bit his lip as he peered out from behind the grubby net curtain that stretched across the equally grubby window. He knew he couldn't stay here for long; the number of cops that had turned up to batter down his door told him that much. He turned his attention from his own front door to the two figures that were standing directly below him on the pavement, underneath a dimly lit street lamp. The taller one of the two he didn't recognise, but the other one . . .

James Quinn prided himself in never forgetting a face.

Reaching into the hastily packed holdall that sat by his feet, he pulled out a copy of last night's *Evening Standard*.

Unfolding the newspaper, the front page confirmed his suspicions.

DI Jack MacIntosh.

A small, black and white photograph of the detective inspector sat alongside an article charting the apprehension of the serial killer known as the Bishop.

MacIntosh.

A small smile crept across James Quinn's face.

MacIntosh.

It couldn't be a coincidence.

Returning the newspaper to his holdall, Quinn pulled out his wallet from his back pocket and slid out a well-thumbed photograph from in-between two crumpled ten-pound notes.

He had her eyes, he could see that now. And the shape of her nose, too. He remembered her two little brats, always clinging to her and demanding her attention. It riled him, the way she would pander to their every whim. And when she said she was giving up the escort and prostitution business to concentrate on her boys, well — he couldn't let her do that.

Stella MacIntosh.

Looks like I've found your boy, Stella, my darling.

CHAPTER THIRTY-NINE

Time: 11.30 a.m.
Date: Monday 11 November 2013
Location: Walker, Frampton and Dunne Solicitors, Guildford, Surrey

The room smelled somewhat musty, much like an old library. Three of the walls were lined with shelves full of tan-coloured leather bound tomes, kept locked away inside glass fronted cabinets. Isabel took her seat next to Jack at the large, oval mahogany table in the centre of the conference room at Messrs Walker, Frampton and Dunne Solicitors. "Remember," whispered Jack, his voice low. "Just nod and say yes. That's all you need to do." His eyes flickered towards the closed door. "And when they mention the name Roger Bancroft, you recognise the name as a family friend. That's it." He paused and turned his gaze back to Isabel. "Trust me."

Isabel found herself nodding. When Jack had told her about Joseph Geraghty — her old Uncle Clive — she'd struggled to comprehend it all. The fact that he was now dead hadn't affected her the way she thought it might. Instead, she merely felt somewhat numb. Maybe that part would come later.

Isabel's thoughts were interrupted by the conference room door being swiftly opened, and a small, beady-eyed man with a closely cropped beard and a receding hairline entered. "Sorry to keep you waiting," he breezed, scuttling over to the other side of the table and depositing a thin, buff- coloured folder in front of him. "I'm Richard Dunne. Partner in the Wills and Probate department." He leaned across the table, thrusting a small hand out towards Isabel. "And you must be Isabel Faraday?"

Isabel raised herself out of her chair slightly, and shook the man's hand. "Yes," she replied, flashing a quick sideways glance at Jack. "Yes, I am."

"Good, good." Richard Dunne sat down opposite. "And you are?" He turned his attention towards Jack, eyebrows raised above a thin-framed set of spectacles.

"Jack MacIntosh. I'm a friend." Jack shifted in his chair, suddenly feeling how warm and stuffy the room was. His shirt collar was clinging to his skin and he ran a finger around the inside edge, loosening his tie. He felt the solicitor's gaze boring into him from across the table.

"Good, good," Richard Dunne repeated. "I'll try not to keep you too long — shall we get down to business?"

Isabel nodded, as instructed, but remained quiet. Jack swallowed, and placed his sweating hands in his lap. Although he'd scrubbed them mercilessly since his visit to The Glade, he was somehow convinced the blood was still visible from across the table. Scrunching his hands up into balls, Jack watched as the solicitor opened the buff-coloured folder.

"We're handling the estate of the late Mr Roger Bancroft and here I have his last will and testament." Richard Dunne slid a thin document out from inside the file. "You are aware that Mr Bancroft is now deceased?" The solicitor peered at Isabel over the rim of his spectacles.

Isabel felt Jack stiffen slightly at her side. After another sideways glance, she began to nod. "Yes, yes I am."

"My condolences. Was he a close friend?" enquired the solicitor, turning over the first page of the Will.

Isabel's mouth felt dry. "I . . . I . . ." She flashed another quick glance at Jack who was again staring down at his hands in his lap. "I know he was a close friend of my parents."

"I see," nodded Richard Dunne. "Well, Mr Bancroft left strict instructions with us in the event of his death, including the reading of his last will and testament." The solicitor paused as he ran his eyes once more over the contents of the document in front of him, before returning Isabel's expectant gaze. "In a nutshell, Mr Bancroft has named yourself, Isabel Faraday, as the sole beneficiary of his estate."

Isabel's jaw dropped and her eyes widened.

A smile crossed Richard Dunne's lips. "I can see that this has come as a bit of a surprise. But it's all here in black and white." The solicitor tapped the document with a well-manicured finger. "Shall I go through the details with you?"

Isabel nodded, unsure what else she should do.

"Mr Bancroft has an estate worth approximately seven and a half million pounds — we're still working out the final details, but that's our initial estimate."

Isabel's jaw fell further. And Jack's shirt clung tighter to his back.

"There is the sum of approximately £2,750,000 in various bank accounts. Then he has two properties in his name — one is a town house in Rome, and the other is a property in the village of Albury, Surrey."

Isabel visibly started at the mention of her home village. Her already pale skin leached yet more colour and she slowly turned towards Jack. He met her wide gaze and merely gave the smallest of inclinations of his head.

Don't ruin it now, Isabel, he prayed silently to himself.

Not after everything I've done.

He unconsciously began to pick beneath his fingernails.

Richard Dunne's eyes were still focused on the will set out before him, oblivious to the looks being exchanged between Isabel and Jack. "Both properties form part of the estate," he continued, "together with an expected sum of two and a quarter million pounds from a life insurance policy. With Mr Bancroft's unfortunate demise, you've become a very wealthy young woman, Miss Faraday." The solicitor looked up and saw Isabel's startled expression. He smiled. "Would you like a cup of tea?"

CHAPTER FORTY

Time: 1.30 p.m.
Date: Saturday 7 December 2013
Location: The Glade, Church Street, Albury, Surrey

"I can't believe I'm really back here." Isabel sipped the chilled glass of prosecco, her eyes watering as the bubbles tickled her nose. "It feels so unreal." She began to stroll away from the patio, heading towards the trees at the rear of the garden, leaving behind the faint chattering coming from the house.

Jack found himself following, and they ducked down beneath the wide boughs of a large oak tree. The day had dawned bright and clear, but temperatures had struggled despite the weak sunshine. Frost clung to the grass and crunched underneath their feet. "Unreal in a good way?" he asked, taking a swig from the bottle of Budweiser that he'd opted for in place of the prosecco.

Isabel hesitated and cocked her head to one side. Slowly, she began to nod. "Yes. I think so. It does feel good to be back."

They'd stopped outside the wooden summerhouse which still nestled underneath the branches of an ancient oak tree. Isabel nodded towards it, taking another mouthful of bubbles. "You know what I found in there earlier?"

"Woodlice?"

Isabel gave a snort. "As well as that. A box of my old toys. They must've been there this whole time." Shivering, she pulled her cardigan closer around herself and turned away from the summerhouse. "Part of me feels sorry for the man."

"Geraghty?" Jack followed Isabel as she set off across the lawn back towards the patio. "Why would you feel sorry for him? He caused you nothing but grief." *And he killed your parents*, Jack wanted to add — but restrained himself. He still hadn't had the courage to divulge his thoughts on that.

"I did say only a part of me," replied Isabel, flashing a quick look at Jack over her shoulder. "A very small part." She climbed the small steps that led up to the patio. "But I don't think he can have been all bad. He left this place to me, didn't he? And returned all my money?"

Jack merely grunted and placed his empty beer bottle down on the patio table. They needed to get off the subject of Joseph Geraghty before he said something he shouldn't. Isabel led him back through the patio doors and he had no option but to walk, once again, across the very spot where he'd left Geraghty lying in a pool of his own blood.

The amount of blood that had pumped out of his dying body had startled Jack. He hadn't been prepared for the damage that single gunshot had caused. Absentmindedly, he began to pick at his fingernails. He knew they were clean, having scrubbed them red raw for weeks, but somehow they'd always be stained, carrying with them the memory of that night.

That night.

Jack turned away from the tiles and headed towards the kitchen in search of more beer. He swallowed a small laugh as he grabbed another bottle of Budweiser. Dr Riches would despair if she ever managed to get him back on her couch again. Yet more haunting memories to try and get under control. He could almost hear her sighing from here.

"Something amusing you, bro?" Mac appeared in the doorway, sporting a huge grin. He stepped forwards and grabbed the open bottle out of Jack's hand and took a swift gulp. "Sorry," he added, noting his brother's raised eyebrows. "Dutch courage. My insides are all over the place."

Jack grabbed two more beers, spying Carmichael making his way into the kitchen. Passing one of the beers across to the detective sergeant, he turned back to his brother. "You'll be fine, Stu. She'll say yes."

Mac gulped down the rest of the bottle and wiped his lips with the back of his hand. "You can't be a hundred per cent sure of that, Jack. I might just end up making a tit of myself."

"And we'll all be right here to see it!" grinned Carmichael. "No, seriously, mate. She'll say yes. No question." He took a large mouthful of beer before adding, "plus, I want to start organising the stag do."

Jack managed a smile, brushing all thoughts of Geraghty and his bloodied body out of his mind. He momentarily caught Carmichael's eye and they exchanged a look. Jack was sure that Rob at least suspected something about Jack's involvement that night — the man wasn't stupid — but so far the secret was still Jack's to keep. For now.

The investigation into the disappearance of James Quinn was being handled by those much higher up the food chain than Jack — something he was quietly thankful for. The regulars at the Baker's Arms had been only too pleased to recount the evening that Quinn had stumbled into their village pub, and a forensic sweep on the hire car outside Quinn's address had shown up particles of Roger Bancroft's blood. Without any traceable next of kin, Bancroft's link to Geraghty remained hidden. And, so far, Jack MacIntosh's name had not been mentioned.

Lily McArthur had gone back home to recuperate. Willie had told Jack she was insisting on returning to London to continue with her studies in the New Year. She was made of tough stuff, the Scotsman had informed him.

Jamie Rivers had regained consciousness and was charged with six counts of murder and one of the attempted murder of a police officer. The Bishop was currently languishing on remand at Her Majesty's pleasure and Jack secretly hoped he was having a rough time.

Rivers' motivation for the murders had yet to be publically disclosed, although the forthcoming trial would no doubt provide many a newspaper headline. When asked in interview about the taking of flesh from his victims, he'd remained mute. Theories ran like wildfire throughout the station, most favouring Rivers wanting to exert his own style of punishment for a lifetime of rejection. Jack had a feeling they would never know for sure.

DC Trevor Daniels was discharged from hospital after three weeks. He then made the journey back to his parents' home on the south coast in order to continue his recovery from his brush with death. Jack had sent him a private message that, as soon as he felt fit enough, he was welcome back on the team anytime.

Martin Rivers had been laid to rest in a quiet ceremony — with just Jack and his team in attendance. DS Cassidy had insisted that they go: it seemed like the right thing to do.

The only fly in the ointment was Vince Butler. The letters from his room at New Green had all been analysed, but the CPS were dragging their heels on what charges they might authorise. A similar search of 13 Lorimer Street, home of Jamie Rivers, hadn't thrown up what they'd hoped. No letters from Butler, no evidence that he'd communicated with The Bishop. All they had was Jamie's fan mail in Butler's room.

Jack knew it wouldn't be enough to implicate Butler in any wrongdoing. He could almost see the look of forced surprise on the man's face. It wasn't rocket science — someone with Butler's intellect would have instructed Jamie to destroy his letters, and Jamie would have obliged. All that would be left would be Jamie's 'fan' letters — but nothing to prove there was a two-way communication. The CPS would take it as far as they could but Jack knew a dead horse when one was being flogged right in front of him. They had the Bishop and, as far as they were concerned, it was case closed. Jamie's rejection by his own family, and his unhealthy interest in animal mutilation from a young age, would no doubt be enough of a motive to satisfy any jury.

"Come on." Carmichael broke Jack's thoughts, nodding towards the living room. "Looks like it's show time."

Jack took a swig of his beer and followed his brother and Carmichael out of the kitchen.

With a final deep breath, Stuart MacIntosh stepped forward, an engagement ring burning a hole in his pocket — ready to ask Isabel Faraday the most important question of his life.

THE END

MESSAGE FROM THE AUTHOR

Although, many of the locations used in this book are real, I have used artistic liberty with inventing many of the road names. The New Green Psychiatric Unit is a figment of my imagination, although it does sound like a fascinating place . . .

Readers often ask me if I base my characters on anyone I know. I'm sure that subconsciously I must do, although it is never intentional (however, I will confess to the delightful Dr Erskine having one or two characteristics from a person I have indeed met before).

As always, there are a large number of people I need to thank for bringing *Sixteen Carved Pieces* to publication. As always, I thank Suffolk Police and in particular PS Rebecca McCarthy for being on hand to answer any procedural questions. If there are any remaining inaccuracies, then I can assure you that they are mine and mine alone!

I must also thank Tracey Proctor — always my 'go-to' person for anything to do with forensics. Your help and support has been invaluable as usual.

Thanks must also go to Sarah Bezant who has the task of reading the first 'final' draft of all my books — your eye for detail and plot holes is second to none!

I also must thank everyone at Joffe Books for believing in me and bringing my stories to life. Enormous thanks to Kate Lyall Grant for continuing to help shape the books into the versions we have today.

And finally, it is you — the readers! Without you, none of these books would ever see the light of day. I thank each and every one of you.

THE JOFFE BOOKS STORY

We began in 2014 when Jasper agreed to publish his mum's much-rejected romance novel and it became a bestseller.

Since then we've grown into the largest independent publisher in the UK. We're extremely proud to publish some of the very best writers in the world, including Joy Ellis, Faith Martin, Caro Ramsay, Helen Forrester, Simon Brett and Robert Goddard. Everyone at Joffe Books loves reading and we never forget that it all begins with the magic of an author telling a story.

We are proud to publish talented first-time authors, as well as established writers whose books we love introducing to a new generation of readers.

We have been shortlisted for Independent Publisher of the Year at the British Book Awards three times, in 2020, 2021 and 2022, and for the Diversity and Inclusivity Award at the Independent Publishing Awards in 2022.

We built this company with your help, and we love to hear from you, so please email us about absolutely anything bookish at feedback@joffebooks.com

If you want to receive free books every Friday and hear about all our new releases, join our mailing list: www.joffebooks.com/contact

And when you tell your friends about us, just remember: it's pronounced Joffe as in coffee or toffee!

ALSO BY MICHELLE KIDD

DI JACK MACINTOSH MYSTERIES

Book 1: SEVEN DAYS TO DIE
Book 2: FIFTEEN REASONS TO KILL
Book 3: SIXTEEN CARVED PIECES

Printed in Great Britain
by Amazon

23715954R00202